Roses *in* December

HAMILTON PLACE, BOOK II

MARK A. GIBSON

Editing by The Pro Book Editor
Interior and Cover Design by IAPS.rocks

eBook ISBN: 979-8-9880747-3-1
paperback ISBN: 979-8-9880747-4-8
hardcover ISBN: 979-8-9880747-5-5

    1. Main category—Fiction / General
    2. Other category—Fiction / Family Saga

First Edition

This book is dedicated to 73 employees and 91 guests.

PROLOGUE

JUNE 1995

I T HAD SEEMED LIKE A good idea at the time. Chalmers wondered how many of life's misadventures began with just such misplaced assurances. Each decision was, he thought, well pondered with the permutations and computations compiled, collated, and analyzed so that the plan for his life was foolproof, or at least *fool-resistant*. As Dr. Horne, his mentor and a dedicated cynic, had once told him, "If you try to make something foolproof, they'll just build a better fool."

Oh, Doctor Horne, if you could only just see me now.

Even in retrospect, his thought processes *seemed* at least *mostly* sound. And yet, here he was, hiking through this steaming, *stinking* jungle, a walking buffet for millions of mosquitoes and biting flies, with forty pounds of equipment strapped to his back and blisters on his feet the size of soccer balls. Well, maybe they were not *quite* the size of soccer balls, but dammit, they still hurt!

"I'm in the Air Force, goddamn it! We don't do this kind of shit in the Air Force," Chalmers muttered to himself. "One joins the Air Force to live in air-conditioned comfort where a 'difficult hike' is traversing a hot parking lot to the

O'Club. The only bag I should ever be carrying ought to have fourteen golf clubs sticking out of it and a flask of Jack Daniels in a zippered pocket."

"Did you say something, Major Chalmers?" The man actually seemed to be enjoying himself.

"No, Sergeant Ryals. Just singing to myself to pass the time." He secretly hated Technical Sergeant Ryals. "Half Navy SEAL and half mountain goat," he muttered under his breath. The thought of *that* unholy coupling actually made him chuckle, and he was still chuckling when the toe of his left boot became ensnared by a vine. His forward momentum being too great to overcome, he fell flat into the mud— or at least he *hoped* it was mud.

"Fuck!" Chalmers yelled as he started pushing up from the ooze.

"You okay, sir?" asked Ryals, trying to suppress a grin and failing.

"I'm fine, Sergeant! Thank you for your concern." And then he mumbled, "Just fucking peachy! How could I *possibly* be any better? I'm just sweating my ass off, having a nice stroll through a freaking jungle, using fucking cobras to play jump rope. I can't believe we actually fought for this steaming dung heap! We should have paid the fricking Viet Cong to just keep it. Geez, what the fuck am I doing here?!" he asked himself for the now thirteenth time that day.

Chalmers had been in Vietnam for ten days, which in his mind was nine and a half days too many. He'd felt professionally trapped by a bad assignment to an airbase in Japan and it really *had* seemed like a good idea to jump at this opportunity at the time, his ticket out of Japan. The initial excitement of escaping that unpleasant military posting had rapidly been replaced by the reality of "camping" in a tropical rainforest. The first few days had been spent tramping through the bug and reptile infested mountain wilderness of central Vietnam in search of a battle site that had been completely swallowed by the jungle. Upon finding it, the next week had been spent sifting, quite literally, through the contents of a twenty-five-year-old bomb crater. Now he was off on another wild goose chase.

"Only three more weeks to go, then I'm out of this pit and out of Yokota...permanently," he muttered. "I wonder if there was another way?"

As his concentration drifted in search of an answer, Robert Frost's "The Road Not Taken" popped into his mind. How did the poem go?

> *Two roads diverged in a wood, and I,*
> *I took the one less traveled by,*
> *And that has made my life this living HELL!*
> *Not an exact quote, but just as well.*

Maybe not exact, but close enough...and his version of the poem summed up his life perfectly. Had he taken the right fork, he'd be on a beach with an umbrella drink in one hand and a hot travel agent in the other. The left fork had him humping it through the jungles of Vietnam.

Instead of the right fork, I took the wrong fork! What the Hell was I thinking!? How, exactly, did I get myself here?

Chalmers supposed it was a lot like World War I. Nobody really *wanted* a war. No leader woke one day and said, "Hey, I know, let's start a war." Instead, they made a series of small moves and seemingly logical decisions that unknowingly and unwittingly edged the world closer and closer to catastrophe. Each step brought them nearer to the precipice until finally, a minor spark turned the planet into a conflagration and an entire generation had gone up in flames.

Chalmers continued muttering to himself. "Give it a rest, Chalmers. Don't be so melodramatic. You're slogging through a jungle, not sucking down mustard gas in some mud-filled trench on the Somme—"

He kicked at a vine and tangled his foot in another, stumbling again, almost falling. He'd just about regained his balance when his right foot came down on nothing but air. Technically, the ground was still there. It was just falling away at a sharp, downward angle. The effect, however, was the same. He pitched forward, tumbling, bouncing, and cursing all the way down the declivity until coming to rest, he thought, against the trunk of a tree.

He lay still for a moment, dazed after his tumble. He tentatively moved first one arm and then the other and stretched his left leg and then his right. Nothing seemed to be broken, and everything moved more or less normally. He tried to open his eyes but couldn't. They were caked with mud. Groping for his canteen, he poured water over his face and rinsed his eyes. As his vision cleared, two huge black eyes the size of Ping-Pong balls came into focus, staring back at him...and then six more. And then eight hairy legs. It was a tarantula the size of a dinner plate.

Startled, he jerked backward and banged his head against the tree trunk, causing a metallic *thunk*.

"Wait a minute!" Chalmers reflected when his slightly concussed and addled mind cleared enough for rational thought. "Trees don't sound like that." He slowly turned to look behind him.

It wasn't a tree but an olive-green painted tail boom.

"Hey! Hey, guys!" he shouted. "Guys! I think I've found something."

In Washington, DC, Senator Alexander Wentworth Prescott, III kicked back with his feet up on his burlwood desk. He liked burlwood. Its unique grain pattern was unmatched in its beauty and complexity. More importantly, it looked *nothing* like the desks in the other ninety-nine senatorial offices. No, this was no polished mahogany, ebony, teak, cherry, or glass behemoth. His desk, unlike those of his peers, featured a swirling honey, sienna, and cinnamon grain pattern painted by the hand of God and merely polished by man.

He held a vintage, unlit Cuban *Romeo y Julietta* cigar between his teeth. Beside him on the blotter, a crystal highball glass held a generous measure of thirty-year-old Macallan. Both the cigar and the Scotch had been gifts from some lobbyist or other. Prescott didn't really like either—the gifts, or the lobbyists—and he didn't smoke, but this was what his father had always done after a win. He'd probably never completely measure up to the old man's standards, but he might still *look* the part.

Prescott stared contentedly out his window, in the general direction of the US Capitol Building. His was a spacious, well-appointed office, perhaps not as nice as his father's had once been, but he wasn't complaining. The old man would've hated the burlwood. He would've said the desk didn't "adequately project the power of office," or some crap like that.

The elder Prescott had been a powerhouse in the Senate for almost four decades. The younger Prescott had been appointed to his Senate seat by the governor of New York after his father's unexpected death in office. He had been only meant to serve as a placeholder until the November elections later that year. That had been almost eighteen years ago.

Apparently, the placeholder had found a place of his own—not bad for a man with precisely zero political ambition. He aspired—*who didn't?*—but his aspirations had never been in the political arena. His motivations were more personal. Unlike the majority of his peers on the Hill, for Prescott, politics was the means to an end; *not* an end in and of itself.

During his years in the House of Representatives and more recently, the Senate, Prescott had fought for veterans' rights and championed the Joint POW/MIA Accounting Command. JPAC's mission was to achieve the fullest possible accounting of all Americans missing as a result of the nation's past conflicts. JPAC's motto was, "Until they are home." He'd forced JPAC through committees and gotten it funded, then sent them out on their first mission into Vietnam. And today, the project had borne fruit. Three previously lost Americans were finally coming home from the war. Without politics, today's win would never have occurred.

Prescott held the tumbler of Scotch to his lips. "Here's to you, Dad...you son of a bitch!"

CHAPTER I

MACK LEE WIPED THE DIPSTICK on an old rag, replaced it, and slammed down the hood on the 1966 Ford Fairlane. It seemed an awfully nice car for an old bat like Mrs. Kline. She didn't even drive the damned thing anywhere other than to church, the corner grocery, and his gas station. He stuffed the rag into the back pocket of his overalls and shuffled around to the driver's side window.

The elderly driver laboriously rolled down the window, stuck her head out, and shouted, "Did you find it this time?" enunciating each word as though he was hard of hearing, or stupid.

Old Lady Kline had brought her car to his service station three times in the past two weeks for a sound she'd claimed to hear emanating from her engine. Mack Lee strongly doubted that she'd ever truly heard anything. The old gal was deaf as a post and wouldn't have been able to hear a .50-caliber machine gun if it had been firing atop her car's roof, much less the ticking sound she was currently describing.

He shook his head and shouted back, "No, everything sounds okay to me." He was fighting a cold and his voice cracked.

"You mean you can't hear that, sonny? I can hear it now. It's going *chttt, chttt, chttt*," she yelled while making a motion with her right hand like a snake striking.

"No, ma'am," he shouted.

Watching the old lady gesticulate, Mack Lee's eyes drifted to the enormous, multihooped bangle earrings swinging wildly from her overtaxed earlobes. Then, he had an idea.

"I just don't hear it, Mrs. Kline. I'm awful sorry! Hey, those are really nice earrings. May I take a look at them? I've been hoping to find something nice to give my girl. She loves fine jewelry. May I see them?"

"You want to see my earrings?!"

"Yes, ma'am. I've been admiring them."

"Well, okay, sonny...here you go," she yelled over the car's engine. Then she unclipped the gawdy bangles and handed them through the window to his waiting hand.

"Can you hear the noise now?" he bellowed.

"No, it's stopped."

Mack Lee handed the earrings back to her and said in a normal voice, "I thought not." Then in a louder voice he called out, "Have a nice day!"

"What do you think? About the earrings? Do you think that girl of yours would like them?"

"No, I think she already has a pair. Thank you, though." Then as her car pulled away, he continued, "Yeah, she has a pair. They're called Hula Hoops." Mack Lee limped back into the relative comfort of the station, muttering under his breath, "Next time, maybe you actually buy something. We *do* sell gas here, you old hag."

His leg ached, but that wasn't unusual. It had hurt for over a decade but was always worse in cold weather, and it had been cooler than normal for November this year. His joints also ached; it felt like rain. He could always tell when it was going to rain. He supposed that was one benefit from the accident eleven years ago. More importantly, it had kept him out of Vietnam.

Woohoo, 4-F, baby! Mister college-boy, goody-two-shoes wasn't so lucky. Little brother is sweating his ass off over there at this very moment. What a schmuck.

Outside, dark clouds were beginning to form and the wind was picking up. "Definitely gonna be rain," he said to himself as he reached over and turned the sign in the door to CLOSED. "Nobody is gonna be getting Mack Lee Hamilton to pump gas in a cold rain—not for a measly thirty-two cents a gallon. Unh-uh, not happ'nin', no way!" he muttered.

Mack Lee locked up the station and trundled home. Mama was making meatloaf for supper, and he didn't want to be late. Many might've found it odd that he'd continued living in the old home place with his mother, but not Mack Lee. After the accident, it had taken months for him to recover from his injuries. Mama was only too happy to play nurse, and he'd milked the injury for all it was worth. He'd always been her favorite, anyway. She'd convinced the old man that he couldn't *possibly* do farm work with a hurt leg, which was all right by him. He hated that damned farm.

It was a good life. He could come and go as he pleased, with no expenses and few responsibilities. He worked at the gas station to keep himself in beer money and in Sherri Lynde's panties. When the old man died, that had removed his only reason to leave. So he'd stayed. If anyone looked askance, he could say he was just there "helpin' out my poor, dear ol' mama after Papa died." It was pure horseshit, but whose business was it anyway?

A few months ago, Jimmy's knocked-up wife had crashed his party when she moved in. She was moody and more than a little bossy, but he had to admit, she brightened up the place. She had a nice, tight little ass he liked to stare at when nobody was looking. Her tits weren't so bad either. They were smaller than Sherri's, but those melons had grown up nice and plump with the pregnancy. He often imagined squeezing them just to see if they were ripe. Even after she'd pumped out her little brat a few weeks ago, they were still pretty sweet looking.

He thought, *Ol' Jimmy-boy's one lucky man! Or at least he would be if he wasn't sweatin' his ass off ten thousand miles away in some stinkin' jungle.*

When Mack Lee arrived home for supper, the sweet, tangy smell of Mama's meatloaf hit him as soon as he walked through the door. Something about ketchup cooked overtop hamburger meat always made his mouth water. Mama was nowhere to be seen, but Jimmy's wife was slumped over the kitchen table bawling her eyes out. In her hand, she held a crumpled handkerchief. From somewhere in the house, Jimmy's little brat was screaming his head off in almost perfect synchronization with his mother.

He walked wordlessly to the stove and lifted lids from the pots, then nodded in silent approval. *Green beans and mashed taters. With the meatloaf in the oven, all that is needed now for the perfect meal is some sweet rolls...and for those two to shut the Hell up! Women can be so damned emotional!*

Only then did he acknowledge his sister-in-law. "Yo, Beck...what gives? And where's Mama?"

"He's dead!" she blubbered through her tears.

"I didn't catch that. Quit blubberin'! I can't understand you," he chided.

Rebecca wailed, "Jimmy's dead!"

"Who?"

"James."

"Naw, I can hear him upstairs cryin' his ass off. He ain't dead. Ya outta' go up and check on him before dinner... maybe get him to shut the Hell up!"

"Not the baby...*James!*" She waved a telegram. "He was killed yesterday in Vietnam," she croaked, her body again racked by sobs.

"Humph. Sorry about that, sis. Guess he shoulda gone to Canada with your brother. Where's Mama? When are we havin' dinner? I'm starved."

Rebecca gave a pained shriek and slumped face-first onto the table, sobbing uncontrollably.

Mack Lee stared at his sister-in-law for a long minute, then turned back to the cabinet and began pulling out plates and setting the table.

A few days later, the family held a memorial service for Jimmy. Rebecca had been too distraught and busy with little James to take much of a role in the planning. Margaret, however, volunteered to take care of all the arrangements. Relieved and appreciative of the understanding and compassion, Rebecca happily ceded preparations to her mother-in-law. Margaret was equally happy to assume the role, as this would allow her to begin the process of erasing James Wiley Hamilton from existence.

The ceremony was held at the First Baptist Church of Boiling Springs with their pastor presiding. Rebecca was dismayed to find the church empty and nearly devoid of decoration. There were no flowers, flags, or guests, other than Shelby, her best friend from high school, who she'd contacted herself.

Shouldn't Uncle Howard be here? And Jimmy's friends from school? Maybe someone from the army? Aghast, she asked Margaret about the obvious absences.

"Dear," Margaret lied, "the army doesn't release funds unless there is a body to bury, and they seem to have lost his. And *we* simply don't have the money to spend on flowers or decorations. As for guests, it's been quite a while since James lived here, and in truth, no one knows him. Sadly, I don't have current contact information for Howard, which is a pity, for certainly he would've wanted to be here. Nor do I have information for his friends from school."

In truth, Margaret had made no attempt to contact the American Legion, VFW, or Department of Defense during her "preparations." Additionally, the obituary she'd placed in the local paper featured an unfortunate and "wholly accidental" typographical error, placing the date for the memorial service as the following weekend rather than for the correct date. As for Howard, her statement had been *partially* true. She'd surreptitiously intercepted and burned each of the letters he and Charlotte had written to Rebecca since she'd moved in, and she couldn't remember their return address. Her old memory just wasn't what it used to be.

Jimmy's ceremony consisted of little more than two prayers and a brief homily. The whole process lasted less than a half hour.

Rebecca was saddened and appalled. Jimmy had been such a wonderful man and a loving husband. He'd died honorably while serving his country, but nobody seemed to care. Nobody but her. She'd thought she'd cried herself dry in the days since the two soldiers had knocked on the door and imploded her world, but she'd been wrong. Hot, fresh tears streamed freely down her cheeks, and she made no effort to brush them away. But for Shelby's steadying hand on her arm, Rebecca would've tumbled down the steps as they departed the church for home. Her eyes were just too blurred to see.

Rebecca and baby James rode with Shelby back to the Hamilton home. There just wasn't enough room in the cab of Mack Lee's old truck to fit all four Hamiltons comfortably—or safely. Besides, Mack Lee had stayed out the night before drinking and still smelled like a distillery. So, when Shelby led Rebecca to her car rather than to Mack Lee's truck, Rebecca had gratefully accepted the ride.

In the cab of Mack Lee's truck, Margaret sat disgusted, looking at her son. Now free from Rebecca's unwelcome ears, she resumed a conversation she'd begun with him earlier that morning.

"Mack Lee, I don't want to hear it. You go and do what's necessary. Marry that girl!" When Margaret Butler Hamilton spoke, wise people listened and only disobeyed at their own peril. Although greatly diminished since Walter's death, she was the unquestioned matriarch of the Hamilton household and remained a force to be reckoned with.

Mack Lee, having never been accused of having wisdom, began to protest. "But, Mama, I don't want—"

"Don't you *dare* 'But, Mama' me!" she hissed. "That girl is the solution to all our problems. All you have to do is marry the little bitch."

"But—"

"No buts! You like having a place to live, right?"

"Yes, Mama."

"You like having money in your pocket, right?"

"Yes, bu—"

She cut him off with a glare. With condescension dripping from her voice, she spat, "Let me spell it out for you so even *you* can understand." She held up her thumb. "One. For your information, we owe back taxes on this house and farm that we cannot now pay. Nor are we likely to be able to do so in the future. Two." Her forefinger went up. "This farm hasn't made any real money since your father died, and your pitiful income wouldn't pay for a cardboard box under the Maple Street railroad overpass."

Behind the wheel, Mack Lee recoiled as though from an invisible blow. It wasn't like his mother *ever* to be critical of anything about *him*. "It's not my fault, Mama! I've got this bum leg. I—"

She glared at him over her reading glasses, and Mack Lee's mouth slowly closed.

"Three. The IRS *will* evict us and auction the property to pay those back taxes. When they do that, *we* will be without a place to live. Four." Another finger rose in the air. "Rebecca has money...or at least she will as soon as she gets the Servicemen's Group Life Insurance money from the army. The army gives all soldiers a life insurance policy before they ship out to a war zone," she explained. "So regardless, *she* will have somewhere to live even if *we* do not."

The pinky rose, and she patted her son on the cheek. "Five, if I deed the property to you *before* the IRS gets it *and* you marry Rebecca, promising to take care of her brat, then *you* will have access to the insurance money. *You* can pay the taxes. After that, what you do with her and *all...that... money* will be solely up to *you*. Once she's wedded and bedded, *we* will be all safe and set. You can even divorce the little tramp the next day if you like."

Mack Lee slowly nodded his head in understanding. "Yes, Mama."

"Good boy! Now give your old mama a hug and go sweep that girl off her feet. It shouldn't be very hard. She doesn't seem particularly bright."

Margaret Hamilton had once been an extraordinarily accomplished cook. Had she the inclination, she might easily have become a chef. She always knew precisely what ingredients were required to make any dish and when to add them, how much to use. And she knew when to stir the pot, both in and out of the kitchen. Toward this latter end, after returning home from Jimmy's memorial service and getting dinner started, she sought out Rebecca, who had come in and gone straight to her room.

Rebecca glanced toward the door in response to Margaret's light knock. She was in a rocking chair in her room, humming softly to James as he nursed. She looked up from the child and focused puffy red eyes upon her mother-in-law. "Hello, Mother," she said in a scratchy, tear-soaked voice.

"Oh, Rebecca dear...poor child! I know that this has all been quite a shock for you. I remember how I was when I lost my dear, sweet Walter...and to have a little one to care for too...and now, all by yourself. You are *so* brave!"

"Thank you, Mother! You have been very kind to me. I don't know what I would have done without you during my pregnancy. After my family disowned me for 'running off and marrying a soldier,' I would've had nowhere to go had it not been for you. And now this." Once again, tears welled in her eyes.

"It was only the Christian thing to do, and you are family, after all, even if only by marriage."

The baby began to grizzle, and Rebecca placed him over her shoulder and began patting his back. Soon she was rewarded by a loud belch, and he resumed his feeding.

"It must be terrible for you too! He was my husband, but he was your son. You must be dying inside."

"Sadly, I have had a great deal of experience with loss... but we all must be brave. It is such a blessing for me that I still have Mack Lee, you, and, of course, my little grandchild here for me to hold on to," she said with a catch in her voice. On cue, a single tear trickled down Margaret's cheek. It was a performance that would have made any Hollywood director proud.

"Oh, Mother, what will we ever do without him?" Rebecca pleaded. A fresh rivulet of tears streamed down her face and dripped onto her nursing baby's cheek, giving the appearance that mother and son were both weeping.

"We will persevere, child. We simply must!" Then she casually set her snare. "You have told me nothing of your plans now that James...is gone."

"My plans?"

"Yes, yes...your plans, dear. Where do you intend to go now that James is no longer able to support you and the little one?"

"Go?" Rebecca parroted dumbly.

"Of course, yes. You see, I barely get by on the Social Security checks I've received since Walter's death, and what little income this farm generates..." She waved her arms expansively. "Mack Lee has a very good job at the gas station in town and is planning to open his own station soon. Thus, he is able to cover *his* expenses. As you know, James sent his military pay back here to defray *your* expenses while he was in Vietnam. Obviously, now he is no longer able. There just is not enough money to allow you and my dear grandson to stay here." Another perfectly choreographed tear stained her cheek. "So...I was wondering what your plans might be?"

"Plans? I...I haven't really made any. I just assumed—"

"Yes, you know what they say about assumptions." Then Margaret's voice grew faint as though she was voicing her inner monologue. "I suppose you *could* get a place on your own. You don't have any marketable skills or job training, but maybe you could wait tables at the diner. No, that won't work. Who would watch little James while you're working? And how would you get back and forth to work? You don't have a car, and there certainly is no public transportation around here."

"Maybe, I—"

Margaret continued her monologue. "Perhaps you could just move back in with your parents. That would solve everything. Maybe they'd take you back now that you're no longer married to a soldier." She knew *that* would never happen, and so did Rebecca. That particular bridge had long ago been rendered to nothing but ashes and scorched timbers.

Rebecca's eyes darted around the room. She'd not thought of any of this. She'd always *assumed* that she and baby James would have a home here for as long as they needed one. After all, this was her husband's, and thereby *her*, family...right? What was she going to do?

She had to take care of her child. At least here on the farm, she could cook, clean, and work like a coolie to survive. Otherwise, she had no marketable skills. Her family refused to take her back after she'd shamed them so. Since her marriage to Jimmy had been a last-minute affair and they had not lived on or near a military base, she was totally ignorant of the military benefit system and didn't realize there would be Social Security and life insurance payments to which she would be entitled.

As Margaret drifted from the room, she added almost like an afterthought, "It's a shame that you and Mack Lee couldn't fall in love and be married. Wouldn't it be wonderful if we could keep our little family together?"

And the snare snapped taught. Three months later, on February 19, 1968, a desperate Rebecca married Mack Lee Hamilton.

CHAPTER 2

FEBRUARY 1968

REBECCA FELT TRAPPED AND TOTALLY alone. With nowhere to turn, she had even tried to contact Uncle Howard and Charlotte. Remarkably, in spite of Margaret's difficulties, Rebecca had had no difficulty whatsoever in finding their contact information. Perhaps the dear old man who'd raised Jimmy to be such a wonderful man would be able to help her and little James somehow. She was heartbroken to find that Howard had died unexpectedly in early January.

After their telephone call, Charlotte mailed Rebecca a copy of an article from the *Scottsdale Sun*:

The Scottsdale Sun
January 6, 1968

A former North Carolina man was found dead yesterday at Scottsdale Municipal Airport. The man, later identified as Dr. Howard Pittman Hines, was found in the cockpit of his antique Stearman biplane a little after 4 p.m.

According to airport sources, Dr. Hines was an avid flier and had spent the day flying. Witnesses reported seeing his distinctive red-and-black biplane flying under, and twice looping, nearby Navajo Bridge on Marble Canyon earlier in the day. After returning to the airfield and taxiing to the hangar, Dr. Hines failed to exit the aircraft after shutting down his engine. Groundcrew approaching the aircraft found the doctor dead at the controls, still wearing his vintage WWI flight helmet and goggles.

Dr. Hines, aged 79, had a long history of heart problems. Foul play is not suspected.

According to Elwood Yeager, chief instructor at Sirocco Flight Academy, Dr. Hines had been flying for just under two years but was already an accomplished aviator who loved flying. "If I know Howard Hines, and I do, the good doctor died with a big grin on his face. He will be sorely missed by our aero club!"

Dr. Hines is survived by his wife, Charlotte.

How perfectly like that dear old man to die in such a fashion, Rebecca had thought at the time. She'd both laughed and cried upon reading the excerpt. Knowing what it was like to lose a wonderful man, her heart went out to Charlotte. It gave her a modicum of peace, however, to know that her Jimmy—wherever he was—was no longer alone.

Lost, isolated, and desperate, Rebecca had agreed to marry Mack Lee.

It might have been expected that for one whose first marriage ceremony took place at the county jail, any change in venue or circumstance would have to be an improvement. That expectation could not have proven more wrong in Rebecca's case. The root cause behind this failed expectation had multiple origins, not the least of which was that Rebecca was still in mourning over Jimmy's death. No doubt the fact that she did not love, or even particularly like, her new husband also played a role. And, lust notwithstanding, Mack Lee seemed to have no strong feelings toward Rebecca either.

Calling this wedding a "ceremony" was overly generous. The Justice of the Peace hadn't even looked up from his blotter. He simply took the twenty-five-dollar licensing fee, verified that everyone's syphilis test had returned negative, gave them forms to sign, and pronounced the "happy couple" husband and wife.

With her marriage to Jimmy, Howard and Charlotte had been there. They'd loved him almost as much as she had and, because of that, their presence at the ceremony had made the day even more special for her. The day had been magical. This time, no one was there for Rebecca, not even her friend Shelby. The only witness to the ceremony was Margaret, Mack Lee's mother, a woman Rebecca tried to love, though she was finding the task increasingly difficult.

If the wedding ceremony had left something to be desired, Rebecca's second wedding night had been even worse. Upon leaving the courthouse, Mack Lee and Rebecca drove back home, where she went upstairs to check on James. By the time she returned downstairs, Mack Lee was already well into a bottle of Scotch.

On her first wedding night, Jimmy had been a gentle and attentive—if inexperienced—lover, and the experience had left her feeling loved and wanted. Afterward, they'd fallen asleep tangled in one another's arms.

By the time Mack Lee finally dragged Rebecca into the bedroom to consummate *their* marriage, he was fully drunk. As a lover, he was rough and selfish, and the experience— thankfully brief—had left her painfully bruised and wanting to cry. Afterward, Mack Lee immediately began snoring and Rebecca went downstairs to take a *long*, hot bath.

In the fourteen months since her wedding with Jimmy, fully one-third of her first wedding party had died. After her wedding night with Mack Lee, she would have considered it a mercy to join the departed and increase the fraction to one-half.

After a few weeks, that outcome wouldn't have bothered Mack Lee one bit. He'd had his life going just the way he'd wanted it before the witch and her brat showed up to ruin it. Before, he could stay out all night doing whatever—or who-ever—he chose, and whenever he wanted to do them. Now, it was, "I need money for the baby. The baby needs clothes. Where were you last night?" Nag, nag, nag! It never ended. Even slapping her around a bit only provided the briefest of respites from her incessant bitching. Hell, she wasn't even a good lay!

On the other hand, Margaret was happy as a clam. Her plans had played out just as she'd designed them. She'd signed the farm over to Mack Lee. The insurance check had arrived by mail less than a week after the wedding was consummated—*talk about cutting things close*—and, as Rebecca's husband, he took immediate control of the money. Now, all back taxes and penalties had been paid and there were no longer any active liens against the property.

As for the girl, Margaret was sure Mack Lee would have her shaped up in no time. She'd learn to be a good wife and keep him happy. Until then, it was amazing what a good, quality foundation makeup would cover up. Come to think of it, if the little princess didn't start pulling more of her weight around the farm, she might add a couple bruises herself.

CHAPTER 3

AUGUST 1973

I N THE NORTHWEST CORNER OF the Boiling Springs town square, across the street from the courthouse and in between the Goforth General Mercantile Building and the Law Offices of Barrow & Parker, sat Blanton's Barbershop. It was a classic single-chair operation that had been open on the square since the late 1940s. Over its near quarter-century existence, it had become *the* place for local men to drop in, chew the fat, and have a little taken "off the top" by the shop's proprietor and sole employee, Albert "Bert" Blanton.

In the middle of the shop was the same old red-leather and chrome barber chair that Blanton had opened the place with in 1948. Behind it, the wall was dominated by a massive mirror with shelves and drawers bearing various scissors, clippers, and combs soaking in glass beakers full of Barbicide. Along the opposite and back walls were a dozen chairs for waiting customers, and to keep them entertained should the local gossip prove inadequate, there was an ancient coffee table stacked with back issues of *Field & Stream*, *Outdoor Life*, *Popular Science*, and *National Geographic*, among others. A large plate-glass window at the front of the shop looked out into the square beyond the shop's entryway. By the door, an ancient cash register sat beside a rack of shampoos, hair gels, hairsprays, and complimentary plastic combs with Blanton's Barbershop emblazoned on one side. The tile ceiling, once white, was stained a dull yellow-brown by a quarter century of nicotine.

As was Mack Lee's Saturday morning ritual, he drove into town to have Bert work his usual magic on his flattop mullet and muttonchop sideburns. He usually arrived right as the shop was opening, but this morning he'd been delayed by his idiot wife.

The dumb bitch *knew* he liked his breakfast with eggs over easy, but this morning she'd brought them out to him over hard. It had taken her just short of *forever* to clean up the shards of broken plate and splattered eggs and then fix his breakfast the *right* way. Consequently, he was much later arriving at Blanton's than was his usual practice, and there were already eight people ahead of him waiting and one in the chair when he arrived. Making matters even worse, the wife had sent her dawdling, snot-nosed kid along with him, and after the dust-up in the kitchen this morning, he was moving even slower than normal. This little trip to the barber was gonna blow half his day. He might even be late getting to the fairgrounds for that afternoon's dirt track race. If that was the case, that bitch was really gonna pay!

Mack Lee limped past the spinning red, white, and blue barber pole and pushed open the door. Immediately, he was greeted by the tinkling bell over the door and a chorus of, "Mornin', Mack Lee" from Bert and his waiting patrons. He mumbled return greetings as he pushed through the layered strata of cigarette smoke and took a chair in the back, next to an overflowing spittoon. With Bert never having been accused of being a speedy barber, Mack Lee selected the

December 1972 edition of *Outdoor Life* from the pile on the coffee table and settled into reading about hunting whitetail deer.

"Only nine months out of date...that's gotta be a new record for Bert," he muttered.

Bebopping in behind Mack Lee, Bert's patrons noticed his little boy, James, who, emulating his father, also wore his hair in a mullet. Although only five years old, he spent significantly more time selecting reading material than his father. Remarkably, the little boy eschewed the illustrated Bible story book and issues of *Weekly Reader* Bert kept on hand for his younger customers. Instead, James selected the February 1972 edition of *National Geographic*.

James had once wanted to be an astronaut, but after watching a Red Skelton skit on TV in which Skelton's character was accidentally left on the moon during a mission, he'd decided another career path would be a better choice for him. That did not, however, curb his interest in space. Soon, to the astonishment of the other barbershop patrons, he was engrossed in Kenneth Weaver's article about *Apollo 15*'s mission to explore the mountains of the moon.

If the child's precocity was even noticed by Mack Lee, he gave no indication. Instead, he plowed into his own magazine and made himself comfortable for what was likely to be a long wait. He was not a fast reader, and a casual observer would have noticed his lips moving as he read. He'd not yet gotten through the first paragraph when J. D. Smith interrupted his reading.

"Hey, Mack Lee, you see that article in *Popular Science*?" he asked.

"Nawh, J. D., I'm readin' about shootin' deer in Wyoming." Annoyed by the interruption, Mack Lee held up his copy of *Outdoor Life* and resumed reading.

"Well, you really oughta read it!"

Mack Lee let out a long sigh. "And why's that, J. D.?"

"It's about your ol' buddy, Bob Morrison."

"Really?" Now his interest was piqued. He'd heard nothing about his former best friend since a few months after their accident in 1957.

"Yeah, according to the article, Morrison was the hero of the *Apollo 13* moon mission. You know, the one where the spaceship blew up and the astronauts nearly died before they made it back to Earth."

"Yeah?"

"Accordin' to the article, it was Morrison who figured out how to cobble together the carbon dioxide scrubbers so they'd have enough air for the return trip. He did all that even though he was confined to a wheelchair. He's probably the most famous person ever to come from Boiling Springs! Hey, didn't you guys play football together back in the day?"

Instantly jealous of his old friend, Mack Lee grumbled, "Yeah, we played ball together, and he cost me my shot at going to college. Bear Bryant was recruiting me to play for him at 'Bama, when Morrison got drunk and rolled our car, left me with this bum leg. He mighta brought back three astronauts, but he'll never be *my* fuckin' hero!" Alternative history was Mack Lee's "speciality." Only he, Bob, and God knew that he, and not Bob, had actually been the driver that fateful night. Besides, this story sounded better, anyway—at least, it did to him.

After Mack Lee's outburst, an awkward hush fell over the barbershop.

After a moment, J. D. broke the silence. "Didn't you guys graduate in '56?"

"Yeah, that was the year we won State," Mack Lee responded, puffing out his chest. "What of it?"

"Coach Bryant didn't start coaching at Alabama until 1958. In '56, he was still at A&M."

Mack Lee's eyes bulged, and his face flushed crimson. He slammed down his magazine and stomped out of the barbershop, eddies of smoke and laughter swirling in his wake.

As the door slammed shut, James quietly returned his magazine to the table and got up to follow his father. If he'd been fazed by Mack Lee's behavior, he gave no indication. In his five years, he'd seen it all before, so his father's outburst was nothing unusual. Instead, he paused at the door and waved. "Bye, Mr. Bert. Guess I'll see you next week."

Outside, Mack Lee yelled, "Get in the truck! We're goin' home."

"But I thought we were going to get a haircut today?"

Mack Lee cuffed the child on the back of the head. "I said get your ass in the truck!"

"Yessir, Daddy," James replied, clambering up into the cab.

No sooner than James's door closed, Mack Lee spun the truck's wheel and tore out of the parking lot, peppering nearby parked cars with a spray of loose gravel and curses.

CHAPTER 4

OCTOBER 1977

OUTSIDE BEVERAGES WERE CLEARLY AGAINST the rules, and doubly so if those beverages happened to be alcoholic. But the rules seldom applied to Mack Lee Hamilton—at least from his perspective—and certainly not when he was at the scene of his greatest triumph. No one paid him any heed anyway, as he sat in the stands at the high school football stadium with a cooler of Miller High Life at his feet.

On the field below, a little league football game was being played. Mack Lee knew he should have been the coach. After all, didn't he know more about the game than anybody else in this Podunk little town? He'd led his team to the state championship on that very field back in '56, a fact he was more than happy to describe to anyone within earshot...repeatedly.

Rebecca's kid was down there. Mack Lee had insisted the child sign up for football, figuring the game would toughen him up a bit, and God knew the little panty-waste needed it.

Although he'd recently turned ten years old, James was least three inches shorter and twenty pounds lighter than the next smallest kid on the team—and *he* was still just eight.

James had little interest in, or aptitude for, football, but his dad wanted him to be there. So there he was, protecting his end of the bench with a ferocity seldom seen in one of his stature.

It was the last game of the season, and as usual, it was a blowout. James's team, the Jets, were behind 63–0 and, thankfully, there was less than a minute left before the game and the season ended. Rather than paying attention to the rout on the field before him, James was on his hands and knees behind the bench, riffling through a patch of clover, searching for one with four leaves.

So it was quite a surprise to James when his coach turned and shouted, "Hey, you...number fifty-five, grab your helmet. You're going in."

James leaped to his feet and bumped into the water cooler on the end of the bench, nearly knocking it to the ground. "Me, Coach?" he asked, clearly stunned. He hadn't even realized the coach knew he was back there. He certainly hadn't called on him before that moment.

"Yeah, you," Coach Jones answered. "You get out there and replace number sixty-seven. Don't just stand there! Go!"

"Yes, Coach!" James yelled as he ran onto the field in search of number sixty-seven.

The Jets were on defense, and James soon found his man. He sent him to the sidelines and assumed a spot somewhere behind the defensive line. He hoped that was the position number sixty-seven had been playing, not that it really mattered. For the first time all season, James was getting to play. He was going to be a football star just like his dad, and someday he'd lead his team to a championship!

James was still busy imagining the accolades soon to be coming his way when the opposing center snapped the ball.

The offensive player who'd been crouched in front of him fired forward at the snap, buried his helmet into James's gut, and rolled over him. James immediately found himself flat on his back, staring up at the sky through tear-filled eyes, gasping for breath and unable to move.

The play ended and, mercifully, so did the game.

The referee came over and asked, "You okay, son?"

James had a mouthful of bile and couldn't draw in enough breath to speak, so he just nodded and then struggled to his feet. Over the buzzing in his ears and the sounds of the departing spectators, he heard a familiar voice, his father's, shouting to him from the stands.

"Get up, you *pussy*! You're embarrassing me..."

After the game, James trudged back to his father's truck, head held high, proud of the mud and grass stains on the back of his jersey. For the first time all season, his mom would have to wash his uniform. During the ride home, he chattered almost nonstop. "The coach must have noticed me in practice. I've been working real hard. He finally let me play in a *real* game. Did ya see, Dad? I bet next year, he'll even let me start."

Mack Lee grunted, too disgusted to speak.

When they arrived home, James burst from the truck and ran into the house in search of his mother, anxious to show off his dirty uniform. He found her in the kitchen preparing supper.

Rebecca listened attentively, smiling broadly as James babbled on and on about the game. Although he'd played for less than thirty seconds, his excited narrative went on for several minutes. When he finished, she knelt and gave the boy a big hug, flinching involuntarily from the pain in her ribs. Mack Lee had been in a particularly dark mood last night.

At that instant, Margaret strode into the kitchen. Before James could launch into an account of his gridiron heroics, she snapped, "Get out of those dirty shoes! You're tracking up my nice clean floor."

Her rebuke did nothing to dampen James's ebullience. That was just his grandmother's way. So, after a contrite, "Yes, ma'am, Grandmother," he slipped off his football cleats and scampered upstairs to his room.

When he'd left, Margaret turned her attention to Rebecca. "I expect you to have this mess mopped up before supper." Then she turned on her heel and stalked from the kitchen.

Rebecca lowered her eyes. "Yes, Mother," she replied after her mother-in-law's retreating figure.

CHAPTER 5

FEBRUARY 19, 1978

R EBECCA GAZED AT HER REFLECTION in the mirror, staring into the face of a stranger. The past decade had taken its toll. Thankfully, the bruises had faded well enough that makeup could cover them. She might even be able to attend church today. That would be nice. It had been a while.

Mack Lee didn't like church. According to him, everybody there was a hypocrite and only went to church so they could look down their noses at "normal" people. Rebecca had given up trying to get him to go years ago. She only went herself when he was out of town watching a stockcar race... and when makeup could cover the bruises. Her husband was a mean drunk, and he was drunk most of the time.

Today was their tenth wedding anniversary. Today was also the twentieth running of the Daytona 500, and Mack Lee had left on Friday to watch the event.

Good riddance, she thought. "God, please help David Pearson to win! Mack Lee's always in a better mood when *his* driver wins," she said aloud, face upturned toward the heavens.

Ironically, it did not bother Rebecca one bit that her husband was absent for their anniversary or that he probably didn't even remember the date. If she was being totally honest with herself, she preferred his absence. It provided a welcome respite. Even had he remembered the date, she wouldn't have felt inclined to celebrate their union. Only fools choose to celebrate a bad decision. She'd been young, desperate, and totally under the thrall of her evil mother-in-law when she'd agreed to marry Mack Lee.

And stupid...let's not forget stupid! No point in crying about it now, she thought as she dabbed at her makeup. Going to church again would be nice.

Church would be good. Rebecca knew James *needed* to go. He was a sweet child, but recently she'd begun noticing the emergence of a few less-than-savory characteristics. She supposed that should've come as no great surprise. After all, he *had* dwelled his entire life beneath the malevolent shadows of Margaret and Mack Lee Hamilton.

Like most little boys, James was desperate to please his "father"—she of all people, could attest to the impossible nature of *that* task—and to do so, he had to be tough. For a child, it is often difficult to discern the line between being tough and just being mean. He'd started making rude comments to her at home. Heaven knows he'd heard enough of them from Margaret and Mack Lee. James was very bright and certainly neither deaf nor blind. It pained her terribly that her sweet little James might grow to manhood thinking that all of the vitriol around the house was normal, that this was the way people who loved one another were *supposed* to act.

Yes, church would be good for them both. All she needed was a touch more foundation to cover up the bruises.

It was a perfect day for racing. The temperature was a mild seventy-three degrees with a light easterly breeze. Heavy rains earlier in the week had thoroughly washed the track, and racing conditions were "green." Mack Lee was in his version of heaven. David Pearson was running near the front of the pack and appeared to be just biding his time, waiting to make his move on race leader, Richard Petty.

Although his dreams of becoming a professional driver had ended in 1957 after his accident with Bob Morrison, Mack Lee was an avid NASCAR fan. Bob had told him over twenty years ago that NASCAR was going to be huge someday, and damned if he hadn't been right! Whenever Mack Lee was at a racetrack, he didn't simply watch the race, he was *in* the race. It was *him* driving fast, turning left, and leading the draft. It was *him* trading paint and spinning out unwary, less worthy drivers. It was *he* who executed a perfect slingshot on the back stretch for victory and got doused with champagne on Victory Lane. And it *could've* been him too.

His favorite driver, David Pearson, had grown up in Spartanburg, a scant twenty miles away from the Hamilton farm. It was Mack Lee who *should* have been driving the #21 Wood Brothers Purolator Mercury, and in his heart of hearts, he knew this to be the truth. Had it not been for the wreck that messed up his leg, *he* would have been the one biding his time behind Petty's ugly blue #43 Dodge instead of Pearson. In spite of the fact that Pearson had practically "stolen" the job with Wood Brothers Racing away from him, he was still Mack Lee's favorite driver on the NASCAR circuit.

Mack Lee had met David Pearson once. One day, he happened to stop by Mack Lee's filling station for gas. While filling his tank, Mack Lee had offered him some sage advice about how to drive at Charlotte Motor Speedway and beat Petty. The very next weekend, Pearson won the World 600 there for his first victory. That was the story Mack Lee recounted to anyone who'd listen. Of course, in reality, the story played out quite differently. Indeed, Pearson had once purchased gasoline from the filling station where Mack Lee worked and subsequently won the World 600 the following weekend. However, the only direct interaction between the two had been when Pearson complained that Mack Lee had "shorted him five bucks" on his change and then drove away from the station with his left hand, middle finger extended, sticking out the driver's side window.

A record 140,000 screaming race fans packed the grandstands and infield that year for the Daytona 500, and Mack Lee fit right in. He was having a grand time drinking beer and cheering on his driver. Beside him, Sherri Lynde had her hand on his thigh, idly caressing his inseam. That made him remember last night. How he'd missed being with a "real" woman. Whereas Rebecca just lay there in bed like a scared mouse, Sherri was a tiger and he had the scratches on his back to prove it.

Mack Lee mused over their previous evening's nocturnal activities until, on lap sixty-one, Petty cut his left rear tire, spun, and took out the cars of both Darrell Waltrip and Pearson. His attention brought back to the present moment, he leaped to his feet in sudden rage. In a tantrum, he threw down his beer can and began screaming obscenities at the top of his lungs. The can hit the ground and spun wildly, spewing Old Milwaukee over the back of a female fan two rows in front of him. She shrieked, and her husband, a mountain of a man in a tank-top muscle shirt spun around, ready to protect his lady's honor.

Mack Lee took one look at the guy's rippling biceps and Marine Corps tattoo on his forearm and did the only thing he could do in the situation. He blustered and lied. "What's your problem, man?! You got a problem, huh? Even with this knee full of Viet Cong shrapnel, I'll kick your ass. I dropped my beer. It was an accident. Big whoop! You wanna make somethin' of it?"

The big guy said, "*You*? Kick *my* ass?! Yeah, right! Like *that's* ever gonna happen. I'd like nothing better than to show you exactly how wrong you are, but I'll never raise a hand toward another Vietnam vet. Everything's cool, man. Semper Fi."

The remainder of the race was classic NASCAR. Benny Parsons blew a tire and spun out, catching A. J. Foyt's fender and sending his car tumbling across the Turn 1 infield in an impressive crash. The remainder of the race was without much excitement, and it looked like Buddy Baker was going to win easily. But, with just eleven laps remaining, Baker's car began belching the "blue smoke of disaster" as his engine blew. That handed Bobby Allison the race on a silver platter, and he cruised on to his first Daytona 500 victory.

Mack Lee had to admit. It had been a good race and a good day, even if Pearson didn't win. But now it was over, and he had to go back to the gas station and that mousy Rebecca. He supposed all good things had to come to an end. With a sigh, he picked up his near-empty beer cooler, and he and Sherri began making their way back to his car. It was already 6:30 p.m. and they had a seven-hour drive back to Boiling Springs ahead of them. Since he was scheduled to open the station in the morning, he'd better get a move on whether he wanted to or not.

CHAPTER 6

FEBRUARY 20, 1978

A CID TEST WAS A CLASSIC "Shaggin' Wagon," a highly customized Chevy van belonging to a pair of fifth-year Music Appreciation majors from Rutgers University. The interior of the former cargo bay had been gutted and now featured wall-to-wall electric-blue shag carpeting lighted by lava lamps built into wall niches. The bay had been accessorized with a high-fidelity sound system with built-in eight-track tape player, a mini fridge, and a well-stocked wet bar. Its most prominent feature, however, was a full-sized waterbed. The van's exterior paint job sported a urethane clear-coat that made the artwork shine. The custom side panels displayed excellent reproductions of Van Gogh's "Starry Night" and Munch's "The Scream." The rear-panel artwork depicted the molecular formula for LSD, for those familiar with chemistry, and the custom license plate read, "ACD TST."

The van's owners had taken time away from their grueling academic schedules to catch a Grateful Dead concert in Tampa and were working their way back north to school. With any luck, they would arrive back on campus in time for spring break. A little after midnight, they were traveling north on I-95 near Bluffton, South Carolina, when a deer bounded across the interstate in front of them. The driver, Bennie Karpezian, immediately slammed on the brakes and yanked the steering wheel to the right. He overcorrected, and the van went up on two wheels, teetering for several seconds before slamming back down on four wheels and skidding to a stop.

"Dude! That was *awesome!*" passenger Darryl Murphy said. "That deer was like, woah...and you were like, wow...and then the van was like—"

At that instant, the van's left front fender was struck by a Chrysler Cordoba driven by Raymond and Sarah Rabinowitz of Boca Raton, Florida. The pair was traveling to Virginia for their granddaughter's fifth birthday. Sarah had urged Ray to stop at a motel as soon as darkness had fallen, but he'd wanted to push onward. She was still in a huff when, almost six hours later, a stopped van materialized on the interstate in front of them. Raymond swerved left but was too late. The Cordoba clipped the van's front fender just ahead of the wheel well and spun the van into the guardrail so that it sat in the emergency lane facing oncoming traffic. Raymond pulled past the van and into the emergency lane and hit his emergency flashers.

In the seat beside him, Sarah berated him as her nose bled onto the rich Corinthian leather seats of their car. "See, I told you we should hab stobbed...now look what habbened. We should hab..."

Raymond tossed a handkerchief onto the seat and slammed the door on his wife's ranting. He limped to the driver's side window of the van. A thick blue fog billowed out when the driver rolled down his window. Immediately, Raymond was struck by a pungent, earthy aroma with just a hint of skunk. He disgustedly waved away the smoke, and asked, "Everybody okay in here? Your van just appeared in front of me. I didn't see you in time. What happened? Is everybody all right?"

"Like, wow, man. Everybody's great. It was Rudolph, man. He was, like, coming through the windshield," slurred the driver.

"Dude, it wasn't Rudolph," the passenger said, laughing. "He didn't have a red nose. Everybody knows Rudolph has a red nose."

Raymond shook his head and rolled his eyes. *Kids these days,* he thought before shuffling to the side of the road and propping against the guardrail to await the first responders.

A passing trucker used his CB radio to notify the Highway Patrol about the accident.

The fender bender had been relatively minor but still backed up interstate traffic for a mile as the Highway Patrol worked to clear the accident. It might have been cleared more rapidly had the responding officers not found drug paraphernalia and two clearly impaired college students in one of the involved vehicles.

In the left-hand lane at the tail of the backed-up traffic, Dwain Crawford sat idling in his ancient White Freightliner. His load of auto parts was due in Richmond in the morning and this delay wasn't going to help him meet his deadline. Management was *not* going to be happy, but there was nothing to be done about it. With little to do but wait, he sat watching the dashboard clock and singing along in a gravelly tenor to Merle Haggard's "Mama Tried" on his eight-track. Movement off to the left caught his attention, and he glanced in his side mirror, finding a pair of headlights coming up fast behind him. As the lights drew closer, they showed no sign of slowing.

That guy better slow down soon! he thought. Then, *Damn, he's* not *slowin' down!* He reached to the dash panel and set his trailer lights to strobe. A moment later, he blurted out, "Oh *shit!*"

Mack Lee's pride and joy was his 1971 AMC Javelin AMX. It was mustard yellow with a black T-stripe on the hood and a 330 horsepower, 401 cubic-inch V8 with a four-barrel carburetor. With racing tires and suspension and several tweaks he'd added in the garage after hours, the car topped out at 125 mph. That night, the engine was humming like a beehive and Mack Lee had the AMX cruising along comfortably at just above 90 mph.

David Pearson's got nothin' on me, he thought as he weaved past slower traffic on I-95 North.

"Yo, babe, you know I'm gonna miss you when we get back home, don't ya?" he said, sliding his hand underneath Sherri Lynde's skirt. Conveniently, she wore nothing beneath.

Sherri gave a gasp as his fingers began to massage between her legs. Almost immediately, he was rewarded by a gush of wetness. "Ummmmmm, baby...that feels so good," she purred. Before too long, she gave a strangled moan and her body jerked spasmodically. "Oh God...*ohhhh...God!!*"

Definitely more fun than Rebecca, he thought.

When her breathing had returned to normal, she said, "You know, baby, you don't *have* to miss me when we get back. You can dump that limp dishrag you're married to and we can be together *all* the time. *Aannnnnnd*, you can have one of *these* any...time...you...like!" She slowly unzipped his fly as she spoke, then took his erect penis into her mouth.

Mack Lee depressed the accelerator farther as he watched Sherri's blonde head bobbing up and down in his lap. Outside, trees and slower traffic flew past his window in a blur. He gave a low groan just as a flashing of light ahead drew his attention back to the windshield.

An instant later, the Javelin plowed into the rear axle of Crawford's trailer at 100 mph. The floor of the trailer cleanly peeled back the top of the car and everything in it just above hood level. Mack Lee was decapitated and died instantly. Sherri Lynde's head was below the level of the dash at the time of impact, thus she escaped decapitation but was pinned between the steering column and Mack Lee's torso. So trapped, she was unable to clear her airway and died a few minutes later from asphyxiation.

A few minutes before five a.m., Rebecca was awakened by a knock at the front door. Initially, she thought she'd dreamed the knocking, but after a short while, the knocking became an insistent pounding. She was certain Margaret would not hear the knocking through her drug-induced stupor and equally certain she knew the cause for the knock. So, she rose from bed and donned her housecoat and stepped into her slippers.

The jackass has probably lost his keys again. Then, she realized the pounding was coming from the front rather than the usual back door. *Or more likely he's too drunk to get his key in the lock. This is going to be ugly. Well, at least I had one good day...*

She sighed and swung the front door open, fully expecting to find Mack Lee falling-down drunk and equally prepared to duck his first wild swing. It wouldn't matter. He would eventually catch her and there'd be more bruises to hide. To her surprise, instead of a drunk and belligerent husband, two men wearing the brown and tan uniform of the South Carolina Highway Patrol stood on the front porch.

"Is there a problem, Officers?" she asked.

"Mrs. Hamilton?" asked the officer on the left.

Rebecca nodded.

"Mrs. Hamilton, I am Officer Spencer and this is Officer Purdue of the Highway Patrol. May we come inside?"

"Certainly, Officers," Rebecca stepped aside and led the two men to the kitchen. *I bet that dumbass man has gotten himself another DUI. How many is that now...three or four? Either way, it's going to be expensive...more money we just don't have.* Then, to the officers, she asked, "Would you like me to put on a pot of coffee?"

"No thank you, ma'am," answered Spencer. "Ma'am, I'm afraid we have some bad news. You might want to sit down."

They're being awfully nice about telling me my husband is a repeat offender drunk driver. She cinched her robe a little tighter but elected not to sit. She was pretty sure that whatever the fool had gone and done, she could stand up through it.

"Ma'am, your husband was involved in an accident. It occurred a little after midnight, and I regret to inform you that neither he nor his passenger survived. I am terribly sorry for your loss," said Purdue.

Rebecca's hand flew to her mouth, and she collapsed into a chair. "Oh dear! Mack Lee...he's dead? Mack Lee Hamilton?"

"Yes, ma'am. We're afraid so," answered Spencer.

"Wait a minute. You said there was a passenger? That's impossible. My husband was alone. He was in Florida for the Daytona 500, but no one was with him. Clearly there has been some mistake. I'm sorry that you officers have wasted your time..."

"No, ma'am. There's been no mistake. The vehicle was registered to your husband, and his driver's license was found at the scene. The female passenger has been identified as one Sherri Lyn—"

Rebecca's eyes flashed. "That son of a bitch!"

CHAPTER 7

FEBRUARY–MARCH, 1978

G IVEN THE GRUESOME NATURE OF his injuries, Mack Lee's funeral service was performed with a closed casket. After the service, the usual collection of family friends, coworkers, and distant relations filed past, expressing their condolences and doling out meaningless platitudes. Through it all, Rebecca's eyes remained dry and free of makeup behind the black veil she wore.

"Where the *Hell* were all these people ten years ago?" she muttered through gritted teeth.

Margaret, on the other hand, was totally consumed by grief. With the passage of each well-wisher, pat of hand or hug, she seemed to sink deeper into her pit of despair. This time, she was going down and the meds were not even going to slow her fall, much less arrest it.

From behind her veil, Rebecca gazed scornfully at her mother-in-law. She couldn't help but notice the difference in Margaret's affect now compared to when Jimmy had died. Back then, she'd shown no more emotion than might've been expected had she been informed that the neighbor's annoying dog had been struck and killed by the mail truck. At the time, Rebecca had interpreted her mother-in-law's lack of outward sentiment to strength and resolve and had even admired her for it. It hadn't taken long for her to see things as they truly were. Margaret had shown nothing because she'd *felt* nothing. She'd been too busy scheming to feel anything.

Well, you're feeling it now, you old witch. Welcome to my world!

After the funeral and burial services, the family returned home for a repast. Rebecca, James, and Margaret welcomed a parade of condolences and casseroles that continued until well into the evening. Rebecca rolled her eyes as she cleaned up after everyone left, thinking, *Does tuna casserole have magical restorative properties for those grieving a loss?* People must have thought so, for she'd put seven of them into the freezer, along with several fried chickens, three pans of baked beans, and enough cakes and pies to keep poor James on a sugar high until Halloween.

Rebecca was exhausted. All she wanted to do was get out of her heels and dress and soak in the bathtub for at least an hour. Most of the bruises were gone, but some of the day's well-meaning hugs had aggravated her cracked ribs. The hot water would help, she was sure of it.

No sooner than she'd settled back into the steaming water, a blood-curdling scream emanated from James's room. She leaped from the bath and ran upstairs, pulling on her bathrobe as she ran. Arriving at her son's door, she saw James lying in his bed, bleeding from a deep gash on his forearm and another on his chest. Margaret stood over him, raising a bloody chef's knife for another strike.

"James!" Rebecca cried. Then she grabbed her son's baseball bat from the end of the bed and, without thinking, swung it with all her might.

The bat struck the knife, sending it cartwheeling into the wall, where it struck, point first, into the wallboard.

"Mother! What are you doing?!" Rebecca screamed, dropping the bat and kneeling by James.

The boy wailed in pain and terror.

Eyes wide and bulging and spittle flying from her lips, Margaret ranted, "He has to die! He has to die! He killed them! He killed them all."

"What are you saying, Mother?" Rebecca screamed. Then to the boy, in a soothing tone as she wrapped his injured arm in a pillowcase, she said, "It's okay. Mama's here."

"He killed them! He killed my baby! He killed my little girl! He killed Walter, and now he's killed my little boy! He is evil—the devil's spawn! He must die! I should have killed him already!" Margaret's eyes were rolling wildly as she yanked the knife free from the wall and lurched toward James. "He has to die!"

Rebecca made no attempt to aim the bat at the knife as she swung. Instead, it connected with her mother-in-law's skull with a sickening thud. A second later, another thud followed as the older woman's head thumped against the floor, where she lay unmoving.

Rebecca scooped James into her arms and ran downstairs, somehow still grasping the bat. She deposited her son on the kitchen table and after three attempts, her trembling fingers managed to dial the police.

A patrol car was immediately dispatched to the Hamilton house. On its arrival, Rebecca explained events to the responding officers who in turn raced upstairs with weapons drawn. Two ambulances were dispatched, one for James and the other for Margaret.

By the time the first ambulance arrived, Rebecca was nearly hysterical. James was covered in sweat and breathing rapidly in short, ineffectual gasps. His lips were a dusky blue and were opening and closing like a landed carp. Her son was dying right before her eyes.

The first attendant into the room, a dark-haired man whose name badge read Cabrera, took in the tableau and sprang into action. He ripped open James's shirt, exposing his chest. Then, he found a huge needle and was preparing to stab it into the boy's heaving chest, only to have his hand caught by a terrified Rebecca.

"What are you doing to him?!" Rebecca screamed as she grabbed the man's hand with both of hers.

"It's okay, ma'am. I saw this kinda thing a thousand times back when I was in 'Nam."

Something in the way he spoke and the look of his opaline-green eyes—unusual given his otherwise Hispanic-appearing features and her swearing they were brown a moment ago—stayed Rebecca's hand, and she allowed him to continue. In one quick motion, Cabrera inserted the huge needle into the right side of James's chest, halfway between the nipple and collarbone, and was instantly rewarded by a *whoosh* as trapped air escaped from within. Immediately, James's respiratory rate slowed and his lips returned to a pale pink.

After stabilizing the boy, Cabrera bandaged the forearm wound and, with the second attendant, lifted James onto a stretcher and rolled him to the ambulance. The attendants climbed in, and as they pulled out from the driveway, the second attendant turned to his partner and asked, "What the Hell was that, Cabrera? I thought you said you were a mess sergeant in Vietnam."

"Yeah, that's right. I was," Cabrera answered, winking one of his dark brown eyes as he flicked on the ambulance's red flashing lights and siren. "What of it?"

The second ambulance arrived a short time later and transported Margaret to the Psychiatric Ward. Some weeks later, she was moved on to the state hospital for the criminally insane in Columbia.

In his grandmother's attack, James had suffered a collapsed lung and a nasty laceration to his left forearm that narrowly missed severing his radial artery. After emergency surgery, he spent a week in the Intensive Care Unit with a chest tube and seventy-two stitches in his arm. Still, he recovered quickly from his wounds and was soon able to return to school.

Children can be cruel. Consequently, his return was not a pleasant one. A week later, he was sent home early from school for fighting. Rebecca was shocked because James had never been in any trouble before at school. He'd always loved school.

"James, what happened?" she asked. "You know better than fighting."

"I don't want to talk about it, Mom." James's words came out thick through a split and swollen lip.

"I don't recall *asking* you what you *wanted* to talk about," she snapped. "I asked what happened."

"Yes, ma'am. Some kids were making fun."

"You know better than that. Remember, when you roll in the mud with a pig, you both get muddy and the pig likes it."

"I know, but this was different."

"No excuses. What could they *possibly* say to make you lose control like that? Who were you fighting with?"

"Terry Brennon. He was making fun of Grandma, calling her Loony Granny and saying, 'The nut doesn't fall far from the tree,' and stuff like that."

"Well, that wasn't very nice, but it doesn't merit fighting," she scolded.

"That's not all. He made fun of Dad too. He said that Dad got decapitated twice. 'He lost both his big head and his little head.' And that he 'lost his head while getting head.' I didn't know what that meant, but I hit him..."

Rebecca's face turned scarlet. "That little shit!" she hissed.

"...and blacked his eye, and I think I might have knocked one of his teeth loose," James said, staring at his shoes.

Her desire to scold her son faded in an instant. "I think I have some ice cream in the freezer to make your lip feel better, but no more fighting! Okay?"

James agreed with his mother's request readily enough and might have even been happy to comply. However, he was an angry, confused little boy who was rapidly growing into an angry and confused young man. Mack Lee, after all, had been his only male role model, and James was nothing if not an observant child. Consequently, the day's altercation was not the last. Indeed, it was the first of many over the years to come.

CHAPTER 8

1979

REBECCA HAD BEEN TRAPPED IN history's longest total solar eclipse. For ten long years, her world had been cold, gray, and dark. The birds rarely sang and only the faintest corona of her previous luster was evident to anyone who saw her. While Mack Lee lived, Margaret Butler Hamilton had reigned supreme in their home. Rebecca had been beaten down, literally and figuratively, almost every day of those ten years. But in an instant, the twin moons that had blotted her sun were taken away, and her radiance was soon, once again, obvious to all.

Remarkably, it had been the pair's scheming that ultimately helped to elevate Rebecca after Mack Lee's death and Margaret's committal to the asylum. When a distraught Rebecca had been manipulated into marrying Mack Lee, she'd been young, naïve, and trusting of her mother-in-law. She'd had no knowledge of military death benefits or insurance, and it had been a complete surprise to her when, a week later, she received a check for ten thousand dollars from Jimmy's Servicemen's Group Life Insurance policy. Of course, as her husband, Mack Lee had immediately assumed control of Jimmy's entire death benefit. To her chagrin, rather than being a good steward of the money meant to provide for her and Jimmy's child, he'd paid a few bills, bought himself a hotrod, and then blown the rest drinking, whoring, and gambling.

Having learned the painful lesson that her mother-in-law and new husband were not to be trusted, Rebecca had wisely neglected to inform either of them when, under Public Law 89-214, she began receiving fifty-five dollars per month from Social Security as Jimmy's widow with one child. Most of this money she'd used to provide necessities for herself and young James, but with the rest, she'd opened a savings account at Boiling Springs State Bank and purchased a twenty-five-thousand-dollar life insurance policy on Mack Lee. Given his reckless nature, she paid an additional $1.65 per month to secure double indemnity for accidental death. Consequently, upon Mack Lee's death, his widow assumed sole ownership of the house and farm *and* received an insurance payout for fifty thousand dollars.

In his best year working at the gas station, Mack Lee never made more than ten thousand dollars, much of which he wasted on booze and gambling. So, if she was careful with her money, Rebecca and James could live comfortably for at least five years, even if she developed no other source of income. And if she could rehab the farm, she might even be able to afford college for James when the time came.

In stark contrast to her second husband, Rebecca was an excellent steward for her newly received wealth. She hired a foreman for the farm and, with his assistance, began growing soybeans. By the end of the first year, the farm was breaking even. By the third year, Rebecca was turning a tidy profit, most of which she reinvested into the farm. Additionally, she rehabbed the old farmhouse and grounds, bringing them back to a level of splendor unknown since before the Great Depression.

For her final investment, she set aside a college fund for James. Like Jimmy, he was exceptionally intelligent. Rebecca was certain that if his inner demons didn't drag him down, he had a bright future ahead of him. If not, she feared he'd wind up like Mack Lee.

Before his death, Mack Lee had never been particularly close to James. He considered the child little more than a costly nuisance, a drain on family resources, someone to be tolerated and certainly not nurtured.

Like any little boy, James desperately craved his ersatz father's love and approval. He always wanted to show Mack Lee how tough and strong he was becoming because he intuited that these were characteristics his father would appreciate.

Although sweet-natured at home, at school James was belligerent and quick to take offense. Kids being kids, any chink in the armor was seen as an invitation, and Mack Lee was clearly James's Achilles heel.

Recently, one of the boys in the grade above James began calling him "Ichabod Crane" and referring to Mack Lee as "The Headless Whores-man." James immediately punched the older boy in the mouth and knocked out two teeth. This led to medical bills, detention, and threats of expulsion by school administrators.

Jimmy had been a kind and gentle soul, whereas Mack Lee had been something of a lout. Rebecca could see shades of both men in her son. It saddened her to observe Jimmy's kindness and compassion slowly being eclipsed by Mack Lee's more brutish nature.

Nature versus nurture, Rebecca thought.

In retrospect, her agreeing to marry Mack Lee and then have him listed as James's father had been a terrible mistake. Decisions always seemed simpler in hindsight, and this time had been no different.

She had practically sleepwalked through the months after Jimmy's death. When Margaret had suggested that her baby's birth certificate be changed to reflect Mack Lee as father and thereby save the cost of formal adoption proceedings, Rebecca had been powerless to object.

She bitterly remembered the conversation with her mother-in-law.

Margaret had told her, "Since you've been living in the same house as Mack Lee since before the child's birth, almost everyone in town *assumes* him to be the father anyway. Now that you two are married, having your husband's name on the birth certificate makes you look like less of a whore."

Rebecca had been totally taken aback, but what choice did she have? On reflection, many, but she hadn't realized it at the time.

Now, James was struggling because of flawed decisions she'd made when he was an infant. But what could she do about it now? What would be worse for him? Learning that he'd been lied to about his real father? Or leaving well enough alone?

Inertia being hard to overcome, Rebecca elected to "let things ride" for now and hoped the "right time" would someday present itself to tell James about Jimmy.

Besides, she rationalized. *With Mack Lee gone, what difference does it make anyhow? I'm sure he'll be okay. With time, he'll forget Mack Lee and outgrow all this nonsense.*

CHAPTER 9

1980

W HEN JAMES WAS TWELVE YEARS old, he was sent home from school with a note for Rebecca. According to the note, he'd been caught cheating on an exam and, since he adamantly refused to admit to his guilt, been suspended from school. The note also requested that she attend a conference at three o'clock the next afternoon to discuss his offenses and detail the school's requirements for his readmission.

Rebecca was flabbergasted. James was an excellent student. He'd always received top marks on every test or exam he'd ever taken, and his report cards had always shown straight A's.

Rebecca waved the note before James's face. "James! What's the meaning of this?"

Her face was flushed, and the creases between her eyebrows formed an angry-appearing *W*. It was a look he'd rarely seen in his dozen years on earth, and one he hoped not to see again in the near future. "I don't know, Mama," was all he could think to say.

"Don't you 'I don't know' me!" Rebecca hissed. "You certainly *do* know, and you're going to tell me *all* about it *now*, young man."

"But, Mam—"

Rebecca's look silenced his objection.

"*Now*, mister!"

"They say I cheated, Mama, but I didn't." A tear welled in the corner of his eyes. "Really, Mama, I didn't."

Rebecca's anger began to fade a just a little. She'd never known her son to lie to her, and she saw no indication that he was doing so this time either. "Okay, then. Tell me what happened," she directed.

"We had a test in my American History class. Usually, our tests are fill-in-the-blank or multiple choice, but this time, it was an essay test. I answered the questions just like what I'd read in the textbook. The teacher said that I answered the questions *too* well, and said that somehow, I'd copied my essay from the textbook. She said my answer was too exact to be my own."

"And did you? Copy, I mean?"

"No, ma'am. I just wrote what I remembered. I just remember really well."

"Uh-huh." Rebecca seemed unconvinced.

"Look, I'll show you."

James handed Rebecca his History textbook.

"Now, turn to any page."

Rebecca took the textbook and turned to a random page.

"Don't show it to me," he said. "What page did you choose?"

"Page two hundred-fourteen."

James's eyelids fluttered for an instant and then, after a short pause, he recited every word on page 214, including illustration captions and footnotes.

Amazed, Rebecca picked another random page and, once again, James recited the new page's text verbatim. Then he did it again...and again.

"How do you *do* that?" she asked, clearly astonished.

"I dunno," James replied. "It just happens. Whenever I read something, it's like there's a picture of it stored inside my head."

"James, that's incredible!"

He gave his mother a quizzical look. "You mean that doesn't happen for you too?"

"Nope."

"How 'bout for other people?"

Rebecca shook her head, then gave her son a hug and said, "I never should've doubted you. Will you forgive me, James?"

The next day, she brought James with her to the conference at school. To the amazement of his teacher and principal, he again demonstrated his ability to perfectly quote written text after only a fleeting glance at any page of any book. He was immediately reinstated into his classes with a sincere apology from his teacher. Additionally, the principal recommended that he be evaluated by a specialist, Dr. Amos Malone, at the Institute for Memory Studies in Columbia.

On the ride home, James was uncharacteristically quiet. Rebecca glanced in the rearview mirror several times, thinking he looked awfully pensive. He just stared out the window. By the time they arrived home, he looked like he was about to cry.

In the driveway, Rebecca put the car in park, but James made no effort to open his door. She turned to him and asked, "What's wrong, sweetie? I thought you'd be on top of the world, back in school *and* with an apology from your teacher. You're batting a thousand."

"Why do they want to send me to Columbia?"

"They want you to see a specialist there, about your memory."

"But they sent Grandma to Columbia..." James's voice faltered, and the tears he'd been holding back began to flow freely. "I don't want to go to jail or to the loony bin!"

Rebecca practically flew across the bench seat and into the back with her son. There, she drew him into a fierce hug. "Oh, sweetie, no. It's not like that! The school wants you to see Dr. Malone because you are exceptional, *not* because you've done anything even remotely wrong."

James buried his face in his mother's shoulder, his breaths coming in halting sobs. "R-r-r-really?"

"Really, sweetie! I promise. Now, let's go in and have some ice cream. We have butter pecan, your favorite."

The next week, Rebecca and James traveled to Columbia for his appointment with Dr. Malone, a clinical psychologist specializing in memory. According to the "love me" wall behind his desk, he had graduated from Berkeley and held a PhD from Harvard. He was a short, thin man with a high, nasally voice. He was almost bald, and what little strawberry-blond hair he had left grew in tufts over his ears. He had a bulbous nose set over a bushy mustache and a weak chin. To James, he looked less like Sigmund Freud and more like Mr. Drucker from *Green Acres*.

After extensive discussion about James's unique abilities and the importance of understanding them better, Malone convinced Rebecca to allow James to stay at the institute for a few days of rigorous testing and observation. James was initially terrified, believing that he was being committed as had been his grandmother. Dr. Malone, however, assured him that this was not the case and promised that at all times James would be in control over his stay. He could halt all testing, or even leave, at any time he chose. When Rebecca agreed to stay with him at the institute, James acquiesced to staying.

He spent three full days being interviewed and tested. The staff at the Institute for Memory Studies performed brain scans, EEGs, word association testing, Rorschach tests, IQ testing, and various memory challenges. He didn't mind the testing at all and actually found his experience at the institute to be fun. After, James and Rebecca returned to Dr. Malone's office to discuss the test results.

"Good afternoon, Mrs. Hamilton, James," Malone said with a nod.

After their returned greetings, the doctor motioned them to the two companion chairs set before his desk. He pulled a file folder from a drawer and began patting the pockets of his white coat for his eyeglasses. Not finding them there, he riffled through piles of papers on his desk in a continuation of his search.

"Are you looking for those?" James motioned to the pair of wire-rimmed spectacles perched atop the doctor's fore-head.

Dr. Malone reached up and slid the specs onto his nose. "I'm always forgetting where I put my glasses." He looked up expectantly, clearly expecting a response.

Receiving none, he continued with a forced laugh. "Sorry. Just a little Institute for Memory Studies humor to break the tension."

James fought the urge to roll his eyes and lost.

"Well, yes...yes, right...about James's testing," the doctor began.

Both Rebecca and James leaned forward expectantly in their chairs.

"First of all, let me say that James is a *very* bright young man. But, I'm certain that I'm not telling you anything you don't already know, Mrs. Hamilton. His intelligence quotient would easily qualify him for Mensa. On the three IQ tests we ran, he scored 179, 180, and 173, respectively, all three well above what is considered to be the genius threshold of 140.

"Second, James's memory is rather unique and quite extraordinary. He is able to reproduce long written excerpts almost without error, even when written in a foreign language. His memory is not quite perfect as there *were* errors, but the errors that we noted were trivial. For example, an *umlaut* misplaced over an adjacent vowel while writing in German or an *accent grave* instead of an *accent aigu* in French—that's an accent mark that points to the left versus to the right, respectively—even though he speaks neither language. It's almost like he has an enhanced eidetic memory."

"An enhanced what?" Rebecca interrupted. "You lost me after unique and quite extraordinary."

"Ah, yes...I suppose I did lapse a bit into doctor-ese." Then Malone explained, "By way of example, when we mere mortals stare at a page of print and then close our eyes, the image of the page persists in our memory for a second or two and then fades. That transient memory trace is an eidetic memory. With James here, that image, rather than fading, is transferred to his short-term memory and later into long-term memory with almost no lapses or gaps. It's truly remarkable."

Rebecca nodded her understanding...more or less.

Malone continued, "Additionally, his autobiographical memory—that's memories of things he's personally experienced—are off the charts with their detail and accuracy. I've heard about cases like this, but they're exceptionally rare."

"So, you're saying that James has a photographic memory?" Becca asked.

"Not exactly. With a photographic memory, and there is some debate as to whether that condition even exists, subjects remember only images. With James, he remembers not only images but sounds, smells, tastes...any sensory input associated with events within his own life. His is sort of a super-enhanced version of a photographic memory."

James had been following the conversation closely, albeit in silence. When he finally spoke up, it was to ask, "Is that why I can quote whole pages from textbooks?"

Malone nodded. "It is, indeed. That, and you have an extraordinarily high IQ."

"Is there something that caused this, like a brain tumor or something?" Rebecca asked.

"Good heavens, no," Malone replied with a reassuring wave to the heavens. "It's an act of God...an anomaly of creation. Sometimes these sorts of things run in families, but there's no associated pathology. In fact, when we did James's brain scan, the only irregularity we noted was that his amygdala—that's an almond-sized structure at the base of the brain that regulates memory and emotion—was slightly larger than would be typical for a boy his age."

"Is that a bad thing? You know, a larger than normal am-yg-dala?" Rebecca asked, struggling with the word.

"Certainly not, Mrs. Hamilton. In fact, examination of Einstein's brain showed a similar anomaly. In addition, the electroencephalogram we performed on James returned as perfectly normal. There's nothing at all wrong with young

James, here. He is a perfectly healthy and normal, yet quite gifted young man. Now, James,"—Dr. Malone turned slightly in his chair—"if you don't mind, I have a few things to discuss alone with your mother. I'll have my assistant show you to the waiting room."

If James had felt put off by having been summarily dismissed by the doctor or by his condescending tone, he didn't show it. Instead, he complied without protest and returned to the waiting room. None of the magazines there were even remotely interesting to him, so he passed the time watching tropical fish swim about in a large aquarium and mentally calculating the volume of water displaced by the air bubbles emanating from the sunken pirate ship therein to pass the time.

Rebecca had always known that James seemed very smart, especially compared to his peers in school. She'd always assumed that the difference could be explained by his being a year older than his classmates. Due to his small stature and October birthdate, she'd had him start first grade a year late. But this doctor was suggesting there was more to it than she'd suspected.

After James's departure, Dr. Malone turned his focus back to Rebecca. "Mrs. Hamilton, I wanted this additional time with you to speak on two issues about which you should be made aware."

Rebecca arranged her purse in her lap and leaned forward expectantly. "Yes, Doctor?"

"The first is pretty simple. It is clear from the testing we've performed that James is not being challenged in his current academic environment. It is the collective opinion of our staff that he would benefit from private education. Somewhere he will not be, not to put too fine a point on it, held back by his peers. Public schools do a wonderful job.

However, a team of horses is no faster than the slowest horse in the harness. In a public-school setting, James is a thoroughbred sharing the track with a bunch of broken-down pack mules. At best, if he remains in public school, he will simply not live up to his potential. At worst, he will become increasingly frustrated and find other, ummm, less constructive ways to stimulate his mind."

Rebecca remembered Mack Lee and shuddered involuntarily. "Like alcohol, drugs, or gambling?"

"That would be our concern, yes."

"I understand, Doctor, but private school is just so expensive. It's just the two of us at home, and we live on a farm, always one bad year away from total ruin. I don't know if we can afford it."

"Luckily, the IMS has a scholarship program, and there are several grants James would easily qualify for that should defray the costs. I'll have my staff help you in filling out the applications if you'd like."

"That would be wonderful, Doctor. Thank you!"

Dr. Malone gave a nod. "Consider it done. The second matter is potentially more concerning. I do not wish to alarm you, but James's exceptional memory has the potential to be a double-edged sword. Certainly, having such an extraordinary memory may lead him to unimaginable heights, but it also may come with its share of challenges.

"With the vast majority of humans, memory is fleeting and fades over time. For even the most intense of memories, time blurs the lines and softens the edges of the picture. This is a natural, protective phenomenon designed to shield the psyche from harm. James doesn't have the luxury of forgetting. He will remember an event from thirty years past as clearly as though it was from but a moment before. Because his memory is unchanged and unattenuated by time, he will continue to experience the feelings, smells, fears, tastes, and sounds associated with the event, which he may find over-whelming. It may be especially so if the event being relived is painful or traumatic. Because the memories are all "new," even the old ones, it is possible for subjects like James to become *trapped* by the past—doomed to relive every detail as though it happened only a moment before.

"As humans living our lives, memories continue to com-pound and collect, but for James, they'll never fade. Con-sequently, subjects with his type of memory might spend a great deal of time 'looking back.' It could prove daunting and may lead him into anxiety or depression."

"Oh dear! Is there anything we can do...you know, to help him?" Rebecca asked.

"Perhaps I've said too much? It is not appropriate for me to speculate. As I mentioned before, I've never seen anything like James's memory. His memory is neither truly photographic nor eidetic. It's something totally unique. Be-cause of this, *no one* knows what to expect. He may have issues, or he may have none. Only time will tell. Because of this, I would like to continue seeing James in the future to assess his evolution and, if necessary, intervene if he does not appear to be coping well with his gift."

CHAPTER 10

1981–1986

J AMES FLOURISHED IN HIS NEW private-school setting. Allowed to advance at his own speed and into curricular areas tailored to his interests, he enjoyed the challenge of taking advanced, college-level classes while technically still being in high school. In 1986, he graduated as class valedictorian and received full four-year academic scholarship offers from Massachusetts Institute of Technology and Harvard, Brown, and Duke Universities.

An additional positive this change of academic venue provided was that no one knew—or particularly cared— about his family's history. Consequently, there was no more teasing about Mack Lee, and James's more pugilistic tendencies fell dormant. Still, he seemed standoffish and had few close friends. Most of his classmates would have described him as reserved, aloof, and unapproachable. Although not an unusual trait for a teenage male, he was often socially awkward and was easily embarrassed, especially around the girls in his school.

With multiple scholarship offers from which to choose, James ultimately elected to attend MIT and selected a double major of Chemistry and Physics with a minor in

History and matriculated in fall of 1986. When his faculty adviser suggested that perhaps he was being a little optimistic by taking on such a heavy class load, James just smiled... and eventually graduated at the top of his class after only three years.

Back in Boiling Springs, Rebecca couldn't have been more proud of her son. It appeared that in the academic world, he'd found his niche. He seemed happy and well-adjusted. Her favorite part of each week was Sunday afternoon, for each Sunday at precisely three o'clock, James called her to talk about his week. Finally, she could relax. James was emerging from the shadow of his childhood and seemed happy.

Apparently, Rebecca had a knack for the business of farming. Consequently, the farm was thriving. She'd even expanded its acreage by purchasing several surrounding properties. From her perspective, all was well.

She had many friends and acquaintances around town, but her only social activity of note was her church. She was there every Sunday morning and Wednesday night for services and was active on several committees. She'd even taken it upon herself to reorganize and manage the church library and archives. Otherwise, with James away in school, her personal life was as barren as a plowed field in the dead of winter.

That's not to say, however, that she lacked potential suitors. The Widow Hamilton was still very attractive in her late thirties and was considered, in her economically depressed farming community, to be "a woman of means." Consequently, she was seen as quite a catch for the single and divorced men of the town. She even went out on a few dates, but they always ended the same way, with Rebecca requesting to be taken home and dropped off early. Just the idea of having someone rutting atop her like Mack Lee had made her feel physically ill. Besides, the only man she'd ever really love, or want, was Jimmy.

That was not to say, however, that she didn't enjoy going on dates. She enjoyed the company but had no desires beyond sharing a nice dinner and intelligent conversation with members of the opposite sex. When her suitors seemed eager for more, she shut them down, albeit gently and with a manner that left them smiling. Behind her, she left a trail of wistful, wannabe lovers who could think of nothing bad to say about her.

When James returned home for Christmas beak during his freshman year at MIT, he and Rebecca had a wonderful reunion. Although she was happy to hear that his classes were going well, she was disappointed that he seemed to be neglecting his social life. With this in mind, she encouraged him to look up some of his old friends while he was in town.

James was reluctant, but after she played the "All work and no play makes James a dull boy" card, he acquiesced. He knew from experience that when his mom started spouting idioms, resistance was futile. So, he called several of his old friends from high school, and they all went to the movies together. Sadly, he found he had absolutely nothing in common with any of them anymore. He'd gone away from home and seen something of the world. They, on the other hand, seemed content never to leave Spartanburg County, much less the state of South Carolina. Watching NASCAR, bass fishing, and cow tipping—although his former friends clearly enjoyed them and who was he to judge—were not high-value recreations from James's perspective.

However, the film the group had selected, Oliver Stone's *Platoon*, left James totally enthralled. Held spellbound by the Vietnam War flick, he returned to the theater the next day and watched it again...and again on the next day. Something about the chaos of battles without defined front lines and the blurring of good and evil captivated him. It was as though the film *spoke* to him. His profound reaction sent his mind wondering about whether perhaps he should drop out of college for a few years, maybe give the army a try and get out into the world.

Rebecca was mortified, not only that he'd set his education and bright future aside but that he'd put himself in harm's way and risk dying like his father had. Though he didn't know anything about that, she knew the pain of great loss too well and was not willing to risk losing her son.

"Absolutely not!" she said in a shrill, croaking whisper, beginning to hyperventilate.

"But, Mom—"

"Don't you 'But, Mom' me, young man!" she snapped.

Rebecca's icy tone caught James off guard and made him wonder why she was so worked up. He'd never seen her so strident about *anything.* Historically, if they had a disagreement, she would lay out a calm, reasonable argument, which more often than not persuaded him to change his mind—but not this time. Her hands were gesticulating wildly, and her face appeared flushed. She even seemed to be physically shaking.

"You're *not* dropping out of school or joining the army, and that's final!"

"If not the army, then how about the navy, marines, or air for—"

Rebecca's glare cut James off before he could finish. "*No* branch of the military...and I don't want you watching that horrible movie anymore!"

"Horrible movie?" James suddenly became defensive. "Mom, how can you say that? You've not even seen it. They're even saying it has a chance at an Academy Award."

"I don't have to see it to know. I watched that goddamn war every night on the evening news! It's a terrible movie about an awful war."

James was taken aback. He'd never known his mother to curse, and now she was even beginning to cry. "Mom?"

"It was a terrible war...and it took away my Ji—" Rebecca caught herself. "It ruined the lives of so many people." She wheeled and, with hot tears streaming down her face, rushed from the room, sobbing hysterically.

James watched his mother's abrupt withdrawal and, a moment later, heard her bedroom door slam. "What the Hell was *that* all about," he muttered to himself. *Menopause maybe*? He shook his head in disgust.

In January of 1987, James returned to college for Spring Term without giving any additional thought to military service. He didn't want to upset his mother and, clearly, she had been set firmly against it. Besides, he'd never *really* been serious about it anyway. He was enjoying the challenges of college life too much to put his academics on hold, even for a short while. There'd be time enough for traveling the world later, and without anybody shooting at him.

Rebecca had been relieved when James dropped the idea of military service and returned to school. She just could not bear the thought of possibly losing James to the same fate that had taken Jimmy.

CHAPTER 11

1987

REBECCA RETURNED TO HER USUAL prespring planting activities once James went back to school in January. The foreman she'd hired for the farm, although he seemed competent enough, really didn't have a head for business. He was good for keeping the fields plowed, fertilized, planted, and harvested on time but had no capacity for strategic planning. The farm was doing well, but there was always some urgent issue demanding Rebecca's personal attention, leaving her little time for life away from the farm.

Had she more time or interest, she might have pursued having a relationship—more than friends—with Edward Belleau. The scion of Belleau Farms, he would someday inherit his father's multimillion-dollar peach empire. On their first date, he was proud to point out that his family's farm produced more peaches annually than the entire state of Georgia, and Georgia was the Peach State. He was well-educated and articulate. Rebecca enjoyed his quick wit and found that they had much in common. With him, she was able to talk farming and could match him jape for jape, such that their time together was filled with laughter and light banter. However, Rebecca just didn't feel enough of a spark there to move beyond a third date, but thought he'd make a wonderful friend. So, after a kiss on the cheek, Edward dropped Rebecca off on her doorstep and drove away thinking what a wonderful wife she might've made, such a nice person. Maybe he should call her next week so they could have lunch together.

Relaxed after a lovely evening, Rebecca drifted back to her bedroom and pulled out a milk crate packed full of vinyl record albums. Flipping through them, she smiled and selected a few, slipping them from their cardboard sleeves. She gently blew away a fleck of dust from the first and fed it over the extended center spindle, directly onto the platter. The second and third, she placed gently onto the record changer before rotating the pickup arm to hold them in place. She touched the power and play switches, and the turntable began to spin. The tone arm automatically swiveled into place and lowered the stylus onto the spinning record. A moment later, Etta James began singing "At Last."

She undressed and walked into her bathroom to run a bath. She loved the old cast-iron claw-foot tub, but it took just short of forever to fill. With her mind on a time twenty years past, she lit a few candles and added bubble bath to the tub. Slipping into the warm water still filling the tub, she closed her eyes and thought of Jimmy. As Elvis sang "Can't Help Falling in Love," she shaved her legs with long, slow strokes.

As another LP dropped onto the turntable and the Righteous Brothers began singing "(You're My) Soul and Inspiration," she rested her head back against the tub's porcelain rim and closed her eyes. With each "Girl" from the song's lyrics, her subconscious mind automatically substituted Jimmy's name. She smiled and slid one hand beneath the water to the mound of soft, curly hair between her legs and the other hand to her left breast.

An instant later, Rebecca's eyes flew open. She sat straight up, sending a tidal wave of soapy water and bubbles cascading over the bathroom floor.

A lump!

She had noted breast lumps for years, but they came and went with her menstrual periods and felt ropey, easy to move. Her doctor had called them fibrocystic lumps and assured her they were nothing to worry about. This one felt different. It was just at the edge of her breast, near the armpit, and was hard, round, and completely immobile. Rebecca was immediately worried.

She spent the rest of the night tossing and turning, unable to sleep. As soon as her gynecologist's office opened the next morning, Rebecca called and booked an appointment. Unfortunately, the first available date was not for two whole weeks. She would've liked to have been seen sooner, but sighed, thanked the receptionist, and resigned herself to waiting.

Over the next two weeks, her mind actively rationalized, repudiated, and generally refused to accept that she may have a serious problem. By the day of her appointment, her denial was in full swing and she'd totally convinced herself there was nothing wrong. She almost canceled her doctor visit entirely, chastising herself, *Why should I waste the doctor's time with something silly like this?* Ultimately, since she was due for her annual exam and Pap smear anyway, she showed up at the gynecologist's office at the appointed time, convinced the doctor would soon be telling her that all was well.

Rebecca calmly paged through a copy of *Woman's Day* as she waited for her turn to see Dr. Mitchell. She wondered casually which magazines men waiting to see their urologists selected before *their* appointments? *Probably* Field & Stream, Rebecca thought, suppressing a giggle.

Once the nurse called Rebecca back and showed her into an examination room, she performed the usual intake vitals—weight, heart rate, blood pressure, and temperature—then collected basic medical history, noting in particular any new or changing symptoms and the date of her last menstrual period. Then she gave Rebecca the obligatory paper gown and instructed her to disrobe and wait on the exam table for the doctor.

After forty-five minutes of shivering on the exam table, she dismounted and began pacing the exam room, trying to keep her body temperature up while looking for a thermostat. Periodically, she glanced at her backside—clearly visible through the split in her paper gown—to verify that she'd not yet frozen her ass off.

After another half hour of shivering, Rebecca peeked into the hall and was relieved to see Dr. Mitchell walking her way with a nurse in tow. Mandy Mitchell had been Rebecca's gynecologist for about ten years. She was in her midforties and barely over five feet tall. With her ever-present smile and sandy blonde hair, which she wore in a pixie cut, she always looked like she was auditioning for the title role in *Peter Pan*. Instead of her usual office attire, she was wearing scrubs that day.

"Rebecca," said Dr. Mitchell, "I'm so sorry to have kept you waiting."

"That's okay, Doc," Rebecca said, trying to keep her teeth from chattering. "Looks like you came straight from surgery."

They stepped into the exam room as the doctor replied, "Yes, emergency C-section. I figured you'd probably waited long enough already, so I didn't add to the delay by taking time to change clothes. I hope you don't mind."

"Not at all," Rebecca replied reflexively. Really, what else could she say?

"Babies tend to come at schedules all their own. How rude! They're so selfish that way. I guess it's to help get us ready for their teen years."

Rebecca laughed half-heartedly.

"Now, let's get you all taken care of before another birth interrupts us. Go ahead and lie back on the exam table. Good. Now scooch down to the end...a little farther...a little more."

Just when Becca felt like she was going to fall off the end of the table, Dr. Mitchell informed her that she'd slid far enough, and the nurse helped place her feet in the stirrups for her pelvic exam.

The nurse handed the doctor a speculum, but as soon as the doctor touched her with it, Rebecca flinched and hissed, "Jesus Christ! That's cold!"

"Geez, I'm sorry, Rebecca. We usually put these in warm water before an exam," Mitchell said, turning to the nurse.

"But, Dr. Mitchell, I *did* put it in warm water, just like always," the nurse replied defensively.

Dr. Mitchell glared over the rims of her glasses. "When? An hour and a half ago?"

The nurse dropped her head to her chest as realization washed over her. "Yes, doctor. I'm so sorry, Mrs. Hamilton!"

Rebecca mumbled a begrudging acceptance.

"Well, now that you've passed your Polar Bear Challenge, let's get on with the exam," Dr. Mitchell said. She ran warm water over the speculum and resumed Rebecca's exam, all the time chatting amiably. Soon she asked, "Rebecca, I noticed from your intake paperwork that you are not using any form of birth control?"

"That's correct, Doc," came Rebecca's reply from the other side of the pelvic drape.

"You realize, of course, that as long as you're still having menstrual periods, you can still get pregnant. And you know what they call people who use the rhythm method as their primary form of birth control, don't you?" After a beat, the doctor answered her own question, "Parents."

"That would assume that I'm having sex."

"You're not?!" Dr. Mitchell pulled down the drape a fraction so she could see Rebecca's face.

"Nope."

"But you're young. You're healthy. You're attractive..."

"Never."

"But your husband's been dead for like ten—"

"*Twenty* years," Rebecca interrupted wistfully.

Dr. Mitchell glanced at the intake form and then up at her nurse but elected not to pursue the discrepancy.

"Well, physical intimacy is a normal part of life, and if sometime in the future you wish to become sexually active again, let me know. I have enough interruptions in my daily clinic without you getting pregnant and adding to my tardiness," Doc said with a smile. After a moment, she changed the subject. "So, I understand your son's a junior at MIT this year. Impressive. Does he have any plans?"

Rebecca welcomed the topical divergence. "Yes, James is there and doing very well! So far, he's undecided about what he wants to do after graduation. He has a 4.0 GPA, majoring in Chemistry and Physics. I think he could do just about anything he sets his mind to doing. I couldn't be more proud!"

"I can see why."

As the doctor completed Rebecca's pelvic exam, Pap smear, and bimanual exam, they continued to talk about random subjects.

Rebecca asked, "Silly question, Doc, but how do you do it?"

"Do what?"

"Well, I'm hanging off the end of the table with my legs up in the air in these stirrups and you're able to chat like you're in the chair next to me at the beauty parlor. How do you do that?"

"Oh…that…well, I've never really thought about it." She passed the speculum to the nurse and helped Rebecca remove her feet from the stirrups. "To me, yours is just another face in the crowd."

"Apparently, you walk in different crowds than I do," Rebecca said with a laugh as she scooched up and lay supine on the exam table.

Dr. Mitchell came to Rebecca's side. "Now we'll complete your breast exam and then we're done. I understand that you recently felt a lump?"

"Correct," Rebecca replied, suddenly feeling nervous.

"Well, let's take a look, shall we?"

The doctor uncovered Rebecca's right breast and began her examination. "Mm-hmm, I feel several small lumps here. They all feel fibrocystic to me. Nothing to worry about." She smiled. "Now, let's take a look at the left."

When Rebecca's left breast was uncovered, Dr. Mitchell's expression became suddenly serious. The smile was still there but now appeared forced. The skin between the areola and the armpit, in distinction to the rest of Rebecca's breast, appeared indurated and slightly pitted, like the skin of an orange.

On exam, the doctor felt a one-by-one-and-a-half-centimeter firm, immobile mass. She turned to the nurse and said, "Get Dr. Rubenstein on the phone, please."

The visit to Dr. Mitchell's office began a whirlwind of activities for Rebecca, none of them pleasant. There were mammograms, ultrasounds, CAT scans, and biopsies interspersed with visits to the surgeon, oncologist, and radiation oncologist. Soon thereafter followed a mastectomy, radiation, and chemotherapy. Trapped in the vortex though she was, Rebecca resolved to be strong and to be a fighter. She was determined that she would fight and *win* her battle against breast cancer.

Luckily, she wasn't alone in her fight. In addition to her medical team, she had James and her many friends from church to help her along. Almost the entire town rallied to her side. Her Sunday School class organized weekly schedules to make sure there was always someone available to drive her to and from doctor visits and treatment appointments. Every day, someone dropped by the house with food. Invariably, when she returned from her doctor visits, she came home to a freshly cleaned house, and usually to fresh-cut flowers on the kitchen table. The men of the community took turns mowing the lawn, and the farm's foreman developed skills he'd heretofore never shown for farm management.

When James came home from school, he pitched right in with everyone else to help wherever he could. He showed amazing tenderness in caring for Rebecca. When she was sick, he was always by her side helping to clean her up, wash her clothes, or change the sheets on her bed. He never complained.

But in every battle, there are casualties—and so it was with Rebecca.

Rebecca's surgeon performed a modified radical mastectomy with lymph node harvest. When pathology returned showing three abnormal nodes, he recommended proceeding with radiation and chemotherapy. He also recommended reconstructive breast surgery for after her chemo and radiation treatments had been completed and she'd fully recovered from them. The surgery left her with an angry, puckered scar cutting diagonally across her left chest. Additionally, her left arm was prone to swelling to monstrous dimensions after traumas as minor as having her blood pressure checked on that side. Radiation therapy left her with a case of thrush and an erosive esophagitis that made it painful and difficult to swallow. Consequently, she lost weight at an alarming rate. Already thin, she soon appeared dangerously so. Her clothes hung loose from her shoulders, making her look like a little girl playing dress-up in her mommy's clothes—a very sick little girl.

It was the chemotherapy, however, that seemed to hit Rebecca the hardest, at least psychologically. The nausea and vomiting were intense but didn't hit until a few days into each cycle of treatment. With medication and perhaps a little marijuana that she bought from some high school kids, they were at least manageable. The fatigue and brain fog were the worst. After chemo, her energy level and anything she'd even *thought* about putting into her stomach were soon in the toilet. She became increasingly forgetful and found herself constantly needing naps during the day.

After one such midday nap almost three weeks into her first round of chemotherapy, Rebecca woke feeling confused and disoriented in her bedroom. Her scalp felt tender, almost sore. Thinking she must have bumped her head while asleep, she reached up to feel around for a bump or bruise and came away with a large wad of hair in her hands.

In a panic, she looked down at her pillow. It was covered by clumps of hair—her hair.

Rebecca had always loved her hair and thought it her prettiest feature. It had always been silky-shiny and long. Jimmy had loved running his fingers through it and teasing her about how her hair tickled his nose when they were asleep together.

Jimmy used to call me Miss Ponytail, she thought as tears streamed down her face.

Feeling another wave of nausea coming on, she slipped into her bathrobe and stumbled to the bathroom where she began retching violently. Afterward, she leaned over the sink to rinse her mouth. Too fatigued to find a glass, she drank directly from the faucet. As she stood, her bathrobe fell open and, for the first time, she caught sight of her reflection.

Gone was the bright-eyed, fresh-faced girl with a cute body and long, shiny coal-black hair. In her place was a gaunt old woman with only a few random wisps and tufts of hair. Her cheeks were sunken, and dark circles were visible beneath lifeless blue eyes. The ugly red scar where her breast had once been was clearly visible over the washboard that was her ribs.

Rebecca put her hands to her face and ran to her bedroom, collapsing on the bed, racked with sobs. For the first time, she was glad that Jimmy was dead so he would never see her this way.

The next morning, James told his mom he had an errand to run and left her in the care of her best friend, Shelby. When he returned an hour later, his head was shaved as smooth and shiny as a cue ball. Upon hearing the reason for his new look, old man Blanton hadn't even charged him for the haircut.

A week later, James received a package in the mail from his friends at MIT. In it was a Boston Red Sox cap signed by Roger Clemens, Dwight Evans, and Wade Boggs, which he proudly presented to his mother. She wore it to every doctor visit and therapy appointment and never shed another tear over the loss of her hair.

To say that the whole town rallied behind Rebecca was slightly inaccurate. Remaining as belligerent neutrals were Rebecca's mother and father who, even after twenty years, hadn't forgiven her for marrying Jimmy. Consequently, they still refused to acknowledge their daughter's existence, much less help her in her hour of need.

In a community as closely knit as Boiling Springs, the conspicuous absence of her parents from "Team Rebecca" did not go unnoticed. Later that year, Rebecca's mother inexplicably lost her long-held seat on the School Board, and Emmitt couldn't seem to find the votes in City Council to block the building of a brand-new ACE Hardware directly across the street from his hardware store.

By the end of the summer, Rebecca had completed her treatment regimen and was declared cancer-free. She'd won. It was over. Her hair began to grow back—only about an inch, but a welcome improvement all the same—and she was regaining some of the weight she'd lost. Looking at her reflection in the bathroom mirror, she thought, *I have eyebrows again!* and did a little dance as she tossed her eyebrow pencil triumphantly into the trash.

Rebecca's surgeon scheduled her reconstructive procedure for the end of the year, giving her body plenty of time to recover from the stress of the cancer treatments. The delay would also allow her nutritional status to improve, which in turn would facilitate her eventual wound healing and recovery after surgery. Until then, she'd wear a prosthetic breast in her bra. She giggled a little at the thought. She'd not stuffed her bra since high school.

In order for him to graduate in three years as planned, James was taking summer classes at MIT when Rebecca received her first cancer-free scan. Busy though he was, he surprised her by flying home and taking her out for a fancy dinner at her favorite restaurant. Over chateaubriand for two, they toasted her victory over cancer with a 1979 Château Mouton Rothschild. How her son could afford such an expensive bottle of wine, Rebecca neither knew nor particularly cared. She'd beaten cancer!

In church and among her community, Rebecca slowly resumed the activities she'd allowed to fall by the wayside while being ill and spent a great deal of time thanking all the people who'd been so kind to her over the past six months.

She even gave Edward Belleau a call. He'd been particularly sweet and supportive during her illness but—with the peach harvest being in full swing—was too busy to break away for coffee or lunch. Unfazed, she resolved to call him again in the fall, after things had slowed down. She *might* even give him a *real* kiss...

Rebecca had won. Nothing else mattered.

CHAPTER 12

1988

A SHIP WITH NO DESTINATION HAS little need for rudder or compass.

James Hamilton was brilliant, inquisitive, and well suited to life in an academic world. He enjoyed learning purely for the joy of acquiring knowledge and was a font of useless, and occasionally even useful, information. Were it possible to make a living from amassing trivia, he would have been as rich as Croesus. However, short of playing Trivial Pursuit in the taverns around MIT's campus or applying to the TV gameshow *Jeopardy*, his options were limited.

His problem was not with the acquisition of knowledge or information but rather with having the focus to apply it. Everything interested him—at least for a time. He flitted from one project or interest to another like a butterfly in a field of poppies.

All too aware of this personal failing, he secretly envied his classmates. Although they struggled far more than he in the classroom, they were able to concentrate and apply themselves in a way he was unable to imitate or duplicate. And they vastly outshone him in life skills.

To this point in his life, the only thing about which James was certain was that he wanted to be nothing at all like his father. Mack Lee Hamilton had been mean to the point of cruelty. He was selfish, lazy, and manipulative. He had been a bastard beyond compare, and James hated him—or at least he did as much as any boy can hate his father. What his mother, a saint of a woman, ever saw in that man, James could not begin to fathom. Thus, his life had been structured around avoiding a negative rather than pursuing a positive, which was hardly a recipe for success.

All that had changed when James returned to MIT for his third fall term. His mother's illness had given him a point of reference from which he could chart the course of his own life. No longer did his vessel lack a destination. He resolved to set sail for the realm of medicine and test the waters.

After dropping by his faculty adviser's office, James discovered that he'd already completed the prerequisites for medical school, but if he still planned to graduate at the end of Spring Term and start medical school in the fall, he'd better get a move on. He needed to sign up for and pass the MCAT (Medical College Admission Test). To score well, he'd need to brush up on Biology, an area he'd neglected with his double major of Chemistry and Physics, and the test was only a month away.

James woke on the morning of the MCAT with a low-grade fever and a severe sinus headache. He dropped by MIT's Student Health Services, where he was diagnosed with a sinus infection and given a ten-day course of antibiotics. By the time he sat for the exam, the pain behind his eyes was so severe he could hardly focus on the test booklet before him. With just over five minutes remaining in the six-hour timed exam, he got to the final question and found that he'd already penciled in the dot while answering question 159. Scanning back over the rows of answer bubbles, he found that somehow, he'd missed a line after question number 41. He had less than five minutes to fix more than a hundred of his answers. Frantically, he went back through the answer sheet, erasing the errant dots and replacing them with the correct answers.

Unfortunately, when time was called, he'd only been able to correct up through question number 133. There was nothing to be done. No answers could be added or changed after time had been called. Of course, he could retake the exam, but with his late start, this exam was already the last offered before the current medical school admissions cycle ended. Convinced that he'd allowed his opportunity for medical school to slip away, he was crestfallen.

Six weeks later, James received his scores in the mail. With a pounding heart, he tore open the envelope and scanned the contents. He found his score and his heart fell. He'd scored a forty-four. With a dejected sigh, he glanced around for a garbage can into which he could toss the page, and with it, his dreams of a career in medicine.

As he turned toward his dorm room, James noticed a second page in the envelope. Dejected, he removed it and gave the page a desultory glance before tossing it into the trash. Three steps later, his eidetic memory kicked in, allowing the information on page two to percolate into his conscious mind. A moment later found James riffling through the garbage can, searching for his discarded letter. Finally, under the bun of a half-eaten hamburger, he found it. After wiping ketchup from the letter, he read both pages through in detail.

What he'd not realized until glimpsing the second page—the one holding his percentile scores—was that his forty-four was out of a possible forty-five. His score placed him above the ninety-ninth percentile for all students taking the exam. His score *wasn't* terrible. On the contrary, it was nearly *perfect*, and likely would have been totally perfect had he not miscued on the final section's Scantron sheet.

James let out a loud whoop and began dancing around the campus post office like a madman, which was *precisely* what the work-study student behind the mail counter thought as he dialed the phone for campus security.

After assuring the rent-a-cops that, no, he was *not* a student suffering from a mental breakdown, James rushed back to his dorm room to call Rebecca.

When Rebecca answered the phone and heard James's voice on the other end of the line, she became immediately alarmed. James called at three o'clock every Sunday afternoon, like clockwork. She looked forward to his weekly calls, but for him to be calling outside of his appointed time surely meant something catastrophic had occurred.

After calming his mother, James explained about the MCAT and his plans to attend medical school.

Rebecca's heart swelled with pride as James described his chosen career path and the motivation behind his choice. She supposed, only a truly ill wind that blows no good, and if her brush with cancer had provided the impetus for her son to find direction in his life, maybe it hadn't been such a malignant draft after all.

No...cancer still sucked.

CHAPTER 13

SPRING TERM 1989

J AMES SUBMITTED APPLICATIONS TO MEDICAL schools around the country, and with his perfect grade point average from MIT and near-perfect MCAT scores, he was offered interviews everywhere he applied.

At each school, either as a written essay accompanying the initial application or at some point during the interview process, some variation of the same question was always asked. "What made you want to become a doctor?"

Invariably, James responded with the story of his mother's battle with cancer. He discussed how impressed he'd been by the medical professionals who'd cared for her and how he wished to emulate them. Sometimes, if more of an answer was sought, he'd expound upon his experiences with Dr. Malone and the Institute for Memory Studies as a child.

There was usually also a follow-up question about his father and *his* role in James's choice of medicine as a career. And typically, James would smile and say, "Well, I was fairly young when my father died in an accident. I suppose his role was in teaching me what I *didn't* want to be."

Almost every time, this prompted another question. "And what was your father?"

At this, a litany of possible descriptors flew through James's mind: wastrel, drunkard, licentious profligate, wife-beater. But in the end, he always answered, "He was a mechanic. I never remember seeing him when there wasn't grease under his nails." *And a beer in his hand*, he would think to himself. Then he'd continue aloud, "And that just isn't who I wanted to be."

Rebecca was with him every step of the way. During their weekly phone conversations, they discussed the pros and cons for each school, and there were no bad choices. Secretly, she was hoping for Duke so James would be closer to home, but she knew he'd thrive wherever he chose to attend. Under her stewardship, the farm had thrived, so he shouldn't worry about paying his tuition.

In the end, he was accepted by every school to which he applied. Overwhelmed by the veritable cornucopia of blue-chip choices, he struggled with deciding where he should attend school. It was an embarrassment of riches. However, when the Vagelos College of Physicians and Surgeons at Columbia University offered him a full, four-year scholarship, his decision was made easy. In spite of her assurances, James didn't want to burden his mother with his educational expenses.

With the acceptance into Columbia's medical school already in his pocket, James allowed himself to relax just a little. Up until that point, with a double major and his plans to graduate after only three years, his class load hadn't allowed for much free time. For his final semester of college, he wanted to take a little time for himself and, perhaps, enjoy a little of the "college experience" before he became totally absorbed by the rigors of medical school.

By design, he'd crammed the most difficult and technical classes into his first five semesters and four summer sessions at MIT. By his final semester, he had fulfilled all the required classes for his twin majors but still needed thirteen credit hours of *something* to graduate. So, he filled them with random electives.

Because he thought it might come in handy in later life, he selected a three-credit-hour class in General Insurance, which he took pass/fail. His second class was Introduction to Flight, a three-credit-hour class in which he'd be able to complete ground school for flight training. With the additional one-credit-hour practical lab, he'd actually learn to fly! With any luck, he'd be able to solo before graduation. Next, he selected a four-credit-hour field biology course in ornithology—basically, bird watching. The only other class available with the requisite number of credit hours that would also fit into his schedule was Introduction to Theater, which proved to be the most challenging and rewarding of his final semester of college.

James felt like the desiccated, fossilized bones of what might *once* have been a fish—back when the Mojave Desert was still an ocean. To suggest that he felt *merely* like a fish out of water would've been an understatement of monumental proportions.

All around him were singers, dancers, musicians, and wannabe actors. They were theater geeks, every one of them. Of course, James had no problem with geeks of any stripe. He himself was a self-proclaimed science and history geek, but in the world of geeks, these classmates were from an entirely different hemisphere.

James loved music, but his interest was more in the math behind the compositions than in the melodies themselves. His musical talent was limited to changing stations on the radio—a radio that he could've built from scratch using a few feet of copper wire, a wooden spindle, and a bit of crystalized lead. Neither was dance his forte. He was stiff, awkward, and uncoordinated. He just couldn't seem to get out of his own head and move with the beat of the music. It was as though he couldn't hear it. An MIT coed he'd dated briefly once described his moves on the dance floor as shuffling around "like a cigar-store Indian." It had been a brutally accurate comparison but insulting to cigar-store Indians everywhere.

James hoped the class would be purely theoretical, with no end of semester class production. Looking at his classmates, he didn't like his chances. Maybe if there *was* a production, maybe he could pass the semester by working props and set design. Certainly, not *everybody* associated with a stage production had to be an actor. He didn't mind the idea of working props. Although no da Vinci, he'd always enjoyed sketching. As a child, he had often mailed in sketches of pirates, turtles, and teddy bears to the "So You Think You Can Draw" contest he found on the backs of magazine covers, although never even once had he received a prize notification in reply. Still, he thought he could draw a respectable backdrop if required.

Each of James's hopes for the class were dashed on day one. First, indeed there *would* be a class production at the end of the semester. Second, to pass the class, *everyone* was expected to act in the play. When he volunteered to work props or set design instead, the professor disabused him of this thought immediately.

"This is an *acting* class," Professor Lloyd said. "Besides, all our props and set design are done through another class in the Art Department. If you want to work props, you need to change classes."

Figuring there was no point in antagonizing his professor on the first day, James wisely elected not to point out that the class was Introduction to Theater rather than Introduction to Acting.

There was *one* piece of welcome news. There'd be no singing or dancing this semester. The show the class would present as their final examination was *not* to be a musical. Instead, Lloyd had selected George Bernard Shaw's *Pygmalion*. To James's immense relief, the professor summarily dismissed the entreaties of the more musically inclined students who'd lobbied hard for *My Fair Lady*, the musical adaptation of Shaw's play.

There was a veritable feeding frenzy among James's classmates when auditions opened. Most were interested in the leading roles of Professor Henry Higgins, Colonel Pickering, and Eliza Doolittle, or the major secondary roles of Alfred Doolittle, Freddy Hill, and Mrs. Higgins. James, however, was quite satisfied at being cast in the minor role of Bystander Number One, with but a trivial speaking part. For the rest of the production, he'd be allowed to set up props and arrange backdrops.

Cast in the leading roles of Henry Higgins and Eliza Doolittle were Harold Rynar and Elliana Petrenko. It came as little surprise to anyone present at the auditions that Harold Rynar was cast as Henry Higgins. Although only nineteen, he had been acting on the stage for thirteen years. At age seven, he'd landed the role of Marian the Librarian's little brother Winifred in the community theater production of *The Music Man*. There, he'd belted out "The Wells Fargo Wagon" and "Gary, Indiana" in his hometown *of* Gary, Indiana, to rave reviews. And his acting career had taken off since. He hoped someday to perform on Broadway, and no one doubted that someday he'd do just that.

The female lead went to Elliana Petrenko, who was new to acting but had a flair for accents and dialects, perhaps owing to her family's international heritage. Her grand-parents had been Ukrainian Jews who'd emigrated to the United States in 1941. She had been raised in a bilingual household. A polyglot, she spoke English, Ukrainian, Russian, and French like a native and was fluent in both Spanish and German. A natural mimic, she easily mastered Eliza's tortured Cockney accent.

Elliana was just under five-and-a-half feet tall and had a ballerina's body—thin and flexible with small breasts—and delicate features. Her hair was bright red. The spikey pixie cut she preferred perfectly accentuated her porcelain complexion and high, Slavic cheekbones. From behind round, wire-rimmed glasses, a pair of huge, brown doe eyes took in the world around her, constantly looking for something *else* to make her lips curl into the mischievous, elfin smile her face usually exhibited.

James was immediately smitten.

Elliana didn't even know he existed.

James's big break came two weeks into rehearsals. He only had one line, "It's all right. He's a gentleman. Look at his boots." It was a line meant to be delivered in a thick Cockney accent. Try though he might, James could not turn his natural South Carolina drawl into Cockney. He could intone a respectable upper-class Brit, but the Cockney accent escaped him.

Finally, out of frustration, Professor Lloyd threw up his hands and called Elliana over to work with James on his enunciation. And so it came to pass that Eliza Doolittle, who in the play was trying to lose her Cockney accent and speak like a lady, was tasked with teaching gentleman-James to speak like a Cockney guttersnipe.

James was elated, Elliana less so.

Still, she worked her magic and, after a week, James was able to belt out, "It's aw rawt. E's a gen'elman. Look aa e's bae-oots," as naturally as a street urchin fresh from the London fish markets.

The coaching, as it turned out, was not all one way. Elliana, although a master of accents, was dyslexic and struggled with remembering her lines in their proper order. James, with his superior memory, had no such difficulties. So, after she had worked her magic on his accent, he spent the rest of the semester running lines with her.

One evening a few weeks into their mutual tutelage, James and Elliana became engrossed in a scene and worked right through the serving time for the campus cafeteria. They ordered pizza, and over a half-empty pizza box, worked well into the night at her apartment, on the scene in which Henry Higgins realizes he's become infatuated with Eliza. By the time Elliana mastered the scene, it was well past midnight. Tired and with a bird-watching field trip early the next morning, James rose to leave. Elliana followed him to the door, stood on her tiptoes, and leaned in to give him a friendly peck on the cheek. Not realizing she was so close, James turned his head suddenly to say goodnight and, to their mutual surprise, their lips met.

For an instant, they stood frozen by their furtive, accidental kiss. After a moment, the kiss became no longer accidental. James dropped the sheaf of script pages he'd been carrying and took Elliana into his arms. She roughly pushed him against the door, and they began kissing passionately. After a moment, she slipped her hand inside his shirt and began caressing his chest.

Coming up for air, James quipped, "You know, if I tried something like that, you'd probably slap me."

Elliana pulled her sweater over her head and tossed it onto the couch. "Why don't you try it and find out, big boy?"

He did...and she didn't.

At five the next morning, James tiptoed back to the apartment door, donning discarded articles of clothing along the way. He paused at the door and gathered up the scattered *Pygmalion* script pages, then slipped quietly into the hall and whistled tunelessly all the way to the Ornithology field trip rendezvous point.

CHAPTER 14

SPRING BREAK 1989

A S THEIR BUDDING RELATIONSHIP TRANSI-
TIONED into full bloom, James and Elliana became
increasingly inseparable. With his light class schedule, he met her for lunch almost every day. Unless he was off
bird watching with his Ornithology class, he waited for her
outside MIT's Theater Arts Building and walked her back to
her apartment after her last class of the day. And it was a
rare occasion that did not see James leaving her apartment
in the wee hours of the morning, if he left at all.

For the first time in his life, James Hamilton was in love.
Elliana was pretty, funny, smart, and fun—everything James
could've hoped for in a woman. He loved seeing the world
through her eyes. His day was not complete unless and until
he'd told her about it and she'd told him about hers. She
dragged him out of his comfort zone and into her world, and
he *liked* it there. Best of all, Elliana loved him too.

In bed one night after doing what lovers do, James
and Elliana lay together, her head on his chest and one leg
thrown across his. He absently stroked her hair and listened
as she told him about her family.

"Baba and Gigi, my grandmother and grandfather, once lived near Mariupol, Ukraine, in the Soviet Union. Before you ask, they were *not* members of the Communist Party. They were both Jewish and fled the Soviet Union, escaping on a freighter barely a week before the Nazis occupied that part of Ukraine in 1941. Afterward, they emigrated to the United States, settling in Norwich, Connecticut.

"My gigi was a master clockmaker in Mariupol but could find no work in his trade in Norwich, so he took a job sweeping floors at a factory that made Thermos bottles. He saved his money and, after five years, opened a watch and clock repair shop that he named It's About Time. He worked five nights each week at the factory and half days at his shop. He was a very good clockmaker and could fix anything. Soon, the shop was profitable enough that he could quit his factory job. After a time, he began building cuckoo clocks. At first, it was just for fun, but then he sold one...then another...and another, and soon an industry was born. He loved woodworking and handcrafted the caseworks and decorative pieces for all his clocks. Now you can find his clocks throughout New England. Gigi died when I was a little girl.

"My baba was eight months pregnant with my father when they boarded the freighter in Mariupol. She began having labor pains a day out of port and ultimately gave birth to my father in the back of a taxicab in New Haven. They named my dad Karol, which means *free man*, because he was the first of our family to be born free in America," she explained.

James nodded. "That's pretty cool!"

"Some of my fondest childhood memories are of my baba baking. She makes this bread she calls 'salt rising bread.' It's to die for!"

"Salt rising bread? What's that?" James asked.

"It's a bread that doesn't use yeast to make it rise, kinda like sourdough but different. I think it's my favorite food in all the world. Even just remembering the smell of Baba's kitchen with her bread in the oven...it takes me to my happy place," she said, lightly stroking his chest.

"When he was old enough, my gigi taught my dad how to make clocks, and after Gigi died, Dad took over the family business. Rather than meeting a nice Jewish girl and settling down like Baba had hoped, Dad fell head over heels for a WASP Broadway chorus girl, got married, and had me. There were complications with my delivery, so no brothers or sisters for me. Dad always teased that I didn't want to share the stage with anybody else. Mum always said that she just got it right the first time, so there was never any need for an encore."

She popped her head up and looked adoringly into his eyes. "I can't wait for you to meet Mum, Dad, and Baba! They're gonna adore you," she gushed. "Now, tell me about your family."

James told her about the farm and his mother and about her recent victorious battle over breast cancer. "She's really an amazing woman. Independent, strong, intelligent—she's a lot like you. She's made me everything that I am today, for better or worse," he said with more than a hint of pride.

"She sounds great! What about your dad?"

James visibly stiffened.

Elliana drew back so she could better see his face.

"He wasn't a very nice person, and we didn't really get along," he said flatly.

"Oh... Is he still..."

"He's dead."

"I'm sorry, Jimmy. I—"

"Don't be. I'm not!"

Elliana sat up in bed. "Wow! That bad? What happened?" she asked.

"Car accident. He and his *mistress* were killed driving back from the Daytona 500 when I was ten." The bitterness in his voice was unmistakable.

"How about your grandparents?" she asked, clearly hoping to find safer ground.

"Not much better. I've never met my mom's parents. Apparently, there was some kind of blow up with them before I was born. My grandfather on my dad's side died before I was born—heart attack, I think—and my grandmother on that side of the family is in the loony bin."

"You're kidding, right?"

"Nope. She tried to kill me," he said in a matter-of-fact voice, totally devoid of emotion.

"You're just saying that?"

James shook his head gravely and tapped the scar on his chest. "She's how I got this. When Dad died, she went off her rocker and tried to kill *me* with a butcher's knife."

"Jimmy, you're really not kidding, are you?"

"Elle, I wish I was. I wish I was..."

"Well, you're going to absolutely *love* my family. I'm more than happy to share my baba with you!" With that, she kicked her leg astride James and sat straddling him. She took his nipple gently between her teeth and tugged slightly, then kissed the long, jagged scar on his chest and slowly slid backward until their bodies coupled.

"Does this make it feel better," she purred, moving her body rhythmically.

"Oh, *God*, yes!" he gasped.

Afterward, they lay together, breathing hard, their bodies bathed in a light sheen of sweat.

When she'd caught her breath enough to speak, Elliana propped on an elbow and said, "I really want to meet your mom and see the place where you grew up."

James laughed. "Kind of an odd time for me to be thinking about my mom, don't ya think?"

Elliana giggled. "Maybe a little, but I really want to meet her!"

"More than a little, I'd say," he said, blushing. "And I want to meet your family too."

"Maybe we should go there over spring break," they said together.

"I can meet your baba."

"I can meet your mom."

"Which one? We can't do both. Your folks are in Connecticut, and my mom is in South Carolina. There's not enough time," James replied.

"We can see one over spring break and the other after you graduate this summer."

"How do we choose?" he asked.

"How 'bout we flip a coin. Winner chooses, and the loser..." Elliana whispered something in James's ear and began nibbling on his neck.

James's eyes flew open wide, then rolled back in ecstasy. "I forfeit," he moaned.

And with that, it was settled. James and Elliana would travel to South Carolina over spring break so that she could meet Rebecca.

Rebecca was thrilled when James called to tell her he was coming home for spring break and planned to bring along his new girlfriend. She knew he'd been dating while in college, but this was the first time he'd ever wanted to bring anyone home. During one of their weekly telephone calls, he had even suggested that this Elliana was "the one." The very idea caused a shiver of delight to run up Rebecca's spine. Although it had been a while for her, she remembered *vividly* what it felt like to be young and in love and was thrilled to hear her son experiencing it.

In preparation for James and Elliana's visit, she cleaned and dusted the spare bedroom upstairs, changed the linens, and bought a new comforter for the bed. She put fresh flowers in a vase on the bedside table. If this was to be Elliana's room, then Rebecca wanted it to be cheerful and homey, somewhere her son's girlfriend would feel comfortable. In James's bedroom, she simply changed the linens and tidied up a bit. Rebecca was less worried about his reaction to his accommodations than she was Elliana's, on whom she wanted desperately to make a good first impression.

Rebecca arrived at the airport a full two hours before James and Elliana's flight from Boston's Logan International was scheduled to arrive. It just would not do for her to be late. After all, this might someday be her daughter-in-law.

She might be my daughter-in-law someday, Rebecca thought, almost giddy with excitement.

By the time their flight arrived, Rebecca was a nervous wreck. As she waited in the arrival area, she fretted to herself, *What if Elliana doesn't like me? I could ruin everything for James...or worse, I could lose him forever.* Then, in the distance, she caught sight of James and Elliana and her fears melted away.

As the young couple strolled hand in hand along the concourse toward her, James caught sight of his mother and gestured to Elliana. Intently following the line of his gaze, she picked Rebecca from the crowd and gave a little leap of excitement. As she came down, a little boy of no more than three years old broke free from his parents and darted in front of her, causing Elliana to lose her balance. Before she could fall, James swept her into his arms and into an embrace. They laughed, kissed, and began to wave to Rebecca.

Rebecca was astonished by her son's careful attention and adroitness in catching Elliana. She'd never known him to be so attentive to anyone or *anything* in the past. She smiled inside, remembering how Jimmy had once caught her in just such a fashion when she'd tripped on their wedding night. *Like father, like son,* she thought, breathing a sigh of relief. Everything was going to be okay. Even the most casual of observers would've seen that her son was in love. By all appearances, so was Elliana. There was no force on earth, and certainly not a loving mother, that could possibly tear the two asunder.

During the drive home from the airport, the three chatted comfortably. As she drove, Rebecca got basic biographical information about Elliana and her family. She glanced in the rearview mirror from time to time and smiled inwardly. The two, although sitting a chaste distance apart in the backseat, were holding hands.

Forty-five minutes later, Rebecca parked the car in the driveway. She popped the trunk and said cheerily, "James, you take the bags upstairs while I show Elliana around the house. You're in your old room, and Elliana's across the hall in the spare bedroom."

For an instant, Rebecca caught the briefest flash of disappointment on his face, but he lodged no complaint. Instead, he resignedly lugged the bags upstairs to their approved destinations.

When he returned downstairs, Rebecca suggested, "James, why don't you take Elliana on a tour around the farm. After traveling so long, I'm betting you two would like to stretch your legs a bit."

"Wanna take a walk around the place?" he asked Elliana.

"Sure," she said, popping to her feet.

"Dinner will be in about an hour. It's pot roast with apple pie à la mode for dessert—your favorites."

"Thanks, Mom," James called as the door closed behind the two love birds.

An hour later, as Rebecca was setting the table, James and Elliana returned from their walk. She observed that both of their faces appeared a little flushed but made little of it. There was a tiny sprig of hay in Elliana's hair, and Rebecca absently reached out to remove it. Then she noticed that Elliana's blouse was also misbuttoned and froze in mid-reach.

Oh my God! They've been out in the barn, she thought.

"Mrs. Hamilton, are you okay?" Elliana asked.

After a moment, Rebecca spluttered her response, "All right? Yes, I'm fine...probably just chemo-brain. I'll start to do something and then my wires short circuit." She pointed to her own head, "I'll figure it out eventually. Now, let's eat."

As she served everyone's plates, Rebecca's mind kept going back to the hay and the misbuttoned blouse. What would the neighbors think? She made desultory attempts at dinner conversation, but until dessert was served, Rebecca was distracted by her discordant thoughts. As she carried the pie back into the dining room, she paused unseen at the door.

James was sitting across the table from Elliana but had reached his hand across the table and placed it atop hers. He was smiling like she'd never seen him smile before, and Elliana was smiling right back with a look of total adoration on her face.

With the aroma of baked apples, sugar, and her famous cheddar crust filling her nostrils, Rebecca appreciated the tableau before her for what it was—two young people in love. The tumblers in her mind clunked into place, causing her to smile. She said to herself, *My son is in love. Who gives a damn what the neighbors think? This might be my future daughter-in-law. If my parents had cared more about me and less about the goddamn neighbors, they might've been here tonight, enjoying this time with their grandson too.*

Rebecca served pie for everyone and, for the first time that evening, thoroughly enjoyed the table conversation. She laughed uproariously when learning that James's inability to pull off a Cockney accent had been the catalyst to bring him together with Elliana.

After hearing the accent firsthand, she said, "While I'm certainly no expert on accents, I can see why your professor recommended voice coaching."

Elliana laughed and patted his hand. "He's a work in progress."

"Aren't we all," said Rebecca, nodding her agreement.

As they were clearing plates, Elliana said, "Mrs. Hamilton, everything was wonderful tonight. I'm not much of a baker, but will you share your pie recipe with me?"

Rebecca deposited the plates on the countertop and turned slowly to Elliana. "Let's get one thing straight." Her voice sounded stern. "I am *not* Mrs. Hamilton. *That* was my mother-in-law, and *thank God,* I'm not her!" She donned an inviting smile. "Call me Rebecca or Becca—anything except Mrs. Hamilton! Becca...that's what my husband used to call me," she said wistfully, a faraway look in her eyes. "And of course you may have the recipe."

Startled, James began, "Really? I never heard him—"

"Never you mind," Becca interrupted. "Now, you two scram. James, while I'm finishing these dishes, why don't you go and show Miss Elliana around the town before it gets dark. You can take the car. The keys are—"

"On the hook by the door," James finished her sentence. "I know."

Becca swatted him with her dish towel.

"I don't mind helping with the dishes, Mrs. Ham—I mean, Becca," Elliana volunteered.

"No, you two go and have fun," Becca said with a warm smile, picking the sprig of hay from Elliana's hair.

Becca smiled as the door closed behind them.

An instant later, James burst back into the room. "I forgot to say bye," he said, kissing his mother on the cheek.

As he pulled away toward the door, Becca caught his sleeve. "I like her...a *lot*!

"Me too," he said with a grin, then he bolted out the door.

After they'd gone, Becca finished the dishes and then, while humming an old Righteous Brothers tune, ascended the stairs to James's room. There, she picked up his suitcase and walked it across the hall to Elliana's room. As an afterthought, she closed the door to *his* room and thought about locking it. Ultimately, she decided against it. She reckoned two bright MIT students could figure it out all by themselves.

In her own bedroom, she put a few albums on the turntable and ran herself a bubble bath.

CHAPTER 15

MAY 1989

A FTER THEIR RETURN TO CAMBRIDGE, life rapidly returned to routine for James and Elliana. Both were relieved that Becca seemed to like her and was supportive of their burgeoning relationship.

Theirs was not the only romance spawned within their *Pygmalion* castmates. Indeed, Mike Holland, cast as Colonel Pickering, had begun seeing Phoebe Gilmore, who'd been cast as Mrs. Doolittle, about the same time as James and Elliana. By all indications, their love affair appeared to be progressing at a similar rate and direction.

It was another blossoming relationship, growing in the shadows, that had the greatest impact upon James, albeit indirectly. Wendall McCabe, known to everyone as Mack, had been cast as Bystander Number Two, alongside James's Bystander Number One. Mack's secondary role was to play the understudy for Harold Rynar's Professor Henry Higgins. Any other year, Mack would've scored the role himself, but this semester he was narrowly edged out for the male lead by Rynar. Had the semester's selected play been *My Fair Lady*, or any other musical, it was likely that with his strong dance background and clear tenor voice, Mack would have won the lead role.

Mack haled from Alameda, California, just across the bay from San Francisco. He was a little under six feet tall and had movie-star good looks. He kept his body toned to perfection through dance and a grueling daily workout regimen. Women swooned at just a glance from his ice-blue eyes. If a girl happened to catch his eye and prompt a smile, she'd immediately be dazzled by perfect white teeth and a pair of dimples deep enough for her to bathe in. More often than not, soon thereafter, the lucky lady, unless she had more willpower than Mother Teresa, would soon get to see his carefully waxed chest and washboard abs somewhere more...private.

Much to James's relief, Elliana seemed to be totally immune to Mack's charms. Over the course of the semester, James, who happened to live on the same floor as Mack, had watched a parade of women come and go from Mack's dorm room. Never did he see the same woman twice. After seeing a particularly attractive lady leaving Mack's room, he broached the subject of Mack's parade of ladies with Elliana.

"Elle, not that I'm complaining, but why haven't you ever been interested in Mack? I mean, you're like the only attractive woman on campus I've *not* seen coming out of his room."

Elliana rolled her eyes. "Because I'm with you, silly."

"And I'm thrilled about that, but you weren't always... you know, with me."

Elliana laughed. "He's just not my type."

"He's got a perfect body and a face that belongs on a magazine cover. How can you *not* be attracted to him? Hell, I almost am a little myself..."

"And Mack would probably like that."

"What?" James asked.

"He's gay," she replied nonchalantly.

"No way! But all those women..."

"It's a ruse, all for show. I tell you, he's gay."

"Really? How do you know?"

"I just know."

"Seriously? But all those women..."

She nodded her head solemnly. "He's gay, or he's hung like a hamster...or both."

James laughed heartily, dropping the subject.

Early the next morning, while returning from Elliana's apartment, he stepped off his dorm's elevator and passed Harold Rynar coming from the direction of Mack's room.

"Hey, Harold! You're here awfully late."

Rynar appeared tense, almost defensive. "Yes, umm, Mack and I, we were just running lines. He is my understudy for Henry Higgins, you know."

"That's what I figured. I've seen you over here a bunch lately."

"Yes, the play opens in less than a week and we *all* must be prepared, even the understudies." Gone was the tension in Rynar's voice. In its place a more pompous tone had been substituted, as though on suggestion of some hidden stage director.

Realization dawned slowly over James. "Yeah, right... even the understudies. Hey, see you tonight for rehearsal," he replied.

Rynar brushed past without another word.

After he'd gone, James thought aloud, "Never the same woman twice, but Rynar's over here at least twice a week. Holy shit, Elle might be right."

Indeed, Elliana *was* correct, and a few nights later outside a nightclub named Round-a-Bout Bar & Grill—a club frequented by patrons with alternative lifestyles—Mack and Rynar were set upon by a group of drunken frat boys. What began as a game of Jeer the Queer rapidly escalated into a full-on altercation. In the ensuing melee, Mack and Rynar defended themselves admirably, but in the end, their opponents were too many and the two of them were too few. Consequently, both boys were beaten savagely. Mack suffered a ruptured spleen, several cracked ribs, a broken nose, and a boxer's fracture to his left hand. Rynar suffered similarly with a broken jaw, fractured orbit, a broken rib, a bruised kidney, and a concussion. In addition, both suffered multiple contusions, lacerations, and abrasions. After the fight, both boys were hospitalized and required surgery, Mack for his ruptured spleen and Rynar for his orbital fracture.

The news of the assault on their classmates hit the Intro to Theater class like a sledgehammer. As a group, the class was shocked and appalled. Many had been aware of the pair's sexual preferences, but nobody cared. There seemed to be a shared consensus that who one chose to love was no one's business but their own. Even if another person disagreed with Mack and Rynar's lifestyle, nothing gave that person the right to beat either of the two perfectly harmless, perfectly likable individuals senseless or put them in the hospital.

When informed of the calamity that had befallen two of his students, Professor Lloyd was appropriately sympathetic. Then he reminded the class that the final examination for his class was, and would continue to be, the completed production and *performance* of Shaw's *Pygmalion*. Without the final exam, all students would receive an Incomplete on their semester grade reports. He informed the class in no uncertain terms, "The loss of the show's male lead and his understudy, while unfortunate, does not absolve the class of this requirement."

His edict was met by a chorus of objections from the students.

"What?"

"No way? How are we supposed to..."

"This is so unfair!"

"But there's not enough time for somebody new to learn the role. We're scheduled to open in two *days*! Nobody could do that!"

"We can't..."

Professor Lloyd wouldn't budge. "You can, and you will. Or, as the Greeks said to the Persians at Thermopylae, 'You shall not pass!' This is show biz, kids. Get used to it. As they say, the show *must* go on."

After enduring several minutes of collective mumbling and grumbling, Elliana held up a hand for quiet. "Guys, wait. We don't have to find somebody new. We already *have* someone who knows the role."

"Oh, thank God! Who?" asked Mike Holland. Colonel Pickering was going to be his first major role and he'd worked for months learning his part, thus he was particularly eager for the show to start.

There was a murmur of collective relief from the rest of the class.

"James," Elliana said in a matter-of-fact voice.

Hearing his name, James was snapped from his reverie. He'd been quietly pondering options for how to still graduate at the end of the term if he didn't have the credits from this class.

The murmur of excitement degraded into disappointed groans. The rest of the class, having had their hopes raised by Elliana, now found them dashed upon learning the identity of their ersatz savior. The entire cast had heard James struggle with his one line as Bystander Number One, and that memory did *not* give cause for optimism. Even Professor Lloyd looked skeptical.

"No, seriously...he can do it. He's been working with me on my lines, so he knows—"

But nobody was listening. Her classmates had already dismissed her suggestion and were casting about for other options.

Undaunted, Elliana pushed on. She stood, and in a voice loud enough to drown out the rest of the room, she said, "James, Act I, Scene 2. What does it say?"

Reluctantly, James stood and recited the scene in perfect detail, and not just Henry Higgins's part but all the parts.

"Act IV, Scene 1," Elliana commanded.

Again, James recited the scene perfectly.

The class was dumbstruck. Even Professor Lloyd was rendered speechless.

"Act V, Final Scene."

As James recited the scene, there were murmurs of amazement as his castmates followed along with their scripts.

"I think he's got it! By George, I think he's got it!" Holland exclaimed, borrowing and slightly rewording one of Henry Higgins's famous lines from the play to the animated titters of the rest of the cast.

As luck would have it, James was about the same height and build as Harold Rynar, therefore no modifications were required for costuming. Additionally, James's stiff movements and stodgy British pronunciations seemed to fit well with those of a haughty, absent-minded, rude, and totally brilliant professor of phonetics. To everyone's surprise and relief, after just two rehearsals and a trip to the video store for a copy of *My Fair Lady* with Audrey Hepburn and Rex Harrison, James totally owned the role.

Pygmalion opened on time and was an unmitigated success. At the end of each of the five scheduled performances, the entire cast received thunderous applause. The most enthusiastic and most extended ovations, however, were always saved for James and Elliana.

CHAPTER 16

1989–1990

As James's final semester in college was drawing to an end, he began having second thoughts about his decision to graduate after only three years. With the monstrous course load he'd taken on for the first two-and-a-half years, his college experience had felt more like a full-time job than anything he might've liked to extend. The last semester, however, had showed him how fun college life could be.

He could've done without the class in General Insurance and found that he became airsick far too easily to enjoy becoming a pilot in his Intro to Flight class. Still, he supposed, the information he learned about insurance was, theoretically at least, useful for his life after academics. And, had he not taken the flight class, he would've always wondered what if. Thus, neither class was a total waste.

Much to his surprise, James had thoroughly enjoyed his Ornithology class. He'd always mentally rolled his eyes whenever he heard about people going bird watching, but by the time his class had ended, he actually *liked* it. He had to admit, it was pretty cool being able to identify a bird from a distance by silhouette, flight pattern, or just its call. Probably the only piece of *useful* wisdom Mack Lee Hamilton had ever passed along to him was, "Don't knock, knock, knock what you haven't tried, tried, tried."

The biggest surprise for him had been his Intro to Theater class. He'd loved it. Although if he was being perfectly honest with himself, was it really the class or the relationship that had begun *because* of the class that he'd found so appealing? That he had no strong desire to act in another play would suggest the latter. The applause had been *fun*, however. Ultimately, a leopard cannot change his spots no matter how many curtain calls one might receive. James was still a science and history geek. His future would be in the sciences, not the arts.

Had he not taken the class, James knew that he would've never truly understood Elliana's passion for the stage, and since he loved *her*, he desperately *wanted* to understand.

On June 5th, James graduated from MIT with Becca and Elliana in the audience, cheering him on. They listened attentively as former US Senator Paul Tsongas delivered the commencement address. The senator opened his speech by stating that he had no recollection who his commencement speaker had been for his own high school, college, or law school graduations. He lamented that he would likely spend history forgotten, little more than a trivia question for the class of '89.

Elliana nudged Becca in the ribs and whispered into her ear, "Clearly, he doesn't know our James."

Becca, who'd been taking a sip of water at the time, nearly spit it all over the row of spectators in front of them. When she'd recovered sufficiently from her giggling fit, she nodded her enthusiastic agreement.

After speaking for just twenty-three minutes, Tsongas yielded the stage to MIT's president, and soon a train of black-gowned graduates walked the stage. When James accepted his diploma and shook the president's hand, it was all Becca could do to suppress a cheer. Since the president had earlier requested that all applause be held until the end of the ceremony, she had to content herself with snapping half a roll of snapshots with her camera.

After the ceremony, Becca treated James and Elliana to a celebratory dinner at Harvest on Harvard Square. The three enjoyed a wonderful meal, laughing and talking until the restaurant closed and they had to leave. Afterward, Becca left the young lovers to their own devices and returned to her hotel, bursting with pride.

The next morning, they met at her hotel for breakfast. Afterward, Becca left for the airport and James and Elliana the train station, for the promised trip to New Haven to meet her family. There, James fell in love all over again, and with someone new. Remarkably, Elliana didn't have any objection to his new relationship. On the contrary, she encouraged it.

Had she stood on her tippy-toes, Oksana Petrenko *might* have been able to elevate her height to five feet. That supposition, however, was purely academic, for Elliana's baba would *never* have tolerated standing still long enough to be measured. Baba was a force of nature, a virtual perpetual motion machine. James could easily imagine her spinning seven plates on sticks and juggling five eggs, all while simultaneously whipping up a Chicken Kiev and potato pancakes. Baba's face was as brown and wrinkled as the walnut-stuffed prunes she plied upon James within the first minute after their introduction, all while chastising Elliana for allowing her man to be so thin.

"Ellya, ees not so healthy a man be so skee-ny," Oksana chided, her blue eyes twinkling. "You must feed heem better!"

Elliana dropped her head penitently. "Yes, Baba!"

"Ellya, you go take and show heem around. Then bring heem back. I feed heem. Boy needs to eat. Now, out of my keetchin. I make food."

As she shooed them from the room, Oksana pinched James on the rump. He jumped and spun around. She winked mischievously, and James was in love.

So this *is what it's like to have a grandmother,* he thought, absently rubbing at the scar on his chest.

James was equally charmed by Karol and Angela Petrenko. Karol was almost completely bald and had the perpetual squint of a man who'd spent his entire adult life looking through magnified lenses, which James assumed, as a watch and clock maker, he had. He was quick to laugh and reveled in regaling James with funny stories about Elliana's childhood.

Angela, who insisted that James call her Angie, had maintained her dancer's body. Even though she was probably in her early fifties, he strongly suspected she still could high kick like the Radio City Music Hall Rockettes.

By all indications, both parents approved of their daughter's choice for a mate and made certain James felt welcome during his stay.

After the visit to New Haven, it was time for James to move to New York for medical school. He found an apartment near the Columbia campus, a fifth-floor walk-up, and, with Elliana's help, moved his few possessions there. A piece of plywood set atop two milkcrates became his desk and dinner table. He bought a set of pots and pans, and together they laid in basic supplies. That evening, Elliana—

channeling her inner Baba—taught him how to make Purina Bachelor Chow, also known as spaghetti. And that night they made love on an inflatable mattress set on the floor of his new bedroom.

In the morning, they made love again, and after a tear-filled goodbye, the couple walked silently to the train station. He promised to visit her in New Haven or Cambridge as often as his class load would allow. She assured him that the trains ran in both directions and offered similar assurances. Then, she boarded her train for New Haven and was gone.

James watched the train pull from the station. He stood motionless, staring down the tracks for several minutes, then turned and trekked back to his apartment, ready to start medical school.

Individually, the classes taken in the first two years of medical school were no more difficult than advanced college-level coursework. The challenge for most medical students was not the complexity of the individual courses, but rather the fact that they were taking eight classes of similar difficulty contemporaneously. Having graduated from MIT with a double science major after only three years, James actually found his medical course work to be relatively simple. His brain, with its superior memory, and his experience from MIT made him feel quite comfortable with the volume of material. All he had to do was listen in class and read the requisite textbook assignments, and he could ace any examination. Consequently, it was a rare weekend when he was unable to keep his promise to visit Elliana.

After completing his first year at Columbia with a perfect 4.0 grade point average, James received a very welcome surprise. After playing Eliza Doolittle in the spring with Jimmy, Elliana was cast as Margaret "Hot Lips" Houlihan in *M*A*S*H* the following term and received outstanding reviews. During the spring term, her class put on a musical, Andrew Lloyd Webber's *Evita*. Although not cast as the lead, Elliana understudied the role. Additionally, she was cast in the role of Perón's Mistress, a part with a solo. Her baleful mezzo-soprano rendition of "Another Suitcase in Another Hall" practically brought down the house.

In the audience that night was Malcolm O'Leary. Until a botched surgery for a vocal cord nodule cut short his career a decade before, O'Leary had been an up-and-coming performer on Broadway. Currently, he was employed as an instructor at NYU's prestigious Tisch School of the Arts. O'Leary sought out Elliana after the final curtain, and after complimenting her effusively on her performance, he offered her a business card and suggested she call him the next morning.

Intrigued, Elliana called the number at precisely eight the next morning, and O'Leary answered on the first ring. In the conversation that followed, he offered her the opportunity to audition for a scholarship to attend Tisch. Extremely flattered, Elliana accepted on the spot.

Without telling a soul about the audition, she traveled to New York the next week. She didn't think anything would come of it and didn't bother to prepare for it. She figured the worst thing that could come from auditioning was an all-expense paid trip to the city where she'd get to see James.

When she arrived at the Tisch Auditorium for her audition, Elliana had expected to be part of a cattle call, so she'd brought along a paperback to read while she waited her turn. She was surprised to find the auditorium empty except for three judges who waited for her on the stage. To her immense relief, one of them was O'Leary. The other two judges introduced themselves, but in her nervousness, Elliana promptly forgot their names. One of them asked her what she'd prepared for the audition.

"Prepared? I, ummm, didn't know that I…"

"Most candidates come to us with taped musical accompaniment," one of the judges explained.

Elliana's mouth opened and closed like a landed cod.

O'Leary's gravelly voice came to her rescue. "It's not a problem, Miss Petrenko. You recently performed in *Evita* for your school, and as I understand, you also understudied the lead. Why don't you give us the number you performed, 'Another Suitcase in Another Hall,' and, perhaps, 'Don't Cry for Me Argentina'?"

After a moment of stunned silence, Elliana cleared her throat and began to sing *a cappella*. When she finished the two numbers, O'Leary and the judge to his left were smiling broadly.

The third judge sat stone-faced for a moment and then asked, "Do you have anything else, perhaps something outside your comfort zone? Outside your usual range?"

Elliana's mind went blank. What could she possibly sing? Suddenly, it came to her. *What the Hell,* she thought, and then she blew the judges away with her rendition of Janis Joplin's "Piece of My Heart."

Afterward, the stone-faced judge rose from his chair, gave three loud claps, and offered Elliana his hand. "Miss Petrenko, thank you for joining us today. The Carnegie Scholarship offered by NYU-Tisch is our most prestigious. It covers all tuition and fees after matriculation, and also provides for voice and dance coaching. Additionally, the scholarship provides for a small stipend to defray our ridiculous New York cost of living throughout the time the student is enrolled. Only one such scholarship is offered each year, and competition is, understandably, intense. Consequently, only the crème de la crème is even asked to audition. We'd actually closed auditions before Mr. O'Leary arranged for you to come here today."

Elliana's heart began to sink. Although she'd expected to be rejected, she'd allowed herself to hope...always a dangerous proposition. She supposed rejection wouldn't be all *that* bad. She could still pursue her dream of becoming a Broadway performer without attending Tisch. Her mother had done it. So could she.

The judge continued, "I fear that my colleague was remiss when he did not explain to you about the scholarship's particulars." He glared briefly over his spectacles at O'Leary, who just smiled. "Of course, I too, was remiss. When introducing myself earlier, I failed to mention my position here at Tisch. I am the Dean of Admissions." After a brief pause, he continued, "I'm certain I speak for my two colleagues when I say your performance was magical. My colleagues and I are in total agreement. We'd like to offer *you* this year's Carnegie Scholarship."

With downcast eyes, Elliana smiled weakly and said, "Thank you, sirs. It was an honor just being asked to—" Then, her brain finally caught up with the words she'd just heard. "What? You want *me*? I won? I really won!"

The three nodded in unison.

Elliana let out a squeal and ran about the stage in circles, jumping about and giggling like a lunatic. She gave all three judges a hug, and O'Leary a kiss on the cheek. Suddenly she froze, her eyes wide. "I've got to tell James!" Without another word, she leaped from the stage and raced to the exit door, leaving the three dumbfounded judges in her wake.

Shaking his head with amusement, O'Leary called after her retreating form, "Miss Petrenko, you can just come back tomorrow to sign the award paperwork."

The auditorium door thudded closed, and she was gone.

An hour later, to James's delight, he was informed that he would soon have a roommate, if, of course, he wanted one.

James did.

CHAPTER 17

1990–1993

A T THE END OF HER academic year, with scholarship in hand and dreams within reach, Elliana
transferred to NYU-Tisch and moved into James's
apartment, wasting little time in making it home.

James, who'd lived alone in the apartment for the past
year, had put little thought into creature comforts and even
less into decorating. The spartan environment didn't bother
him at all. He still slept on the floor on the same cheap air
mattress he'd purchased on his first day in New York, and
his only piece of furniture was a single folding chair placed
before his milk crate and plywood table/desk. The walls and
windows remained bare.

Usually blissfully unaware of his surroundings, he began
noticing little changes almost immediately after Elliana's
arrival. First, movie posters and playbills appeared on the
walls. He didn't mind, and they *did* brighten up the place,
even if they were a little artsy for his taste.

After she'd been there for about a week, Elliana glanced
someone in the apartment across the alley from theirs
peeking at her as she got dressed one morning. Unfazed,
she showed the person her middle finger, and when James

came home that evening, there were curtains on all their windows.

Soon thereafter, the air mattress disappeared, replaced by a simple metal frame with a full-sized mattress and box spring. It was nothing fancy—there wasn't even a headboard—but it got them off the floor, and for Elliana, it was heavenly. Soon thereafter, a tiny dinette table and chairs appeared in the breakfast nook. When a loveseat and television magically appeared in their living room, James finally inquired about their origin. Elliana gave a coy smile and pointed to the cuckoo clock, newly mounted on their wall, and that was all the explanation he required.

Elliana continued to feather her nest throughout the summer. By fall, when classes resumed for both, she'd transformed James's little apartment into a comfortable living space for them both.

For James, it didn't matter. He'd been perfectly happy living his spartan existence. It had been simple. However, he appreciated the joy Elliana received by decorating and transforming the apartment into a home, and wisely raised no objections. If she was happy, then so was he.

The summer ended all too soon for the young lovers and soon both were quite busy with coursework.

The second year of medical school was much like the first had been for James. It was purely classroom material, albeit with a slightly more medical bent. During his first year, only Gross Anatomy and perhaps Biochemistry had seemed even remotely applicable to the practice of medicine. During his second year, with classes such as Physiology, Pathophysiology, Microbiology, and Pharmacology, he finally felt like he was in medical school and found the year much more interesting.

For his birthday that year, Elliana took James to Yankee Stadium to see the Red Sox play the Yankees. She had no interest in baseball but knew James loved the game.

He'd once told her that when he was a kid, there were only three sports offered in his tiny little home town: football, basketball, and baseball. His small stature precluded much success in football or basketball, but he'd discovered that if you could run, catch, and throw, you could play baseball. He might never hit home runs, but he still could be competitive while playing the game. So baseball had become his sport of choice. So when one of her professors, a season ticket holder, had offered up his seats for the game, she'd jumped at the opportunity. Their seats were in a field-level box just behind home plate. James was in heaven. A good sport, Elliana stood and cheered whenever he did. Between those occasions, however, she read a book.

A month later, James had the opportunity to return the favor. Whereas he'd enjoyed his brief run at playing Professor Henry Higgins in *Pygmalion*, he had less interest in musical theater than Elliana had in baseball. Thus, it was quite a surprise when, for Elliana's birthday, he acquired tickets for Cameron Mackintosh's *Les Misérables*. The seats he'd selected were in the first row of the balcony and provided an unobstructed view of the stage. Elliana was thrilled.

James purchased the tickets because he knew she would enjoy the show. It was *her* night, and he was determined to be a good sport about it. Still, he fully expected that he'd pull the Broadway equivalent of reading a book at a baseball game—he'd sleep through it. He could not have been more wrong. If it was possible, he actually enjoyed the show more than Elliana. He'd always thought that because he was tone deaf, he wouldn't enjoy musical theater. He'd read *Les Misérables* as a boy and, sitting in the balcony beside Elliana, was surprised to find himself mentally following the plot as it was conveyed in song. He might not have recognized the notes, but the story was just as compelling and the emotions expressed in song just as real to him as had Victor Hugo's prose.

As James and Elliana walked arm in arm along West End after the show, he was left with two absolute certainties. The first, a great surprise for him, was that this would not be his last foray into the world of musical theater. Of course, he'd always known that if Elliana succeeded in her dream of becoming a Broadway performer, he'd attend her shows just to be supportive. The surprise was that he'd actually *enjoyed* it! He wondered if Elliana would enjoy seeing Andrew Lloyd Webber's *Phantom of the Opera* as a Christmas present. His second certainty was that the world could use a lot more men like Jean Valjean.

After James's second year of medical school ended, there was no prolonged summer break. Instead, a short two weeks after his final examinations in June, the third-year clinical clerkships began. For the first time, he found himself out of the classroom and out of his comfort zone. No longer could he simply read and regurgitate a textbook and expect top marks. Now he was expected to think on his feet and make decisions in the often murky waters that are clinical medicine.

Initially, he struggled a bit, but ultimately, James found his footing and thrived. Because of his superior memory, it was easy for him to formulate differential diagnoses based upon patient symptoms, complaints, and sundry test data. For him, medicine came to life at the bedside. Every patient was a jigsaw puzzle just waiting for him to place the final piece and see the whole picture for what it truly was. Sometimes the picture was the *Mona Lisa*, and other times, no matter what he did, it turned out to be a Rorschach ink blot.

By the time James completed his third-year core curriculum of clinical rotations, he remained undecided about which area of medicine he'd most like to pursue. Except for Psychiatry, which with his family history hit a little too close to home, he found something to like about each field. Still, he'd narrowed it down a bit.

In Pediatrics, he liked the children but found that the parents annoyed him terribly. Additionally, really sick kids—the ones with cancer or birth defects—were depressing to treat if their prognosis was poor. He found himself growing very attached to each child, so every loss was gut wrenching. Consequently, Pediatrics was out.

Internal Medicine held the allure of being very cerebral. He enjoyed puzzling out diagnoses but felt that he'd become rapidly bored with caring for chronic disease states for years on end. Cardiology and Critical Care Medicine were areas of interest, but one had to go through an Internal Medicine residency before subspecializing into either field, making the concept less appealing. He didn't entirely exclude Internal Medicine but doubted that he'd ultimately go in that direction.

James enjoyed Obstetrics. It was generally a happy time in patients' lives, making it fun, though joyous could turn tragic on a dime and office Gynecology held little appeal for him. Therefore, he doubted his future career path would lead him there.

That left Orthopedics or Surgery. With each, there was a discrete problem that could be corrected with a procedure. Of the two, Orthopedics was the least appealing. Ortho cases often seemed almost brutal to him. The hammering, sawing, and casting seemed too much like carpentry for his personal taste.

Although many surgeons were cowboys—"Cure it with cold steel," a surgery attending had once quipped during rounds—there was a degree of finesse required to repair an artery or to dissect away diseased or cancerous tissue while preserving the healthy tissue around it. Postoperative surgical patients could be every bit as sick as those in the Medical ICU, so the field provided more than a little of the Critical Care Medicine that he'd so enjoyed. And with surgery, he could dabble in each of the fields of medicine he'd liked without becoming ensnarled by any of them. Thus, by the end of the required third-year core rotations, James was leaning toward an eventual career in General Surgery or one of its subspecialties. He wasn't worried about the decision. There was no rush. James knew his fourth year, with its allowance for elective clerkship rotations, would help him solidify his career plans.

At the end of his third year of medical school, Elliana graduated from NYU-Tisch. To celebrate, James took her out for dinner at Tavern on the Green in Central Park. The wait for their table took longer than anticipated. When they were finally seated, their waiter apologized profusely for the delay, explaining that the restaurant was terribly short-staffed. James thought nothing more of the delay, and he and Elliana shared a delightful meal. Elliana's pan-roasted halibut was superb and, if his empty plate was any indication, so was his Scottish salmon. After dinner, the couple tarried and finished off the Pouilly-Fuissé their waiter had recommended as an accompaniment for their meal. The wine was too good to waste.

As she savored the last sips of her wine, Elliana glanced about. Although it was rather late, the restaurant remained packed and the staff still appeared harried. During a brief lull in their conversation, she off-handedly asked, "I wonder if they're accepting applications?"

James was caught off guard by the sudden change in the course of their after-dinner conversation. "Applications? Who? For what?"

"For here, silly. And to work," Elliana replied.

"Yeah, but why?"

"Ummm...to make money, duh," she said, rolling her eyes.

"I get that, but why?"

Elliana took another sip of wine. "I want to stay in New York. I *need* to be here if I'm going to make it on Broadway."

"I get that, but—"

"It's expensive living here, and my scholarship stipend ended with graduation. If I'm going to stay, I'll need a job to pay my way."

"But you live with me. I can take care of you," James objected.

"I know you would, sweetie, but I've no desire to be a kept woman while I pay my dues. So, I need a job. Besides, isn't it a cliché that struggling actors are supposed to wait tables until they're discovered?"

James's mouth opened and closed much like the Scottish salmon he'd enjoyed for dinner might have done in the minutes after it had been landed. There was no point in arguing, so he just nodded his head and sighed. "Okay."

As they left the restaurant, Elliana picked up an employment application from the manager. A week later, she began work bussing tables at Tavern on the Green. After a month, she began training to join the waitstaff. Six months later, she was promoted to shift leader.

During James's fourth year of medical school, his inclination toward a career in surgery was further solidified. He enjoyed procedures and liked the rapid turnover of patients. Patients came in with a problem, underwent a surgical procedure, got better, and went home. Afterward, they followed up in the office a few times and were replaced with new patients with new problems.

James graduated with high honors from medical school. Once again, Becca and Elliana were there to cheer him on. As before, the dean encouraged family and friends to refrain from applause until *all* graduates had crossed the stage, an instruction that the New Yorkers in the audience—and soon Becca and Elliana with them—happily ignored.

After a celebratory meal at Le Petit Bijou in Lynwood, Becca queried "Dr. Hamilton" about his postgraduate plans.

Before James could answer, Elliana proudly chimed in, clearly excited for him, "James has been offered a General Surgery residency here at Columbia."

"James, that's wonder—" Becca began.

"Actually, I *was* offered a position at Columbia, but I've decided to accept another surgical residency instead, one offered by Massachusetts General in Boston. The chief of the Columbia surgical residency tried his best to get me to stay, but I think the program at Mass General is the better option for me."

Although it was late May, an arctic wind swept over their table, freezing the smile on Elliana's face. "I thought you said you were staying at Columbia?" she said slowly. And that was the longest sentence she'd speak for the rest of the evening.

CHAPTER 18

1993–1998

I N THEIR APARTMENT THE NEXT morning, it rapidly became evident to James that the surgical chair from Columbia was not alone in his disappointment over his election to leave New York for his surgical training. Elliana was heartbroken. Following James to Boston was not an option for her if she wanted to pursue her own dreams. His move was going to force them to be apart, and she wasn't happy about it—not even a little.

James did his best to reassure Elliana that although he was leaving the city, he'd always be with her, but she wasn't buying it.

He maintained his apartment's lease in New York and sublet it to Elliana. His was a rent-controlled building, and if he'd allowed the lease to lapse, her rent there would have increased by over a thousand dollars per month. Still, she wasn't convinced.

Over breakfast, James did his best to explain why he felt changing programs was important. In short, he wanted to be the best surgeon he could be and did not think that possible if he remained at Columbia.

"But the residency program at Columbia Presbyterian is world class. You told me that yourself," she argued.

"True, Columbia's program is outstanding," he agreed.

"Then why can't you stay?" she pouted.

James put down his slice of pizza and paused, collecting his thoughts. "You love dogs, right?"

Clearly bewildered by the abrupt change in tack for their conversation, she replied, "You know I do. You met Mr. McRuff when you came to New Haven with me to meet my family. For sixteen years, that dog practically raised me. But what's that got to do with anything?"

"That's precisely my point!"

"Because I love dogs, you're going to leave me and move to Boston?" Elliana flopped back into her seat, a look of exasperation on her face.

James shook his head.

"Well, what is it then?" She hated when James went off on tangents like this.

"You've had McRuff for sixteen years," he began.

"We're not talking about the damned dog! We're talking about why you feel it necessary to leave me."

"What kind of dog is he?"

Elliana sighed. "There you go again with the fucking dog."

James raised his hand to stop her from continuing. "Just answer the question and then hear me out...please?" he begged.

Now Elliana was practically shaking with rage. "You know damned well he's a mutt. Heinz 57. Part terrier, part poodle, part Labrador, and God knows what else. Who the Hell cares?"

"Well, I want to be a mutt," James said in a matter-of-fact tone.

"What?" Deflated, Elliana was more confused than ever. Loving a genius was taxing.

"I want to be a mutt," James repeated. "You told me once that you used to have two other dogs: a French bulldog and a dachshund. Both were purebreds, right?"

Elliana nodded.

"And you told me both had scads of medical problems? And both died fairly young?"

Again, she nodded.

"There's a lot of inbreeding with purebred animals. Because of that, they are prone to medical issues. Mutts, on the other hand, tend to be healthier and more robust. You can't kill a mutt. Look at Mr. McRuff—he's sixteen and still going strong. Well, inbreeding also happens in medical training. There are 'purebreds' from Duke, Columbia, Stanford, Washington University, Minnesota—all the top programs—and they're all great. I believe that a hybrid mutt will make a better doctor than one who stays within a single program for his entire training. If I want to be the best, I need to be a mutt."

Elliana was little placated, but at least now she could better understand James's reasoning. It didn't matter now anyway. It was too late for him to change programs. The Rubicon—or, rather, the Hudson—had already been crossed. James was on his way to Boston.

And so, amid a sea of tears and promises of frequent visits, James moved to Boston to begin his formal surgery training.

James's surgical residency lasted for five grueling years. His attendings recognized his unique abilities very early in his training. If he read it, he remembered it, so his capacious memory made him a walking medical library. He also had the uncanny ability to collate random factoids from widely disparate sources, allowing him to be a master diagnostician. His surgical technique was superb, and after learning about new techniques from reading articles in the surgical literature, he was quick to apply them in the operating room. In his interactions with patients and family members, he was empathetic and had the ability to explain complex issues in a manner all could understand, and without coming across as condescending.

Perhaps the attribute that best served James in his chosen career was his ability to make decisions and deal with the aftermath. Often, and especially in emergency situations, it is better to make a wrong decision than it is to do nothing at all.

Early in James's training, one of his mentors had related a story from his childhood as an object lesson. He had grown up in a rural area and, for extra income one year, his mother had taken a job with the Census Bureau, which entailed driving out into the boonies to fill out census data with the folks living out there. Before going out on her first assignment, her supervisor had given her a bit of advice. "Never go down any road farther than you can back yourself out." James's mentor had explained, "As long as you know how to back yourself out of a situation, you can't get yourself into too much trouble."

James had taken these words to heart and always operated within himself. He was quick to make decisions and had a knack for making the right ones and for already having a plan in place for those rare occasions when he made the wrong call. Consequently, in Dr. Hamilton's operating room, even the most complex and chaotic of cases came off appearing planned, almost choreographed.

By all appearances, James had the makings of an out-standing surgeon, but he was not perfect. According to his staff mentor, he had one-and-a-half flaws. The half flaw was his perfectionism. The pursuit of perfection is not in itself a damnable affliction for a physician. After all, who would want their surgeon to embrace mediocrity? However, James took this pursuit to the extreme. If a case did not go per-fectly for *any* reason, he was relentless at ferreting out and correcting the mistake—real or imagined—so that the same error never occurred twice. In cases with an absence of any discernible errors and a less-than-perfect outcome, James couldn't let it go. After one of these random acts of God, or twists of fate, he relived and reviewed the case cut by cut, suture by suture, over and over again. Sometimes, during his mental play-by-play, James would unearth a trivial deviation from perfection. If that deviation was his own, he'd immediately correct it. If it was committed by one of his colleagues or the operating room staff, his second full-on flaw revealed itself. He had little patience for others and possessed a volatile temper. He'd fly into a rage and, not un-commonly, his tirades ended with thrown instruments, and one or more of his OR staff being ejected from his operating theater, often in tears.

Mack Lee Hamilton would have been proud. Like father, like son.

Even with this personal failing, James's positives as a surgeon vastly outweighed his negatives. Consequently, by the end of his five-year residency program, he had his pick of fellowships from blue-chip training programs all across the country.

Most of his attendings at Mass General expected James to select Cardiothoracic Surgery for his subspecialty. At-tention to detail and skill in the operating room were prerequisites for coronary artery bypass grafting or valve replacement and repair, and he had both of these attributes in spades. Others believed Transplant or Micro-Vascular Surgery to be his calling. Another attending even suggested that James might find Plastics, specifically Reconstructive Plastic Surgery, to be a good fit.

It was a surprise to everyone who'd *not* seen the scars on his forearm and chest—and no one other than Elliana had—when he eschewed other offers and accepted a Trauma Surgery Fellowship from Stanford University at the completion of his surgical residency.

James was certain that his relationship with Elliana would survive the greater distance while he was in California. Besides, the fellowship was only for a year...and she might even find she preferred the big screen to the stage.

Never happen, he thought to himself. *That girl was born for the stage.*

During his five years in Boston, James had been as good as his word. Whenever his training schedule allowed, he traveled back to New York to see Elliana. On weekends when she was not working, she traveled to Boston. The young couple weathered the hardships caused by distance, and their relationship thrived. By the end of the five years, their relationship was stronger than ever and James felt ready to take it to the next level.

Three months before the end of his residency, James began shopping for engagement rings. He knew he'd have two weeks between the end of his residency and the start of his fellowship program, so *that* was when he'd pop the question. Just the thought made him giddy.

Other than an antique gold locket her baba had given her when she turned sixteen, Elliana didn't usually wear jewelry, so he wasn't sure what she might like. He hoped that magically, he'd know whenever he saw it in a showcase.

After more than a month of shopping at malls, jewelry stores, and even pawn shops for the perfect ring, James had his doubts. It was becoming apparent to him that *the* ring wasn't going to magically appear, illuminated in a shop window by a shaft of sunlight beaming down from heaven. He was terribly discouraged and began to wonder if he should just give up on his idea of picking out a ring and surprising Elliana and instead let her pick out one for herself.

After another long afternoon of fruitless shopping, he was ready to give up and go home. Dejected, he walked down Tremont Street toward the Orpheum Theatre, where he'd parked his car. As he passed an alley, he noticed an ancient appearing bronze plaque that read, Feigenbaum Fine Jewelry, Est. 1919. Muttering, "What the Hell," he turned down the alley. He'd been to every other jeweler in Boston, so why not try this one?

Inside, he was met simultaneously by the shop's proprietor, one Carl Feigenbaum, and the incongruous mixed aromas of Lemon Pledge and stale pipe tobacco. The latter almost made him turn for the door. The former, however, begged him to stay.

"Come in! Come in, young man," insisted Feigenbaum, extending a plump pink hand in greeting.

By James's estimation, Mr. Feigenbaum was easily in his seventies. He wore a rumpled tweed jacket over an equally rumpled open-collared white shirt, the front pocket of which held the source of the pipe smoke. But the old man had a welcoming smile, so James elected to stay. He accepted both the hand and the greeting, all while thinking the old fellow looked more like somebody's grandpa than a purveyor of fine jewelry.

"I'm looking for a diamond engagement ring for my girl-friend," he began.

"Of course you are. Come, come," the old man said, leading James to a lighted display case. "Do you have anything in particular in mind?"

James assured him that he did not and gave a detailed account of his search and frustrations up to that point.

Feigenbaum listened attentively while occasionally the old man's bushy white eyebrows wriggled as James related especially troublesome details. Then he said, "Well, come and sit down. Maybe I can help. I've been doing this for almost fifty years, and my father and grandfather before that. If I can't help you, then maybe I can steer you to someone who can. Would you like something to eat or drink? I was just putting on a pot of tea when you came in."

"Yes, thank you. Tea would be wonderful."

In every other shop, James had been hounded by a cadre of perfectly tailored, coiffed, and manicured salespeople, all wearing expensive jewelry and fake smiles. They'd beaten him about the head and shoulders with the "four C's of diamond buying" and tried hard to sell him something—anything, really. They talked but didn't listen...or care. Here was someone who did both, and the only pieces of jewelry the old man wore were a wedding ring and an understated vintage rose gold Omega Seamaster wristwatch with a simple leather band.

"The most important thing to remember when you're picking out an engagement ring..." Feigenbaum began.

James sighed. *Here come the four C's again,* he thought.

"...is to know about the girl. Tell me about the girl you want to make your bride. It'll be easier to help you find the right ring if I know more about her."

Stunned, James's mind raced. *No lecture? No sales pitch? Just interest?* If he hadn't liked the old gentleman already, he was solidly in Feigenbaum's camp now. He launched into a litany of facts, thoughts, and impressions about Elliana, little of which was cogent to the point of Feigenbaum's question.

The old man sat patiently, nodding and smiling beatifically. When James finally came up for air, Feigenbaum redirected. "So, does she usually wear jewelry?"

"No...wait. She wears an antique locket, a cameo her grandmother gave her. That's all."

"Ahhh, that says a lot about her. Do you mind?" Feigenbaum asked, taking the pipe from his pocket.

"Not at all," James heard himself saying. He hated pipe smoke, but somehow, right now, that didn't seem to matter. He calmly watched as Feigenbaum produced a can of tobacco from an inside pocket of his jacket and filled the bowl.

When the pipe was lit and drawing well, Feigenbaum continued. "Yes, that's very important. See, if she doesn't wear jewelry, she probably won't care for anything overly flashy. Of course, she will like anything given her by the man she loves, but a big, showy ring isn't one she'd naturally select for herself."

James nodded, reflecting that the cherry-and-vanilla aroma of the pipe smoke wasn't so bad after all.

"No," Feigenbaum continued as though to himself. "The setting shouldn't be anything too ostentatious. She wouldn't like that. And the stone..."

James looked into the old man's bespectacled eyes in anticipation.

Feigenbaum continued his musings, almost at a whisper, his thoughts far away. "The stone...it should be something classic, elegant, not too loud or too modern. Definitely not a round or brilliant cut...same for a princess cut, cushion, or radiant. Doesn't sound like the kind of girl who'd go for an emerald or marquise cut..."

"Definitely not marquise," James agreed.

The old man's head snapped up triumphantly, and he practically shouted, "I've got it!"

James jumped back, almost spilling his tea at Feigenbaum's exclamation.

"Asscher cut! Definitely an Asscher." Feigenbaum beamed.

"I'm not familiar with that one," James admitted.

"It's like an emerald cut, only more square...like this." Feigenbaum produced a pen and pad of paper and began to draw as he explained, "Asscher cut diamonds are an older style cut less commonly employed today, largely out of laziness, in my opinion."

"Why's that?" James asked, instantly curious.

"Like with an emerald cut, the table—that's the flat part of the diamond—on an Asscher is larger and has fewer facets. Therefore, this forces the cutter to select a finer quality stone and to make more precise cuts. Flaws in the stone or imprecise cuts, which might be hidden inside a round or brilliant cut diamond, would be clearly evident inside an Asscher cut stone."

James smiled, nodding in agreement. "The perfect girl deserves the perfect diamond."

"Precisely, my boy. Now, let's go pick a diamond for your bride-to-be!"

James rose and eased back to the showcase, eager to find the perfect stone.

"Not there, my boy. Those baubles are not for you...or for your girl. *Here* is where you'll find *Elliana's* diamond."

James was amazed that Feigenbaum had remembered Elliana's name. Without a word, he followed him to a table covered in black crushed velvet in the back corner of the shop.

"One moment, please." Feigenbaum locked the front door before ducking into the back room.

James waited patiently, surprised to find himself actually *enjoying* shopping for engagement rings.

Feigenbaum returned a moment later with a velvet-lined metal box. "Three times each year, I travel to Mumbai, Cape Town, and Tel Aviv to procure my stock of diamonds. I buy directly from the cutters and personally inspect and select every stone I purchase. This removes the middleman from all dealings and allows me to provide higher quality stones at a more reasonable price for my customers." Feigenbaum began scattering the contents onto the velvet-topped table and switched on a brilliant white light. "I brought these stones back from Tel Aviv just last week."

Dazzled by the diamonds cascading onto the tabletop, James donned the white gloves proffered by Mr. Feigenbaum.

Offering James a jeweler's loupe, Feigenbaum asked, "I presume you've developed a familiarity with one of these during your ring shopping odyssey?"

James nodded, selecting a diamond at random. He picked it up easily with tweezers, like the surgeon he was, and examined the stone with the loupe. After a moment, he put it down and selected another, then another. After several minutes of silent scrutiny and dozens of stones, he returned to the third diamond he'd examined and placed it before Feigenbaum. "This one. What can you tell me about it?"

Feigenbaum took up the stone, gazed at it through his own loupe, and nodded appreciatively.

"I can tell you that you have an outstanding eye, young man. If ever you decide that surgery's not for you, come see me and I'll give you a job here in my shop."

James replied sheepishly, "My eyes can't be that good, because they don't see the inclusions in this one."

Feigenbaum beamed. "That's because there *aren't* any." He briefly consulted an indexed list, then continued, "You just picked out the finest stone in this collection. Look here on the girdle."

James picked up the diamond again. On the girdle, he saw a series of letters and numbers he'd overlooked before. He looked up again in puzzlement. "What are those?" he asked.

"It's a laser engraving." Feigenbaum consulted his list again to be sure, then continued, "GIA 5515221467 is an Asscher cut, 1.52-carat, D-color diamond certified by the Gemological Institute of America to be internally flawless with a Signature Ideal cut. It's a beautiful, near-perfect stone with a near-perfect cut. Bravo, my boy!"

After James selected the stone, it was time to choose a setting. He and Feigenbaum returned to the display case. After several minutes of gazing through the glass, James shook his head in dismay. Nothing *looked* like Elliana to him.

Feigenbaum was unfazed. "I didn't think you'd find the setting in there to match your girl—too modern. Will you humor an old man for a moment?"

James nodded, and once again, Feigenbaum produced his pad and pen. "Jewelry design has always been something of a passion for me," he explained as he began sketching.

James watched in amazement as two views of an engagement ring took shape. Feigenbaum incorporated an Asscher cut center stone and flanked it with two small baguettes. The result was stunning.

This was a ring Elliana would wear. This was a ring Elliana would love.

———————

After completing his surgical residency in late June, James had two weeks before he'd be expected at Stanford and intended to spend every possible second of it with Elliana. No doubt, his mom might have enjoyed having him visit too. But this time, he was sure she'd understand his absence— she'd told him as much during one of their recent Sunday afternoon telephone calls.

James wanted to find the perfect time to pop the question, but neither Elliana's work schedule nor the weather seemed to want to cooperate with his plans. On the last Saturday of June, the stars aligned—finally.

Throughout the evening, James felt keenly aware of the weight of the ring in his jacket pocket. Although platinum was heavier than gold, he knew it was only his imagination, born out of anticipation, that weighed on his mind. Every few minutes, he nervously fingered the pocket to confirm it was still there. The damned thing was burning a hole in his pocket, and it was all he could do not to drop to one knee, whisk the ring from his pocket, and offer it, along with his undying love, to Elliana.

Usually very attentive, James was totally distracted. Several times over dinner, he posed questions to Elliana in casual conversation that she'd answered clearly only a moment before.

Always quick to pick up on his moods, Elliana noted his distraction but wrote it off as anxiety over his pending move to California and the start of his Trauma Fellowship. If she was being totally honest with herself, and she usually was, she was anxious too. Yes, she knew that while he'd been in Boston, James had visited often, and she was certain that he'd do so from California if he could. But still, he'd be a whole continent away instead of a few hours by train.

Elliana adored James. He was the man she'd dreamed about finding when she was a little girl, and she couldn't imagine a future without him. She imagined the two of them sitting in matching rocking chairs, holding hands, watching and laughing as their grandchildren played together in their backyard. What would she do if he forgot about her while he was so far away? How could she go on?

The thought sent a chill down her spine. "After all, absence makes the heart go yonder," Elliana mumbled, not realizing she was speaking aloud.

"What was that? I couldn't catch what you said," James asked, absently fingering the lump in his jacket pocket.

"Oh, nothing. I was just thinking about your move to Stanford next week and how much I'm going to miss you," she said with a smile that didn't quite make it all the way to her eyes.

James didn't notice. "Right, right...yes, that *is* next week," he said. "Luckily, I don't have very much to pack. I just wish you were coming with me."

"You know I can't, not if I want to work in the theater."

"I know." James reached across the table and took her hand. "You know, there's a great theater program in San Francisco."

Elliana withdrew her hand from his. "I know, but it's—"

Nodding his understanding, James finished her sentence. "It's not Broadway."

The two had been over this ground repeatedly. Just as James's dream was to be the best surgeon he could possibly be, Elliana's dream was to make it on the Great White Way. To date, she had been less successful than James in achieving her goals. She'd appeared in several off-off-Broadway productions, but none had propelled her into the big time yet. She figured she still had a few years left to chase her dream. After that, she didn't know. He clearly loved her, and she loved him, but he seemed too focused on his career to settle down or start a family. Having children had always been a touchy subject between them. Early in their relationship, after Elliana had cajoled James into talking more about his family, he'd sworn to her that he'd never have children. His hatred for his father ran way too deep.

Elliana remembered the conversation vividly. "His genetic line ends with me," he'd said. When she'd tried to convince him that he wasn't Mack Lee Hamilton and instead was a good, kind, and loving man, regardless of how bad his father might've been, her entreaties had fallen upon deaf ears.

Someday, Elliana knew, she'd have to push the issue. She'd fold her arms across her chest and declare, "You'll just have to decide which is more important to you, your hatred of your father or your love for me." Someday, she would draw that line in the sand, but certainly not today, not with James leaving for California in a week. And...she really wasn't ready to give up *her* career dreams just yet either. So, *that* was a conversation for another day.

After dinner, James and Elliana had just enough time to reach their seats at the Minskoff Theatre before the curtain rose on Disney's *The Lion King*. Elliana hoped that Simba's coming-of-age tale might nudge James further down the road toward *wanting* to be a father, but she doubted it. Still, the ticking in her ears, or was it her ovaries, was becoming deafening. She figured she only had a few years during which she could pursue her dream of a career on Broadway. After that, she really wanted children. And she wanted James to be their father. Becca promised her that she shouldn't worry. He'd come around. Still, if Elliana couldn't convince him... Well, that just might be a deal-breaker for her.

The heat of the day had dissipated by the time the show ended, and James suggested they take a walk before heading home. He said he'd never been to the Empire State Building and wanted to see the city from the observation deck at least once before he departed for the West Coast. Since it was only a fifteen-minute walk and she was wearing comfortable flats, Elliana raised no objection.

On arrival, Elliana was surprised to find that James had already purchased the Express Pass for the 86th and 102nd floors. Apparently, his "last-minute" impulse to see the Empire State Building hadn't been such a simple caprice after all.

It took a full minute for their express elevator to reach the 86th floor. Although it was almost midnight, Elliana was surprised to find the open-air observatory deck still packed with people. They walked arm in arm, enjoying the view. James dropped a quarter into one of the swivel-mounted binoculars, and they took turns gazing across the harbor toward the brightly lit Statue of Liberty. After several minutes, James urged Elliana back to the elevators, and a moment later they were at the 102nd-floor Observatory. The views were essentially the same, but they were at least out of the wind and away from the crush of people.

Everything was new for James, though he seemed uncharacteristically anxious. Maybe he had issues with heights? Certainly, Elliana didn't. She'd seen all these views before, albeit from the slightly different perspective of her new employer's location. Earlier that month, she had left her longtime position at Tavern on the Green and accepted a junior waitstaff position at Windows on the World. Although she'd enjoyed working at Tavern, she had the opportunity to learn more about wine at Windows—they had a phenomenal wine cellar—and the tips would be better there too.

Elliana turned to point out her new place of employment on the Manhattan skyline and found James kneeling, apparently to tie his shoe. Instead of tying his shoe though, he was just down there looking up at her, holding something in trembling fingers.

That's odd, she thought. *James's hands never shake.*

He had tears streaming down his face and was saying something, his voice just a croak, barely above a whisper.

She couldn't hear what he was saying. *Speak up, dammit*, she thought.

Then she saw the ring, and the rest of the world disappeared.

"Oh my God, oh my God, oh my God, James! Are you? Are we? Oh my God, yes! Yes, yes, a thousand times, *yes!*"

His hands were shaking so much that it took James three tries to get the ring onto Elliana's finger. The ring whisperer, Mr. Feigenbaum, had guessed her size correctly and it fit perfectly. Then he rose unsteadily and, to the sound of applause from the 102nd-floor onlookers, kissed his bride-to-be.

CHAPTER 19

B ECCA HAD SEEN JAMES AND Elliana's engagement coming for quite some time, so when he'd called her in late May to help plan his proposal, it came as no surprise and she was more than happy to "assist" in the planning.

James had always been fiercely independent and a meticulous planner, so "assistance" meant listening as he mulled through the various permutations and combinations of every decision, all in nauseating detail. All that was really required of her was to say "uh-huh" or "huh-uh" at the appropriate times and smile at his enthusiasm. She thought it wonderful that even a big-time, hotshot surgeon still wanted his mom's approval.

He had wanted everything about his proposal to Elliana to be perfect, memorable, and a total surprise. He felt she deserved no less and thus didn't want to do anything ordinary like proposing over dinner in some fancy restaurant. No, the venue had to be perfect too.

Originally, he'd thought to propose at the Statue of Liberty. That, he'd thought, would be the perfect place in light of her family's immigrant heritage. However, he could think of no subterfuge that would get Elliana out to Liberty Island without her becoming suspicious.

Next, he'd considered proposing during a carriage ride through Central Park. Elliana *did* love horses and they'd always enjoyed picnicking there. But what would he do if it was raining that day?

Becca listened to James fret on the other end of the phone, all the while absently fingering the ring she wore beneath her blouse, next to her heart. Although the day was over thirty years distant, she remembered it like it was yesterday—Jimmy kneeling before her in the Rexall drugstore; holding that pathetic little, magically *wonderful* ring; and asking her to be his bride. James didn't get it now, but she knew someday he would. It's not the ring or the venue that makes the proposal perfect but rather the man holding the ring who matters. He would be all Elliana remembered, and for her, his proposal *would* be perfect.

Becca gave a conspiratorial smile, thinking she'd lead him to the right answer if it was the last thing she'd ever do. So, she came up with a plan. Of course, she was wise enough to make James believe *he'd* thought of it all himself.

"Remind me, how did you two meet?" she prompted.

"While working on *Pygmalion* for school."

"And you and Elliana still enjoy the theater?" she began, as though just making conversation.

"Hey, I know, I can take her to dinner and a show. She'd love that and wouldn't suspect a thing."

"Yeah, that's a great idea! I should've thought of that," she agreed. "But you've already ruled out proposing over dinner, and at a show, it'd be too dark for her to really *see* her ring."

"I guess that's out too, then." James sounded dejected on his end of the line.

Really, Becca thought. *For someone so intelligent, he can be really dense sometimes.* She suggested, "Not necessarily. Maybe you could take her somewhere close by after the show?"

"But where?"

"Well, how do you think you're going to feel when you slip that ring on Elliana's finger?"

"I'll be on top of the world."

Becca could almost hear James smiling through the phone.

"How about somewhere *both* of you could be on top of the world?" she suggested.

Becca allowed that thought to marinate in his head for a moment, then shook her head. *Truly dense,* she thought. Then she prompted him again with, "Like..."

"The Empire State Building! That's perfect. I'll tell her I want to see it before I go off to Stanford. She'll never suspect a thing."

Mission accomplished.

Over the past few weeks, Becca had replayed that conversation repeatedly in her mind, and every time, it made her smile. Aside from the fact that she loved seeing her son happy, she was looking forward to having grandchildren. She was, of course, aware of James's antipathy toward having children, but she was pretty sure that, together, she and Elliana would successfully wear down his resolve and be able to persuade him over time.

At Stanford, James grew rapidly into the role of Trauma Surgeon. His training from Mass General had prepared him well for the challenges of General Surgery. Dealing with major trauma, however, was General Surgery on steroids.

He still performed the entire panoply of general surgical procedures, treating appendicitis, bowel obstructions, bad gallbladders, etcetera. But now, he also dealt with blunt and penetrating trauma, vascular injuries, and burns.

During the day, he spent his time in the operating room like any other general surgeon, performing mundane surgical procedures or dealing with the occasional traffic or farm accident. When not operating, he'd be in the Trauma ICU dealing with postoperative complications of the critically ill patients residing there. Nights and particularly weekends were the realm of the Knife & Gun Club. There were always shootings or stabbings to be stabilized, with the occasional bar fight thrown in for good measure.

James took overnight call for Trauma every third night. The schedule was grueling, but he thrived. It was almost as though he had a genetic predisposition toward dealing with trauma patients and the aftermaths of their injuries. He'd found his niche.

His schedule during his one-year fellowship made it challenging but not impossible to visit Elliana, and her schedule was only a bit less hectic than his. Still, they managed to see one another at least once every few weeks, though not as often as either would've liked. Between visits, they generated monstrous long-distance telephone bills. Many were made even larger because of James's propensity for falling asleep mid-conversation. Elliana, it seemed, enjoyed listening to him sleep.

James's year at Stanford passed quickly, and after graduating from his training program, he accepted an offer to join the faculty for the surgical residency program at Washington University in St. Louis. The senior staff there believed, with his capacious fund of knowledge and superb surgical technique, James would be a natural at teaching. And, by all rights, he should have been. Unfortunately, his exacting standards and lack of patience made him exceptionally difficult to work with. His patients almost always did well. There was never an issue with his judgment or clinical skills, but nobody—not colleagues, surgical residents, anesthesiologists, or scrub techs—wanted to work with him. Behind his back, the house staff referred to James as "the BB," short for Brilliant Bastard.

If James was aware of his reputation around the hospital, he gave no indication. It certainly wouldn't have bothered him. To his way of thinking, patients' lives were more important than the tender sensitivities of hospital staff. If the truth was to be known, the only feelings that were worth a fig to him were Elliana's. She was an island of serenity in his sea of strife. To cause even the ghost of a smile to briefly cross her lovely face, he would've moved heaven and earth. With Elliana, James had near-infinite patience. Around her, his volatile temper was tamed. Although they'd had many disagreements over the course of their relationship, he'd never spoken a harsh word to her and certainly never would he *ever* raise his hand to her, except perhaps to lovingly caress her cheek as she slept.

The main selling point for accepting the position at Washington University—other than, perhaps, its proximity to a National League baseball stadium—was that James would be about 2,300 miles closer to Elliana than he'd been in California. And it was easy to find flights to JFK or Newark from the international airport in St. Louis, so even with his busy clinical schedule, James could spend time with his fiancée more often.

James and Elliana planned to wed in December of 2001. With Elliana's family all living in New Haven, that seemed the most logical location to hold the ceremony. As long as he got to spend his life with her beside him, he didn't care one whit about the venue. For Elliana, however, it was important. After all, it *was* her big day.

Planning a wedding is supposed to be a happy time for the betrothed, though even in the best of situations, it can also be stressful. With the ceremony being held at a location four hours distant from the closer of the two participants, working out details for the event was even more challenging than normal. With the hectic work schedules for both members of the bridal couple, planning was a nightmare.

Had it not been for Elliana's baba jumping in and taking the reins—even at her advanced age—Elliana likely would have said, "to Hell with it" and just eloped. By summer 2001, James, having observed Elliana's rising stress levels, was finding the concept of an elopement increasingly appealing. Besides, if they eloped, that would make her his wife even sooner, a thought that always brought a smile to his face.

On Elliana's urging, James took his first full week of vacation to assist with wedding planning. It was the first real vacation time he'd had since his second year of medical school. It was evident to all that he was becoming a workaholic. He spent most of his time at the hospital, and even when not on call, he frequently slept in one of the hospital's On-Call rooms. He loved what he was doing and did it well, so why shouldn't he make himself available, just in case.

Having read the writing on the wall, by August, Elliana felt an intervention was indicated. So, that evening during their nightly phone call, after chatting for a half hour, Elliana laid down the law.

"I love you too, sweetie," Elliana cooed into the phone. Then, in a much less flirtatious voice, she continued, "You know, I could really use your help with our wedding plans. December's not that far away."

"I'll be there this weekend. We can knock everything out then," James replied.

"Knock everything out then? Are you nuts? Do you have any idea at all how much planning it takes to coordinate and to pull off a wedding?"

"Just calm down. We'll get..."

"Calm down? Don't you tell me to calm down, James Wiley Hamilton!" Elliana's voice rose another octave.

"I—"

"No, *you* listen. There's too much to do here to get it all done on weekends or in snippets. I need you here for a *block* of time."

"But—"

"There's the caterers. We have to try the foods for the rehearsal dinner and reception. Then there's the florist. We haven't even chosen colors yet. And there's the..."

At some point during her litany, James zoned out.

"Are you even listening to me?"

Damn! Busted, James thought. "Yes, of course...I'm right here."

"Then what's the last thing I just said?" she challenged.

James squinched his eyes closed and took a stab in the dark. "Choosing...col...ors?"

"No! I can't even hold your attention long enough *to talk* about planning our wedding. How am I supposed to arrange everything by myself with you so far away?" Elliana's voice broke slightly as she fought to hold back a sob.

"Look, babe, don't cry...I can ask for vacation." James consulted a calendar, then continued, "Maybe the first week of September? I can book a flight for after work on the thirty-first and come back here on the ninth. We can have the whole week in between to work on the wedding. How's that sound?"

Elliana squealed with delight and began chattering excitedly, already making plans for their time together. "And if you're *not* here, *Mister*-Doctor Hamilton, you're gonna have to get married wearing a robin's-egg-blue tuxedo and the 'puffy shirt' from *Seinfeld!*" she threatened sweetly, followed by another little squeal. Clearly, she was excited about *something*. "And...I have some really, really big news."

James's mouth went dry. "Wait! Are we? Are we going to have a—"

"No, silly...not that!"

James could breathe again. "Well, what, then?"

"I'll tell you when you get here and not one minute before. And don't even think about begging. That's *so* unbecoming. Beneath you, really."

Did I just get played? he thought to himself after he hung up the phone. If he had, he didn't care. He smiled. It would be good to spend some quality time with the woman he loved.

Throughout James's training, Elliana's schedule had been only slightly less taxing than his. As she had at Tavern on the Green, she advanced rapidly to the role of shift leader at Windows on the World and her career as a performer was starting to take off too. She'd been noticed by the Broadway talent scouts and was routinely being invited to *non*-cattle-call auditions for major productions, even being cast in the ensemble on several.

The need to be available for rehearsals and evening shows dictated that Elliana transition from the dinner to the breakfast shift at Windows. Since she'd always been a dedicated employee, never missing a shift, her manager was more than understanding and happy to accommodate her request. Adding someone of her caliber to the breakfast crew would be a boon for the restaurant. So, when Elliana requested to be transferred, he bade her, "Break a leg," and happily authorized her change of shift, effective the first of September.

Elliana took the first week of September off from work to spend it with James, reconnecting and working on wedding plans. The couple's week together in New York was all either one of them might have hoped for. The weather was mild, and even the rain on the first and fourth of September didn't dampen their joy for being together.

During their days, the happy couple sampled catering for the rehearsal dinner and reception. They selected flowers, generated guest lists, and worked at composing their wedding vows. They picked music. They dreamed. They talked. They laughed. They dined. And at night, they loved.

Midweek, they made time to pop over to New Haven to see Elliana's parents and visit with her baba—who, once again, chided Elliana for allowing her man to be so thin.

While in New Haven, Elliana took James for a tour of their wedding venue, allowing him to see it for the first time. The cathedral she'd chosen was beautiful. Inside, James stood at the altar, imagining Elliana, on her father's arm, floating down the aisle toward him, holding a bouquet of pink sweet peas as the string quartet played Pachelbel's *Canon in D Major*. From his perspective, December 15th couldn't arrive quickly enough!

Before leaving for New Haven, and almost constantly during their stay, Elliana badgered James, trying to entice him to share with her the location he had planned for their honeymoon. Though her powers of persuasion were impressive and her attempts relentless, James kept the secret to himself. All he deigned to tell her was that she should pack for warm weather and she'd need her passport.

With James being so stubborn about their honeymoon plans, Elliana resolved to withhold her big news from him. She'd share when he did—quid pro quo. When even this inducement failed, and with their vacation week nearing an end, Elliana finally gave in and spilled the beans.

On Saturday evening, after dining in their favorite restaurant, Elliana led James on a walk down Broadway. As they strolled along, he noticed that she was even more ebullient than usual. By the time they arrived before the Winter Garden Theatre, she was practically bouncing with excitement.

There, she paused.

"There's a new musical scheduled to open in this theater in October," Elliana explained. "It's called *Mamma Mia!*, and it's based on music by ABBA."

James laughed incredulously. "ABBA? The seventies pop group from Sweden? You gotta be joking!"

"No, really," she said. "It's going to be great..."

"Yeah, but *ABBA*?"

Elliana scowled at James briefly, rolled her eyes, and continued. "Yes, and I, for one, think it's going to be wonderful! There's going to be a preview of the show on October fifth before it opens officially on the eighteenth."

"So, shall I try to score us a pair of tickets whenever they go on sale?"

"No need. I already have them."

James cocked his head. "How'd you manage that if they've not even gone on sale yet?"

"I'm in the show."

"Still, the tickets shouldn't be...wait...what? You're in the show?!"

Elliana gave a squeal and began hopping and skipping about on the sidewalk. "I've wanted to tell you all week."

"Babe, that's wonderful!"

"And that's not all," she continued, totally unable to check her excitement. "I'm cast in the ensemble, but I'm *also* cast as first understudy for the role of Sophie Sheridan...the second female lead!"

To be selected as understudy for a lead role in a major Broadway production represented a huge leap forward for Elliana's career.

"Yes!" James cried, joining Elliana in her dance on the sidewalk. After a few minutes, he drew Elliana into an embrace, kissed the side of her face, and whispered into her ear, "I knew you could do it. I knew it! I'm so proud of you, babe. Congratulations!"

As they walked home, Elliana chattered nonstop about the show, rehearsals, and her castmates. That night, they made love passionately before falling asleep tangled in loving arms.

James's love-filled sojourn in Manhattan ended all too soon. Both he and Elliana were due back at work bright and early Monday morning, James at Washington University Hospital and Elliana at Windows on the World. They woke early on Sunday morning, showered together, and Elliana accompanied James to Newark International Airport for his flight back to St. Louis.

It appeared James was getting out of New York just in time. Hurricane Erin was out in the Atlantic, churning toward New England. Simultaneously, a cold front was pushing down from Canada toward the city. The weather for September 10th had the potential to be nasty, and flight delays were almost guaranteed.

James and Elliana enjoyed a prolonged embrace in the departure lounge.

Overhead, a speaker crackled, "This is the final boarding call for United Flight 93 to San Francisco. Now boarding all seats and all rows. All ticketed passengers should now be boarded. Repeat, this is the final boarding call for United..."

United Flight 93 was the flight James used to take for his return trips to California while he was still at Stanford. *I'm glad I'm not taking that flight anymore!* he thought before boarding his flight to St. Louis. "Love you, babe!"

"I love you too."

Elliana gave James a lingering kiss, then longingly watched as he disappeared up the jetway.

During his flight back to St. Louis, James reminisced over the week he'd spent in New York with Elliana. It had been everything he might have hoped it could be. And it had given him a clear picture of what life would be like with her after their wedding, and he *liked* what he saw. Of course, they'd lived together while he was finishing medical school and she was starting at NYU, but this was different. Before, one or the other of them was always busy with *something*. There was always some responsibility that precluded them from focusing attention entirely upon one another. For this visit, however, it had been just the two of them together, being themselves.

On his first morning back in New York, James had awakened somewhat startled to find the bed empty and Elliana gone. She wasn't in the bathroom, and there were no places to hide in the tiny little apartment. Wondering where she was off to so early, James had slipped on a pair of boxers and padded to the living room, settling onto the couch to await her return. There, before him on the coffee table, lay a three-ring binder. Curious and with nothing else to occupy his time, he'd picked up the binder and begun to read. Turning to the title page, he'd seen, *"Benny Andersson & Björn Ulvaeus' Mamma Mia!* A musical by Catherine Johnson."

James had smiled and skimmed the pages, noticing the lines for Sophie Sheridan were highlighted in yellow. Realization dawned upon him. From the sheer number of marked lines, it was clear that Sophie's role in the play was significant, maybe even a lead. He realized that this must be the big secret Elliana had wanted to share with him. She'd been cast as lead, or more likely, understudy, for the lead in a new Broadway play. This was going to be a huge move forward for her career, and he'd beamed with pride.

Just then, James had heard a key rattling in the apartment's front door lock. For an instant, he thought to meet Elliana at the door and congratulate her for her upcoming role but reconsidered. *Let her have her surprise*, he'd thought before replacing the script binder on the coffee table and sprinting back to the bedroom. He'd just ditched his boxers and slipped back beneath the covers when she came in with coffee and bagels from the little shop around the corner.

"Wake up, sleepy-head! We've got a big day ahead of us," Elliana had practically sung as she entered the bedroom.

James had pulled her onto the bed and a moment later, they were making love. Afterward, while she was in the shower, he returned to the living room. The binder was no longer on the coffee table. In fact, it was nowhere to be seen.

James had nodded his head. "So *that's* the way she wants to play this. So be it," he'd said to himself before joining his fiancée in the shower.

The entire week had gone that way. They'd had a wonderful visit with Elliana's parents and her baba. James had hoped to make a day trip to Boston so Elliana could meet "the ring whisperer," but time did not allow. It was no big deal. There'd be plenty of opportunities for them to go in the future.

All good things must come to an end, even perfect vacation weeks with the ones we love. Thus, James returned to St. Louis on Sunday and to work Monday morning. He was not the Trauma ICU attending that month, and it would be the next weekend before he'd be back on primary Trauma call. Until then, he'd take such general surgical cases as came his way. It looked like it was going to be a fairly easy, low-stress week.

CHAPTER 20

SEPTEMBER 2001

T HE DAY DAWNED BRIGHT AND clear. Yesterday's cold front had pushed through New York and was now out in the Atlantic, nudging Hurricane Erin farther out to sea. All signs of the previous day's thunderstorms were gone. It was going to be a beautiful day.

Elliana hiked briskly uptown from her subway stop. It was a good morning for walking, just sixty-nine degrees with none of the previous day's humidity. She arrived at her building at 5:45 and took the elevator to the 106th floor. As she waited to clock in, she chatted with coworkers and gazed briefly out the window to the Empire State Building some four miles away. She smiled, remembering James's proposal there and contemplating their future together. If she'd had any doubts—of course, she didn't, but if she had—the last week with him would've totally dispelled them. James was wonderful, and she only wished he was more receptive to the idea of having children. She wanted *desperately* to hold a tiny little life they'd made together to her breast. Becca, of course, had assured her that he would eventually come around, and she was probably right. But still...

James had thought himself so clever to withhold information about his honeymoon plans, and Elliana had been
quite happy to play along with the charade. She'd found a
pair of first-class airline tickets, a travel guide, and a half-
dozen brochures about Tortola in the British Virgin Islands
in his sock drawer during her last visit to St. Louis. She
hadn't been snooping. She'd just stumbled across them
while putting away his laundry. Of course, none of the laundry had been socks, but that was beside the point. After all,
a woman needed to know these things and it was all for *his*
benefit. After that visit, she'd purchased a bikini that was
going to *absolutely* rock his world.

Elliana clocked in promptly at six. This was only her
second day working the breakfast shift at Windows on the
World, but she was pretty certain she was going to like it.
The breakfast service was less frantic than the dinner service. The sounds were the same—the murmur of patrons
chatting at their tables, pots and pans clanking, knives
chopping, silverware scraping, dishwashers steaming—but
the air seemed more relaxed.

Elliana paused briefly between orders to take in the sun-
rise as it crested the horizon to the east. The view through
the picture windows was spectacular. "James would love
this," she said to herself, already planning to bring him to
the restaurant during his next visit to the city.

Her shift progressed smoothly with a fairly quiet section
to attend. She'd not been assigned to the large Risk-Waters
conference group, but she had no objection. Tips were better
not working a conference, and having fewer diners allowed
her time to mull through matters not related to work. With
Mamma Mia! opening in just over a month and her wedding looming in December, she had more than enough to
occupy her mind.

She collected a tray of food and a fresh carafe of orange juice from the pass for a group of businessmen at a table near the window. As she left the pass through the narrow kitchen hall, she heard a loud, high-pitch shriek coming from outside the building. The sound rapidly increased in volume to a deafening roar, and at 8:46, it was punctuated by an ear-splitting explosion. Accompanying the explosion, the entire building whipsawed violently back and forth. Elliana was driven forcefully into one hallway wall, only to be thrown against the other a moment later. Her head struck the wall hard, and the tray of food she'd been carrying crashed to the floor, shattering the carafe of juice and sending French toast and bacon flying.

Elliana woke a few moments later on the floor. The air was heavy with oily, black smoke and the odor of kerosene. She carefully tested her arms and legs. Nothing seemed broken, though her head ached and a gash on her temple was bleeding freely. She cast about for something to stanch the bleeding and found one of the napkins from the tray she'd been carrying. She pressed it tightly against the wound and struggled unsteadily back to her feet. Immediately, her head began to throb and the room spun, forcing her to sit back down on the floor.

"What happened?" she asked no one in particular, unable to hear her own voice after the blast. She sucked in a lungful of smoke and coughed spasmodically. "Fire?"

Her thoughts seemed sluggish, like they were coming to her through an ocean of molasses. Out of the corner of her eye, she glimpsed a patron standing motionless between tables eleven and nineteen in what had once been her section of the restaurant. He was wearing what appeared to be green army jungle fatigues, and though the tower still swayed like a thirteen-hundred-foot metronome, he stood tall and erect, totally unaffected. Oddly, she'd not noticed him in her section before the explosion, and dressed as he was, it seemed unlikely to her that she would've missed him. Seemingly oblivious to the chaos around him, the soldier appeared perfectly calm—almost tranquil—and was gazing right at her.

Elliana briefly glanced away, and when she looked back, the soldier was gone. In what was left of the dining room, patrons and staff members lay on the floor moaning. Others stumbled like zombies around the room. All appeared dazed and were coughing. After a moment, the emergency lighting came on, but with the smoky air, it did little to illuminate her surroundings.

Realizing she had to get out of there, Elliana found the elevators out of order and then turned toward the stairway. As she groped back through the murk from the elevator, she almost tripped over an elderly lady lying on the floor in a pool of blood. Like Elliana, she was bleeding from a scalp laceration but also appeared to have a broken arm. Elliana knelt beside her, tore a strip from a tablecloth, and bound it about the woman's head. Then she tore another strip and splinted the arm against the woman's chest. It wasn't perfect, but it would have to do until the paramedics arrived. The woman mouthed what Elliana assumed was a thank you, but over the roaring in her ears, she couldn't make out the words.

At least now she heard ringing instead of dead silence. That had to be an improvement. Elliana smiled inwardly, thinking how proud James would be of her newly realized diagnostic and first-aid skills. Upon thinking of him, she felt an overwhelming need to hear his voice. He'd be so worried, and she had to let him know she was okay.

Elliana forgot about the stairs and made her way through the flotsam and jetsam that had once been the world's highest grossing restaurant, feeling her way along the wall to the employee locker room. Whenever she found someone injured along the way, she rendered such first aid as she could before resuming her trek. By the time she reached the employee lockers, she was having to walk bent over—almost to her waist—just to breathe, but at least she didn't see any fire.

When she arrived at the locker room, she found the bank of lockers had fallen on its side. Her locker's metal door was dented and badly warped. After several minutes of banging and prying, she managed to wrench it open. Thankfully, she found her cell phone inside to be unbroken and with an almost fully charged battery.

After another paroxysm of coughing, she powered up the phone, found James's number, and hit SEND.

Across the screen, she read, "CALL FAILED."

For an instant, Elliana saw not one but two cell phones in her hand. She blinked hard, and after a moment, her vision returned to normal. The bleeding from her scalp wound had stopped and the ringing in her ears had toned down to a dull roar, but her head was still pounding and seemed to be getting worse. She was pretty certain that when she eventually got in touch with James, he'd tell her she'd suffered a concussion. In desperate need for relief, she removed her purse from the locker and riffled through its contents. Jackpot! She found two Midol tablets rolling loose among the detritus and immediately dry-swallowed both. Not a perfect remedy but better than nothing.

She attempted her call again.

"CALL FAILED."

Again, and again, she tried to place the call but each time received the same error message.

Scared and frustrated, Elliana slumped to the floor and began to cry. She leaned back and rested her pounding head against the wall. No sooner than she'd gotten settled, she heard another screech followed by a second nearby explosion. It was loud but didn't seem as close as the earlier one had been. Still, the blast buffeted the building and slammed the back of Elliana's aching head against the wall behind her, knocking the phone from her hand.

Dazed, she retrieved the phone from the floor and glanced at the display. It was 9:03. Then, miraculously, the cell phone in her hand began to ring.

On the morning of Tuesday, September 11th, James arrived at the hospital at promptly six o'clock to make rounds. Since he'd been off the preceding week, there were only a few patients he needed to see that morning and so he was finished with rounds by seven-thirty. With time to kill before his morning clinic, he ducked into the doctor's lounge for breakfast.

He selected a bottle of orange juice and a strawberry Nutri-Grain bar—probably not the healthiest of choices, but an improvement over the eggs, bacon, and toast most of his colleagues were enjoying that morning. Then he eased into one of the overstuffed recliners and settled back to watch CNN on the big screen and learn about the news of the day.

He was still there at 7:50 when across the ticker on the bottom of the screen, he read, "Small aircraft strikes World Trade Center."

James remembered a story he'd once read about a B-26 bomber that had crashed into the Empire State Building in the fog back during World War II. Fourteen people had been killed. He was regaling his colleagues with this recollection when the picture on the screen changed to a view of Manhattan and the Twin Towers.

Instantly, James was struck by three observations. First, there was not a cloud in the sky. Second, the diagonal slash belching smoke and fire across the face of the tower was far too large to have been created by a "small plane." Third, and most chilling, it was the North Tower of the World Trade Center that had been hit. He recognized it since it had the television antenna on top instead of a helipad. That was Elliana's building!

Struck by a wave of nausea, he immediately halted his commentary about the Empire State Building crash, grabbed the TV remote, and increased the volume on the lounge's television. Offscreen, the news reporter was saying, "...received reports that at just after 8:46 Eastern Time, a small plane crashed into the World Trade Center's North Tower and has started a fire on the upper floors. We have received no reports of casualties but have been informed that fire and emergency response vehicles are en route."

Elliana! She's been working the breakfast shift at Windows. Was she supposed to work today?

James snatched the cell phone from his jacket pocket and thumbed in her number.

The screen read, "CALL FAILED."

"Shit!" He tried again, with no better luck than the first time.

Thumbing to redial the call repeatedly, he thought, *Is she at work?* He was staring at the live feed of smoke pouring from the rent in the North Tower when a bloom of fire, smoke, and debris suddenly appeared on the face of the South Tower.

On the television, the reporter shouted into his microphone, "A second...oh my God, a second aircraft appears to have struck the South Tower..."

James thumbed in Elliana's number again and hit SEND. Miraculously, her phone began to ring and then was quickly answered.

"Jabes, is that you?" came Elliana's voice.

A wave of relief swept over him. "Oh, Elle, thank God! I was afraid you'd gone to work this morning."

"I ab at work..."

The connection was terrible. Words kept dropping, every *M* came out sounding like a *B* through her stuffy nose, and it sounded as though Elliana had been crying.

"...there was...xplosion. What happened?"

A chill ran through to James's marrow. The relief he'd felt at hearing Elliana's voice only an instant before now seemed a cruel and distant memory. "Elliana, babe, are you okay?"

"I hit...head. The bleeding's stopped...bad headache."

James flipped the switch into doctor mode. "Nothing broken? How's your vision? How about your balance?"

"No breaks. Sometimes I...double. It's hard to...lots of debris...building keeps shak..."

From what James was hearing, Elliana at a minimum suffered from a concussion and might be developing a subdural hematoma. He prayed not, but for now, there were more pressing matters.

"Elle, someone crashed a plane into your building several floors below you."

"An airplane? How could that happen?" she asked. It was such a relief to hear James's voice, even through the crappy cell connection.

"Not important right now, but it wasn't an accident. Both towers have been struck."

Elliana said something unintelligible.

"Elliana, listen to me very carefully. We've *got* to get you out of there. Can you walk?"

She tried to stand but was immediately hit by a wave of dizziness and nausea. "I think so. Just very dizzy when I stand up, and there's heavy smoke everywhere. The elevators are out."

"Can you make it to the stairs?"

"I think so. The smoke's really heavy and it's hard to breathe, but I should be able to get there."

"Use your phone like a flashlight."

There are worse things, she thought, *than being engaged to a genius.* She smiled and activated her phone's screen, though it did little to cut through the murkiness. Still, it was better than nothing.

Elliana held the cell phone before her as she picked her way back to the main dining room. There, the chaos was unabated. The smoke was even heavier now, billowing from the elevator shaft and stairwell like a pair of chimneys. Elliana thanked God there were no flames—at least, not yet. Some men were using a table like a battering ram, attempting to break out windows. *An excellent idea,* she thought. It was already uncomfortably hot in the room and the air was almost unbreathable and getting worse with each passing moment.

Out of desperation, she stumbled to the stairwell and wrenched open the door. Immediately, she was hit by a blast of super-heated air and smoke and was nearly overcome. Still, she managed to reach the stairwell landing. Almost immediately, the rubber soles of her shoes began to melt against the hot metal. She carefully peered over the edge and nearly had her eyebrows singed off.

Below her, barely two flights down, the stairs ended abruptly and dangled broken over a raging inferno. Elliana snatched her head back and burst coughing through the stairwell door, back into the restaurant's main lobby. There, after her breathing had recovered sufficiently, she returned to the stairwell and sprinted the four flights to the roof. Finding the door padlocked—dammit, she'd forgotten that tidbit of information from her new-hire orientation—she returned to the restaurant and reported her findings to James.

This was not good. With the stairs out and the elevators nonfunctional, James knew there was no way firefighters or rescue personnel would be able to reach the 106th floor. Elliana and the rest of those people were trapped. Additionally, the fire suppression system, with its pipes running through the stairwell would also be broken, though even undamaged, the system wasn't designed to deal with a fire fueled by ten thousand gallons of jet fuel. The fire was going to have to burn itself out on its own. It *had* to burn itself out. The alternative was too terrible to fathom.

Data from his college physics days flowed through his mind in an unwelcome stream. Jet fuel, depending upon conditions, burns at between 800 and 1,517 degrees Fahrenheit. Structural steel melts well above those temperatures, about 2,777 degrees Fahrenheit, so the tower's beams were not at risk of melting. However, he also knew from the engineers with whom he'd shared classes at MIT that the heat *would* be sufficient to cause the steel to expand and thereby weaken its structural integrity. The structural steel used in the construction of the towers, in its unattenuated condition, was more than capable of bearing the balanced load of the weight of the entire structure above it. Both of the towers had already endured the physical loss of structural support caused by the kinetics of the crashing jets. James wondered if the steel would still remain sound if weakened by heat-induced expansion. If not, one floor would collapse to the floor below it, carrying with it the entire weight of the floors above. The sudden increase in load would overstress the steel supports below and cause that floor to collapse as well. The same process would be repeated with increasing rapidity with the next and the next floors in sequence until the entire structure had pancaked to the ground.

In James's analytical mind, the South Tower would serve as the canary in the coal mine. Although it had been struck after the North Tower, the strike had been much lower on the building. Thus, the steel there had more weight above it to support. If the South Tower survived, no doubt, Elliana's North Tower would as well. If not, both towers and everyone inside them were doomed.

Elliana coughed, hacked, and gasped for breath. While she'd been at the stairwell, several of the dining room's windows had been successfully smashed, and people were waving white tablecloths out of them, attempting to get the attention of the rescuers below. She made for one of the windows and enjoyed a few lungsful of the fresher air.

Through her phone, James asked, "Can you...the stairs to the roof? Maybe...helicopter—"

A burst of static drowned the rest of his words. Their cellular connection was getting worse, and it was nothing short of miraculous that the connection had held up even this long.

Elliana shouted back into her phone, "Can't get to the roof. They keep the doors locked."

At 9:59, the floor beneath Elliana's feet began to shudder and a low-pitched rumble was audible above the cacophony of noise already around her.

"James, what was that?"

In the doctor's lounge in St. Louis, James watched in horror as the canary died. "The South Tower...it just collapsed," he answered mechanically. Knowing it could happen did nothing to lessen the shock of seeing it on live TV, especially since he understood the ramifications. "Elliana, listen to me *very* carefully. I know the doors to the roof are locked, but you've *got* to try. The roof's your best possible chance. Go to the kitchen. Find something you can use as a pry bar to force the doors. Get up to the roof!"

"James, you're scaring me."

"Elle, just go! *Now!* There's no time to waste."

Hearing the urgency in James's voice, Elliana made her way through the kitchen where she found a fire axe. She returned to the stairwell door but burned her hand when she grasped the metal latch. When she swung the door open, she was met by a gout of flame and tripped over her own feet as she retreated from the door. On the floor, she crab-walked backward, chased by a wall of flame.

The heat was intense. Observing her clothing beginning to smoke, she regained her feet and sprinted back to the dining room. There, to her horror, she saw a man in an expensive suit helping a lady, possibly his wife, onto the sill of one of the broken windows. A moment later, he scrambled up beside her and, hand in hand, they stepped out into the abyss and disappeared over the edge.

Elliana screamed. Whirlpools of smoke, ash, and flames billowed about her. She gasped for air and coughed violently. "James! The floor, it's starting to buckle. Oh my God, they're jumping. Can't breathe. So scared..."

From out of nowhere, the soldier Elliana had noticed earlier suddenly materialized before her. He appeared totally calm and unaffected amid the chaos around him. She glanced at his face and mused briefly about how much the soldier looked like James. The soldier said nothing as he folded Elliana into an embrace. An instant later, everything was gone.

Back in St. Louis, James shouted into the phone. "Elliana, I—"

On the television screen, the North Tower crumbled to the ground in a cloud of concrete dust, smoke, and debris.

"—love you!" The final word came out as little more than a squeak before James dropped the phone.

On the floor, the display read, "CALL FAILED."

CHAPTER 21

SEPTEMBER–OCTOBER 2001

FOR THE REMAINDER OF SEPTEMBER, James had no recollection. For an individual whose mind is physically incapable of forgetting, that represented quite a departure. And it was also, technically, inaccurate. A more accurate statement would've been that James had no recollection of *new* events occurring in his life over that period of time.

In truth, he remembered it all—the sound of Elliana's choked scream, the sight of the North Tower pancaking to the ground, the smoke, the dust and debris, the taste of refluxing orange juice from his breakfast that morning, the smell of Dr. Smith's Old Spice aftershave wafting from the chair beside him in the doctor's lounge, the condensation dripping from the ceiling air-conditioning vent, the cockroach that skittered across the floor beneath the big-screen TV as the towers fell. James remembered it all, and in such vivid detail, nothing else around him existed. It was as though he was in the world's most advanced multisensory 4-D simulator, trapped in a continuous replay loop.

Most of the time, the playback loop was limited to the eighty-five minutes between 9:03 and 10:28 a.m. Eastern

Time on September 11, 2001, corresponding to his last, frantic conversation with Elliana. Other times, the loop began August 30th, when he arrived in New York for his final visit or back in college preparing for *Pygmalion* and falling in love with Elliana. Still other times, the loop began with his grandmother stabbing him when he was ten years old. Regardless of where or when the loop began, the loop always ended at precisely 10:28 a.m. when the World Trade Center's North Tower, and with it, all of his hopes and dreams, crumbled into dust.

Throughout the month of September, friends, colleagues, and hospital staff would've accurately described James as catatonic. He displayed minimal response to even the most painful stimuli. Day or night, it didn't matter, he stared unseeing with an unblinking gaze. Nurses came into his room twice each hour to apply eyedrops to forestall the development of corneal ulcers. He was totally unmoving, requiring staff to turn and reposition him several times each day to prevent bedsores and administer shots in his stomach to decrease the risk of blood clots. Physical therapy came by each day to keep his muscles and joints from locking up. He was unable to assist with feeding or toileting. He had a tube from his nose to his stomach for the former, and a catheter and kind nurses for the latter.

Becca arrived in St. Louis late on the thirteenth. She would've been there sooner, but all air travel had been grounded. By the time someone thought to contact her on the twelfth about James's condition—Elliana had been listed as his emergency contact—it was too late for her to start the nearly seven-hundred-mile drive. Sitting at his bedside, she couldn't help but remember her last cross-country odyssey, that time to see Jimmy at Walter Reed. James looked so much like her Jimmy, it hurt, and especially seeing him like this.

The doctors caring for James were baffled. His blood diagnostics revealed no abnormalities, and his drug and toxicology screens returned negative. Both his CAT scan and MRI revealed no structural anomalies in his brain, and his electroencephalogram demonstrated no abnormal brain wave activity. It was as though he'd just shut down, and no one was certain how to proceed toward making it better. Nothing helped. He showed no response to benzodiazepines, antidepressants, or stimulants. There was talk of performing ECT, electroconvulsive therapy, if no improvement was observed over the next few weeks.

It was a shock to everyone, therefore, when out of the blue on October 5th, James turned to Becca, who'd been standing vigil at his bedside and, in a raspy voice said, "The preview shows for Elliana's play are supposed to start today. I hope it will open as planned."

Becca, lost in Mitch Albom's *Tuesdays with Morrie*, nearly fell out of her chair at the sound of his voice.

CHAPTER 22

OCTOBER 14, 2001

P
AULIE SCHACCATANO WAS A MASTER welder by trade and a proud member of Local 580, the Iron Workers Union, with jurisdiction over Staten Island. His wife, Edith, made him breakfast, packed his lunchbox, and gave him a kiss on the cheek as she did every morning before he left for work. Then, Carl took the ferry to Manhattan and made the twenty-minute walk from the Whitehall Terminal to Ground Zero for another sixteen-hour day working on the Pile.

The Pile was the name workers gave to the five-story mass of twisted steel, concrete, glass, and dreams that had once been the North and South Towers of the World Trade Center. The Pile held 200,000 metric tons of steel and 325,000 cubic meters—780,000 metric tons—of concrete. Another 400,000 cubic meters accounted for windows, elevators, and internal fixtures. Additionally, there was an untold volume of internal walls, desks, chairs, office plants, and family photos, and whatever mass remained of two 767 aircraft. A final grisly statistic, if one assumes an average of seventy kilograms for each victim who died in the towers that day, buried within the Pile was another 175,000 kilograms of human remains. All told, the Pile held over 1.8 million tons of wreckage.

By October 14th, with no survivors having been found for over a month, the efforts at Ground Zero had shifted from rescue to recovery and removal. Beneath the Pile, fires continued to rage, and the air above it remained a miasma of dust, smoke, and decay. The bucket brigades from the early days post collapse were gone, replaced by "yellow iron"—grapplers, cranes, and excavators. Workers and cadaver dogs continued to crawl through the debris in search of human remains.

Schaccatano's responsibilities at the Pile included cutting through the iron and steel debris and attaching it to recovery cables. It was dangerous work. The Pile, although significantly more stable than it had been a month ago, was still a treacherous worksite. The steel was jagged, sharp, and often quite hot from fires still burning below. The air was hard to breathe, and even though he wore his respirator religiously, his asthma dictated that he stop for frequent puffs on his rescue inhaler...and maybe a cigarette or two.

Over the weeks he'd been working the Pile, Schaccatano, thank God, hadn't located any human remains. He'd uncovered a number of shoes—thankfully all empty but *never* in pairs—but nothing more substantial. Still, even finding those had been sobering. He'd just freed a particularly large section of steel I-beam and was contemplating another smoke break when he happened to peer down into the void created after the beam had been lifted away.

A shaft of sunlight flooded into the chasm and at its base, he caught a glint of light. It was just a flash, but it piqued his curiosity. Schaccatano called for the basket in which he was dangling to be lowered so he could better investigate his find. After being lowered no more than a meter, he cried out, "Stop!" and flailed his arms wildly, trying to attract his supervisor's attention.

Below him, teetering on the edge of another beam, was what appeared to be a horribly burned, severed human forearm. On the claw that might once have been a hand shone the source of the glint that had caught Schaccatano's attention—a battered diamond ring.

CHAPTER 23

OCTOBER–NOVEMBER 2001

J AMES WAS ABLE TO DRAW himself from his catatonia through monumental strength of will. Technically, he'd never lost *complete* contact with reality. It had always been there. Every attempt he made to describe what he'd been experiencing to his doctors came up woefully short, but the description that came closest to his reality played something like this:

Since the collapse of the Twin Towers and Elliana's death, James's mind experienced the world as though a picture on a big-screen television, one possessing the capability of "picture-in-picture" viewing. While he was deepest in his catatonic state, he experienced the constant replay loop of his life up until Elliana's death on one screen—the larger one—while present-day reality played on a much smaller one in the corner of his consciousness. On October 5th, his mind finally figured out how to change the channels. The looping simulation continued to play in his mind, but now he'd managed to relegate *it* to the smaller screen while present-day reality played on the larger.

James's doctors were amazed. They'd never heard of anything even remotely like this. Residents, fellows, and attending physicians queued outside his door just to hear his story, many hoping to use it for future publication in Psychiatric literature.

The one person who *didn't* seem shocked by James's story or recovery was Becca. Dr. Malone from the Institute for Memory Studies had warned her of just such a possibility—patients getting lost in the past after traumas—when he was describing the potential negative ramifications of James's extraordinary memory and inability to forget to her over twenty years before. What likely would've amazed the good doctor, however, was James's ability to find his way back to the present. She was pretty certain that a lesser mind than James's would never have been able to follow the trail of breadcrumbs back to reality.

With no structural pathology, James's physical recovery was rapid, although his body was terribly deconditioned after a month of total inactivity. With physical therapy, he was soon up and walking. It would be some time before his muscle tone returned to that present before 9/11, but there was little doubt it would return. His mental health was another matter. The perfect memory, which previously had been James's superpower, in an instant, had become his kryptonite. Although he was generally able to sequester the replay simulation to the smaller screen of his consciousness day or night, it *always* played in the background and with no commercial breaks. Consequently, he suffered post-traumatic stress disorder on steroids.

Once again, through sheer strength of will, James was able to function well enough around the hospital. He found that whenever his mind was fully engaged, for example, by a complex, high-risk surgical procedure, the replay loop shrank in size. No matter what he did, it never went away. The replay loop was a constant stressor—a festering thorn in his paw—impossible to be relieved. His interactions with staff, especially in the operating theater, had never been particularly cordial. Now, with the constant replay of watching his fiancée die before him, he became prickly to the extreme. It was rare that he ended a procedure with the same anesthesiologist, scrub nurse, circulator, or surgical resident as had been there for the start. He was brilliant—no one would argue against that—but he was impossible to work with. Staff actually began calling out sick if they found out far enough in advance that they were scheduled to be in his operating room. It was not uncommon to find James in the Human Resources director's office defending his actions. HR was unable to touch him, however, for *technically*, his objections were all sound and he never used inappropriate or offensive language before or during the expulsion of offenders from his cases.

Not wanting to be an intrinsically cruel individual like Mack Lee had been and realizing the stress from the constant replay of the worst day of his life was taking its toll upon him, James decided to self-medicate. He tried alcohol, sedatives, and even marijuana, but they only made matters worse. As the higher-functioning portions of his brain slowed down, it became increasingly difficult to constrain the traumatic replay to the smaller screen. Attempts at the opposite approach, with stimulants such as Adderall, were dangerously ineffective. With them, even while relegated to the small screen, the events became so painfully intense as to become unbearable, threatening to return him to his catatonic state. Tricyclic antidepressants, tetracyclic antidepressants, MAOI inhibitors, and selective serotonin reuptake inhibitors had no positive effects at all. No matter what he tried, the pressurized boiling magma of anger and loss was always there, just beneath the thinnest of crusts, ready to erupt after the slightest provocation.

Still, anyone with an understanding of James's exceptional memory would've thought he was performing remarkably well. That he was able to function at all, much less on a highly professional level, in the real world after such a trauma was little short of miraculous. An event in late October nearly wiped away all of his progress, however.

After completing a grueling six hours of surgery on a patient who'd been run over by a dump truck, James returned to the locker room for a shower and to catch up on messages. The fourth voicemail on his phone was from an unknown number with a New York area code. Since it was clearly nonclinical, he responded to the messages ahead of it and took his shower as planned.

Afterward, he retired to the hospital's medical library—James hadn't stepped foot in the doctor's lounge since 9/11—and returned the call.

After three rings, the phone was answered. "Staten Island Medical Examiner's Office, Klugman speaking."

"This is Dr. James Hamilton. I received a message from this number."

"Dr. Hamilton, thank you for returning my call." Klugman's accent pegged him as a lifelong Staten Islander so that "call" came out as "cuawl." "The reason we called is..."

James braced himself for news he knew was coming but didn't want to hear.

"...while excavating and clearing Ground Zero..."

The picture-in-picture in his mind began to flicker.

"...the remains of a terribly burned..."

On TV, the North Tower pancaked to the ground in a rush of smoke, dust, and debris.

"...human forearm and hand were recovered."

James was momentarily overcome by the smell of Dr. Smith's Old Spice aftershave. The guy practically bathed in the stuff. Above him, the air-conditioning vent dripped. He felt heartburn from the orange juice he'd had with breakfast earlier. OJ always exacerbated his reflux. A cockroach skittered across the floor beneath the screen.

"On the hand, we recovered a ring. Examination of the ring revealed..."

A new image flashed into James's memory. It was of a ring sliding onto the fourth finger of Elliana's left hand as they stood atop the Empire State Building. In an instant, this image was replaced by another, a series of letters and numbers he first saw through a jeweler's loupe in the ring whisperer's store. The next image was of a table from his old Physical Chemistry textbook, the melting point for platinum appearing highlighted, 1,768° C/3,215°F. This image was immediately replaced by another table in another textbook, this one displaying the burning temperature for jet fuel, 825°C/1,517°F. Still another table showed the usual temperature within a crematory oven, 982°C/1,800°F. Images flickered and whirred before his vision with dizzying rapidity.

"GIA 5515221467," James murmured into the phone.

"That's right," Klugman's astonished voice replied. "You must have a pretty good memory to remember that. Anyways, we found the number and tracked it back to you. Can you identify the person who..."

James's picture-in-picture wavered unsteadily before current reality once again played on the larger screen. "The ring belongs—" His voice cracked as a single tear ran down his cheek. He squeezed his eyes closed, swallowed hard, and continued, "...belonged to my fiancée, Elliana Karolovna Petrenko.

The remainder of the conversation was lost in a kaleido-scope of mental images for James. When he returned again to the present, he still held the cell phone in his hand, but there was no one on the other end of the line. Had he spoken with Klugman five minutes ago? Or was it five hours?

After he'd recovered sufficiently, James called Elliana's parents to pass along the news that her remains had been located. The Petrenko's had always been kind and welcoming to him, and he didn't want them to hear this news from a stranger. Besides, if he was the one conveying, he could temper the awful facts to make them, if not more bearable, at least less ghastly. There was no reason they had to know that all that remained of their daughter, the little girl they'd loved and nurtured into adulthood, was a horribly burned forearm and hand. If he could save them from this final gruesome memory of Elliana, then he had to try. They'd suffered enough already.

The call went much as might've been expected. On James's end of the line, reality flashed between the large and small screens of his mind's internal display. On the Petrenkos', tears ran freely as James, in as gentle a manner as possible, dashed even their most irrational of hopes. Denial, it seemed, would no longer be a refuge from grief for the Petrenkos...or for James. With denial no longer an option, theoretically, they could move on to and through the other stages of grief—anger, bargaining, depression, and acceptance. While the Petrenkos moved forward, James never made it past anger.

There was, however, one unexpected outcome from James's call. The Petrenkos—technically, Baba—somehow managed to wrangle a pledge from him that he would accompany them to the memorial service for families of the victims of 9/11 in November in New York City.

As the date for the memorial service neared, James formalized his travel plans. He'd drive to New York from St. Louis. The trip would take him just under fourteen hours, but he had no desire to fly *anywhere* for the foreseeable future. While he'd been catatonic, Elliana's apartment had been cleared and leased to new tenants, so he reserved a room at the Westin Times Square. It was just as well because being alone in the apartment they'd shared for so long would've crushed him.

He arrived in New York on the afternoon before the memorial service and settled in, then called the Petrenkos at their hotel. After a brief conversation, they invited him to join them for dinner later that evening, and to James's surprise, he accepted the invitation. He'd not seen his in-laws since the visit to New Haven the first week of September, and frankly, he didn't know how he'd react. Would he be able to interact normally? Or, would the experience cause his psyche to shut down again? He supposed he'd have to find out eventually, so it might as well be that night.

The Petrenkos were already at the restaurant when James arrived. He was immediately struck by their appearance. When he'd originally met Angela, he'd been impressed by how well put together she'd seemed. Like Elliana, she'd had an elegant beauty and a dancer's body, one she'd assiduously maintained though decades removed from the stage. Now, however, there were dark circles beneath her eyes that makeup did little to hide. Her hair, formerly silky-shiny and perfectly coiffed, now appeared straw-like and limp. She'd never been large but now appeared physically wasted, almost cachectic. Frankly, she looked much like Rebecca had after she'd completed her sixth round of chemotherapy.

Karol, it seemed, had fared no better. The weight Angela lost, he'd added to his midsection. His nose was reddened as though by frequent blowing or the result of heavy drinking. James suspected a little of both. To say that Elliana's dad had bags beneath his eyes would not have done justice to the luggage he carried. His were steamer chests. The easy smile and litany of silly "dad jokes" James had enjoyed each time he'd been around the man, clearly hadn't been packed for this trip. Instead, he suspected they'd been sold for scrap.

The biggest shock, however, was the change in Oksana Petrenko. Gone was the spritely little elf who bounced about like Tigger on steroids with the look of devilment on her face and a perpetual twinkle in her eye. In her place was a haggard old woman with eyes totally devoid of their previous spark. She now was using a cane and shuffled about slowly with an unsteady, wide-based gait. Her lips and lower jaw quivered constantly as though fighting back a sob. Baba looked lost...and broken.

James was reasonably certain that he looked no better to them than they did to him. He supposed it was to be expected. Although the entire nation had experienced a loss, his and the Petrenkos' was more acute...more personal... more...*real*.

It was good to see the Petrenkos again, even under such terrible circumstances. Like him, they wanted to put meaning to Elliana's senseless death but were failing. That being impossible, they sought to celebrate her life. At dinner, they told funny stories about her childhood with much laughter, albeit muted, around the table. James joined in the laughter at appropriate times, but his was forced. It was hard to laugh about the person he loved when the video in his mind was actively displaying the instant of her death.

After dinner, he eschewed the taxi, instead choosing to walk back to his hotel. As he walked, he reflected on the evening. The Petrenkos were trying to heal and, over time, probably would. Their memories, and with it their pain, would fade with time. James envied them.

The memorial service was set to be held in lower Manhattan the next morning, beginning promptly at eight-thirty. The service would entail family members of the victims reading the names of those killed in the September 11th terrorist attacks. Six moments of silence were scheduled during the reading. The first would occur at precisely 8:46, the time corresponding to American Airlines Flight 11 striking the World Trade Center's North Tower. The second occurred at 9:03, corresponding to United Airlines Flight 175 striking the South Tower. The third, fourth, and fifth moments of silence were held at 9:37, 9:59, and 10:03 to coincide with American Flight 77 striking the Pentagon, the collapse of the South Tower, and United Flight 93's crash into a field in Shanksville, Pennsylvania. In between moments of silence, family members read the names of 2,983 men, women, and children killed in the terrorist attacks of 9/11 and the 1993 World Trade Center bombing.

The sixth and final moment of silence, scheduled for 10:28, the time corresponding to the collapse of the North Tower, by coincidence came immediately before Elliana's name was to be read. At dinner with the Petrenkos, James had agreed to read her name on behalf of the family, but when the time came, his picture-in-picture flipped and current reality was minimized while the tower's collapse played all around him in IMAX clarity. His tongue just would not form the words. His mouth opened and closed like a landed carp, but no sound escaped.

Oksana immediately came to James's rescue. She stepped up beside him at the microphone, grasped his arm, looked up into his eyes and smiled. Then, almost as though it was planned, in a steady, clear voice, she read, "Elliana Karolovna Petrenko." After a beat, Baba added, "Hamilton."

Later, James retained no recollections from the remaining portions of the memorial service, or from him taking his leave from the Petrenko family, although clearly, he'd done so. When he returned to the present, he simply found himself alone, back in his hotel room.

His reaction to the reading of the victims' names had left him mentally and emotionally exhausted, so he extended his stay for another night. He figured that tomorrow, after a good night's sleep, he'd be better prepared to make the fourteen-hour trip.

Perhaps it was the stress and riled-up emotions of being at the memorial service, or maybe it was because he was now alone in a city he and Elliana had loved together. Regardless the cause, James found it exceedingly difficult to keep the 9/11 replay relegated to his mind's small screen. Consequently, his afternoon and evening were neither restful nor relaxing. No matter what he did, the replay kept jumping back to the large screen. The level of concentration required to keep himself in the present was extraordinarily taxing, leaving him drained. He stretched out on his bed and, after a while, the fatigue overcame him and he fell into a troubled asleep.

When James awoke, it was almost midnight and his growling stomach reminded him that he'd not eaten anything since that morning. With the bagel he'd grabbed in the hotel lobby that morning now just a distant memory, he dialed room service. Unfortunately, the kitchen had already closed, but the helpful front-desk clerk suggested several excellent restaurants who provided late-night service. James was in no mood for a taxi ride though, so he settled on the hotel bar, thinking the food there should be more than adequate to tide him over until morning and, so long as nobody told his cardiologist about it, there should be no harm.

To James's surprise, the bar downstairs was packed. Apparently, he'd decided to have bar food on karaoke night at the Westin and the acts were in full swing. It took almost forty-five minutes just for him to get a seat at the bar. After attracting the bartender's attention, James ordered a burger, fries, and a Coca-Cola. Cholesterol be damned. After his meal came, he snacked on fries and listened to the performers on stage. Some of the acts were really pretty good. Others, not so much. In the latter category, James would've placed a group of highly intoxicated Asian businessmen who tried—and failed—to match Frankie Valli's falsetto while singing "Sherry." In the former category, was a cute, thirty-something brunette who belted out a near-perfect rendition of LeAnn Rimes's "How Do I Live."

The lyrics from *that* song hit far too close to home for James, especially that day. As the woman sang the tune, he wheeled about to the bartender, intending to ask for his check, but then thought better of it. Instead, he requested the bartender to add rum to his Coke. He drank it immediately and asked for another.

James was halfway through his second rum and Coke with 9/11 playing on the big screen in his mind when the small screen registered a presence to his immediate left. It was the woman who'd been singing "How Do I Live" only a moment before.

James woke the next morning with a pounding headache, totally naked and very much alone. He groaned and padded to the bathroom, seeking the aspirin in his shaving kit. Oddly, he had no recollection of returning to his hotel room the night before. The last thing he remembered was the brunette singer-lady sitting next to him at the bar. Then, he'd had the weirdest dream. In it, *he* was up on the karaoke stage singing Harry Nilsson's "Without You."

"What a messed-up dream. *I don't sing,*" he mumbled as he gulped down the aspirin. "Funny, I don't even remember coming back to the—"

James abruptly stopped talking as other vague recollections eddied about in his consciousness. Awareness swept over him, and he rushed to the trousers he'd apparently draped over the back of a chair last night. There, just as he'd suspected, his wallet was gone.

"I've been roofied!"

He reached for the phone, intending to call hotel security and file a police report, but froze mid-dial. Suddenly, he'd been struck by the realization that he *didn't* remember the night before. More importantly, this morning there was *no* picture-in-picture playing in his brain. The only reality that he was aware of today *was* today. The Rohypnol had closed the second screen in his consciousness.

James slowly returned the telephone receiver to its cradle. Instead of calling security, he began packing his clothes for the long drive back to St. Louis, all the while tunelessly whistling "Without You." After calling to cancel his credit cards, he checked out of his room and retrieved his car from the hotel garage to begin his trek back home. *Is St. Louis really home?* he wondered. If home is where the heart is, then his home was being trucked away to a landfill called Fresh Kills somewhere on Staten Island.

James took I-95 South out of the city and was still musing over where he should consider his home to be when, just north of Philadelphia, the picture-in-picture playback of his life resumed playing in his head. Disappointed, he supposed the Rohypnol had by then metabolized completely from his system. There was no legal means through which he might acquire another dose because the date-rape drug was banned in the US, and it wasn't like he could just hang out in bars in hopes of being roofied again.

As James traveled west on I-70, the weather deteriorated. Over the entire breadth of Ohio, there'd been a cold drizzle falling. By the time he crossed the Indiana line, the temperature had dropped and the sky was spitting snow, slowing his progress. A tractor trailer clipped a sedan and sent it spinning into a temporary retaining wall east of Indianapolis, slowing him still further. It was well past midnight when he passed through Terre Haute, Indiana. He considered stopping for the night but instead elected to push on. Even with the bad road conditions, he should still make it back to his apartment in about three hours.

After crossing the Illinois line, James stopped for gas and coffee at a truck stop near Marshall. No sooner than he'd gotten back up to highway speed, his car hit a patch of black ice and began a slow pirouette down the empty interstate. After four complete revolutions, the car came to rest, undamaged, in the median, pointing back toward Terre Haute. He was shaken but unhurt. It could've been *so* much worse.

As he paused to allow his heart rate to return to normal, two realizations became evident. First, hot coffee in the lap *is hot*! As for the second, for a second time in twenty-four hours, his picture-in-picture playback had blinked entirely off. He was, once again, totally in the present.

Much to his chagrin, less than an hour after his spin-out, his picture-in-picture returned. As he drove, James considered the nature of his mental playback. Twice it had gone away, and the respite had been heavenly. Why would it go away? Why did it come back?

The first instance with the Rohypnol was easier for him to understand. The drug altered his brain chemistry. If only he could reproduce the effect and give himself a modicum of peace. Sadly, he knew he could not. LSD might be expected to have a similar effect, but he had no desire to lose his medical license trying to purchase illegal substances off the street. He also considered, and excluded, ketamine as an option. The drug's propensity toward causing nightmares was enough to steer him away. James was already living a nightmare and certainly didn't need a drug that might make it worse.

As for the second instance during and after his car's spin down I-70, that one was more intriguing. James had previously noted, during particularly stressful surgeries, the smaller picture seemed to shrink from his consciousness, although it never went away entirely. He postulated that the common thread between high-risk surgery and his near-death experience might be adrenaline. Certainly, there would've been a surge during his spin and probably when disaster loomed imminent during surgery. He wondered what other activities might trigger a similar surge. Maybe he could take up skydiving or BASE jumping? Rock climbing without safety equipment might be another option?

Of course, none of these options would be available while he was working, and even spinning down an ice-slicked highway at seventy miles per hour had only provided but the briefest of respites from his overdeveloped memory. Still, the thought that there may be a sport or activity that could give him even a short-lived reprieve from his mental anguish merited additional consideration.

CHAPTER 24

DECEMBER 2001–MARCH 2002

I T BROKE BECCA'S HEART TO see James suffering and, so much more so, knowing that she was powerless to help. Had James been anyone else, she would've assured him that time would deaden the ache in his soul—as it had for her after Jimmy died—and someday, the hurts would heal. Sadly, "tincture of time" was an unguent denied to someone like James, whose memory would not allow him to forget. *Curse his goddamn perfect memory!* All she had to offer her son was her unconditional love and support and, perhaps, religion. Neither of which did anything to assuage his grief.

James appreciated his mother's efforts and loved her all the more for wanting to help. He thought she shouldn't feel too badly—nothing *else* worked either. No matter what he tried, the picture-in-picture remained unabated and unendurable. He jumped out of airplanes. He nearly killed himself rock climbing. He was arrested—but later released—when he got caught trying to base jump from the St. Louis Arch. James drove his sportscar at dizzying speeds at a local speedway and nearly lost his license trying the same on local highways and back roads. He began hanging out in local bars and experienced a dizzying series of one-night stands. Nothing gave him any relief.

Out of desperation, he once even tried ketamine. It temporarily suppressed his mental playback, but if possible, he found the experience even more disturbing than watching the towers fall. And, within an hour of awakening from the drug-fueled nightmares, his usual nightmare returned to the video screen of his consciousness.

In spite of his best efforts to find a means of suppressing the constant video feed from his overly developed memory, James seemed to be getting worse rather than better. His sleep pattern, already suboptimal due to the nature of his job, became even more fragmented. His affect and patience when dealing with others, already strained, became even more volatile and toxic. Only the thinnest of veneers protected the world around him from the seething cauldron beneath. Errant staff members considered themselves lucky *only* to be dissected by his acerbic wit after a miscue in the operating room or ICU.

Finally, the director of Human Resources had had enough. The straw that broke the camel's back was James's particularly vicious flaying of a surgical intern that had prompted the intern's subsequent resignation from the training program. The intern, sleep-deprived after working a double shift, had administered an antibiotic to a patient recovering from surgery for uterine cancer. Her chart clearly stated that she was severely allergic to that particular antibiotic, but the intern gave it anyway. The patient suffered an anaphylactic reaction and, had James not happened to be walking through the ICU at the time, would've died.

"Dr. Hamilton, you simply *must* get your anger under control. You're a gifted surgeon, but we cannot afford to have you out there running off our house staff."

James had always found the HR director's nasally voice annoying. He replied, "Running off our house staff? Siracuse, you're joking, right? That intern—"

"You may refer to me as *Doctor* Siracuse, Dr. Hamilton. I hold a PhD in Philosophy from Bethany Community College and will *not* be disrespected by *you*!"

James glared over the officious prick's pristine desk. Not so much as a paperclip was out of place. It was the desk of a meddlesome bureaucrat. For an instant, he imagined diving over the spotless surface and strangling the effete little man using the chain of the director's pince-nez reading glasses for the deed, but instead, he continued, "That intern is dangerous, and this institution—Hell, the practice of medicine—is better off without him, as were the two programs that released him before he landed in our laps. Today's incident represents the *fourth* major screw-up from him this month, and he's only been on the surgical service for a week and a half."

"It doesn't matter. This is a teaching institution. You should be training your house staff more carefully," Siracuse said.

"First of all, *Doctor* Siracuse, the intern in question wasn't *on* my service. I just happened to be available in the ICU to save the patient and prevent this institution from writing a *really* big check to her next of kin."

Before James could enumerate his follow-on points, Siracuse interrupted him again. "Dr. Hamilton, the university appreciates you doing your job—"

"Doing my *job*?!" James was incredulous.

Siracuse continued, "...but if you're to continue being employed by this institution, we—read that, the dean and I—expect you to issue a formal written apology to your intern—"

"He's not *my* intern."

"And enter into anger management counseling."

"You've *got* to be kidding me?"

"I do not kid, Dr. Hamilton. When may we expect your written apology?"

"About the time pigs fly. By the way, you're not looking to book any trips anytime soon, are you? I'm outta here!" James rose and stomped from the office, slamming the door so violently, a framed diploma fell from the wall. The glass shattered, spilling Siracuse's hand-lettered PhD certificate onto the floor.

The next morning, James returned to the HR director's office, knocked on the open doorframe, and politely waited for an invitation to enter.

Siracuse smiled smugly, noticing James was holding a letter in his hand. "So, I see that you've come to your senses and have brought along your letter of apology? Well, it's all for the best."

James stepped forward and wordlessly slid the letter, face up, across the polished surface of the desk.

Siracuse's face went white. Rather than a letter of apology, it was James's letter of resignation, effective immediately.

Without a word, James turned on his heels and strode to the door. There, he paused, tapping the glass on the newly reframed diploma. In a conversational tone and without turning around, he said, "FYI, *Doc*, 'College' is spelled with an *E*, not an *A*." He fluttered his fingers in a wiggly wave, then was gone.

Although he harbored less respect for Siracuse than he did for the average sewer rat, James had to admit the little man did have a point. He needed to do something about the constant anger that boiled within him. He didn't like the person he was becoming, too much like his father. Knowing the cause of his anger already—the constant replay loop of his memory—he held out little hope that counseling would be beneficial. Nothing short of a lobotomy was going to fix *that*. If there was a way he could channel his anger, then perhaps he might be able to do some good before it destroyed him.

That evening, while surfing through two hundred and seventy-six cable TV channels, he stumbled upon a favorite movie from his youth, *Platoon*. As he watched, Willem Dafoe's Sergeant Elias sprinted from the jungle, pursued by North Vietnamese army troops. They fired, striking him in the back. Elias collapsed to the ground, dying, with arms raised toward the sky and the retreating helicopter before him. It was an effective scene. Oliver Stone got that one right. No wonder he'd used the still from that shot for the movie's poster.

James watched for several minutes before surfing onward. Two channels later, he landed on CNN. There, the anchor was discussing Operation Anaconda, currently underway in Afghanistan, with a former army colonel. As James listened, an idea began to germinate in the recesses of his mind.

The more he thought about it, the more appealing the idea became. What if he, now that he was technically unemployed, volunteered for the army? There, he might successfully channel his anger and grief while bringing down a little retribution upon the people responsible for Elliana's death and *maybe* even do some good.

Comfortable with his decision, James flipped off the television and went to bed. Then he enjoyed his first restful night's sleep, being roofied notwithstanding, since September 11th.

CHAPTER 25

MARCH 2002–JANUARY 2008

S TAFF SERGEANT MIKE SHEEGOG SAT in the bar, nursing a Budweiser. In all his years as an army recruiter, he'd never scored such an outrageous coup as the one he'd finalized earlier that day, and he was more than happy to brag about it to his buddies. 9/11 had been a boon to recruiters, but today took the cake.

"So there I was, just sittin' at my desk, doin' paperwork and mindin' my own business, when this guy walks in. He's wearing a business suit and for all the world looks like a fuckin' lawyer. And I'm thinkin', geez, some mama's boy with connections ain't happy with army life and his family sent this guy down to bust my balls, like I really need *that*."

There were nods around the table, each man a recruiter who had suffered through such an onslaught at least once. It went with the territory.

Sheegog continued, "So I ask him if I can help him with somethin', and you know what? He just sits down at my desk and tells me he wants to join up. I kinda roll my eyes a bit, like the army needs another fuckin' lawyer. Then he tells me he's some kinda bigshot doctor. Okay, not a lawyer, I tell myself. This is gonna be okay. Then he says he's a surgeon, and now I'm getting real interested."

At this point, Sheegog had them on the edge of their seats, right where he wanted them.

"It gets even better. Then he tells me he's a fuckin' trauma surgeon from some Ivy League school and Stanford and has just quit his job at Wash U, here in town. He wants to join up immediately."

Sheegog's buddies stared open-mouthed, silently cursing him for his good luck.

"So I'm lookin' all around, thinkin' there's gotta be a camera somewhere and it's just you guys prankin' me or some shit like that. But it wasn't no prank. The best part? He wants to volunteer for *front line*, combat shit, and here it comes...this dude signed up for a *six-year* hitch. I mean, if this don't get me that next stripe, ain't nothin' gonna! So, drink up, boys. The next round is on me."

———

As was his custom, James planned to call Becca on Sunday afternoon. She looked forward to his calls, and so did he. Usually, their weekly conversations entailed little more than idle chitchat, but this time would be different. James had real news to share with his mother...and she wasn't going to like it one bit!

At promptly three o'clock, he began to dial. Twice in his nervousness, he mishit keys and had to redial. Finally, the call went through and he heard his mother's voice on the line. After a few minutes of light banter, James worked up the courage to drop the bomb.

"Mom, I have something I need to tell you."

Becca couldn't imagine what could be so important or why he sounded so nervous. *Has he started seeing some-*

one? This soon? "Certainly, dear. What is it? You know you can always talk with me about anything." Still, she held her breath.

"I've resigned my job at Wash U—"

Her words came out in a rush. "What? I thought you loved that job?"

"And I've joined the army."

"That is *not* funny, James. Now what is it that you *really* wanted to tell me?"

"Mom, it's not a joke. I'm going to be a part of the War on Terr—"

"No!" she gasped.

"Mom, I've got to do something. They attacked us. They killed Elliana." James's voice cracked. "What's to keep them from doing it again? I can't let that happen. I just can't."

Becca knew there was no argument that would change her son's mind. He'd always had a stubborn streak. She could argue with him, or she could love and support him. Ultimately, she elected the latter.

Several minutes and many tears later, she ended the call. As she put down the phone, she said to herself, "How could he do this? Doesn't he know—?"

No, he doesn't know...and that's all on me. Then she buried her head in her hands and sobbed until she had no more tears left to cry.

Becca was as good as her word and, when James took his oath of office and received his army commission on April 1st, she was there to support him. Although firmly opposed to his decision, she attended the ceremony and proudly pinned the gold oak leaves of a Major onto his uniform, and with a minimum of tears.

Due to his years of medical training and experience, James was sworn into the army as a Major and could expect to be promoted to Lieutenant Colonel after just two years' active service. As with everything he'd ever done, he embraced his new role wholeheartedly, without regrets or second thoughts. He was a soldier now. If it became necessary to forfeit his life to protect the people and the country he loved, so be it. In an instant, James became Major Hamilton.

After his commissioning ceremony, Hamilton traveled to Fort Benning in Georgia for the army's Direct Commission Course (DCC). There, he'd learn military customs and courtesies, how to wear the uniform, and become familiarized with the Uniform Code of Military Justice. Additionally, he'd learn to march and would undergo basic physical and firearms training.

The only portion of DCC that was a struggle for him was the firearms training. Like the other officers in his training group, he was issued an M9, a 9mm Beretta 92 pistol. He received the same training and range time as his peers, but in the words of the Fort Benning Range Master, "Major Hamilton, sir, you couldn't hit the broad side of a barn from ten feet. Damn good thing you're a doctor, sir!" It didn't matter what he tried or how long he practiced, his marksmanship never seemed to improve. To qualify with the M-9, he had to place just twenty-five of forty rounds into a man-sized target from only fifty feet away. Even so, it took Hamilton an embarrassing four tries to achieve even a minimum passing score, and even then, he was left with questions.

It was a relief to all when, on the penultimate day of the DCC, the Range Master informed him that he'd finally qualified. Hamilton was elated, but his sense of accomplishment was short lived.

On the day of his eventual qualification, in the firing lane to his immediate left, there had been a crack pistol shot.

This person routinely put forty of forty shots into a neat, three-inch cluster near the X-ring from fifty yards. On the day of Hamilton's qualification, there had only been thirty-eight holes found in the crack shot's target. The Range Master, well aware of the man's skill with a handgun, knew there was not even the *remotest* possibility that this man would totally miss his target. He suggested that perhaps the two missing rounds had passed through the same hole. That *had* to be it.

Upon hearing this, Hamilton examined his target. The dispersion pattern on his own target was embarrassingly diffuse and from a much shorter range than the crack shot's. Holes were scattered from forehead to groin and shoulder to shoulder on the man-sized and -shaped silhouette. Oddly, two rounds had formed a perfect figure eight, obliterating the X in the center of his target's chest. The next closest bullet hole was a good three inches away. Having passed with a score of just twenty-six out of forty, he wondered... *Nah! He couldn't have...*

After leaving Fort Benning, Hamilton traveled to San Antonio for part two of the Basic Officer Leader Course specific for Army Medical Department officers. With his background as a trauma surgeon, he easily could've taught this portion of the course. However, he declined to undermine his instructors' authority and held his tongue, even when they were wrong. Clearly, he was learning the finer points of being an officer in the military.

Hamilton continued to struggle with the incessant picture-in-picture display inside his head. Usually, through force of will, he was able to suppress the past well enough to remain "in the moment," but still he occasionally slipped. Multiple times during his post-commission army indoctrination and training, his instructors noted that the major seemed to "zone out" at times. But due to his general level of competence, they elected to overlook the episodes. To retain the services of a surgeon of his caliber, they would've happily overlooked far more serious idiosyncrasies.

After completion of his stateside training and as per his request, he received his first orders to Afghanistan. Early in his first tour in Afghanistan, the Taliban attacked Hamilton's base with a combined rocket and mortar barrage. A young private caught outside at the onset of the attack immediately sustained severe wounds. Upon hearing the man's screams from just outside the hospital bunker, Hamilton, without thinking, grabbed a medic bag and sprinted to the wounded man's side.

The soldier had been struck in the groin and was bleeding profusely from a severed femoral artery. If something wasn't done quickly, the man would bleed out and die long before he made it to an operating table. The wound was too high for a tourniquet, and the artery had retracted well above the inguinal ligament. Manual compression might keep the artery from bleeding out through the wound but wouldn't prevent it from continuing to bleed into the abdominal cavity until the man exsanguinated.

Hamilton assessed the situation in seconds and immediately intuited what had to be done. As shells continued to explode and shrapnel rained down about him, he gave the soldier a shot of morphine, found a scalpel, and extended the wound toward the abdomen. Through the enlarged wound, he located and clamped the lacerated artery. The bleeding slowed to a trickle immediately. The procedure wasn't clean, but infection was the least of the man's worries. Then, he lifted the wounded soldier into a fireman's carry and conveyed him to the relative safety of the hospital bunker and operating room.

Hamilton immediately scrubbed for surgery. There, he found and removed the offending piece of shrapnel, and on the fly, performed a complex vascular repair. He reconnected the damaged vessel and then debrided and cleaned the wound. Immediately, the soldier's mottled blue-and-white leg turned a healthy pink. Hamilton looked at the clock. The vascular repair had taken him less than twenty minutes. He took his time assessing his patient for other injuries and additional damage from the shrapnel but found nothing significant. He placed drains, started antibiotics, and closed the wound.

An hour later, he checked on his patient in post-op. His vitals were stable. Plasma and packed red blood cells were still infusing, but the man's foot was warm and had palpable pulses. Hamilton was pleased. All was well.

The hospital commander, however, was *not* pleased. He was thoroughly pissed and wasted little time in telling Major Hamilton about it. "What in the holy Hell did you think you were doing, going out there in the middle of a goddamn attack?"

Hamilton stood at rigid attention before the commander's desk, braving the onslaught, then replied, "There was a man hit—"

"Don't interrupt me, Major! That was a rhetorical question. You're a goddamn trauma *surgeon*, not a combat medic. Your job is to take care of the wounded men once they're *inside* the hospital, not wander out into the compound to bring them back yourself. If you get yourself wounded or killed, who do you think's gonna patch *you* up?"

Hamilton didn't answer.

"I asked you a question, Major."

"Sorry, sir, I thought it was rhetorical. Sir, if I'm dead, it won't matter. If I'm wounded, there are three other—"

"Don't be a smart-ass, Hamilton! I know all about our staffing. I *am* the goddamn commander here, after all."

"Yes, sir."

"Now, what do you have to say for yourself, Hamilton?"

"Permission to speak freely, sir?"

The commander gave the slightest of nods.

"The soldier who is now in recovery is Private Fred Leuschner of Duluth, Minnesota. I found a photograph Private Leuschner had tucked inside in his helmet when I brought him in from the compound. According to the back of the photo, it was a picture of his wife holding his newborn baby girl. Sir, someday in the not-to-distant future, he's going to get to *meet* that little girl of his, and someday in the *more* distant future, he's going to walk that same little girl down the aisle with *two* good legs. That's what I say." Then belatedly, he added, "Sir."

"Goddamn it, Hamilton!" The commander slammed his fist on the desk hard enough a framed photograph bounded off the desk and crashed to the floor. "The point is you're right...and now I've got to write you up..."

Hamilton sighed. He supposed *some* kind of punishment was to be expected after his rash action, but *damn!*

"...for a goddamn medal. Now get out of my office!"

"Sir?"

"You heard me. Get! And, Hamilton..."

"Yes, sir."

"Be more careful in the future. You're worth more to the troops out there if you're alive rather than dead, you hear?"

"Yes, sir. Will that be all, sir?"

The commander nodded.

Hamilton gave a crisp salute, performed an about-face just like he'd been taught, and marched from the room. It felt good. In fact, it felt damned good. He'd made a difference.

After ducking into the mess tent for chow, he returned to his quarters and lay back on his bunk, replaying the day. Suddenly, he sat bolt upright. He just realized there was no picture-in-picture playing inside his head, nor would there be for the rest of the week. He dozed off and dreamed happy dreams.

The following morning, an aeromedical evacuation flight took off bearing a stable Private Leuschner to Landstuhl Regional Medical Center in Germany. From there, after additional treatment, he'd travel back to the States and the loving arms of his family.

A month after Leuschner's departure, at Commander's Call, they awarded Hamilton a Bronze Star with a *V* for *Valor*.

When his picture-in-picture playback eventually returned, as Hamilton had always known it would, there was an additional screen for Private Leuschner, although this one, he didn't mind. Nor did he mind the other "wins" he experienced while serving in Afghanistan and Iraq. The screens depicting the losses, however, were less welcome and more disturbing.

Upon hearing the news of James's military decoration, Becca was equal parts proud and afraid. She'd felt the same way when Jimmy received the Silver Star for rescuing another soldier from the middle of a minefield. She supposed the apple didn't fall very far from the tree. Of course, this should not have come as a surprise to her. James looked exactly like Jimmy. He had the same opaline-green eyes and lopsided smile she'd fallen for so, so long ago. Their voices were even the same and, temper notwithstanding, he even *acted* like his father.

James was so much like Jimmy it hurt, and she'd *nearly* told him that many times. Of course, with him being unaware of the identity of his *actual* father, that revelation would've triggered a *very* awkward conversation and she hadn't been ready for *that*, especially not via overseas email. She resolved to tell him as soon as he came home from the war. Certain conversations should not be had by remote. She needed to have him here, to see his eyes and to answer his questions. Jimmy had been a wonderful man, caring, loving, and responsible. He'd been the kind of man every girl dreamed of marrying someday. A son deserved to know that about his father...that, and so much more.

Although Becca was still unhappy about James's decision to join the military, she had to admit, he seemed happier than he'd been at any time since Elliana's death. Perhaps *happier* was not quite correct. *Less unhappy* seemed the more accurate descriptor, or perhaps, *more at peace*. It seemed to her that James believed he was making a difference. Although the path was not the one she would've chosen for her son, she was glad he was finding a measure of peace over there. But while fighting a war? The very idea seemed bizarre to her.

For six years, Becca waited for James to come home from the war so they could have their conversation about Jimmy. Somehow, he managed to never quite make it there. She'd hoped he'd return home for his pinning ceremony when he was promoted to Lieutenant Colonel but had been disappointed. Instead of returning home on leave or in between combat tours, James spent his entire six-year term of duty overseas, rotating between Afghanistan, Landstuhl, and Iraq.

The only time he had even attempted to come home had occurred in 2005 during his second tour in Afghanistan. After being informed of Oksana Petrenko's death, he'd applied for Emergency Leave to attend her funeral. His commander, however, denied his leave request, stating, "Emergency Leave is intended to be used in instances of death or critical illness of *immediate* family members, *not* family friends."

Becca heard the story through the Petrenkos. She could only guess at James's reaction. It couldn't have been good. She hoped the commander lived. During their weekly telephone and video chat, James didn't bring up the topic, and she, wisely, elected not to ask. She figured just because one sees a low-hanging hornet's nest doesn't mean one should use it as a piñata.

In January of 2008, during one of their weekly chats, James reminded Becca that his six-year term of service would end in March. He'd had enough of the war and had no intention of signing on for another term. Becca was equal parts thrilled and relieved by the news. James was coming home, safe and in one piece. Nothing, not even the migraine headache she'd been suffering with for the past week, could temper her joy. As for her headache, it was nothing a nice long, relaxing bubble bath wouldn't cure.

CHAPTER 26

FEBRUARY 2008

THE BATH DIDN'T HELP. NOR did aspirin, ibuprofen, or acetaminophen. With over-the-counter remedies proving ineffective, Becca scheduled an appointment with her family doctor. The doctor was busy, but his nurse practitioner told her she had a sinus infection and provided prescriptions for an antibiotic and an antihistamine decongestant. Two weeks later when her symptoms hadn't improved, Becca returned to her doctor's office. The doctor, annoyed about having to yet see another neurotic, drug-seeking patient, wrote a prescription for pain medication just to get her out of the office.

Had either the physician or his extender elected to perform the physical examination for which they'd both billed Becca's insurance, they might've noticed an abnormality. Specifically, they would've observed swelling of the optic disc, a condition known as papilledema, indicative of increased intracranial pressure. This might have led one or the other of them to request a contrasted CAT scan of Becca's brain, which in turn would've revealed a large parietal mass on the left and three smaller masses on the right. With her remote history of breast cancer, these findings most assuredly would've triggered a referral to an oncologist.

Granted, such diligence would not likely have had a great effect on her prognosis, but it may have prevented Becca from suffering a seizure while driving home from their office that day. Instead, she was involved in a car crash and taken to the local Emergency Department for evaluation. There, the physician performed a thorough exam, noted the papilledema, ordered the CAT scan, and contacted her oncologist. The oncologist, in turn, ordered a bone scan that also showed the lesions in the brain but additionally revealed multiple abnormal areas in the bone and liver.

Becca was sitting up in her hospital bed when the oncologist came to her room to discuss the test results with her. She shuddered and gave a weak smile. Before he could say a word, she said in a matter-of-fact voice, "You don't play poker, do you, Doc?"

This startled the oncologist. "I beg your pardon?"

"You have the worst poker face I've ever seen. If you ever go to Vegas, I recommend you just watch the shows. Otherwise, you'll lose your shirt. So, my cancer's back. How bad is it? How do we treat it this time?"

"Well, we don't know for certain."

"Don't BS me, Dr. Schlabach. It's written all over your face and the faces of the technicians who've been doing all these fancy tests you ordered."

"We can't be one hundred percent sure until we've done a biopsy."

"And what do you *think* the biopsy will show?"

"Well, I don't like to—"

Becca cut him off with a harsh glare. "And *I* don't like doctors who beat around the bush. In all your years of training and clinical experience, what does it look like to you?"

The oncologist was taken aback. "Certainly, in a patient with a history of a breast malignancy, the pattern on your scans would be consistent with a recurrence and widespread metastases."

Becca closed her eyes and released a long sigh. "That's kinda what I figured. Everybody who even walks past my room looks like their dog just died. So, when's the biopsy?"

"I have you scheduled for tomorrow morning in Interventional Radiology."

"And how soon after that will we know?" Becca asked, her voice beginning to falter.

"We'll have some idea almost immediately. Of course, the pathologists will want to do special staining, and that might take up to a week."

"I guess we'll talk then," Becca said quietly. She lay back in the bed and turned toward the window.

"Of course, we'll talk then."

After a moment of silence in the room, the oncologist left, shutting the door behind him.

Only after the door clicked closed did Becca allow herself to cry.

Two weeks later, she sat in the consultation room at Oncology Associates of America, waiting to hear her fate. As she waited, she thought what a terrible name "Oncology Associates of America" was for an oncologic practice. The initials, O-A-O-A, spoken rapidly sounded like "away, away," not the most reassuring words a patient contemplating their mortality, and the possibility of going away forever, wants to hear. But then, she supposed, maybe a patient might instead interpret the name as a sign that their *cancer* would go "away, away" instead?

"I guess it depends on whether they see the glass as half-full or half-empty?"

"I'm sorry, Mrs. Hamilton. Did you say something?"

Becca jumped. She'd not heard the doctor enter the room nor realized she'd been speaking aloud. "Oh, no, I was just thinking about your... Oh, never mind. Your office called and told me you have my biopsy results."

"Yes. Mrs. Hamilton..."

"Please, call me Rebecca. Mrs. Hamilton was my mother-in-law."

"Rebecca...yes, of course. Yes, we have your results, and I'm afraid it's as we feared..."

Becca zoned out, lost in her thoughts. When she returned to the conversation, the doctor was talking through treatment options.

"Let me stop you there, Doc."

Dr. Schlabach paused.

"One question. How much time do I have left?"

"Well, I don't like to—"

"We've been through this before. Tell me, in your professional opinion, what can I realistically expect? And no, I won't hold you to it if you're wrong."

"With radiation and chemotherapy, maybe six months."

"And how about without?"

"With new treatments coming available every day and clinical trials, I—"

"How much time without?"

"Three, maybe four months."

"And how would I feel up until the end?"

"Well, much like you do today. There will be pain and more seizures nearer the end."

"And if we start treatment, when would treatment start?" she asked.

"Why, immediately, of course."

"Let me get this straight. I die either way. One way, I feel relatively normal for a couple of months before it all falls apart. The other, I might live another two or three months but will *wish* I was dead the entire time."

"Well, Mrs. Ham—" Schlabach caught himself. "Rebecca, that's not the way we like to look at things."

"Maybe not *you*, but it *is* how I look at it. I've been through all of this before. I know what it's like. My son's coming home from the war next month. As long as I'm still here and functional for that, I'll be satisfied. But I have to be *me* when he gets here. I can't have chemo-brain and be puking up my toenails all hours of the day and night. Huh-uh."

"I can understand how you feel, but—"

Becca shook her head.

"I suppose we could talk about hospice..."

Becca was no longer listening. In her mind, she was already with Jimmy...and at peace.

CHAPTER 27

FEBRUARY 2008

I N 1995, MAJOR STEVEN J. Chalmers had accepted orders assigning him to the inaugural mission of the Joint POW/MIA Accounting Command into Vietnam. During the mission, his team had located and repatriated three sets of American remains from a helicopter crash dating back to 1967, associated with the Battle of Da'k To. Two of the three had been identified and returned to their families. The third remained unidentified.

Chalmers had joined the mission for all the wrong reasons. He'd had no understanding of the mission or its importance. Back then, the thirty-day trek through the jungle meant little more to him than a way out of a dead-end job, an opportunity to advance his career, and a great way to impress a girl. The mission had ended up being all these things, and so much more. Seeing the effect those returns had upon both family members and strangers had had a transformative effect on Chalmers. Before going to Vietnam, he'd been selfish, churlish, and self-centered. After, he fully embraced the mission of JPAC. When given the opportunity to select any job within the Department of Defense, he'd eschewed plumb positions in major medical centers and instead chosen to become the newest project officer for the Joint POW/MIA Accounting Command. From there, his military career had skyrocketed. He'd been promoted to Lieutenant Colonel and gotten the girl.

Over the next four years, Chalmers organized and participated in four more missions into Vietnam and one each into Cambodia and Laos. For two of the missions, he served as Medical Officer, and for the other four, he operated as Team Leader.

At the end of his tour, Chalmers, then a full Colonel, left JPAC with a sterling record. His teams had been responsible for the identification and repatriation of an additional seven sets of remains from service members lost during the Vietnam War. With each return, he personally accompanied the fallen soldiers, sailors, airmen, or marines on their final journey back home to their families. Never before or since had he departed a posting with a greater sense of satisfaction than he had for his time with JPAC.

It always nagged at him, however, that the third set of remains from his inaugural mission into Vietnam had never been identified. There were no artifacts found to provide clues to his identity. It was as though the man had fallen from the sky, but no helmet or parachute hardware was located near the site. The skeleton had been incomplete at the time of discovery, and none of the bones his team unearthed had any identifiable antemortem injuries to match with military records. The mandible had never been located, and damage to the maxilla had been too great to allow for an identification match through dental records. DNA had been successfully recovered, but with no family members against whom it might be compared, the technology was useless.

During the Second Gulf War, Brigadier General Chalmers was assigned to the Pentagon as a staff officer. It wasn't a particularly exciting job, but it was important and some-one had to do it. Besides, there were worse things for one's career than to have a job in which one reported *directly* to the Chairman of the Joint Chiefs of Staff.

Each day, Chalmers culled through hundreds of emails and memos for General Myers. Those he thought had merit, he passed along. For those that did not or that could be handled at a lower level, he'd been empowered to quash or deal with them as he saw fit.

One afternoon during January 2008, while going through his daily trove of emails, he found one that, in his estimation, needed to be passed to the boss. It was a request for the chairman to lobby the House Armed Services and Appropriations Committees for funds. Beginning about 1985, DNA samples were obtained for all servicemen and reservists upon their entry into the military. The capac-ity for the initial repository of DNA information had been exceeded and a new, larger facility was now required. The funding request seemed reasonable, and Chalmers dutifully passed it along before forgetting about it and returning to his message queue.

Later that evening, he and "the girl"—now his wife, Holly—enjoyed a bottle of their favorite Australian Caber-net Sauvignon, a 1999 Penfolds Bin 707. They sat watching their son, Austin, play in the backyard with his best friend, a six-month-old Boston Terrier puppy. The two took turns chasing one another around their cramped backyard. First, Austin chased the puppy. Then upon some unseen signal, they both turned and the puppy chased him. During one turn as the chased, the little boy glanced over his shoulder to check his lead over his pursuer. As he looked back, the four-year-old tripped over a discarded toy and tumbled across the grass. He immediately began to cry at the top of his ample lungs, holding his injured knee with both hands.

Holly began to stand, intending to comfort the boy, but Chalmers put a hand gently on her arm and held her back for a moment. "Wait," he said. "Give it a sec…"

In an instant, the puppy was in Austin's face, licking and yapping excitedly and pulling at his sleeve to resume the game. Almost immediately, the little boy, who only a moment before had been bawling about his *grievous injury*, was transformed into a giggling, writhing mass of sheer joy. His skinned knee was totally forgotten, just as Chalmers had suspected.

Smiling, Chalmers said, "Ah, a boy and his dog…"

Holly rolled her eyes and shook her head. "Amen! I mean, look at him! You'd never need a DNA test to prove that he's *your* son. Not only does he have your lack of coordination and totally looks like your shrunken clone but he even has your short attention span. Show him a puppy, or in your case a little leg, and the rest of the world ceases to exist," she teased. Holly loved ribbing Chalmers. It, at least in her mind, was a big part of what made their marriage fun.

Chalmers stared toward his son. In the back of his mind, something clicked. "What did you say?"

"He looks just like you, and has zero coordination…just like you."

"No, not that…about the DNA?"

"That you don't need a DNA test to prove he's your son. Geez, don't be so sensitive! It was only a joke."

"No, no…of course. That's perfect! God, I love you! It was 1967. That just might work." Chalmers put down his glass, gave Holly a quick kiss, and almost ran to his study.

Holly shook her head as she watched him race into the house. *I love him. I don't understand him, but I love him.*

In his study, Chalmers booted up his computer, which took forever. "Come on, come on, come on. I have *got* to upgrade this thing. Whoever came up with that damned spinning hourglass thing should be drawn and quartered and have their entrails eaten by rabid squirrels," he grumbled aloud.

Finally the computer booted up, and he logged into his Pentagon email account. "Where is it, where is it, where is it? If I deleted that email, then *I* should be draw— Yes! Here it is. 1985...*hot damn*!" Chalmers punched the air in triumph, then printed the email and practically danced back outside, waving the printed page as he walked.

"Oookaaayyy...should I go ahead and send your measurements to your tailor now so he can get started on your straight jacket, or is there some explanation that will make me believe you *haven't* lost your mind?" Holly asked.

Chalmers showed her the email.

"Got it. Now let me just get my phone," she said. "I keep him on speed dial for juuusst such an emergency. Maybe he'll throw in a few tranquilizer darts...you know, just in case you don't come quietly. You're gonna love your new huggy-jacket!"

"No, no, no, no. This might be it!"

Realizing that Chalmers wasn't going to be drawn into her banter, she said, "It? Okay, I'll bite. To which *it* might you be referring?"

"The remains from that first mission to Vietnam...the ones we couldn't identify. You remember!"

"I remember, but I think I'm still missing something. Maybe you'd better start at the beginning."

"We couldn't use dental records for ID because there were for all intents and purposes no teeth."

"Okay?"

"Similarly, we couldn't use DNA because we had no comparison samples. There will probably be DNA out there from family, but we had nothing about the site to suggest who we could use for a comparison. Here is a database with hundreds of thousands of DNA samples!"

"Sweetie, I hate to break it to you, but the DNA collection program started in 1985, and the Vietnam War ended in 1975, and Da'k To was in 1967. Nice try," she said, patting his hand. "But he's not going to be in there. I'm sorry."

"No, not *him*...his potential children. If he was from the Battle of Da'k To, any children he had would have been at least eighteen in 1985. They would have been old enough to be serving when the program started. If any of *them* joined the military, then we might get a hit out of the database we already have!"

Holly nodded. "It could work, assuming that he had kids."

"Here's to hoping," he said, touching his wineglass to hers.

For the first time in Chalmers's working life, Monday morning couldn't arrive quickly enough. He absolutely could not wait to make the call to the JPAC Central Identification Laboratory at Hickam AFB. On arrival to his office, however, he realized that he would *have* to wait at least until noon, owing to the time difference between DC and Hawaii.

Every few minutes, Chalmers checked the clock on his office wall. Once, he even got up to check to see if the damned thing was working. Time dragged. He realized the last time he'd felt this nervous was on his wedding day, waiting for Holly to walk down the aisle. The thought made him smile.

Noon *finally* came, and Chalmers was quite pleased that he had the self-restraint to wait until *12:01* before placing the call.

After four rings, the call connected and a bored-sounding voice came across the line. "JPAC CIL, this is Airman Jennings. How may I direct your call?"

"Airman, this is General Chalmers calling from—"

"Yeah, right?! Joey, is that you again? You gotta cut the crap, man. You can't keep calling and pulling this kinda shit!"

In a measured tone, Chalmers said, "Airman Jennings, I have no idea who *Joey* is, but I assure you that I *do* know your commanding officer, Colonel Bosa, very well. So kindly put him on the line *now* and tell him that *General* Chalmers is waiting. Thank you."

"Y-yes, sir! I'm sorry, sir! Right away, sir. May I place you on hold, sir?"

"Certainly."

A moment later, the phone clicked and the line went dead.

Chalmers shook his head and redialed the number.

"J-JPAC C-CIL, this is A-Airman J-Jennings."

"Airman Jennings, it appears that we were disconnected."

"Y-yes, s-sir...I accidentally hit the wrong button. I-I'm sorry, sir!"

"Take a breath, son! You're hyperventilating. Just slow down and breathe. If that's the worst thing that happens today, then this is going to be a good day for both of us. Now, may I speak with Colonel Bosa?"

The phone clicked, and a moment later he heard, "This is Colonel Bosa."

"Ted? Steve Chalmers calling from DC. How are things at JPAC?"

The two chatted for a few minutes before Chalmers made his request. Bosa said that he'd be happy to email him a copy of the unknown's DNA profile and wished him luck.

"May I ask a question?" Bosa asked.

Chalmers, of course, agreed.

"I'm curious, sir. It's been over a decade since those remains were recovered. Why now? What's changed?"

"Fair question. I don't know if you know this, but I was involved in that recovery mission. It's always bothered me that we were never able to make an ID, even a tentative one. Somewhere there is somebody's mother, somebody's husband, somebody's father, or somebody's friend. Whoever they may be, they deserve to know, and he deserves to be recognized for his service and for his sacrifice. Recently, I had an idea—a hunch really—about how we just might be able to make all that happen. If this works, it should open the playing field for you guys. Even if it doesn't, it's still worth running to ground. This could be a proof-of-concept test for the future. Thanks for your help, Ted," he said, then ended the call.

Gaining access to the Armed Forces Repository of Specimen Samples for the Identification of Remains (AFRSSIR) was more challenging. It took the intervention of Chalmers's boss before the information was finally released. Three weeks later, his email pinged. They had a hit!

According to the email, there was a 99.9997 percent probability that the remains were a first-degree relative, most likely the father of Army Lieutenant Colonel James Wiley Hamilton of Boiling Springs, South Carolina. Lieutenant Colonel Hamilton was presently a Medical Officer assigned to the 212th Mobile Army Surgical Hospital south of An Najaf, Iraq, in support of Operation Iraqi Freedom.

Chalmers stared at the email and thought about an officer currently serving half a world away. *After forty-one years, your dad's finally coming home.*

CHAPTER 28

FEBRUARY 2008

L IEUTENANT COLONEL HAMILTON HAD SPENT six long years supporting a war that showed no sign of ending, at least not for his country. For him, it was over and it was time. He'd done his part. Now it was time for him to go home.

Physically, Hamilton hadn't stepped foot upon the soil of his native country in 2,148 days. Mentally, however, was an entirely different story. With his picture-in-picture playback now upgraded to *multiple* screens—currently resembling the news wall in the White House Situation Room—he'd never left. Even for a mind as capacious as his own, such a constant psychological barrage was taxing in the extreme. He needed a break.

How, or from which vector, that break might come, Hamilton had no earthly idea. That was tomorrow's problem.

Another problem for tomorrow would be his plans for life after the army. He supposed he could return to his position at Washington University. The director of Human Resources had been terminated the same day Hamilton first met Staff Sergeant Sheegog. It seemed that someone *anony-*

mously slipped a sheaf of papers under the door of the university president during the night, bringing into question the HR director's academic bona fides. When it was discovered that Siracuse had falsified his employment application, he'd been fired. On that same day, the president declined to accept Hamilton's letter of resignation, insisting instead he would be classified as on an extended leave of absence, since he was leaving to serve his country after the 9/11 attacks.

Today's problem was the Pentagon. It had been quite a surprise when, on his penultimate day of out-processing from his post at An Najaf, Iraq, he received an amendment to his Discharge and Travel Orders. Certainly, *he'd* not requested any amendments, appendixes, or deviations. His new orders dictated that he was, upon returning stateside, to report to the Pentagon for an interview with some Air Force general. Hamilton wanted to go home, not suffer through an exit interview from some rear-echelon desk jockey. But orders were orders, and he *was*—at least for the moment—still in the army.

"Why the bloody Hell, on my last day of wearing a uniform, am I being summoned to the Pentagon? It's not like it's part of the standard Out-Processing Checklist," Hamilton muttered to himself as he cleared security at the world's largest office building. "Looks like they rebuilt nicely after 9/11. That's good. Wounds need to heal."

As he stood outside the office of Air Force Brigadier General Steven J. Chalmers, Hamilton rapped lightly on the door. A voice from inside immediately bade him to enter. Hamilton entered the room as directed and turned to close the door. By the time he'd turned away from the door but before he could render a salute, the general was already around his desk, pumping Hamilton's hand in a vigorous handshake.

Chalmers directed Hamilton to one of the chairs before his desk and, to Hamilton's surprise, rather than returning to the power position behind the desk, the general selected the companion chair next to his own and sat down. Hamilton observed the general as he settled into the chair. The man's face, above what could only be a genuine smile, glowed and he practically jittered, like a kid next in line for a visit with Santa Claus.

"Lieutenant Colonel Hamilton, I cannot adequately express how excited I am to meet you or how long I've waited for precisely this moment." The general's excitement was almost palpable.

Hamilton assumed that he must have treated someone from the general's family during the war. The man appeared far too young to have had a son or daughter old enough for military service. Maybe it was a brother, sister, or even father? A quick mental roll call of every patient he'd treated over the past six years failed to reveal anyone named Chalmers, however. Even had that been the case, such an extravagant amendment in his Travel Orders would never have been approved, not even on the behest of a brigadier general. So, for the moment, Hamilton remained clueless about why he was there.

As though reading Hamilton's mind, Chalmers said, "I'm sure you're wondering why I've asked you to come here."

"Yes, sir," Hamilton replied mechanically, pretty sure he hadn't been *asked* to be *anywhere*.

"Allow me to explain," Chalmers said with a smile. "In 1995, I was part of a Joint POW/MIA Accounting Command mission to Vietnam, searching an area in the Central Highlands where the Battle of Da'k To was fought in November of 1967. During that mission, we discovered the wreckage of a helicopter crash associated with the battle. From that crash site, we unearthed three sets of remains. Two were readily identified, but until recently, the identity of the third remained unknown. However, within the past week, we've confirmed the identity of the third set of remains. According to DNA technology, Colonel Hamilton, the third set of remains belong to *your father*."

"That's impossible! My father died in a car accident in 1977 in South Carolina. That's a decade and nine thousand miles removed from your site in Vietnam." Hamilton's mind reeled. "I'm afraid there's been some kind of mistake."

Through the strobing effect of a hundred different memory pictures from his childhood, Hamilton only registered snippets of General Chalmers's remaining words.

"No mistake...closure for your...finally coming home...should be proud...honorably served...remains to be interred...Arlington National Cemetery...June.... Lieutenant Colonel Hamilton, thank you for *your* service," Chalmers said, smiling as he stood. Again, he eschewed the customary salute and extended his hand for Hamilton to shake.

An hour after his arrival, a stunned, confused, and thoroughly distressed Hamilton staggered from the general's office with a maelstrom of memories swirling about on the IMAX screen of his mind.

CHAPTER 29

MARCH 2008

M ACK LEE HAMILTON HAD BEEN cruel, narcissistic, and abusive, both physically and mentally. He was a human wrecking ball who destroyed everything and everyone he touched. His menacing shadow had loomed over James Wiley Hamilton as a child, and his specter continued to be a malevolent presence in his life, even three decades after his death. Hamilton had hated the man, and the thought that he might be even *remotely* like him made him feel physically ill.

The news he'd received from Chalmers was, to say the least, shocking, and Hamilton reacted precisely as the man he'd *believed* to be his father would have. He flew into a blinding rage and lashed out against the person he blamed for perpetrating and perpetuating this lifelong hoax—his mother, Becca.

After the revelations he'd learned during his brief time in DC, all thoughts of a happy homecoming were forgotten. When he arrived home to the family farm, James wasted little time in confronting his mother.

"*My* father was an abusive, lazy, philandering drunk who died with a whore's head between his legs," James snarled at his mother. "*That* was what I was told. *That* was the truth of my childhood. *I* lived with that shame. *That* became a part of me and who I am today. For *forty years*, I've lived with that *truth*. For forty years, I didn't want to get married or have children because I didn't want to take the *chance* of passing along that *bastard's* DNA! Now I find out it was all a lie...that just maybe my *real* father was a *great guy* who honorably served, and died, in Vietnam."

James continued to rage, a scornful expression distorting his usually placid features. "And how did I find out about this miraculous transmutation of my pedigree? Certainly *not* from the loving mother who watched me suffer for my entire life! Noooo, why would *she* want to ease my struggles?" His voice dripped with sarcasm. "Not a chance! Not her! No, my genetic alchemist was some *bureaucrat* from the goddamn Department of Defense, informing me that they'd used my DNA to identify the mortal remains of my *real* father. In what alternate universe does *that* happen?!"

"I'm still your mother, and you *won't* talk to me like that!"

"Really?! Can I be sure about that? Or is some desk jockey from Washington gonna show up some day and tell me otherwise, just like they did with dear old Dad?"

Becca's slap came out of nowhere. "You *will not* talk to your mother that way!"

James rubbed his cheek in stunned silence.

"Yes, I know I should have told you. I almost did dozens of times, but never quite found the words. I guess I didn't know how. Then, after Mack Lee died, I figured, what did it matter anymore. Maybe I should just let sleeping dogs lie. I'm *sorry*, James! I never meant for you to be hurt. It was all so long ago. It's almost like a dream."

"I'm sorry too, Mom. It was just a shock, and I shouldn't have taken it out on you. Honestly, I'd suspected that Mack Lee wasn't my real father. God knows I *hoped* he wasn't! I guess I just wanted to hear it from *you*, not the DOD."

"Really? How'd you figure it out?"

"Eyes. I have green eyes. Your eyes are blue. Dad, err... Mack Lee had brown eyes. It's a genetic impossibility for blue- and brown-eyed parents to have a green-eyed child. I couldn't be completely certain, of course, because I do look a little like him and pictures I've seen of Grandma and Grandpa Hamilton," he said with a shrug. "I convinced myself there might have been a primary mutation in the gene for eye color."

"You always were too smart for your own good." Then she added in a wistful, faraway voice, "Just like your father... your *real* father." The faintest of smiles creased her lips. "He was the sweetest, most intelligent person I'd ever known. That is, until *you* came along."

"Who was he, Mom?" James asked with a crack in his voice.

"You really don't know? As smart as you are, you haven't figured it out?"

James shook his head. "No clue."

Becca smiled a radiant smile. "They wanted *your* DNA because your real father was James Wiley Hamilton."

A look of puzzlement crossed his face. "Excuse me?"

"You're the one with the genius IQ. Puzzle it out," she said with a laugh. "You're a Junior...or a Second, if you prefer. James Hamilton was your father. He was Mack Lee's younger brother...my first husband...and the love of my life."

"First husband? That's a relief. I thought I was a bast—"

"No, you are fully legal and legitimate. James and I were only married five days before he shipped out to Vietnam," she said with a blush, her blue eyes twinkling.

"What about my birth certificate? It lists Mack Lee Hamilton as *father*."

"You were just a few weeks old when James died. After I married Mack Lee—"

"Why *did* you marry him? I can't imagine."

"Because I was young, ignorant, and naïve, whereas your grandmother was a manipulative, evil witch. It was she who manipulated me into marrying him—she wanted the money from Jimmy's life insurance—and it was she who insisted that your birth certificate be changed. She'd already purged every record with any mention of James Hamilton from existence. She wanted the world to forget he'd ever lived. She sure as *Hell* wasn't going to leave *that* document unaltered. Her friends in the county records department pulled strings and got the birth certificate reissued."

"But why?"

"Because she is a bitter, crazy old crone who hated your father with a rare and abiding hatred," she answered with loathing in her voice.

"Again, why?"

"That's a long story. Suffice it to say, she is crazy. That's why she's still locked up in Columbia at the hospital for the criminally insane. They finally tossed her in the loony bin after she tried to kill you when Mack Lee died. My God, if I hadn't walked in when I did. I shudder to think. But that's a story for another day. Today is about your father."

"Will you tell me about him?"

"Better yet, why don't I let *him* tell you about himself?"

"I beg your pardon? Him tell me? Little late for that, isn't it?"

Becca laughed. "Let me show you." She led him to an antique rolltop desk.

"This was always locked when I was a kid," he said, gesturing to the desk. "I always dreamed about what might be inside."

"And it's locked now too," she said, extracting a small, brass key from a hidden compartment in the chair-well.

"Has that key been there all these years?"

She nodded and rolled back the tambour, opening the desk.

"Damn! If I'd only known..."

"Don't feel bad," she snorted. "Mack Lee and your grandmother couldn't find it either. The desk was a present from James's Uncle Howard. It had been in his office before he retired. He was a doctor, you know. It galled the two of them that they didn't have the key. I'm pleasantly surprised the old witch never took a crowbar to it!"

According to the desk's lock plate, it had been fashioned by the Gunn Manufacturing Company of Grand Rapids, Michigan. Its red oak panels bore a honey-wheat stain and had been lovingly maintained since its purchase sometime in the 1890s. Inside, the cubbies and drawers were crammed with letters and drawings. There were *hundreds* of them. Some were bound together with twine, others by rubber bands, and more than a few were loose-scattered over the writing surface as though they had recently been read...or reread.

Observing James's puzzled expression upon seeing the mass of letters, she explained, "Jimmy and I knew each other when we were kids, but he left home for ten years. We met again just before he was inducted into the army in 1965. His relationship with his immediate family was, let's say...strained. So, he asked if he could write letters to me. I said yes, and he did. I wrote him back, and he wrote more. He told me about his life. Some parts I already knew...or thought I did. The rest was all new and fantastic. Through our correspondence, we fell in love.

"With us having been married for less than a week, your father knew that I didn't really *know* him, at least not as well as he wanted me to." She stared sightlessly into the middle distance for a moment, then continued, "During his second tour in Vietnam, he redoubled his letter writing. He said that he wanted me to know *everything* in his past, everything he thought was important. That way, I might understand him better when he finally came home, but then...he didn't come home."

Shaking her head slowly and dabbing away a tear, she said, "I'm sorry!"

After a moment, she regained her composure and said with a wistful smile, "It's all here."

On Becca's bidding, James sat at the desk. The old swivel chair creaked and groaned in protest. He selected a random letter from the stack and began to read. After a few moments, he paused. "Mom, how is it that you have letters in here addressed to Howard Hines? Was that the Uncle Howard you mentioned?"

"Yes, he was your fathers grand-uncle, your great-grandmother Mary's younger brother. He took your father in when he left home after his little sister died. James absolutely adored the man. Some years after Uncle Howard died, Charlotte, his wife, came across a bundle of correspondences from James. She called and asked if I'd like to have them, and of course, I did, which reminds me." Becca turned and walked out of the room. "Come with me. I'm going to need your help."

James rose and obediently followed his mother to her bedroom closet.

"That shoebox up there, on the top shelf." Becca pointed. "See if you can reach it and bring it back into the living room. When Charlotte sent the other letters, she sent this box along too."

Returning to the desk, Hamilton smiled. It was an old Buster Brown shoebox and *damn* if that dog didn't look creepy! He sat in the creaky old desk chair and opened the box. Inside were more letters, hundreds of them. He riffled through and noticed they'd been chronologically filed with postmarks dating from 1956 to 1965. Over the years, the handwriting on the addresses evolved from a childlike scrawl into tiny, crabbed, adult-appearing script.

Across the front of each letter, written in a flowing hand he vaguely remembered, James read, "Return to sender. Addressee unknown."

"Isn't that Grandma Hamilton's handwriting?"

Becca nodded.

"But why?"

Becca gave a rueful shake of her head. "Why did that woman do *anything*? You should read them. I have." She gestured to the letters. "They were all unopened until then."

James selected the first letter and began to read. In it, a little boy, Jimmy—his father—described his new room to his mom and dad. He wrote of how much he missed them and how he hoped he'd be able to come home soon. In another, he described a cat named Kitty Lamarr and the silly things she did.

James smiled, thinking about the bond between a little boy and his pet, then continued to read. It appeared that his father had written at least one letter each week for nine years. He chronicled his daily life, the things he did and the books he read. He wrote about mowing lawns, learning to draw, and learning to shoot. Later, he described his adventures in college. Regardless the topic, he ended each letter with an affirmation of love for his parents and an expression of hope that he'd be allowed to come home soon.

Becca sat in a rocking chair, knitting as James read. When he finished the last letter in the box, he looked up and asked, "Why'd he have to leave?"

"On his eighth birthday, your father accidentally shot and killed his little sister. Your grandmother never got over the loss. Even though he was just a little boy, she blamed him solely for her death. Of course, Mack Lee had carelessly left a loaded gun for your father to find, but Margaret always had a blind spot when it came to Mack Lee. In her eyes, he could do no wrong. Your father, on the other hand, could do no right. As Margaret's mental health declined, your grandfather began fearing that she'd do your father bodily harm, so he sent him away to live with Uncle Howard."

James listened attentively to his mother's explanation. "Man, that's harsh!"

"In truth, Jimmy was much better off living with his uncle. He absolutely adored Uncle Howard. I only met him once, at our wedding, but I assure you, the feeling was mutual. He was a delightful man. When he retired and moved to Scottsdale, he had his old desk sent here for Jimmy, saying he could use it someday when he eventually became a doctor. Like father, like son."

"How'd he wind up in Vietnam? I mean, if he was in college, wouldn't he have had a draft deferment?"

Becca nodded. She lay aside her knitting and walked over to the desk. She riffled through the letters before selecting one. "Here, read this one," she said, handing him a letter from October of 1965. "I think he explains it better than I could."

James accepted the proffered letter and began reading. A moment later, he put it down again. "So, Grandpa Hamilton died. Jimmy takes a semester off from school, thinking Grandma needs him at home, and while he's there, he gets drafted. Talk about rotten luck."

James continued reading throughout the afternoon. Becca left him to his reading, answering questions whenever they arose. Twice the phone rang but was allowed to go to the answering machine. As the day dragged on, she brought him a mug of coffee, but he was so engrossed in the letters, it was long cold before he tried the first sip.

Becca was about to ask him when he'd like to pause for supper when, suddenly, he dropped the letter he was reading onto the desk. He rushed to the window and held his arm out straight with his right thumb out, like he was thumbing a ride. As she watched in puzzlement, he blinked one eye closed and then the other. He cycled from the right to left eye repeatedly, then replicated the entire process, this time using his left arm and thumb.

"I'll be damned," he said with a laugh. "I'm left-eye dominant! Mom, do you have a pie plate or something else I can use as a target?"

A bewildered Becca fished a foil pie pan from the cabinet. No sooner than she handed it to him, James was out the door. Her bewilderment became alarm when he opened the trunk of his car and removed a locked gun case and a box of ammunition from it.

"James?!"

"It's okay, Mom. I'm left-eye dominant," he replied, as though his answer explained everything. "Come see!"

Equal parts worried and curious, she followed James to the compost heap behind the barn and watched as he carefully positioned the pie pan at its base.

James stepped off fifty feet and removed the pistol from the case. It was a .45-caliber Kimber Ultra Carry Model 1911 he'd purchased after 9/11. Back then, it had *almost* seemed like a reasonable way to *permanently* turn off the constant playback loop in his head. He shuddered at the memory.

He loaded it and told Becca to cover her ears, then he emptied the magazine in the general direction of his target. Only one round struck the pie pan. Unfazed, he ejected the magazine and reloaded. Once again, he took aim and emptied the pistol, but this time he fired lefthanded. The grouping wasn't particularly tight—he'd never tried shooting lefthanded before—but all seven rounds struck the pie plate.

"Yes," James exclaimed, pumping the air with his fist. "Left-eye dominant, baby!" Then he policed his spent brass—old habits never die—and collected the pie pan. It was a shame, he thought, that he couldn't pass along the news of this finding to his old Range Master. "It's not striking a match with a .22 rifle from fifty yards away, but nobody's gonna tell *me* I can't hit the broad side of a barn again, either," he mumbled.

"What was that, dear?"

"Nothing, Mom. Just remembering something."

Together, they walked back to the house. There was a slight grade, and James noticed that Becca seemed to tire easily, but he made little of it. As they walked, he happily explained the concept of eye dominance to her in nauseating detail. By the time they reached the house, Becca appeared markedly short of breath, pausing to rest in a lawn chair before climbing the stairs to the back door.

"Mom, are you okay?"

"It's nothing, James," she panted. "I just need a minute."

"It certainly doesn't look like nothing to me. Maybe we need to get you in to see a doctor?"

"Already been."

"And..."

"We can talk about that later. Besides, I'm better already. See?" Becca rose and climbed the stairs. "Now, are you about ready for supper? The pot roast should be about ready, so go and wash up!"

James did as he was told. By the time he returned to the kitchen, Becca already had the plates filled. Pot roast had always been his favorite meal as a kid. and the aromas wafting through the kitchen were already making his stomach growl.

During the meal, Becca managed to keep the conversation going along avenues other than her health. Only once, when James casually mentioned the large array of pill bottles on the counter, did the conversation near the edge of her comfort zone. Luckily, it was time to serve the key lime pie she'd made for dessert, allowing her to deftly elude his query yet again. She knew her condition would have to be discussed eventually, but not tonight. Tonight was all about her son getting to know his father. Her health would wait... it had to.

James rose from the table and began clearing dishes just like he'd done as a boy. Old habits never die. "Mom, that's probably the best meal I've had in six years," he said, rubbing his stomach.

"That's some high praise coming from somebody who's been eating MREs for the past six years," Becca quipped. The military's Meals Ready to Eat were known more for being filling than for being even remotely palatable. She smiled at his compliment all the same.

"There is that," James agreed. Then, as though the thought had just struck him, he asked, "Hey, whatever happened to Uncle Howard? I don't remember meeting him as a kid."

"No, you wouldn't have. He died back in 1968. I think still I have the newspaper article." Becca scurried back to the desk in the study. She returned a moment later brandishing a newspaper clipping, yellowed with age.

James accepted the proffered article from the *Scottsdale Sun* and read. After a moment, he asked, "Do you think he *really* flew loops beneath Navajo Bridge?"

Becca nodded. "Yeah...probably."

James laughed, handing the clipping back to Becca. "He sounds like quite the character! I wish I could've gotten to know him."

"Me too."

James and Becca chatted companionably as they washed and dried the dishes. Afterward, he returned to the old roll-top desk and stacks of letters as she puttered around the kitchen a bit longer. He read them chronologically, mentally collating the letters written to Uncle Howard with the ones written to Becca, and two points became immediately evident.

First, it was clear that his father—James still struggled with the concept—tried to protect and insulate Becca from the horrors of war. He smiled thinking about it. He'd done the same with his letters and calls home from Afghanistan and Iraq. Maybe the apple hadn't fallen far from the tree? In contrast, the letters Jimmy had written to his uncle pulled no punches. In those letters, he freely expressed his doubts and concerns about how the war was being waged.

The second point was equally clear. Jimmy Hamilton was falling in love. He may have begun his letter-writing campaign as just a soda jerk who used to help Becky Hansen with her homework, but by October of 1966, the boy was totally besotted. At first, this seemed odd to James. How does someone fall in love just from writing letters? But the more he thought about it, the more it made sense. In the days before telephones, telegraphs, and jet travel, would not a boy write a letter and send it by sailing ship to a girl? She'd receive it a month or so later and write him back. They never saw each other, but over time, through their correspondence, they grew close. Eventually, after months or even years of nothing but letters, they'd meet and marry. Hamilton smiled. Jimmy, his dad, had been an eighteenth-century romantic trapped in a twentieth-century world.

After finishing up in the kitchen, Becca briefly joined James in his letter-reading marathon. She stood beside the desk, providing a running commentary to accompany each letter. However, she fatigued quickly and soon retired to her bedroom.

James watched Becca as she left the room. She'd lost a lot of weight since he'd seen her last. *What, six years ago?* Her clothes hung loose over her gaunt frame. His mother looked and acted old. But she wasn't. She was only sixty. Something was wrong. He could sense it. He almost followed her to her bedroom to get some answers but thought better of it. Maybe she really *was* just tired? He resolved to ask her about it tomorrow, then selected another letter and began to read. In it was a description of how a drunken soldier named Ballentine wandered into a minefield and got his leg blown off. Apparently, Jimmy had plunged right out into the minefield to save him.

Holy shit!

The grandfather clock chimed midnight, and James yawned reflexively. Maybe he should get some rest too. He'd barely put a dent in the collection of correspondence, and there was no way he'd be able to finish in one night. With that, he rolled down the tambour, turned out the light, and padded upstairs to his old room.

CHAPTER 30

MARCH 2008

THE NEXT MORNING, JAMES WOKE to the intermingled aromas of bacon frying and coffee brewing. He took a quick shower, dressed, and went downstairs to join his mother in the kitchen. There, she offered him a cheek that he was only too happy to kiss. It had been *way* too long since he'd been home.

At his offer to help with breakfast, Becca lowered her chin and stared at him over the rims of her glasses. "Yeah, like that's *all* I need. The best way you can help is to sit yourself down at that table and keep me entertained. If you feel like you've just got to do something more tangible, you can set the table while you're talking. But stay out of the way!"

"Ma'am, yes, ma'am!" James stood at attention and rendered a smart salute.

"I guess maybe the army wasn't such a bad thing for you after all," Becca said, turning back to the stove. "You've learned to respect authority and to obey lawful orders."

They enjoyed a laugh as James collected plates and silverware and placed them on the table.

"So, what did you learn about your father last night after I went off to bed?"

James pulled out one of the chairs from the table—the same one he'd sat in as a kid—and sat down. "Well, if nothing else, I think I understand why you almost had a coronary when I developed my fascination with the Vietnam War after watching *Platoon*."

"Ummm...ya think?"

"Yeah. Actually, I'm a little surprised you didn't lie down on the tarmac in front of the plane that was going to take me off to DCC."

"I tried, but with the heightened security after 9/11, I couldn't get past..." Too late, she realized her banter had drifted into dangerous territory for her son.

James froze as a kaleidoscope of images flickered through his mind.

"Oh God, James. I'm so sorry. I was just..."

James was shaken. After six-and-a-half years, nothing had changed. The heartburn, Old Spice cologne, dripping AC vent, and that damned cockroach were all still there. He shook his head to clear the images from the worst day of his life. Then, wrestling the present back onto his brain's main screen, he figured if his dad could run out into a real minefield to rescue a stranger, he could damned well rescue his own mother from this virtual one. It wasn't her fault.

He managed a weak, "It's okay, Mom. It was a long time ago." After a pause, he said, "Just before I went off to bed last night, I read a letter from November 1966. In it, Jimmy—I guess I should get used to referring to him as Dad—asked you to come and visit him at Walter Reed. That seems a pretty brazen ask for some random soda jerk who tutored you in high school math. Did you go?"

A wave of relief swept over Becca at the change of subject. "Silly, of course I did!" she replied.

"Your parents just let you go? Did one of them go with you?" he asked with a smile.

"Oh, I didn't ask. I called them from the bus station in Spartanburg and told them I was going about five minutes before departure. They were *not* pleased!"

"I can't imagine why!"

"Two of life's greatest truisms, my son. It is far easier to get forgiveness than permission, and love conquers all! And I was totally and helplessly in love. Nothing would've kept me away. I figured Jimmy had already closed the distance between us by ninety-four percent, so why shouldn't I be able to cover the last six percent?" Then she added with a wink, "Your father was always fond of using math to support his arguments. You look a lot like him, you know. Same boyish good looks, same lopsided smile, same emerald-green eyes, and the same flyaway hair. And you're both more intelligent than anyone has the right to be. The resemblance is uncanny, really.

"When I arrived at Walter Reed, I'd not seen your father for over a year. The changes were scary. His cheeks were hollow, and he could barely walk, but that lopsided grin was the same. The doctors told him he had a pocket of blood between his brain and the inside of his skull that was putting pressure on his brain. The pocket was slowly expanding, and unless the blood was drained and the bleeding stopped, he could become paralyzed or even die. He needed to have a hole drilled into his head to release the blood and relieve the pressure on his brain.

"On the day after Thanksgiving, he had his surgery. When I saw your father afterward, with all those bandages and wires, he looked like one of those space aliens from Area 51. You know, the ones with the skinny body and huge heads? I was there when he woke up...and he smiled. That's when I knew he was going to be okay.

"I had to leave him on Sunday to get back to school. My parents were mad enough already. I'd already missed a Sunday at church that they were going to have to explain. Heaven forbid I miss a day of school too. They would have been 'irretrievably *scandalized*'!" she said, making air quotes and with a hint of bitterness.

"There was Hell to pay when I got back home. I think I only stopped being grounded...oh, about this time last year," she chortled. "Jimmy recovered quickly after his surgery. His vision cleared and his headaches abated almost entirely. Soon, his balance and gait were both back to normal. After he was released from the hospital, he was given four weeks leave before having to return to that terrible place. He spent those four weeks back here in Boiling Springs. We saw each other every day, albeit on the sly since I was still under *house arrest*.

"One day in late December, I snuck away from home and met him at the Rexall Pharmacy in town. I had a hot fudge sundae. He had a Coca-Cola and kept sneaking bites of my sundae whenever I *pretended* not to be looking. Out of no-where, he asked me to marry him! I thought he was joking, so I said, 'Sure!' But he wasn't joking. He pulled a ring out of his pocket and held it out to me. It had the tiniest little diamond chip you've ever seen. I didn't know what to say, so I said yes."

James smiled. "Was that the ring you used to wear on a chain around your neck when I was a kid?"

"Ha! Still do!" she said, pulling the chain from beneath her blouse. "It really used to piss off Mack Lee, which in ret-rospect was a bonus. The very next day, your father showed up at my father's store and asked to talk with my daddy, wanting his blessing to marry me. He was old-fashioned that way. Daddy turned him down flat and threatened to fill him full of buckshot, said he should anyway for *disgracing me* by seducing me away to Maryland. Like anything could possibly have happened as weak as he was in that hospital bed. Ooooh, it still makes me angry just thinking about it!

"But your father didn't give up. He was determined to marry me with or without Daddy's blessing. So, we eloped. I think somehow he knew we wouldn't have another chance. It was then or not at all. I was perfectly happy having a Justice of the Peace perform the ceremony, but your father wouldn't hear of it. He thought it important that our union be *ordained by God.* He was adamant! So we looked everywhere for a preacher, priest, or rabbi...anybody who'd be willing to marry us. One after another refused. Some didn't believe I was really eighteen, and it was just a week after my birthday. Others wouldn't marry us without six months of premarital counseling. Still others refused because we weren't members of their congregations or parishes.

"Finally, we found a preacher to perform the ceremony. He was the chaplain for the Spartanburg County Jail. Your father got his ball and chain applied *at the county jail*! Can you believe that? I teased him about it for months.

"After the ceremony, he took me back home. After supper, I snuck out of my bedroom window with my suitcase. Your father met me at the street with a car he'd borrowed from God-only-knows-who and we were off to Spartanburg. We spent our honeymoon at the Howard Johnson's on Pine Street. We only had five days before your father had to return to Vietnam. But we loved enough in those five days to last a lifetime...and enough to give me you.

"And *that* was a problem for my family. My parents were livid that I'd snuck off and gotten married. My father was well into annulment proceedings with one of his attorney buddies when my pregnancy began to show. Convinced they'd be ostracized from the Baptist church by my 'scandalous behavior'—they *had* raised a strumpet, after all—I was unceremoniously kicked to the curb, completely disowned by my own family." A lone tear trickled down her cheek.

"I was completely taken aback. I never would've expected such from my own family. Certainly not after they'd been so supportive of my older brother when he decided to dodge the draft and go to Canada! I suppose there are different standards for sons versus daughters," she said bitterly.

"Remarkably, Jimmy came to my rescue from half a world away. Although not on the best of terms with Margaret, your grandmother, he contacted her by telegram, no less, and promised to send the lion's share of his military pay to her to support me. The rest, he sent to me. That's how I wound up living in this house"—she motioned her arms in an expansive gesture—"with her and Mack Lee.

"When your father enlisted in the army, he accrued a two-year active service commitment. Before he was wounded, he'd agreed to serving both years in Vietnam. It may seem foolish and it cost him his life, but he believed in what he was doing. He thought that Vietnam was somewhere he could put his talents to the greatest use for his fellow soldiers and for the poor Vietnamese people. I think it gave him a sense of purpose. Jimmy planned to get out of the army after his commitment had been fulfilled, finish college, and then go on to become a doctor like his Uncle Howard. But you know what they say about making plans. Your father was an avid reader. It might have been better for him if he'd remembered Tolkien's words from *The Hobbit*. 'It does not do to leave a live dragon out of your calculations, if you live near him.' For your father, the war was his dragon.

He didn't count on the dragon having plans of its own, or teeth. He went back to the war in Vietnam and never came home again."

James put a hand on his mother's shoulder. "You know he's coming home now, don't you? They've found him. There's going to be a ceremony for him...at Arlington."

"I know. But I don't think I can go."

James blurted, "What? You've *got* to go!"

"They can never bring back the sweet man I knew...the man I adored. I can never hear his laugh or feel his arms around me. Those are lost to me forever. All that's left of the man I loved are the stories he told me via the letters in this desk."

James took his mother into his arms and kissed away a salty tear from her cheek. "No, you also have *me*, and now you'll finally have a chance to say *goodbye*."

Becca patted her son's hand. "I said my goodbyes decades ago, sweetie. But I'll try to go, if only to be there when *you* meet him."

"You'll *try*?"

Becca pulled out a chair and sat down beside her son. Taking both of his hands in hers, she said, "There's something I've been meaning to tell you, but the time was just never quite right. I'm not so sure there'll ever be a good time, so here goes." She laid out the details of her cancer recurrence calmly and completely.

James couldn't help but think that she'd done a better job of talking about her diagnosis, prognosis, and treatment options—or the lack thereof—than any of his former surgical residents could've done back at Wash U, and probably even some of the attendings. That did not, however, prevent him from suggesting alternative treatment strategies, or at least the consideration of second opinions from the premier cancer centers at MD Anderson, Mayo Clinic, or Sloan Kettering.

Nor did it prevent Becca from declining all. "James, honey, I'm all right with it. We're all going to die sometime. Most people don't know how or when. I do, and I get to go out on my own terms." She stroked his hair like she'd done when he was a little boy. "And with you being home again, I even get to say goodbye to the people I love. Besides, the way I look at it, I've been waiting for *forty-one long years* to be with the *only* man I've *ever* loved. In a month or maybe two, the wait's gonna be over and we'll *finally* be together."

There were no letters read that day.

CHAPTER 31

THE LAST LETTER

J AMES SPENT THE ENTIRETY OF the next day reading the correspondences his father had posted during his second tour in Vietnam. Some were newsy. Many detailed his hopes and dreams, especially those in regard to Becca's growing pregnancy. He wrote about the music and bands he found interesting. He wrote about his cat, friends, and fellow GIs. There was the triumph he felt when each friend rotated safely home, and the sense of helplessness when one was lost or severely injured by the war. It was evident that he took each loss personally. His letters were often about his family and projected a melancholy that practically bled from each page. He discussed his mom and dad and the demons each had battled with varying degrees of success. He wrote of Mack Lee and his Uncle Howard, and, frequently, he wrote about Anna. Clearly, he'd never come to terms with her death. He missed her terribly and most often spoke of his need for atonement. There were letters detailing his childhood, the time spent with his uncle and in college. For many of these, he provided illustrations.

James smiled. *Dad was a pretty decent artist. I guess talents skip a generation.* The overriding tone of his letters was guilt over Anna's death being slowly replaced by a budding hope for the future. His letters were a chronicle of a life lived and dreams for a future that would never be realized.

The stack of letters dwindled as James read. In the next-to-last letter, he recognized his mother's flowing script. Paperclipped to the letter was a typed note.

Letter found in uniform pocket and
returned with personal effects.
Referenced photograph was not located.

James thoughtfully fingered the rust-colored smudges on the page, took a deep breath, and began to read.

October 2, 1967

My darling James,

Congratulations, my love! Instead of being the husband to a wife the size of a barn, you are now officially a <u>daddy</u>! Our baby arrived at 8:21 last evening. He's a big boy and has all the right number of fingers and toes... and he's <u>beautiful</u>! No, I am not biased! Everyone agrees. He's perfect! He has a full head of hair, and his eyes are shaped just like yours. Although they are currently blue, I hope that they will eventually turn green like yours. You have such pretty eyes.

I have enclosed a photograph taken with one of those new Polaroid cameras. Polaroids are really wonderful. You just snap the picture and a few minutes later, you can see the developed photograph. There is no more waiting two weeks to have a roll of film developed at the drugstore. Isn't that grand?! I will send more pictures with my next letter.

Your mother even seems pleased about the baby's arrival and that is saying something since nothing pleases that woman. I mustn't complain. She is allowing me to live in her house, after all.

I am doing well. Labor lasted just short of forever yesterday, and I still feel rather tired. Oh, they are bringing in dinner now. They say I must eat to regain my strength. First, I was eating for two and now they say that I must eat to keep up my strength. I think that the world is conspiring to keep me fat! I want to be slim and pretty for you when you come home. I miss you and cannot wait to introduce you to your son.

Oh, I almost forgot! His name is James Wiley Hamilton, Jr. I hope you like it. He's named after the most wonderful man in all the world. I love you, my darling! Come home to us safe and soon!

With love and kisses,

Becca

James recognized the letter for what it was...and for what it had been. He'd removed and cleaned far too many "last letters from home," unfinished letters to moms, wives, and sweethearts from soldiers' pockets during his six years in the Middle East. He swallowed hard as he reached for the next letter.

October 18, 1967

My darling and most beautiful Wife!

Becca, today, you have made me the happiest man on the planet! I thought when you agreed to marry me last December that I could never be any happier. I was wrong. I was certain when we were married in January that I could not possibly be any happier than I was that day. Again, I was wrong. In April when you told me that you were going to have our baby, I was absolutely <u>positive</u> that there was no <u>conceivable</u> chance that I could ever be any happier than I was then. I have never been more wrong about <u>anything</u> in all my life!!

When I opened your letter and that photo of you holding our little boy fell out, I found out exactly how wrong I was. I started jumping up and down and screaming at the top of my lungs. That scared the Hell out of poor Rikki-Tikki-Tabby. Poor cat is probably down a couple of lives from the fright. Then I went tear-assing around the compound, wearing nothing but my skivvies, holding your letter in one hand and the picture in the other. I showed it to EVERYBODY, all my buddies, the gate guards, the chaplain, the old Vietnamese lady who does laundry, even to people I didn't know. They all got to see! I even ran into the camp commander in the compound and showed <u>him</u>...and he even overlooked the fact that I forgot to salute!

There is so much that I want to do with our son. Is it too early for me to buy a ball and glove? We'll go fishing together, and I'll teach him to shoot. I can tell him stories and read him books. I can give "sage fatherly advice" and teach him to love, respect, and totally adore his mother. That part should be easy. All he has to do is watch me!

Since I've had a few years of college, the army has offered to send me to OCS, that's Officer Candidate School. It is quite an honor but would entail several more years of active military service. Whereas I don't mind serving, I have no desire <u>ever</u> to be away from you again. Consequently, I have officially declined the offer. Instead, in two more months, I will happily put the army behind me, come home, and be the husband you deserve and the best father a little boy could ever want to have.

What's this nonsense about you being as big as a barn? To me, you are as beautiful as the day you walked into Rexall and ordered that first root beer float. Actually, you are more beautiful, for now you've given me our son! I love you more than life itself and cannot wait to show you when I get home!

This morning, I thought the coolest thing that could happen today was seeing an Edwards's pheasant outside the wire. Boy, was I wrong. Your letter blew that one totally out of the water. Still, the Edwards's pheasant was my little sister's second favorite bird when we were kids. It is supposed to be quite rare and it's the first one I've seen in almost two years in Vietnam. Luckily, Rikki-Tikki-Tabby didn't see him or the species would be even rarer! I made a quick sketch that I'll include with this letter. It's no "John Gould," but it's pretty good, if I say so myself. I keep looking for a long-tailed broadbill, that was Anna's very favorite, but so far, I've had no luck.

It may be a week or two before I can write again. Intel puts a fair-sized NVA force somewhere north of here, and I think there are plans afoot for my unit to root them out. So I will probably be busy. Although I may not be able to write, my thoughts will be of you and of our perfect little boy. You shall always be in my dreams. Know that the breeze you feel caressing your cheek as you fall asleep will be my softest and most tender, loving kiss.

And know without any doubt, that I love you and our little son with all my heart! I will write again as soon as I can. Give our boy a squeeze for me!

Your loving husband,

Jimmy

A lump formed in the back of James's throat. There were no more letters.

CHAPTER 32

APRIL 14, 2008

T HE FLUIDITY IN ADJUSTING TO a new reality that James had shown while going through all those letters had been impressive, and he'd assimilated it all so easily. Becca supposed she shouldn't have been surprised. His memory being what it was, all he had to do was glance at a page and it was his forever. Still, her son had digested a lifetime of information in only a few days. She was glad that he seemed so ready to accept Jimmy as his father. He and Jimmy were *so* very much alike—about as much as he and Mack Lee had been different.

Becca shook her head slowly. "I should have told him about his father sooner..." She supposed all decisions are elementary when made in retrospect.

It was wonderful having James home again. Of course, she had talked with him by satellite phone or via video chat almost every week—perhaps not precisely at three o'clock every Sunday, but frequently enough—while he'd been away to war, but this was different. It was better. He gave the *most* wonderful hugs—always had—and you just couldn't get that by Skype. She was glad to have this last bit of time with him before...before the end, though she longed for more.

Becca enjoyed making breakfast for James each morning, and today, she was making his childhood favorite, bacon waffles. She plugged in her old waffle iron and was relieved to find it still worked. Then she took a large mixing bowl from beneath the sink and poured in two cups of flour, a tablespoon of baking powder, and a pinch of salt. She separated two eggs and whipped the whites before adding them to the bowl, along with three tablespoons of melted butter. Next, she added in the yolks and stepped over to the refrigerator for milk.

She hummed to herself as she poured the one-and-a-half cups of milk into the bowl and was startled to feel milk splashing onto her feet. How could she have missed? Confused, she stared at the countertop. But now, rather than one bowl, there were two...and they appeared to be swimming about one another in midair.

James heard a loud crash and ran to the kitchen. To his horror, he found Becca on the floor, actively seizing. He rushed to her side and knelt down, cleared her airway, turned her on her side, and waited for the seizure to pass.

It was Becca's third seizure in a week. With the first, he'd called 9-1-1 and rushed her to the emergency room. When she had recovered enough from her post ictal state to realize where she was and what was going on, she chastised him for taking her to the hospital. "I'm on hospice, you dolt! If something happens to me, you call *my hospice nurse*, not an ambulance."

Chastened, James had learned his lesson. When the seizure passed, he scooped his mother into his arms—she was light as a feather—and carried her to her bedroom. There, he gently washed her, because she'd soiled herself during the seizure, and redressed her in a fresh gown. When he was convinced that she was resting comfortably, he called her hospice nurse to report the seizure and then returned to the kitchen to clean up the mess.

As James cleaned, happy childhood memories of his mother played in a continuous loop on the big screen in his mind. In every phase of his life, she had always been there for him, good times and bad. From scraped knees to spelling bees, she'd always been there. Hers had been the first face he'd seen upon his emergence from the abyss after Elliana died. She'd provided a firm mooring to reality, to the present. But soon, she'd be gone. James knew he had to wrap his mind around the concept and be strong for her, just like she'd been for him.

As pictures from a lifetime of experiences flickered past at lightning speed, James just didn't know how to—or if he even could—do it.

Becca slept throughout the rest of the day, waking a bit before midnight. She needed to go to the bathroom but *really* didn't want to move. Her bones ached and even breathing hurt. She coughed, and immediately, her back was on fire. She glanced to the bedside table to her right. *Thank God!* The MS Contin and Dilaudid were both there, right where they were supposed to be, and James had even thoughtfully left a glass of water beside it for her. Now, all she had to do was reach over and take them.

It just hurt so much to move. She knew she could call for James. He'd be there in a flash to take care of her. *He's such a good boy.* She knew he wouldn't complain but really didn't want to bother him. Instead, she struggled herself into a sitting position and was immediately racked by a wave of pain and nausea. Sweat broke out on her forehead and back, soaking her hair and gown. After a few minutes of sitting perfectly still, the pain abated enough for her to swallow the pain medications. Soon, the meds kicked in and her pain dialed back to manageable levels again.

One problem solved. Next, the bathroom...

Last week, James had procured a bedside commode for her. Although it was right there by the bed, she didn't like using it. The idea of sleeping right next to a pot full of her own waste offended her sensibilities. Besides, her bathroom was only a few feet farther away and certainly she could manage the distance. Couldn't she?

Standing, she was immediately beset by dizziness. It soon passed, and she plodded slowly to the bathroom, one hand on the wall for support. There, she did her business, flushed—much better than a glorified chamber pot—and stood to wash her hands. Pain and dizziness struck her again, and she slumped against the wall by the sink until it passed.

Gazing about the tiny room, her eyes lit upon the old claw-foot bathtub by the wall. She loved that tub. It had always been her happy place, something of a refuge. As she waited for her pain to abate, she thought how wonderfully soothing the warm water would feel against her aching bones.

After a moment, she filled the tub. She dropped in a bath bomb and slowly disrobed. She stepped into the bath, carefully lowering herself into the water. It was the perfect temperature and came up almost to her chin as she reclined. The heat relaxed her muscles, and the water's buoyancy relieved the stress off her screaming joints. It felt heavenly.

After a few blissful moments, Becca began to doze.

"Hey there, Ponytail! One root beer float comin' up."

"Aww, Soda Pop, you always know what I need. You're gonna help me with my homework again today, right?" Becca asked.

She was back at Rexall Pharmacy again. Jimmy was there, tending the lunch counter. Other than the two of them, the place was empty. The record dropped on the old Wurlitzer, and Joni Mitchell began singing "Both Sides Now."

Jimmy slid the float before her, and she took a sip. It tasted heavenly—just like always—but this time, the glass stayed full in spite of multiple sips.

"I'm supposin' I can. Looks like the rush has passed us by today. We have the place to ourselves." Jimmy gestured to the empty lunch counter. "How may I help?"

"It's James..."

The scene changed. Now Becca and Jimmy were back at the Howard Johnson's on Church Street. They were in bed, and she was in his arms. Outside the window, the sign for Burger Chef Hamburgers & Shakes flashed on and off, intermittently illuminating dust motes eddying above the rattling heater vent in their room.

"...he needs me here, but I don't know how much longer I can stay..."

The scene morphed again, and they were back at the lunch counter.

"Actually, the solution is quite simple, Becca. All you've got to do is..." Jimmy began describing a complicated formula full of variations and derivatives, but try as she might, she couldn't make out his words.

The scene changed again. Now Becca and Jimmy were in the chaplain's office at the Spartanburg County Jail on their wedding day. But instead of the chaplain, Uncle Howard was officiating the ceremony while wearing a vintage World War I flight helmet and goggles.

"But I don't understand," Becca was saying.

"That's all right, child. You don't have to." Uncle Howard glanced toward the ceiling. "Someone else does."

"But James..." she began.

Uncle Howard smiled serenely. "I have it on very good authority that your James is going to be just fine."

Jimmy said nothing but nodded his agreement.

Becca woke with a start and bolted upright in the bathtub. She coughed out a mouthful of water and gazed around the room, finding nobody there but her. She released the stopper, and the water began to drain.

Moving like one in a trance, she stepped from the bathtub and dried herself. She brushed and combed her hair before plaiting it into a loose French braid. She had pretty hair. She folded and rehung her bath towel before returning to her bedroom. Remarkably, she felt no pain. From the chest of drawers, she selected her favorite nightgown and slipped it over her head. Then, she reclined atop the bedspread, folded her hands over her chest, and drifted off to sleep.

That's how James found Becca the next morning, totally at peace, her bluish lips set into a beatific smile. As the first tear rolled down his cheek, he reached for the phone and dialed her hospice nurse.

CHAPTER 33

O N THE DRESSER IN BECCA's bedroom, Hamilton found a large manila envelope. His name was written on the front in large block letters and circled twice in red. He smiled. Apparently, his mother had left nothing to chance. In the envelope, she had detailed her wishes. All he had to do was call the associated telephone numbers and everything would take care of itself.

As he read, he determined that Becca wished her body to be cremated and did not desire a large funeral service. She'd figured that after she was dead, she wouldn't care and a circus of mourners and well-wishers would place an undue stress upon him. He clamped his eyes tightly closed at the realization. Even though she'd been dying, his mother had been thinking of *him* and *his* needs. *The woman was a saint!*

Clearly, Becca had known her son. Even the small, relatively intimate memorial service she'd planned, he found to be overwhelming. Although James appreciated the kindness of the well-wishers, he rapidly became stressed and overstimulated. With every kind word or remembrance extended to him, another picture populated his mind's eye, one that nothing could make fade. By the time the final mourner departed, he found it a challenge simply discerning which of the pictures playing in his mind were memory loops and which represented current reality.

Somehow, he made it home after the memorial service. There, he immediately went to his room, undressed, and lay on his bed. He did not emerge from the house for three full days and hardly even moved, as his brain struggled to achieve equipoise. Images of his life danced and shimmered on the screens of his mind like starlight on a calm sea. Every time he tried to focus upon any one, it flitted away and disappeared, only to be replaced by another.

His mother had always provided a safe harbor and a secure mooring. For several years, Elliana had assumed those roles. Now, both were gone. He had no close friends, certainly none in the continental US, and now had no family either. For the first time in his life, James was totally alone, adrift on the tides.

Desperate, and with nowhere left to turn, he thought to call Dr. Malone at the Institute for Memory Studies in Columbia. For a full hour, he fought his way through the Mobius loop that served as the IMS's automated phone tree. No matter which number he selected, he kept getting kicked back to the initial recording. Finally, after completing his forty years of wandering in the desert, James was inexplicably connected to an actual human in the director's office.

There, he learned that Dr. Malone had retired almost a decade earlier.

"Probably tried to call his office and got tired of waiting," James muttered irritably.

The far-too-perky receptionist either didn't hear James's complaint or elected to ignore it. "If you'd like, we can get you in to see Dr. Sydney Freedman."

Through the phone, James heard the clicking of a keyboard.

"It looks like Dr. Freedman has a cancelation for tomorrow. Two o'clock? Would that be too—"

"I'll take it?"

"Very well, Mr. Hamilton."

No one had called him "mister" in ages. It actually felt good.

"We'll see you tomorrow at two. Do you need directions?"

"No," he deadpanned. "I think I can remember them."

The next morning, James drove to Columbia, arriving at the IMS almost an hour before his appointed time. As he waited, he casually flipped through several magazines, some of which he was pretty sure he'd read when he was last there in 1980.

When his appointed time came, the receptionist led him back to Freedman's office. Freedman was moderately obese, and his white, short-sleeved dress shirt looked as though it had been purchased when the man was thirty pounds lighter. He was completely bald and featured a particularly prominent forehead. Taken as a whole with his undersized shirt and perpetual smile, he resembled a small beluga whale.

"Dr. Hamilton, it's so nice to meet you," Freedman said, stepping around his desk and extending his hand.

Shaking the man's hand, James replied, "My pleasure, Dr. Freedman. Thank you for seeing me on such short notice."

"Are you kidding? You're a legend around here. Your file is required reading for all new hires. Hell, they even used you as a case study when I was taking my oral exams back in

'99. This is a great honor, sir. I never expected we'd have the opportunity to meet."

James blushed. "All that for me? You've got to be kidding!"

"Not at all. Your case is even featured in Eddleston's *Encyclopedia of Memory Disorders*. Your memory is really most unusual...very unique. Since you were here in 1980, they've come up with a name for your condition. It's called, hyperthymesia, also known as highly superior autobiographical memory, or HSAM for short. If Malone had chosen to write you up back in '90, you would've been the first documented case in the modern era. As it was, that honor went to a subject known as AJ, out at U. Cal. Irvine just two years ago! Yours is an exceptionally rare condition— only about sixty documented cases—but has been shared by persons such as Julius Caesar, Napoleon Bonaparte, Nikola Tesla, and Marilu Henner."

"Marilu Henner? The actress from that TV show, *Taxi*?"

Freedman nodded reverently before retreating behind his desk and sitting down. James took a chair opposite him while casually glancing about the office. To his left was the requisite wall of diplomas, certifications, and awards. A bookshelf full of textbooks dominated the wall to his right. On the corner of Freedman's desk sat a plaster bust of who James presumed to be Mnemosyne, the Greek goddess of memory, displayed prominently among family photos— wife, children, and *probably* grandchildren. On the wall immediately behind his desk hung a motivational poster featuring a blood-red rose growing from a field of snow. The caption featured a quote from James Matthew Barrie, the creator of *Peter Pan*. It read, "God gave us memory so that we might have roses in December." Another poster, unattributed, read, "Today is tomorrow's memory. The choice is yours, so make it a good one."

James and Freedman chatted amicably for several minutes, engaged in the typical "feeling-out" period between a doctor and a new patient. After some invisible cue, Freedman stopped chatting, put on his doctor hat, and asked, "So, Dr. Hamilton, you've not been here in quite a while. What brings you back to see me today?"

James filled Freedman in on his life since 1980. At one point early in his narrative, Freedman interrupted him briefly, triggering the intercom button. "Miss Duncan, please cancel the rest of my appointments for today. Thank you. I'm sorry, Dr. Hamilton. Please, go on."

After completing his story, he began with a description of his multiscreen picture-in-picture memory display and his inability to turn it off for any extended periods of time. He also detailed the things he'd attempted for short-term relief.

Freedman was fascinated but kept his responses noncommittal. "Um-hum...I see," being the most common.

As James wound down, he practically begged Freedman for help. "Dr. Freedman, I've got to make it stop. Something *has* to give! How do I make these memory loops go away? Otherwise, I'm going to lose my mind. Help me!"

Freedman remained quiet for almost a minute, long enough for James to think he'd zoned out or gone to sleep. When he finally spoke, it was with a non sequitur. "I love roses. I have since I was a child. My grandmother cultivated them, you know. Sadly, I did not inherit Grandmother Freedman's green thumb. I think I could probably kill silk flowers. There are three things I know about roses. First, roses are beautiful. Second, roses have thorns."

James's patience began to wane as Freedman droned on about his damned rose fetish.

"And finally, third, I'd rather live in a world where there are roses than in a world without them."

James was on the verge of standing up and leaving the office.

"Memories are a lot like roses. They can be beautiful. They can be painful. But it is better to have them than to have no memory at all."

James relaxed again in his chair. Maybe there really *was* a point to all this after all.

"The key, Dr. Hamilton, is not to make your memories go away. Instead, it would be much more favorable to create some form of random-access memory, like on your computer, where the memory might be stored until it's needed. You know, to sort of reduce the number of windows open on your display, if I may continue the analogy."

James leaned slightly forward in his seat. This was getting interesting. The tiniest seed of hope began to sprout.

Freedman paused briefly, then, from *way* out in left field, he asked, "Dr. Hamilton, have you read J. K. Rowling's *Harry Potter* book series?"

James wanted to scream but instead managed a muted, "No."

Freedman nodded. "Well, in that case, I'm going to give you a homework assignment. From your file, I see that you are an exceptionally fast reader. I want you to read the *Harry Potter* series start to finish and see me again next week."

Before James could object or ask clarifying questions, Freedman had ushered him from his office and he was holding an appointment card for his one week return visit. Bewildered, frustrated, and summarily dismissed, he did the only thing he could do and still maintain any hope of getting help. He found a Barnes & Noble and, over the next week, read about the boy wizard and his friends. He completed the series as directed but felt no closer to a solution for his problem of being crushed under the weight of his "perfect" memory.

When James arrived at the IMS the next week, Dr. Freedman met him at the door to his office and greeted him like the prodigal son returning.

James, however, did little to conceal his annoyance. "I came here on the verge of losing my mind, and all you did is recommend that I read a children's book?"

If Freedman even noticed James's irritation, he gave no indication. "Indeed I did, although I'd argue that *Harry Potter* is more of a coming-of-age tale than a children's book."

James wasn't sure exactly what reaction he'd expected to his objections, but it certainly wasn't *this*. Consequently, he was left speechless. This man's tangential, often flippant approach was mind boggling. James's mind reeled as Freedman ushered him into the office and into a chair before taking his own seat behind the desk.

"Dr. Hamilton, you seem puzzled by my approach to your concerns. Although my methods may appear, on the surface, unusual, I assure you, I take your problem very seriously."

James nodded.

"Allow me to summarize, if I may. You do not have the capability of forgetting. Your lifetime of memories plays as a continuous loop within your mind. You continually relive every moment of your life, good or bad, as though it was occurring at that very instant. You have many such loops playing at any time that you are unable to suppress, and now they are impairing your ability to function in your current reality. Not an uncommon scenario for people with HSAM, hyperthymesia, if you prefer."

Again, James nodded. The doctor had described him to a T. Maybe Freedman wasn't nuts after all?

"Dr. Hamilton, are you familiar with the concept of the 'memory castle?' "

"That's a memory technique where one changes memories into images placed in a familiar mental location. The idea is that one can mentally walk through their castle looking at the memories to recall them and thereby be capable of remembering long lists of data. But, Doc, remembering isn't my problem. I can't *forget*."

"Precisely. *That's* why I wanted you to read *Harry Potter*."

Maybe he is nuts, James thought.

"You seem incredulous. Allow me to explain. In *Harry Potter*, Lord Voldemort created horcruxes from objects or persons about him to hide pieces of his soul and thereby make himself immortal. I want you to create *memory* horcruxes from objects around *you*. It's sort of the opposite of a memory castle, but you ascribe a certain memory, good or bad, to an object within your world. That object—it can be anything—serves like a thumb drive, a memory stick, there when you need to access the stored memory but off the big screen and in a drawer when you don't. This memory exercise won't make you forget, but day-to-day, it should allow you to function more comfortably."

James had never heard of anything even remotely like the exercise Freedman was suggesting, and it sounded just crazy enough to work. So he spent the next week creating memory horcruxes.

The brushed urn containing Becca's ashes became his first horcrux. To his surprise, the technique actually seemed to work. After he'd focused memories of his mother there, several screens in his mind blinked off. Next, he concentrated memories of Elliana into the engagement ring he'd once given her. Uncle Howard's rolltop desk absorbed the memories of James learning about his father. Other horcruxes included a playbill from *Mamma Mia!,* the caduceus medical insignia from his army uniform, and a photograph of the Twin Towers in flames. With each horcrux formed, another replay screen blinked off.

James couldn't believe how liberating it felt not having to watch the worst—or even the best—moments of his life repeatedly. He felt free. He strongly suspected that he'd be creating horcruxes for the rest of his life, but that would be a tiny price to pay for feeling, if not normal, then his version of it.

When he returned to Freedman's office the next week, Hamilton was a changed man. He was resting well and, for the first time, he felt totally at peace. Freedman's technique had transformed him.

"How did you know it was going to work?" James asked.

"I didn't. I made it up on the fly. The important thing is that *you* believed it would work. The mind has a great capacity to heal itself. We just had to get out of the way to give it the chance."

James laughed. He didn't know if Freedman was joking or serious, and at that instant, he didn't care.

CHAPTER 34

JUNE 6, 2008

A BRILLIANT WHITE, ANVIL-SHAPED THUNDER-HEAD BOILED into a cornflower-blue sky. Intermittently, a strobe of lightning flashed near its darkening base, a harbinger of the storm to come. On the breeze was the sweet, cut-watermelon scent of freshly mown grass. In a nearby maple, a pair of cardinals called, "Tea-kettle, tea-kettle, tea-kettle." Whether urging one another to prepare for harsh weather or simply enjoying the sound of their call, James could only guess.

Every sight, sound, and smell triggered an image in his mind; a vision of the childhood that was, and another of the one that might have been.

The *clop, clop, clop* of a horse-drawn caisson and the marching feet of the military honor guard and chaplain soon drowned out the birds. The detail leader called a halt as the caisson arrived at the gravesite.

James felt oddly detached as these events unfolded. This was his second funeral for a parent in as many months, and this service was for a man he'd never met. Still, the solemnity, precision, and attention accorded by the military to even the most trivial of details moved him. Clearly, this ceremony meant as much to these men and women as to the small cluster of onlookers at the graveside. Perhaps even more. For the hundredth time that day, he wished his mother could've been there. Cancer had robbed her of the opportunity to say a last goodbye to the man she loved. He took solace in the knowledge, or at least the hope, that perhaps they were already together and watching the ceremony from afar.

The Officer in Charge, Noncommissioned Officer in Charge, and chaplain exchanged salutes, and an NCO secured the flag against the freshening breeze. They invited onlookers to be seated, and the military chaplain delivered the homily. Although blessed with an uncannily capacious memory and near-perfect recall, James later couldn't remember a single word the man had said.

James shook himself from his reverie and noticed that everyone was standing. Apparently, the chaplain had finished and the service was over. He scrambled to his feet, and a moment later, three rifle volleys cracked. Somewhere in the distance, a bugler played "Taps." Afterward, the chaplain directed all to be seated.

The Casket Team stepped forward and expertly folded the flag. Their precise and well-practiced movements created a perfect triangle, folded with the union out. The team leader presented the folded flag to the NCO in Charge. She placed three spent cartridges into the folds and passed the flag to the Officer in Charge. The OIC accepted the flag, performed an about-face, and marched to James. There, with great solemnity, he presented the folded flag to James and snapped a crisp salute. He then performed another about-face and marched to the graveside.

"Detachment, left face! Forward march!"

The Casket Team and Honor Guard marched away to a silent count.

A flash of reflected sunlight drew James's attention to a general officer in Air Force blues standing a respectful distance from the ceremony. The officer—*Was that Chalmers?*—gave a slight nod, turned, and walked toward the Visitor Center.

As the officer strode away, James noticed the phalanx of serious-appearing young men in dark suits, each wearing mirrored sunglasses and ear buds. *Had they been there before?* He was about to ask an onlooker if the men were part of the ceremony when he noticed a shiny black Cadillac limousine slowly approaching along York Drive. The limo sported an American flag over the right front fender and another fluttered over the left in the breeze.

The presidential seal?

The first enormous drops of rain began to explode around him. *This is going to be quite a storm,* he thought. He smiled, appreciating the petrichor, the earthy smell rising from the soil.

To his astonishment, the limousine came to a stop only a few yards away, and another serious-looking young man stepped before him. "Sir, would you mind stepping this way, please?" He motioned toward the limousine.

Although grammatically posed as a question, James had spent enough time in the military to recognize a command when he heard one. "Certainly," he said and followed the Secret Service agent to the limo.

Before he had taken three steps, the rear door opened and out stepped the president of the United States. "Good afternoon! Alex Prescott." He held out his hand to shake.

"M-Mr. President," James spluttered, accepting the proffered hand.

"Colonel—scratch that. *Doctor* Hamilton. You've already separated from the army, I understand. I hope you will forgive me for intruding upon your father's interment ceremony?"

"I... Of course, Mr. President."

"Good...good." He nodded. "The weather is about to turn unpleasant. May I offer you a ride?" He gestured to the open limo door.

"With you, Mr. President?"

"Depends on whether you're a Republican or a Democrat." The president laughed. "Of course, with me. The Secret Service would have a conniption if I let you ride in the trunk with all their Uzis and rocket launchers."

After losing the popular vote but winning the requisite electoral vote in his first presidential election, Alexander had won his second term in a landslide. Now, in his final year in office, he still maintained an amazing 59 percent approval rating—an incredible feat in a divisive time where partisan politics was the norm.

After only thirty seconds in the man's presence, James could see why. The man's charisma was palpable.

James settled into the presidential limousine, also known as "the beast." He had to admit, for what basically amounted to a plush decorated tank, the seats were rather comfy.

"Dr. Hamilton, I was very sorry to hear about your mother's death. Metastatic cancer, I'm told. I wish I could've met her. I'm told that she was an incredible woman."

"Thank you, Mr. President. She was. You seem...very well informed."

"Would you expect any less?" The president grinned. "After all, the FBI, NSA, CIA, DIA, and a half-dozen other intelligence agencies *do* report to me. Not to mention my fleet of black helicopters and, if you believe the tabloids, the intel services of a race native to Alpha Centauri."

James chuckled. "Point taken, Mr. President. I suppose the better question is *why* are you so well informed about *my* family, sir?"

The president brushed an imaginary fleck of lint from his lapel, remaining silent for several seconds.

Fearing he had overstepped, James held his breath, poised to make an apology.

"Dr. Hamilton." The president swallowed. "I had...the distinct honor of serving in Vietnam...with your father." The words came as though from far away. "I was there when he died."

James was dumbstruck. "You knew my father?"

"Do you have plans for dinner, Dr. Hamilton?"

James opened his mouth and then closed it. *So many questions...*

"I would be honored if you'd join me and Kimberly. And then, I will tell you the story."

Heat rushed to James's face. *Say something, dammit!* He exhaled, "Of course, Mr. President. I would be honored."

The president settled back, and the limo continued to the White House. He chatted companionably about sports, Hamilton's plans after leaving the military, and what actions were needed, in James's opinion, to improve quality and access to healthcare in America. James, although hardly able to focus on the conversation after the president's revelation, found the man to be an excellent listener and to have a quick and incisive mind.

As the beast pulled onto White House grounds, President Prescott turned to him. "Dinner will be in the family dining room around seven, give or take. Attire will be totally *in*formal. Sneakers and open-collared shirts are okay. I have some issues to attend to in the Oval for a few hours, but I know Kimberly would be delighted to give you the *nickel tour* and show you around the house. It'll only cost you a dime." He winked. "Inflation."

James nodded, biting his lip. *This is wild!*

"Also, the Lincoln Bedroom is open if you'd like to stay the night as my personal guest. I can have your bags delivered from your hotel. The Ritz-Carlton Georgetown, isn't it?"

"Once again, Mr. President, you are remarkably well informed."

The president shrugged.

The president shrugged! He managed to say, "Thank you, Mr. President. I would be honored, sir."

At the White House, the president was immediately ushered away toward the Oval Office with a cadre of staffers nipping at his heels like a pack of rabid chihuahuas.

James's reception was far more pleasant. He was met by Kimberly Prescott, the First Lady of the United States, and a warm smile. She was wearing a peach-colored sundress that contrasted her wavy chestnut hair. Other than her wedding ring and a pair of simple pearl earrings, she wore no jewelry. But for tiny crow's feet at the corners of her eyes, she might easily have passed for a woman twenty years her junior. His first impression of her was that of elegant beauty. If what he'd heard about her was true, *she* was the brains behind the Prescott presidency.

"Madam First Lady, it's a pleasure to meet you," James said, extending a hand.

She accepted his hand with a firm shake. "The pleasure is mine, Dr. Hamilton, and just call me Kim. 'Madam First Lady' is too much of a mouthful." Her reply seemed as genuine as it was disarming.

James found himself smiling in spite of himself. "Yes, ma'am, but only if you'll call me James."

"Very well, James." She linked her arm through his and motioned to a corridor on the left. "Shall we?"

Over the next hour and a half, Kim Prescott led James through hallways, nooks, and back rooms. He found the First Lady to be charming, funny, and informative. She talked about Dolly Madison and how she'd saved many priceless works of art from destruction as the British burned Washington during the War of 1812. She recited dozens of different White House ghost stories and told funny anecdotes about previous presidents and first families. James laughed heartily at the story of how President Taft had once gotten stuck in his bathtub.

Before the tour ended, James asked, "Do you mind if I ask how you and the president met? What's your story?"

The First Lady laughed and, glancing at James's bare left hand, teased, "Are you looking for pointers or are you a plant from the tabloids?"

James flushed.

"Why, Dr. Hamilton, I would never have taken you for the type to blush. This may be something of a protracted tale. Shall we sit?" she asked, gesturing to a bench beneath a portrait of Teddy Roosevelt.

They sat and Kimberly Prescott began her tale.

"Alexander was a senior at Princeton. With his wavy blond hair, boyish good looks, effortless charm, and dry sense of humor, he'd been all the rage at every frat party and sorority mixer. He was considered by all to be quite a catch, but he'd determined early on *not* to be caught! It was in the fall of 1963, after the annual Princeton-Harvard football game, when Alex Prescott finally ran out of line and found himself hooked. Manning the tackle was none other than, *moi*, Kimberly Morgan Arquette. I had him hooked, gaffed, and landed before he even realized there was bait in the water. Funny thing is, I wasn't even fishin' at the time. I think it was just meant to be.

"It was my junior year at Wellesley, and I was just getting over a horrible breakup. One of my friends suggested that I come visit for the annual Harvard-Princeton football game and I agreed. After the game, we went to a bar. Would you believe, Alex rescued me from a bar fight?"

Hamilton laughed. "You're joking, right? I have a hard time wrapping my head around the two of you involved in a barroom brawl."

"Well, that's what happened. After that chance encounter, we started dating. By Thanksgiving, we were serious. By Christmas, we were in love. By Easter, we were engaged. And that, Dr. Hamilton, is our story. Are you sorry you asked?" she said with a laugh. "Shall we continue your tour?"

The tour ended half an hour later, outside the Lincoln Bedroom.

"This is our final stop," she said. "I have it on good authority that your luggage has been delivered, and if Morris is up to his usual tricks, everything will have already been put away. If there is anything you need, just dial number seven on the bedside phone. Someone will be by to collect you when it's time for dinner. In the interim, feel free to explore, take a shower or a nap, or grab one of the books from the shelf. Is there anything you need?"

"No, Mada—Kim." James still could not get used to calling the First Lady by name. "Well, maybe one thing."

"Yes?"

"Why?" He gestured expansively. "Why all of this for me?"

"Ah-ah-ah, *that's* for the president to tell. Not me. Barring the outbreak of World War III, you'll find out this evening." She smiled. "Dinner is *supposed* to be at seven, but more likely it will be more like seven-thirty. I swear that man's *never* on time. If you need a snack beforehand, dial number seven and the chef will whip something up for you. See you seven-ish."

Morris delivered James to the private dining room promptly at seven. After the First Lady's admonition regarding her husband's penchant toward tardiness, James was pleasantly surprised to find the president already there and thumbing through a briefing book. He'd even had an opportunity to exchange his suit and tie for a pair of pressed khakis and a golf shirt from the Ocean Course at Kiawah Island. The First Lady, he noticed, had retained her sundress but added a single strand pearl necklace to complete her ensemble.

The three engaged in small talk as the chef served a grilled chicken salad with a Dijon vinaigrette and an excellent Grgich Hills Estate Napa Valley Chardonnay.

The president tasted the wine and held up his glass. "I try only to serve domestic wines here at the White House, and why not? In a publicity stunt to celebrate the US Bicentennial in 1976, a British wine merchant named Spurrier organized a blind tasting of the six top California wine producers against the top wine producers of France. Back then, it was generally agreed that fine wine *only* came from Europe and nobody gave us 'colonials' a snowball's chance in Hell of scoring well. However, when the scores were tallied, the 1973 Chateau Montelena Chardonnay and a 1973 Cabernet Sauvignon from Stag's Leap Wine Cellars—both from California—won the competition. They were named the best white and red wines, respectively, *in the world*!

This tasting would later become known as 'The Judgment of Paris' and it put US winemaking on the map. A bottle of each now resides in the Smithsonian's National Museum of American History in their '101 Objects that Made America' exhibit.

"Of course, the French poo-pooed the results, saying that although the California wines may have scored well during the initial tasting, the Californians couldn't *possibly* age as well as French wines. So, thirty years later in 2006, they staged another blind tasting using the same wines and vintages tasted in 1976. And you know what? Our American wines kicked their asses *again!*" he said with a smile.

"In 1973 a Croatian émigré named Miljenko (Mike) Grgich was the chief winemaker for Chateau Montelena Winery in Napa Valley. When Mike left Chateau Montelena, he opened his own winery, Grgich Hills. I happened upon it some years ago during a campaign stop in Northern California and made it the official White House 'house white' after I took office. I think that was one of my proudest moments as president. It's one of my favorite Chardonnays, Dr. Hamilton. I hope you'll enjoy it as much as I do!"

James nodded.

"Dr. Hamilton, quite reasonably, you are wondering why I have requested that you join us this evening. I'm now prepared to give you your answer." The president pushed back his chair and stood, raising his wine glass to eye level. "But first, I would like to propose a toast...to James Wiley Hamilton"—he paused for a beat—"*Senior*, a man without whom I would not be here today."

James nearly spilled his wine as he stood to touch glasses with the president and First Lady.

"I'd like to tell you a story," the president said.

CHAPTER 35

JUNE 6, 2008

S OME PEOPLE ARE BORN TO greatness whereas others have it thrust upon them. Alex Prescott III, to his dismay, fell firmly into both categories. It had always been assumed that he would join the family business. And why not? From time immemorial, had not the smith, after a lifetime of toiling at the forge, passed his hammer on to his son? Had not the mason passed his trowel to the younger hands and stronger backs that followed him? Cops begat cops. Firefighters begat firefighters. Miners begat miners. Each father passed a lifetime of knowledge and experience on to the next in line, hoping the subsequent generation will have as much, or even more, success than they'd had themselves. This had been the natural way of the world since time began and would likely continue until its end.

When your name is Alexander Wentworth Prescott III, of the Manhattan Prescotts, there was little difference. That your grandfather was *the* Alexander Wentworth Prescott, Speaker of the United States House of Representatives from 1930 through 1946, and your father was Alexander Wentworth Prescott II, a five-term United States senator from New York and senior-ranking member of several prominent

Senate committees changed your fate not at all. The difference was that rather than wielding a hammer or trowel to create and build, you wielded influence and power to build a political machine designed to propagate still more influence and power.

As a Prescott, it was Alex's destiny to turn the wheels of government and pull the levers of power. It had been so for over five decades, and would continue to be so, if Prescott II had his way. Alex was born to it. He was bred for it. And he hated the very *thought* of it. But no one said "No" to Alexander Wentworth Prescott II. It simply was *not* done. In short, he was screwed.

Disdain for his fate notwithstanding, Alex looked every bit the prototypical politician. He was tall, slightly over six feet, and had an athletic 190-pound frame honed by his time as captain of the Princeton lacrosse team. In addition, he was charismatic, funny, and although not a prerequisite for a successful politician, he possessed a nimble mind.

With a master's eye for election optics, Prescott II had insisted that Alex join the military after graduation. Using his position as Chairman of the Senate Armed Services Committee, he would, of course, arrange for a nice, comfy posting for his son, something close enough to the front to claim "war service" but far enough removed that his son's greatest risk for injury would be a strained back from carrying some three-star's golf bag.

Alex agreed with his father's "suggestion" that he should join the military, albeit with entirely different motivation. He cared not one whit for politics but was a fervent believer that it was the duty of every able-bodied American to serve his country, especially in times of war. He eschewed Prescott II's offer of a cushy staff job and enlisted in the army. Since he was a college graduate, he attended Officer Candidate

School and received a second lieutenant's commission. After OCS, he went to jump school and was assigned as 1st Platoon Leader, B Company, 2nd Battalion, 503rd Infantry, 173rd Airborne Brigade of the 101st Airborne Division in Vietnam.

In October of 1967, US Intelligence reported a division-sized force of North Vietnamese from Pleiku moving into Kontum Province in the Central Highlands of Vietnam. The NVA objective was to attack and crush the American Brigade located at Da'k To in a lead-up to what would later be known as the Tet Offensive. Consequently, NVA forces infiltrated and fortified several ridges around the air base at Da'k To.

In early November, a series of firefights had occurred on Hills 724, 882, and 1416. On November 19th, the 2nd Battalion of the 503rd was ordered to take and hold Hill 875. Lieutenant Colonel Saad, the battalion commander, acting contrary to the "recommendation" of his superiors, divided his force. He sent Alex's B Company to the crest where they were caught in an elaborate ambush and immediately surrounded. With an intense firefight on all sides, his company suffered heavy casualties.

By anyone's estimate, Alex Prescott was having a bad day on November 19, 1967. First, and perhaps most obviously, he'd been shot. Although he would recover fully from his injuries, being shot would never be anybody's idea of a good time.

Second, the platoon the lieutenant commanded—*his* men—had been decimated by enemy action. That he'd been ordered onto the hill upon which his men were subsequently ambushed really wasn't relevant. Somebody had to take the blame for the debacle, and it certainly wouldn't be the ones who gave the orders. That just wasn't the army way. And it sure as *Hell* wasn't the way things got done in Vietnam! And as long as the bigshots were ladling out blame, they might as well tag him for a "friendly fire" incident for which he had no control and couldn't possibly have prevented.

Next, in a more pernicious development, Alex's immortal soul had been sold to the devil. In point of fact, he hadn't even realized his soul was on the market. Had he been, perhaps he might have worked out a better deal. That the bargain basement price, two lumps of silver fashioned into the shape of eagles, was all the sum his immortal soul had garnered? Well, that was nothing short of embarrassing. That his *father* was the devil manning the cash register only added insult to injury. Now that old bastard owned him lock, stock, and barrel, and there wasn't a goddamn thing Alex could do about it.

As if that wasn't bad enough, he had incurred a debt to a man who he would never be able to repay even if he lived for a hundred years. *What is a hundred years,* he thought. *36,525 days...876,000 hours...52,596,000 minutes...* It really didn't matter. Every second, he knew, was borrowed time, a gift from a man he hadn't even known and now never would.

The president took a sip of his Chardonnay and leaned back in his chair. For a moment, he sat silent, staring unseeing off into the middle distance, or back in time. Then, he began to speak.

"I was positioned about twenty yards from the crest of the hill with my radio operator, an M60 machine gunner, and three riflemen. We'd dug in behind a deadfall overlooking the mouth of a draw, up which the North Vietnamese were pushing troops. It was a strong position from which we could enfilade the entire upper section of the draw.

"Our position was holding up pretty well until Charlie brought up an RPG. A round detonated just to the right of Peterson, our machine gunner. The shockwave blew his eyeballs right out of their sockets! A fragment drove through the receiver on the M60, rendering it useless. Another splinter gave one of the riflemen, a private named Basaraba, a scratch under his left eye. Or, at least, he claimed it was a splinter. He'd always been something of a malingerer, so he might have just scratched himself with his bayonet for all I know.

"A medic showed up a few minutes later and immediately started working on Peterson. I didn't know the medic and didn't learn his name until much later. He wasn't from our company and we were too busy for introductions, but I'll never forget how calm the guy appeared. He seemed more like someone sitting down to a family picnic than a guy in the middle of a firefight. He calmly took Peterson's canteen, rinsed off the eyes, stuffed them back into their sockets, and bound them in place with a bulky dressing. The medic was about to cart Peterson down to the aid station when Basaraba started screaming, 'What about me? I'm wounded too!'

"The medic stopped and leaned Peterson against a tree, crawled over to Basaraba, and asked where he was hit. Basaraba gestured to the scratch on his cheek. I'll never forget what that medic said. He examined the scratch and said, 'So...you want a Band-Aid for that, or what?' " He chuckled at the memory.

"Basaraba started screaming, 'Screw you! I'm outta here! This is my third wound, my ticket out of this shithole country! I'm going to the aid station. Then I'm getting the Hell home!' About that time, another of the riflemen, Kaplan, got hit by a burst from an AK. He was dead before he hit the ground. The medic checked him out, but there was nothing he could do to save him. By this time, Basaraba had already started walking down the hill toward the aid station. The medic called out, 'What the fuck, man?! If you're going, at least take Peterson with you.'

"Basaraba held up both middle fingers and kept walking. I was watching this scene unfold when the medic turned back toward me and suddenly drew his pistol, aimed it at *me*! He fired twice, readjusted his aim, and fired again. Two NVA soldiers who'd been coming over the deadfall behind me sprawled to the ground, dead at my feet.

"Our position was about to be overrun. I motioned the radioman over to me and called in close air support. We popped yellow smoke and hunkered down behind cover and waited. A Marine Corps A-4 Skyhawk flying out of Chu Lai piloted by Major Joe Boyd took the call from the forward air controller and rolled into his bombing run. He radioed, verifying seeing our yellow smoke. Although aware that the smoke represented the perimeter of our lines, he pickled two two-hundred-fifty-pound Mk-81 Snakeye bombs well *inside* that perimeter. The first, thank God, was a dud. The second struck a tree and detonated in an air burst directly over the Battalion Command Post and Aid Station. Twenty men were killed instantly, and another forty-four were wounded in the worst 'friendly fire' incident of the war. The bodies of four men were never found and were believed to have been vaporized by the blast. One of the bodies unrecovered was that of Private Basaraba.

"By then, the NVA had brought a heavy machine to bear on our position at the head of the draw. I could hear the deep, rhythmic *pom-pom-pom* of a Chinese .50 caliber ripping through the deadfall. Heller, the last of my riflemen, was practically cut in half by a burst, killed instantly. When Wilson, my radioman, was hit in the neck and shoulder, the medic went to work on him immediately.

"It's funny the things you perceive when in battle. Time slows down, and you notice things. The medic *always* placed himself *between* the enemy and whichever soldier he was ministering to at the time. He got hit twice in the legs by rifle fire but didn't even flinch while he was caring for Wilson. It was like he hadn't even felt his own wounds.

"Then I got hit. Took a .50 caliber round through the right lung, a 'sucking chest wound,' I was later told. As a trauma surgeon, you certainly know all about those, Dr. Hamilton, but I sure as Hell didn't and wish I still didn't. The medic crawled to where I'd fallen and rolled me over. He gave me a shot of morphine and put a plastic patch over the exit wound in my back. I remember him rooting around in his pack for something that apparently wasn't there. Not finding what he was looking for, he hesitated for an instant and then took something out of his shirt pocket. He taped it over the entry wound in my chest, and almost immediately, it became easier to breathe.

"About that time, another NVA soldier hopped the deadfall and came at us. The medic put four rounds into Charlie's chest, dropped his empty .45, and grabbed mine from my holster. He leaned me against the deadfall and was immediately struck twice in the chest by a sniper firing from somewhere back in the brush. I remember seeing him look down at his chest, spurting bright red blood with each heart-beat. He looked back up at me—no, actually, he looked past me—and slumped to the ground. A second later, a grenade rolled between us. I couldn't move. Wilson was down. The medic clearly was dying, but I saw his right arm flail toward the grenade and draw it beneath him. An instant later, it detonated. His body absorbed the entire blast, otherwise all four of us would have been killed. As it was, the medic was the only"—uncharacteristically, the president's voice cracked—"the only one...killed or injured.

"About that time, I heard a Skyraider diving overhead. An instant later, there was a blast of heat, followed by screams as burning napalm washed down the draw. That's the last thing I remember before waking up in the hospital.

"The surgeon taking care of me back at the hospital said that that he'd found a Polaroid photograph of who he *assumed* were my wife and baby taped to my chest when I came in off the chopper. He said using that damned photo had been one of the cleverest battlefield improvisations he'd ever seen and it likely had saved my life. Since he assumed the photo was of *my* wife and child, he thought I might like it back."

The president opened a folder next to his plate and removed an ancient, faded Polaroid photograph and passed it to a stunned James. "I thought I remembered the medic's nametape but was unable to confirm it until years later. But, unless I miss my guess, the infant in this photograph, Dr. Hamilton, is you. On November 19, 1967, a man I believe to have been your father saved my life four separate times. With the third time, he did so by giving me his most prized possession in all the world—this photograph—and with the last, his life. *That* is why I invited you here today, Dr. Hamilton."

James sat thunderstruck. With each of the president's revelations, another tumbler had clicked into place in his mind. *My father was a hero. He loved me...and maybe I'm a little like him.* A tear welled in his eyes but did not fall.

The president continued his narrative. "When I recovered sufficiently from my wound, I sought to find information about the medic so that he could be put in for posthumous decoration. I thought the Medal of Honor would have been more than appropriate for his actions on November 19th. My commander, Lieutenant Colonel Saad, had other ideas. He said, and I quote, 'The army is not in the habit of doling out medals to soldiers for committing suicide.' The bastard! I was dumbfounded. Instead, after finding out who my father was, Saad awarded *me* a goddamn Silver Star for Valor! He said that three NVA soldiers had been found a few feet from me, killed by the .45 pistol found by my feet. When I tried to explain that all I'd done was get shot, he'd hear nothing of it. He said, 'The paperwork was fast-tracked and has already been approved by General Westmorland. There's no changing it now. You're a hero.' Inexplicably, a week later, Saad was promoted to full Colonel, well below the zone and *way* ahead of his peers. Given his rather impressive fuck-up—"

"Language, dear!" Kimberly chided.

"I'm sorry, dear! Given Lieutenant Colonel Saad's *major error in judgment*"—the president glanced briefly toward his wife—"and disregard for orders *against* sending my company up that hill, he should have been court-martialed rather than promoted.

"That medic, your father, saved my life *four* times and lost his own in the process. All I did was bleed, but they gave me a Silver Star...and eventually an office in this house. Your father lost his life to give me this." The president made an expansive gesture with his arm. "Then his remains were lost and his heroism forgotten. But I didn't forget. I could never forget. When I was informed that his remains had gone missing, I made it my life's cause to *find* James Wiley Hamilton and *bring him home*! It was the least I could do. When I'd risen sufficiently high within the government to allow such, I founded the Joint POW/MIA Accounting Command and sent teams into Vietnam to find him and other brave men who paid the ultimate price for their country but never made it back home.

"With the first JPAC mission, three sets of remains were recovered and returned to the States. Two were readily identified. The identity of the third remained a mystery for fourteen years. I was recently informed that a very clever Air Force officer who, coincidentally, had been a part of that first recovery mission, had discovered a means to identify the third set of remains. The remains were those of my medic, your father, Corporal James Wiley Hamilton.

"It had been my hope that I could express my gratitude both to you and your mother for Corporal Hamilton's sacrifice. Regrettably, fate has robbed me of the opportunity to thank your mother, but I hope that you, Dr. Hamilton, will accept my deepest and most heartfelt thanks. Tomorrow, Dr. Hamilton, at nine a.m., there will be a small ceremony held in the Oval Office in your father's honor. He is, among other things, to be posthumously promoted to Staff Sergeant. It is my fervent hope that you will attend. Dress, this time, will be more formal as there will be a photographer and potentially a few members of the press. Will you please join us?"

James was stunned and nearly speechless, but somehow managed a choked, "Yes, sir!"

"Excellent! Whenever you're ready for breakfast, just ring the steward. I shall see you in the Oval at nine."

The president and First Lady rose and took their leave.

CHAPTER 36

LATE EVENING

J AMES WAS USHERED BACK TO the Lincoln Bedroom. It appeared the presidential valet had been busy during his absence. Hamilton found his suit had been cleaned and pressed. His shirt was freshly laundered, pressed, and lightly starched. Three Turnbull & Asser herringbone silk ties hung from the rack. None he recognized, but he liked them. His shoes bore a shine that would have brought a tear of joy to the eye of the toughest Parris Island drill instructor.

These guys don't miss a trick.

He undressed and slipped into bed. Although the bed was quite comfortable, he tossed and turned, unable to fall asleep. Images from his day spooled through his mind like an old-fashioned VCR on a continuous-play loop.

James had always wondered what *possibly* his mother had seen in Mack Lee—what could've induced her to marry the man. With Jimmy, it was easy to see the attraction. *That* union actually made sense. His father, Jimmy, had been a hero. He'd served honorably and even saved the future president's life. James shook his head admiringly and murmured to himself, "And using the Polaroid to seal a sucking chest wound? Well, *that* was nothing short of genius!"

Initially, the president and First Lady's stories had seemed incredible. But as James considered them within the context of other information he'd read or heard, Prescott's unlikely rise to the presidency made sense.

From the president's biography, James was aware that he'd married after his return from Vietnam. Shortly thereafter, at the age of twenty-six, he'd narrowly won a seat in the US House of Representatives for his district in upstate New York purely on name recognition. During three lackluster terms in the House, he put forth no significant legislation. He served on the House Committee on Veterans' Affairs but seemed little more than a "rubber stamp" vote for the chairman. But for fate, his political star might have fizzled and died in the House. Midway through his third term in the House of Representatives, Alexander Wentworth Prescott II, the senior senator from New York and a political powerhouse, died in office with one year left on his term. The governor of New York appointed Prescott III to his father's Senate seat as a placeholder until the General Election the following November.

The death of his father and Prescott's elevation to the Senate seemed to energize the young political scion. Finally, out from beneath the shadow of his larger-than-life father, young Prescott blossomed. The whiff of mediocrity that had suffused his House career seemed to diffuse overnight. He found his legs and his voice, and he exercised both immediately. He was named to a seat on the Senate Committee on Veterans' Affairs, immediately becoming an outspoken champion for veterans and their families. He often bucked the chairman and party leadership and showed a predisposition toward reaching across party lines to achieve bipartisan solutions to veterans' problems.

To the surprise of most Washington insiders, he easily held his Senate seat in the General Election the following November. He won a second and a third term in the Senate and rose steadily within the party hierarchy. After a scandal involving a senior senator from his party created an opening on the Senate Armed Services Committee, Prescott was named to the seat.

The "pet project" in each of Prescott's committee appointments had been Vietnam POW/MIA recovery and repatriation. To this end, he was instrumental in the creation and oversight of JPAC, the Joint POW/MIA Accounting Command. In the mid-1990s, JPAC sent its first search-and-recovery team into Vietnam.

By 1999, Prescott had risen within the Senate hierarchy and was named Chairman of the Senate Armed Services Committee. As a popular, well-respected senator from a state with twenty-nine electoral votes, it was no surprise when he was approached by party leaders about a possible run at the presidency. That he was happily married to his first wife and had no hint of scandal in his background were appealing to moderate voters from both parties, as was his prior military service. Early polling suggested he had sufficient national name recognition to be successful and that he might even be able attract moderate voters away from the opposing party without alienating his party's base.

Senate notwithstanding, Prescott had never considered himself to be particularly ambitious in terms of politics. However, he considered himself to be a good and honest man who had more to offer the country than his likely opponent, the somewhat disreputable vice president of the popular two-term sitting president. So, Prescott had agreed to run.

He'd won the party's nomination and run on a domestic platform of tax and healthcare reform. Additionally, he proposed pouring tax revenue into improvement of the nation's infrastructure and espoused giving people jobs rather than handouts. His ideas were solid, well-considered, and if implemented, would prove beneficial to the country at large. Unfortunately, his platform wasn't particularly captivating for the electorate.

Prescott's opponent was a lifelong politician who had spent the past forty-five years inside the Beltway in DC. Although he claimed California as his home-state, he had spent 107 *more* days in San Tropez over the past forty years than he'd spent at home with his constituents, a point Prescott pounded home during their second televised debate.

His opponent ran on a domestic platform of free college, free healthcare, and a national minimum wage of fifteen dollars per hour. When Prescott asked him to explain how he planned to fund his "free" programs, the VP's response was a "tax on the rich." The electorate loved it. "Free Program" was sexier and far more interesting than "Responsible Growth," especially if *they* were not the ones funding either. That the VP's proposal defined "rich" as anyone with a family pretax income of greater than $100,000, regardless of their number of dependents or local cost of living, was conveniently not mentioned.

Throughout the election, Prescott had held himself to the high ground, repeatedly refusing to green-light negative political ads. He'd always believed, "*If you're slinging mud, you're losing ground.*" His opponent, on the other hand, needed a dump truck for all the mud he was throwing. Still, the election remained close.

Prescott's opponent rode hard the coattails of his popular predecessor and chided Prescott's youth and inexperience in foreign policy. And the electorate seemed to agree. Two weeks before election day, Prescott had fallen behind in the key battleground states of Pennsylvania, Florida, and Missouri. Without a sweep of all three, the election was lost.

With the polls looking increasingly discouraging, Prescott's campaign manager, Alistair Wasserman, pleaded for him to approve an advertisement detailing his military record and decorations while contrasting the fact that his opponent had never served. To date, Prescott had only allowed his ads to state that he had served proudly and been wounded in service to the country. Wasserman begged him to reconsider his objections, pointing out the "large veteran population" in each of the contested states and suggesting that such an ad might sway opinion his way.

Prescott had inexplicably refused.

A week before the election, an independent Political Action Committee released a national TV advertisement with particularly heavy saturation in the battleground states. The ad's title was "The Hero of Da'k To" and quoted verbatim the citation accompanying Prescott's Silver Star Medal from 1967. The final shot of the ad showed a split-screen. On one side was a photograph showing Prescott in a hospital bed, heavily bandaged with a Silver Star pinned to his pillow. On the other was a photograph of his opponent wearing bathing trunks and a straw hat, holding a coconut shell cup and a scantily clad woman who was not his wife in his lap on the other. Beneath was the caption, "In a time of crisis, who would you rather have as *your* president?" Then, "PRESCOTT FOR PRESIDENT."

The following day showed Prescott surging in the polls and slightly ahead in Florida and Missouri. Pennsylvania was still too close to call, a statistical dead heat.

In spite of the good news, Prescott had been livid. He'd stormed into Wasserman's office, demanding to know if he'd had any knowledge of the ad before its release. Wasserman initially denied knowledge but later came clean. He pointed out that, because of the ad, Prescott would likely take the presidency. Although true, Prescott fired him on the spot.

James remembered pundits at the time had been stunned by Wasserman's firing. Wasserman, to his credit, kept quiet, and Prescott refused comment beyond, "We had a difference of opinion." Into this vacuum, the political analysts poured multiple theories attempting to explain Wasserman's abrupt departure, but none bore fruit or any resemblance to the truth.

A week later, Prescott lost the popular vote by 101,063 votes but carried all three swing states with their crucial electoral votes and won the presidency. With the closest election in American history to talk about, Wasserman's departure was rapidly forgotten.

Now it makes sense, thought James as he drifted off to sleep.

CHAPTER 37

JUNE 7, 2008

THE FOLLOWING MORNING, JAMES WOKE and enjoyed a relaxed breakfast in the White House private dining room. The First Lady popped in briefly to say good morning and inquire about his night but couldn't stay. Except for the intermittent staffers wolfing down bagels, fruit, or granola, he dined alone.

After breakfast, he returned to his room to prepare for the Oval Office ceremony. Although he understood the motivation behind the president's desire to honor his father, a ceremony in the Oval Office with *press* seemed over the top. In a political world, this might make perfect sense, but to his surgeon's brain, something didn't compute.

At ten of nine, there was a light tapping at the door. James opened the door, fully expecting to find the valet who'd been so helpful during his brief stay. To his surprise, instead of Morris, standing outside his door was Alan Schulman, the president's chief of staff.

The surprises continued after James's arrival to the Oval Office. Instead of a "few members of the press and a photographer," he found the room nearly packed. Already present and seated in one of the couches opposite the Resolute Desk were the Secretary of Defense, the Chairman of the Joint Chiefs of Staff, and the Army Chief of Staff. Clearly, there was more going on here than a corporal's posthumous promotion ceremony.

Shulman ushered James to one of the chairs flanking the fireplace. A moment later, the president strode in wearing a perfectly tailored charcoal-gray, double-breasted Yves Saint Laurent suit with a striped Salvatore Ferragamo silk tie. He strode to the fireplace, where he stood beside James. Flashbulbs popped, TV lights blazed, and a boom mic slid in place above them.

Without preamble, the president began. "My fellow Americans, we are gathered here today to honor an American hero, Corporal James Wiley Hamilton of Boiling Springs, South Carolina. Corporal Hamilton, who served with the 101st Airborne Division in Vietnam, is being promoted posthumously to Staff Sergeant. In addition, today I offer a citation to his son, Dr. James Wiley Hamilton II, that is some forty-one years overdue."

The president fished into his jacket pocket and put on a pair of reading glasses as a staffer handed him a portfolio. He quipped, "Although I know the story by heart, I want to make sure that I get it right. Corporal, now Staff Sergeant, Hamilton deserves that."

He opened the folio and began to read.

CITATION TO ACCOMPANY THE AWARD OF
THE CONGRESSIONAL MEDAL OF HONOR
TO
JAMES WILEY HAMILTON

Rank and organization: Corporal, U.S. Army, B Company, 2nd Battalion, 503rd Infantry, 173 Airborne Brigade

Place and date: Da'k To, Republic of Vietnam, 19 November 1967

Entered service at: Spartanburg, S.C., 19 October 1966

Born: 27 August 1948, Boiling Springs, S.C.

Citation: For conspicuous gallantry and intrepidity in action at the risk of his life above and beyond the call of duty. Corporal Hamilton distinguished himself by exceptional heroism while engaged in combat against hostile forces. Corporal Hamilton was serving as a combat medic when his unit was ambushed and surrounded by a numerically superior North Vietnamese force. His unit was heavily engaged by intense small arms, automatic weapon, mortar, and rocket fire from a well-fortified and concealed enemy. Immediately, three members of the platoon in an advanced position fell wounded. Corporal Hamilton, with complete disregard to his safety, ran through the heavy fire to his fallen comrades and was himself painfully wounded. In total disregard for his own injuries, he rendered life-saving first aid to the wounded. During the course of rendering aid, the position was overrun. With complete disregard to his own safety, Corporal Hamilton attacked and killed three North Vietnamese soldiers with his sidearm and was, in the process, grievously wounded. Although mortally wounded, Corporal Hamilton observed a grenade thrown into the midst of his wounded comrades. Aware that the grenade could further injure or kill the wounded personnel, he drew the grenade beneath himself, smothering the blast. Through his indomitable courage, complete disregard for his own safety, and profound concern for his fellow soldiers, he averted probable loss of life and additional injury to the wounded members of his unit. Corporal Hamilton's extraordinary heroism and intrepidity at the cost of his life, above and beyond the call of duty, are in the highest traditions of military service and reflect great credit upon himself, his unit, and the U.S. Army.

Twice during his reading of the citation, the president paused to blot a tear from his eye. When he finished reading, he said, "Staff Sergeant Hamilton was the bravest and most honorable man with whom I have ever had the pleasure of serving. So long as there are men in our country like James Wiley Hamilton, then our republic shall have nothing in the world to fear. Dr. Hamilton, I present to you your father's Congressional Medal of Honor, along with the sincere thanks of a grateful nation."

Flashbulbs popped. Cameras whirred. The room erupted in a thunderous round of applause.

James stood in shocked silence, alternately smiling and dabbing away tears of his own. *God, I wish Mom could've been here for this!*

The president leaned forward and whispered into his ear, "Think of this as a first installment toward repaying a debt that I will never fully be able to repay, a small compensation for your father's borrowed valor."

CHAPTER 38

2008–2017

J AMES'S METAMORPHOSIS WAS AS COMPREHENSIVE as it was instantaneous. The weight that he'd carried for over four decades was lifted from his shoulders, and for the first time, he could *breathe*. The cancer that had been slowly eating away at his psyche since birth—Mack Lee— had been surgically removed. Transplanted into the newly cleansed space was the story of a good and honorable man, his true father. This was a man he could look up to and emulate. This was a man who he wanted to make proud.

After leaving the White House, James returned to his childhood home in South Carolina. Although Becca was no longer there, with his hyperthymetic memory, she'd never *truly* leave him. He sat alone at the old rolltop desk, staring at the bundles of letters and contemplating his future. He thought maybe he was ready to get back to medicine. Perhaps he could be the kind of surgeon his father might've been, had fate not robbed him of the opportunity. The president of Washington University had once assured him that his old job would be waiting should he ever wish to return after leaving the military. Maybe he should give him a call?

In retrospect, James had to admit, he'd been something of an ass while he'd been at Washington University before. He was quite relieved, therefore, when the president confirmed his previous offer and informed James he could resume his position there effective July 1st.

James spent the next few weeks putting the farm in order. He leased some of their acreage to a man named Belleau, who wanted to grow peaches on it. The rest, he left in the capable hands of Becca's foreman.

When James returned to Washington University, his colleagues could not get over his transformation. He laughed often and developed a *joie de vivre*, which heretofore had been sorely lacking. He no longer snapped at staff and now took an active interest in the people around him. He remained a gifted surgeon—that hadn't changed, but everything else about the man had, and all for the better.

Still a very private man, he never spoke about the source of his transformation. His colleagues assumed that something miraculous had occurred during his time in the army. It was as though Ebenezer Scrooge had met Marley's ghost somewhere outside of Baghdad. Whatever had happened, they liked it, and there were several additional staff members they'd *like* to send away for similar reverse transmogrification.

Accompanying the shift in personality from Mr. Hyde to Dr. Jekyll, James noted a marked increase in his popularity within the hospital's female nursing staff. Suddenly recognized as an attractive and highly eligible bachelor, he tentatively dipped his toe into the dating pool. Ultimately, no one from Wash U managed to steal his heart. Instead, it was a preschool teacher named Robin who became his wife, and two years later, gave him a set of twins—a boy and a girl.

A few years later, with a river of tears and heartfelt well-wishes in his wake, James left St. Louis to accept the Deputy Chief of Trauma Surgery position at Vanderbilt University Hospital and moved his family to Nashville, Tennessee.

James had almost two full months to kill in between his departure from Washington University and his start date at Vanderbilt. After setting up their house in Nashville, Robin shipped off the kids for an extended visit with the grandparents, and she sent James to South Carolina to oversee a renovation project on the old family homeplace. She wanted everyone out of her hair so that she could feather her new Nashville nest without distraction. James was wise enough to comply without debate. Besides, it had been years since he'd checked in with the folks at the IMS in Columbia. Maybe he could drop in while he was back in the Carolinas.

In Boiling Springs, before the renovation project could begin, all contents had to be removed and stored from the 130-year-old home. While clearing out the attic, James found his father's footlocker from Vietnam that had been returned with his personal possessions back in 1967.

Opening the locker, he found two items of interest. The first was the copy of *The Birds of Asia* his father had spoken of so often in his letters. The second was a letter, still unopened, from Uncle Howard. Apparently, it had been received after his father had gone into the field for the last time in October of 1967.

He opened it and read.

October 29, 1967

Dear James,

It was with great pride and pleasure that I received your letter of October 18. I congratulate you on the birth of your son, James Junior. I am certain that he will grow to be a fine lad and a good man, just like his father.

When you came to live with me, you changed my life. You may not have realized it at the time, but after Doris's death, I found myself in a pretty dark place. Charles had died during the war, and I felt that I had nothing left to live for. Having you there, at the risk of sounding melodramatic, gave my life purpose again. You gave me a reason to live again, and for this, I shall forever be in your debt.

You were quite industrious during our time together, and I was very proud of your lawn-mowing business. It warmed my heart when, rather than spending your money on a new bicycle, candy, or movies, you chose to give the money to me. I think you said it was "to help cover the expense of your board" or something like that. I remember thinking at the time that that was a terribly mature—and sad—thing for you to offer. You were insistent, so in the end, I accepted your money. Unbeknownst to you, I did not, however, apply the funds toward your room and board. Instead, I matched you dollar for dollar and purchased thirty-six shares of stock in the Walt Disney Company on your behalf. The shares have risen nicely in value since 1958, and this morning, I instructed my attorney to place those funds in trust for your son. (I suddenly feel very old—Ha!) He will have access to it when he comes of age. I hope that you will not begrudge an old man's indulgence!

Charlotte and I are doing well out here in Scottsdale. The warm, dry air has done wonders for my lumbago. Charlotte put me on a diet, although I still sneak an occasional slice of pie. I think she's on to me and just looks the other way. She's a good woman! I never thought that I would be happy again after Doris passed, but in this I was, thankfully, mistaken.

As for you, I hope that my letter finds you safe and well. Also, I know that you'd never ask, but know that Charlotte and I would absolutely love it if Becca and young James would come to Scottsdale to stay with us until you are released from your military service. Please bring it up with her and know that I will happily provide air or train fare for the trip out should she choose to come!

Even if the two of you prefer not to move out here—I know Becca's family still resides in Boiling Springs—I hope that all three of you will come to visit us upon your return from Vietnam. Charlotte and I cannot wait to meet our new great-grandnephew!

Warmly,
Uncle Howard

James smiled as he read the letter, and once again, regretted that he'd never known the man. *Wonder what happened to the trust? Maybe I can apply it toward the house renovation project. Every little bit helps…*

After a great deal of searching, he discovered that Uncle Howard had long ago retained Samuel Bellamy of the Law firm Bellamy, Tache & Roberts of Scottsdale, Arizona, for all of his legal needs. Upon contacting the firm, the secretary informed him that Mr. Bellamy had died in 1981, but his son was employed by the practice and had absorbed his father's old client files. So, he scheduled a telephone conference with the younger Bellamy for the following day.

At the appointed time, James placed his call and was connected after a short delay to William Bellamy, the firm's current managing partner. After initial introductions and obligatory small talk, Bellamy confirmed that there was, indeed, a trust fund being held by their firm. The trust had been opened by Howard Hines with a beneficiary listed as James Wiley Hamilton or son, James Wiley Hamilton, Jr. The trust was opened with thirty-six shares of Walt Disney common stock purchased at $13.88 per share during Disney's initial public offering in 1958.

James worked the math in his head. *Great. About five hundred dollars. That'd hardly cover the airfare to Scottsdale to sign the paperwork*, he thought. He thanked Bellamy for his time, preparing to end the call.

"Mr.—I mean, Dr. Hamilton," Bellamy began. "When will it be convenient for you to assume these funds?"

"I'm not sure if it's worth it for me to fly all the way out to Scottsdale—" James began.

"Oh no, Dr. Hamilton! You don't have to travel here. I'll fly to meet *you*. In fact, I insist!"

"You're joking, right?"

"Dr. Hamilton, I assure you, this is no joke. Your uncle's trust has been one of this firm's most important for over half a century."

"I don't—"

"Dr. Hamilton, you don't understand. I said that the trust was *opened* with thirty-six shares of Disney stock.

Over the past sixty-plus years, that stock has split on six occasions. There were two-for-one splits in 1967, 1971, and 1972 at price points of $105, $177.75, and $214.50 per share. Then the stock split four-for-one in 1986 and 1992 at $142.63 and $152.87 per share, respectively. The most recent split occurred in 1998, three-for-one at $111 per share. You don't own thirty-six shares of Disney stock. You own 13,824 shares."

James heard a calculator clicking on the other end of the line.

Bellamy continued, "At a share price this morning of $186 per share, your stocks are presently worth just under two-point-six million dollars. Additionally, there have been dividends that add up to roughly another three hundred-thousand dollars in cash value. So, unless you'd prefer that our corporate jet fly down and pick you up, I will be quite happy to deliver it to you in person."

James dropped the phone.

"Dr. Hamilton? Dr. Hamilton, are you still there..."

CHAPTER 39

FIVE YEARS LATER–MAY 2022

JAMES W. HAMILTON, MD, PHD, FACS
DEPUTY CHIEF, TRAUMA SURGERY

J AMES READ THE PLAQUE ON the door—*his* door—and smiled a wistful smile. *Mom would've loved this,* he thought. *I wish she could've seen it! She would've liked the plaque. The space beyond it, not so much.* His mother had never been into clutter.

The plaque identified James's office, a barely ten-by-ten windowless space deep in the bowels of Vanderbilt's University Hospital. It was cramped. It was cluttered. And he wouldn't change a single thing about it, even had that been an option.

But it wasn't an option. He had need for the room to be precisely the way it was. His daily ritual since accepting the position at Vanderbilt five years ago was to spend several minutes meditating in his office—surrounded by his memories—before starting rounds each morning. It allowed him to focus on other, more important things in the present.

The room was dominated by a large shelving unit that took up the entire wall left of the door. Most, but not all of the shelves, were filled with rows of medical and surgical textbooks, his personal medical library. One of the other shelves displayed photos of his wife and two children. On another there was a photograph of his MASH unit at An Najaf, signed by each member of his team. On a top shelf, in a shadow box, there was a folded American flag. Peeking from behind the shadow box was a framed photograph of James and President Prescott shaking hands in the Oval Office.

Immediately to the right of the door and partially hidden behind it whenever the door was open was the requisite "love me" wall of framed diplomas, licenses, and board certification certificates. The office was never used for patient consultation, therefore in James's opinion, having such a wall was overly pretentious and, frankly, ridiculous. *He* certainly didn't need to be reminded where he'd gone to school or the board certifications he held. Had the wall of diplomas and awards not been dictated by the university, he never would've unpacked any of them from their boxes.

Box checked—bureaucrats be damned! This thought made him smile again.

Sharing the wall to the left of the door was Uncle Howard's antique, oaken rolltop desk and an oak rolling swivel chair that creaked and squeaked with the slightest motion of its occupant. No doubt, a drop of oil or a squirt of graphite would've silenced the protesting chair, but he didn't mind the noise. He thought it calmed him, or at least reminded him not to fidget while working at his desk. On the wall above the desk hung an ancient, framed needlepoint piece saying, "Do Right and Fear Not," that had once been a gift to Elliana from her baba.

Along the wall opposite the door was James's only new piece of furniture—the coat rack in the corner didn't count—

a custom-built, mission-style, white-oak credenza that had been presented to him by Elijah Yoder.

Five years ago, on James's first day on call for Vanderbilt's Trauma Service, Elijah's son, Jeremiah, had been driving along Hillsboro Pike near Nashville when his horse-drawn carriage was struck by a drunk driver. Jeremiah was gravely injured in the accident and not expected to live. He suffered a ruptured spleen, a fractured liver, a lacerated aorta, a flail chest, a subdural hematoma, lacerated bowel, multiple orthopedic injuries, and myriads of lesser injuries.

James had immediately taken the young man to the OR for surgery. It had been Jeremiah's only hope. He led a team of surgeons, anesthesiologists, and orthopedists who rotated in and out of the OR during Jeremiah's eleven-and-a-half-hour surgery. James, however, did not emerge from the operating theater until his patient was stable and ready to be transferred to the Trauma ICU.

During the surgery, twenty members of Jeremiah Yoder's family sat vigil in the waiting room. They looked up expectantly as James strode into the room. With a weak smile, he informed the family that Jeremiah had survived his surgery and, although he was still in critical condition, he fully expected him to pull through. After receiving myriads of handshakes, hugs, tears, and prayers, James had left the relieved family and promptly collapsed in the hallway outside the waiting room, suffering from exhaustion and dehydration. He woke four hours later in a hospital bed, with an intravenous line in his left wrist and Elijah Yoder sitting in the chair to his right, placidly reading his Bible.

Jeremiah Yoder, to the amazement of everyone, walked out of the hospital six weeks after his accident. He had died twice during surgery. Both times, James had resuscitated him—the second with open cardiac massage. Jeremiah had lost his spleen, three feet of small bowel, a quarter of his liver, and sixteen units of blood. Additionally, he had so many metal clips, plates, and screws inside him that he practically clanked with each step, but he left the hospital under his own power.

So began James Hamilton's reputation at Vanderbilt as a miracle worker.

The Yoder family were Amish and carpenters by trade. Elijah was a craftsman extraordinaire. Out of gratitude, he had presented the credenza to James four months after Jeremiah's release from the hospital. He'd perfectly matched the stain to Jamses's rolltop desk and even had taken the time to distress the credenza's wood slightly so that, although it was 150 years newer, it appeared to be the desk's natural companion piece. Additionally, a year later, when the Yoder family welcomed its newest addition, they christened the child with the name "James."

Set atop one end of the credenza, in a glass display case, sat a lovingly maintained copy of Gould's *The Birds of Asia*, open to a color lithograph of a long-tailed broadbill. In the book's crease lay a simple gold band adorned with a tiny quarter-carat diamond chip.

On the other end of the credenza sat a framed playbill from the Winter Garden Theatre for *Mamma Mia!*, opening October 18, 2001. The bill proclaimed a new musical by Benny Andersson and Björn Ulvaeus featuring the music of ABBA. Beside the playbill, displayed in a matching frame, was a photograph of the Twin Towers viewed from across the Hudson. The photo depicted the towers belching smoke and flame on September 11, 2001. If one chose to inspect the photo closely with a magnifying glass, that inspection would demonstrate tablecloths being waved from windows on the 106th and 107th floors of the North Tower. Looped over one corner of the framed photo was a yellow ribbon. The ribbon, in turn, held a battered platinum ring bearing an internally flawless Asscher cut, 1.52-carat center diamond with one missing flanking baguette.

Positioned as they were, on opposite ends of the credenza, the photos and his father's book sat in perfect equipoise. One was Yin, the other Yang. Between them sat a brushed aluminum urn. Although the rest of the office and all corners and crannies were cluttered with piles of patient charts and medical journals, the credenza was spotless.

For a man incapable of forgetting, one might've considered such a space, packed as it was with so many reminders of the past, a dangerous place. But for James Hamilton, it was the opposite. With the memory horcruxes spread before him within the room, it freed his mind to focus more upon the present, secure in the knowledge that these memories would be there waiting should he ever have need to revisit them.

James sat perfectly still, staring sightlessly into the middle distance as memories ebbed and flowed around him. The occasional creaking of his chair was the only indication there was a living, breathing trauma surgeon, and not a mannequin, seated at his desk. After several minutes, he shook his head as though to clear it and blinked several times. He glanced down at his watch, an antique gold Bulova with a Mickey Mouse silhouetted on the face in bas-relief.

It was time for rounds.

James stood, took his white coat from the rack, and slipped it over his scrubs. Then, once again becoming "Dr. Hamilton," he sauntered to the Trauma ICU, tunelessly humming ABBA's "The Name of the Game."

After five years as the deputy, James had recently been elevated to Interim Chief of Trauma Surgery at Vanderbilt

University Medical Center and was, this month, the surgical attending assigned to the Trauma Intensive Care Unit Service. As a higher-up in the Vanderbilt surgical chain of command, James was only expected to work the TICU service once or twice a year, but because he particularly enjoyed it, he ran the service once each quarter instead. Certainly, the other trauma attendings on staff didn't mind him stepping in. It was grueling work.

That morning, James was leading an entourage engaged that morning in "walking rounds" in the TICU. Joining him was the Trauma team, a half-dozen surgical interns, two upper-level surgery residents, and three medical students. On walking rounds, the interns and residents discussed the patient's status at the bedside with the surgical attending. They briefly detailed the patient's general progress over the preceding twenty-four hours. They conferred information regarding diagnosis, procedures, and any complications or issues that may have arisen since the previous day's rounds. In turn, the surgical attending assessed each patient and detailed plans for the next twenty-four hours.

Ideally, house-staff presentations should be brief, succinct, and to the point. Trauma surgeons are not generally known for their patience. How does the old joke go? "How many trauma surgeons does it take to change a lightbulb? Answer: One, and the world revolves around him."

James paused the gaggle of house staff and students at the foot of the first patient bed and turned to one of his interns. "Dr. Lu, would you care to enlighten us about Mr. Jackson this morning? How was our patient overnight?"

"Yes, sir. Mr. Jackson is a twenty-three-year-old African American male who—" began Belinda Lu.

James raised his hand, cutting in on Lu's presentation. "Let me pause you there for a moment."

Lu cringed. *Here it is, my first day on service and already Hamilton's gonna hate me!* thought Lu with a sense of impending doom.

"Please forgive my interruption," James continued in a remarkably gentle tone, his cultured southern accent dripping honey. "Dr. Lu, this is your first day upon my service, is it not? Of course, it is, and it is also for many, if not most, of your compatriots as well."

The senior residents in the group smiled, knowing what was to follow. They'd all been to this movie before and knew how it ended.

"Dr. Lu, as I recall, you attended Johns Hopkins Medical School..."

James made it a point each month to review the file on each member of his surgical team. He liked to familiarize himself with everyone's backgrounds, and with his extraordinary memory, he had an uncanny ability to recall details and discuss them, often at unusual times. If, for example, a surgical resident had mentioned in his Vanderbilt Surgery application that he once had a hamster named Ralphie, James was likely to ask him about it—in the middle of repairing a lacerated aorta. Like as not he'd use the hamster as a segue into some esoteric teaching point. For this reason and many others, James had won Teacher of the Year honors for four of the past five years since joining the Vanderbilt faculty. The only year he'd *not* won, he was away from the university on sabbatical. Even *that* year, he had placed second in the voting.

"...and Hopkins is a truly outstanding institution," he continued. "Certainly, while you were at that bastion of learning, you were taught how to present cases to members of the medical staff? No doubt, you are familiar and skilled at providing a History of Present Illness, Review of Systems,

Social History, Medical & Surgical History, and Family History down to fourth-degree relatives in nauseating detail?"

This is going to be vintage Hamilton, thought the senior resident.

"Y-yes, sir," croaked Lu.

"Please allow me to revise your approach somewhat. First, we know that Mr. Jackson is a male. He was yesterday and remains so today. His *maleness* is implied by the 'Mr.' preceding his name, is it not? So, to restate the fact with every presentation seems tiresome, a little redundant, might you say?"

Lu nodded.

"Second, on my service, unless race bears some *direct* clinical relevance to the case at hand—for example, sickle cell anemia, or thalassemia in persons of African American heritage or perhaps Fanconi's anemia or cystic fibrosis in a patient who is an Ashkenazi Jew—then I don't want to hear about it. Race has no place on a Trauma Service. The same goes for religion or the lack thereof. If it is relevant, say a Jehovah's Witness who might require a blood transfusion, bring it up. If information is salient to the patient's condition, include it. Otherwise, the *Reader's Digest Condensed* version is perfectly acceptable and even desirable. Everyone understand?"

There were nods and murmurs of affirmation from the group. A hand rose from the back of the crowd. It was one of the medical students.

"Mr. Donovan, you have a question? How may I help our young doctor this fine morning? And no need to raise a hand. Just chime in."

"Well, sir, it's just—" he started in a patrician Boston accent.

"Hang on there, Daniel."

Hamilton even knows the medical students by name. Holy crap, thought Lu.

"No reason to be nervous. I haven't eaten a single medical student this week, and besides, whatever question you have, somebody else here probably has too. The difference is that you have the guts to ask." James smiled. "So ask away!"

"Would there be a problem with Muslims or Orthodox Jews receiving bioprosthetic heart valves? Shouldn't we tell you about that too?" Donovan asked in a pompous tone.

"That is an interesting question. But technically, there should be no problem."

"But isn't there a restriction against pigs in those faiths?" Donovan continued with a smirk.

Typical medical student, thought Lu, silently rolling her eyes. *Always trying to look like the smartest person in the room in front of the attending.*

"Again, not a problem," explained James. "To begin with, not all bioprosthetic valves are heterografts. A heterograft or xenograft employs tissues from other species. The two most common in heart valves are bovine, cow, pericardial valves and transplanted porcine, pig, valves. Additionally, there are allografts and homografts. Allografts are valves transplanted from the same species. For example, a cryopreserved cadaver valve. Whereas a homograft is a pulmonic valve from a patient that has been moved to the aortic position in that same patient. So, there are options that do not involve pigs. Even if the porcine valve *was* considered to be the best option, there still would be no problem."

"So you're saying that you'd just put a pig valve in someone over their religious objections?" challenged Donovan.

This kid's pushing his luu-uuccck! thought Lu.

"No, Daniel! No one is going to perform *any* procedure over the patient's objections, religious or otherwise. In this case, however, there is no religious restriction for either of the faiths you mentioned."

"But—"

Hamilton held up a hand in the universal gesture for *STOP*.

The fourth-year surgical resident leaned against a pillar, settling in. *This is gonna be good,* he thought.

"My turn, Doc-y!" James began. "In the Islamic faith, the issue with pigs is in *partaking* of the flesh. Under Sharia Law, *is not* haram for a Muslim to use the animal for any other uses for which the animal is commonly used, and that *includes* its use as a heart valve donor. Look it up if you still don't believe me. Try Al-Baqarah 2:173, 'But whoever is forced, neither desiring nor transgressing, there is no sin upon him.' I think that's the quote—it's been a few years since I've read it."

James continued without the slightest hint of sharpness in his typically gentle tone. "Restrictions are similar for those of Jewish faith. 'And the swine—although it has true hoofs, with the hoofs cleft through, it does not chew the cud: it is impure for you. You shall not eat of their flesh or touch their carcasses; they are impure for you.' Leviticus 11:7–8. According to *halacha,* Jewish law, Jews should avoid *touching* the flesh of a pig during the festivals of Passover, Shavuot, and Sukkot, during which a higher state of purity is required. So, there is no halachic problem with pigskin or pig heart valves on the way to Jerusalem or any other time. Furthermore, there is a very important tenet of Judaism called *pikuach nefesh...*"

This guy's a freakin' encyclopedia, thought Lu.

"...or saving a life. According to Jewish law, any of the commandments in the Torah, except for idolatry, murder, and forbidden sexual relationships, can, and in fact *should,* be violated if necessary to save a life. Thus, when a person's life is at stake, we are allowed and are even *commanded* to do whatever is necessary to save them. What I *would* do if a patient had reservations about their procedure, would be to bring in their trusted local imam or rabbi to explain all of this to them. If they still did not wish to proceed, I'd schedule an alternative procedure. Got it?"

James continued, his voice rising slightly above its usual timbre, "Now, had you *really* wanted to impress me, Daniel, you would have asked about the use of bovine pericardial valves in adherents to the Hindu faith. It's an *absolute* no-no, by the way."

If Donovan could have melted into the floor, he would've long ago been a puddle. The senior resident stared with new fascination at the ceiling air-conditioning vent. Lu was barely able to stifle a giggle. Two of her colleagues were less successful.

"Now for the sake of everyone here, let me give you all my take on questions. I will ask each of you questions from time to time. Please do not view this as 'pimping for minutia,' for it absolutely is not. I don't expect you to know everything. I pose questions to determine your current level of knowledge and understanding so that I'll know where I need to start *teaching*. Going into exhaustive detail about something you already know and fully understand is a waste of your time and mine. None among us has so much surplus time that we can afford to waste any of it. If you do not know the answer, say so. *Do not* try to bluff or BS me. It will *not* work, and I *won't* be impressed!

"Your job on my service is to ask the question, 'Why?' I don't want you to do *anything* by rote. If you cannot give me five minutes off the cuff about *why* we are doing something, ask me. If I cannot give five minutes about it, then I need to reassess whatever it is we're doing. By asking why, you'll help keep me honest and make *me* a better physician. This is the gospel according to Hamilton!" he said. His opaline-green eyes twinkled in the fluorescent lighting, giving off flashes of emerald.

"Now, back to the medical history. Bear in mind, there is nothing wrong with a fully detailed and comprehensive medical history. The hitch is that in *this* setting, we might get to know all there is to know about Mr. Jackson but not have time to learn at all about the *other* nineteen patients in this unit. Abridgment, although an abomination in litera-ture, is *essential* in the TICU. Got it?"

There were nods all around.

James glanced at his watch. It was getting late, and he needed to move rounds along. Without notes or even a glance at the chart, he began talking about Lu's patient. "Now, as for Mr. Jackson, here. Tony is the unluckiest son of a gun you'd ever want to know. Tony, here, was just walk-ing along, minding his own business last Saturday night when he came across a fellow by the name of Some Dude. Now, Mr. Dude is one *bad* dude. He's been implicated in multiple crimes from here to New York City but has *never* been caught. Imagine Tony's bad luck just stumbling across a guy that the police of seventeen states can't seem to find. What are the odds? Well, Mr. Dude was just showing Tony his new switchblade when poor Tony tripped and fell onto the blade. It seems that Tony is something of a klutz too, be-cause he actually fell onto Mr. Dude's knife two more times! Can you imagine it?

"The blade went through his colon and nicked his splenic artery. Another punctured his small intestine in six places and just missed the aorta. The third lacerated the liver, went through the diaphragm and into his right lung. He got a chest tube in the ER, and we took him up to surgery. When we opened him up, his belly was full of blood and stool. We patched the splenic artery, fixed the liver lac and small bowel, gave him a diverting colostomy, packed the wound, and left it open. So, how's Tony doing today, Dr. Lu?"

"His vitals have remained stable overnight. His temp is down to 100—it was 102.4 yesterday—and his white count is down from twenty-three to nineteen, so it looks like the antibiotics are working. The chest tube still shows signs of an air leak. His hemoglobin and hematocrit are stable at nine and twenty-nine without additional transfusions. I still don't hear bowel sounds, but there's no X-ray evidence of obstruction," Lu reported.

"So, what do you want to do with him?" asked James.

"Me, sir?"

"You *are* his doctor. What do we do with him next?"

"Well, ummm...I don't think we do anything with the chest tube for now. Continue the antibiotics and maybe take him back to the OR tomorrow. If his white count is still going down and everything looks clean, maybe we can close the abdomen?" Lu responded diffidently.

"Sounds fair. Book an OR for tomorrow. You'll scrub in, of course?"

"What, sir? Really? You want me to—"

"He's your patient, Dr. Lu. And your plan sounds reasonable and appropriate. Own it. Believe in yourself and make it happen," said James, smiling approvingly.

Before moving on to the next patient, James signed off the orders in the chart with the vintage, tortoiseshell Pelikan fountain pen that had been his mother's wedding gift from Uncle Howard. Then, returning the pen to his pocket, he asked, "Now, who will tell me about Signor Reyes, who

I understand had an unfortunate introduction to a bridge abutment?"

Rounds continued throughout the morning. At each bedside, James paused his entourage and discussed the case. His capacious memory allowed him to file and collate each patient's condition, medications, laboratory data, and backstory in startling detail. Though it was clear to all involved that he was already intimately familiar with each of the twenty patients, he listened attentively to each intern, resident, and student as they stumbled through their presentations. When appropriate, he asked questions to sharpen their focus and understanding. In response to questions, he often queried the questioner, drawing them toward the correct answer rather than directly providing it to them.

James believed a solution developed by logic and derivation was more likely to be remembered than a solution simply given. Even if forgotten, the derivations could be repeated and a correct solution found. "How" and "why" always trumped "what." Give a man a fish, and he'll eat for a day. Teach a man to fish, and he'll eat for a lifetime. Give a man the answer, and he *might* someday remember it. Teach a man to *find* the answer, and it will be his forever.

James Hamilton loved practicing medicine in a teaching hospital. The word *doctor* is derived from the Latin, *docere*, meaning "to teach." Thus, he believed it incumbent upon *all* physicians to pass along the knowledge they have accumulated through years of experience to those who follow them into practice. If there are no students, interns, residents, fellows, or colleagues, then a physician must teach patients, family members...and, indeed, himself. Not only was this his personal doctrine, it was just...well...fun.

After rounds were completed, the trauma team broke up to complete their hospital duties. Some had procedures scheduled for later in the day, while others dealt with post-operative patient management for their non-ICU patients. Those without pressing responsibilities, like Lu, drifted back to the house-staff lounge to study, snack, and gossip.

"My God, Zahra, could you believe Dr. Hamilton today? I mean, the guy's brilliant. He knew everybody in the trauma unit by heart—the patients, us, the nurses, the techs. I'd bet he even knows the janitor's pet goldfish."

Zahra Karanja was another surgical intern at Vanderbilt. Her family had emigrated from Kenya to New York when she was a child, leaving her with an accent that was Brooklyn with just a hint of an Eastern African lilt. It was an odd combination, but somehow, she made it work. Her dark mahogany skin starkly contrasted Lu's porcelain complexion. Karanja was tall with generous feminine curves, whereas Lu was no more than five feet tall and reed thin. The unlikely pair were best friends, and together, they were intent upon cracking into the male-dominated field of surgery.

"Yes, he was most impressive today. I particularly liked how he put that jackass student—what's his name?—Donovan in his place!"

"Score: Dreamy Surgical Attending, 1. Brown-Nosing Asshole Medical Student, 0."

"Dreamy? Belinda, really? He's got to be like fifty or something!"

"Just because there's snow on the roof doesn't mean there's not a fire in the chimney," retorted Lu. "And he seems to be in great shape. And his chestnut hair only has a smudge of gray at the temples, but otherwise he could pass for thirty."

"Give it up, Lu," chimed Randall Coleman, a third-year surgical resident, from the corner of the lounge. "He's got a hot wife who, by all indications, he adores, and a couple of kids."

"Sorry, lover-girl!" Karanja laughed.

"Damn! All the good ones are taken!"

"Hey, what am I over here? Chopped liver?" asked Coleman in mock offense.

"Yep! Pretty much," responded Lu and Karanja in unison.

"I'd say that pretty well sums it up," Lu continued, with Karanja nodding her agreement. "What's his story, anyway?"

"Hamilton's?"

"No, Coleman. Aaron Burr's. Of course I mean Hamilton."

"Ha, ha, ha...the funny intern's here today," chided Coleman. "Are you gonna remind me to *tip my server* when I leave? Nobody knows that much about him. He's been here for a little over five years, way before I got here. They say he was some kind of war hero and started at Vandy after he got out of the army, but I don't know if it's true—probably not. I've not been in his office, but Joey Vinson has. Vinson says there's a folded flag and a Medal of Honor in one of those shadow box things, and a picture on his desk of Hamilton with President Prescott. Of course, that doesn't necessarily mean it's true. Vinson wouldn't know the difference between a Medal of Honor and a Girl Scout merit badge. Maybe Doc sold the most cookies or something."

"Somebody told me that he's loaded...invented some kind of surgical clamp or something, but nobody knows. They say that he works here for just one dollar per year," added Karanja.

"Yeah, and he found a cure for cancer and foot odor too," said Coleman with a roll of the eyes. "All that stuff's bullshit!

What's really true is that he's like some kind of god in an operating room. Nothing fazes him. He's Mr. Unflappable. I swear, if some guy came in with his head cut off, Hamilton would calmly sew it back on, all the while chatting with the scrub tech about her Rhodesian Ridgeback puppies. And when he's finished sewing, the guy would hop up off the table, thank the doc, and walk out of the operating theater. Seriously, I've never heard of him losing his cool—*ever*! They say the only way anybody in the OR would know a patient's crashing is that Hamilton starts talking slower. I've seen it.

"As for that douchebag Donovan, that was vintage Hamilton. Every time Hamilton's on service, *somebody* tries to prove he or she is smarter than him or has bigger balls than him. Every time, Hamilton squashes the perp like a bug. He never uses profanity. He never raises his voice. He never talks down to anybody. But when he's done with them, they're flatter than three-day-old roadkill. And it's not just medical students. I've seen him do the same thing with other attendings, and once, even with the former Chief of Medicine, a guy named Beechard. The guy just withered like a violet on a hotplate. It was a thing of beauty, I tell ya."

"Hmmm, now he is sounding kind of attractive to me too." Karanja laughed.

"If you want to stay on his good side," Coleman offered helpfully, "don't try to bullshit him. If you don't know something, that's fine, provided he knows you tried. If you don't know something because you're too lazy to find out...well, that's another story entirely. *You* will be one who's three-day-old roadkill."

The overhead speaker crackled to life and after a moment of static, "Trauma Team to Trauma One! Trauma Team to Trauma One! Trauma Team to Trauma One!"

Lu dropped her half-eaten bagel in the trash and sprinted out the door, in the direction of the Emergency Department. Karanja was a half-step behind, thinking, *Damn! How do those short little legs move so fast?* Arriving to Trauma Room One in the Emergency Department, the two stood panting, trying to catch their breath.

A moment later, James sauntered in like he hadn't a care in the world. He eased over to the head nurse. "Good evening, Rhonda. How are the kids? Has Alicia decided on a college yet? It's getting to be that time. She must be excited!"

"Oh, thank you, Dr. Hamilton. Everyone is fine. She'll be thrilled that you remembered her from the hospital picnic last year. That child is still undecided but is thinking about UT-Chattanooga or maybe Appalachian State."

"Hmmm...a Moc or a Mountaineer? Well, both have terrific music programs, so I'm sure she'll do great in either." Then, still in a conversational tone, James continued, "So what do we have coming in this evening?"

"Gunshot wound to the chest, Doctor. The ambulance is about one minute out."

"Go ahead and get an intubation tray and set up for a chest tube. Call down for six units O negative blood and have the OR standing by. Has Radiology been notified?"

"Yes, Doctor."

Just then, the ER doors were flung open by a gurney propelled by an EMS crew. "We have a twenty-year-old male with single GSW to the chest. Appears to have been a sawed-off shotgun at short range. Sucking chest wound. Entrance but no exit."

"Vitals?"

"BP 70 over palp, respirations 30 and labored, heart rate 140s. We have 18s in both ACs and an IO in his left tibia. He's had just over two liters Lactated Ringer's en route."

"Name?"

"ID says Lamont Colbert."

"Lamont, I'm Dr. Hamilton. Do you know what happened to you?"

"Got...shot."

"Yes. It looks like you did. Do you know who shot you?"

"Some...dude."

James glanced toward his interns in the corner of the trauma room and winked. "*Him* again!"

After being stabilized in the Emergency Department, Colbert was taken to the operating room for definitive treatment of his chest wound. Since both Lu and Karanja had been present when the patient arrived, both were invited to scrub for his surgery.

Watching James perform surgery was like watching Baryshnikov performing ballet. Everything appeared effortless. His hands hardly seemed to move, yet stitches and clamps seemed to appear everywhere, all at once.

Without looking up from his repair of a rent in the pulmonary artery, he asked Karanja, "So, Dr. Karanja, do you pronounce your name zahRA, or has it been Americanized to ZAHra?"

"ZahRA, sir. It was my grandmother's name. She died before I was born. It means 'brilliant' or 'bright.' "

"Very good! Stay true to your heritage and *never* sell out. I'm sure your grandmother would have been very proud of you," James said, smiling behind his surgical mask. "So, what can you tell me about Mr. Colbert?"

"Um, a gunshot wound to the right chest with an entry just lateral to the nipple in the midclavicular line, causing extensive injury to the right lung and right upper pulmonary artery."

"Okay, that's a start. What did Mr. Colbert look like? Tell me about the wound itself. What did it look like when he rolled in?" James asked. "Tell me what you saw."

"The patient was sweaty, his heart rate was high, and his blood pressure was very low," started Karanja.

"So you're saying that he looked shocky, then?"

"He was breathing really fast and shallow. He seemed a little confused and drowsy."

"So he's shocky and in respiratory distress. What did the wound look like?"

"Um...it was a big, jagged hole?" she responded hesitantly.

"Definitely was that. Was it doing anything? The wound, other than bleeding?" James coached.

"Well, it made wheezing noises whenever he breathed, and it bubbled."

"Bingo! What you've described is the classic sucking chest wound. So, what can you tell me about sucking chest wounds other than it sucks to have one?"

"I heard the EMT say that when he rolled into the trauma bay, but I didn't know what it was. I was going to read about it, but you said that I could scrub in and..." Her voice trailed off to a whisper, fully expecting to be kicked out of the OR by her attending.

James was unfazed. "Fair enough. Let's talk about sucking chest wounds."

Lu realized that she'd been holding her breath. After Zahra's admission that she'd not had time to read about her patient before surgery, she'd fully expected Hamilton to go ballistic and rant about unprepared, half-assed, lazy interns. That's what other attendings would have done, throw a tantrum, kick the poor dumb bastard out of their OR, and then turn to *her*. Knowing no more than Zahra, the entire process would've been repeated, lather, rinse, repeat. Instead, Hamilton was going to use this as an opportunity to teach? *Who is this guy*?!

"How do we breathe?" he asked.

Hamilton's Socratic method of teaching was well honed. Anyone listening to the audio of the session without benefit of the corresponding video would've thought him to be sitting in the doctor's lounge, enjoying a casual chat with his interns rather than being up to his elbows in a complex vascular repair and partial pneumonectomy on an unstable patient. Though his hands flew about the surgical field performing complex maneuvers, the inflection and tone of his voice never changed.

A geyser of blood sprayed toward the ceiling.

James didn't miss a beat. "I mean, mechanically. What are the mechanics of respiration? Dr. Lu, feel free to jump in here, too. You wouldn't want to let your colleague have *all* the fun."

The interns remained silent.

James glanced up at his interns and winked. "Don't both of you answer all at once. Show some decorum."

After another moment of hesitation, Karanja began, "The diaphragm contracts, moving down toward the abdomen. At the same time, the intercostal muscles contract, causing the ribs to expand and elevate. This causes—"

"Dr. Lu, would you mind pulling up a bit on that Allison Retractor? Perfect, thanks. Well, what do we have here? A rifled slug? Who puts a rifled slug in a sawed-off shotgun? Kinda defeats the purpose, doesn't it? I guess Mr. Some Dude needs to go back to gangsta school for remedial training. At the range he was shot, double-O buckshot would have torn a hole the size of a soccer ball in Colbert's chest.

Looks like this was Mr. Colbert's lucky day! Suction. Go ahead…you were saying, Dr. Karanja."

"Yes, sir. This causes negative pressure within the thoracic cavity, which causes the lungs to expand. At the end of inspiration, the diaphragm and intercostal muscles relax and air passively is exhaled from the lungs.

"So what happens when there is a hole in the chest wall and a hole in the lung? Forget about blood for a minute. Let's keep this as simple as possible. Now, Dr. Lu, his middle lobe is pretty well shot, and my wife would shoot *me* for using that pun. Use that Allison Retractor to nudge the upper lobe out of the way and take the Sarot and clamp the middle lobe bronchus. Good. Now, let's see if we can remove it cleanly. Go ahead, Dr. Karanja."

"The negative intrathoracic pressure during inspiration will make air leak into the chest cavity from the outside and also leak from the damaged lung. The air displaces the lung and causes it to collapse."

"You'll forgive me, I hope, for what was something of a trick question? You are partially correct, but the answer actually depends upon the *size* of the hole in the chest wall."

"Why is that?" asked the scrub tech.

"It has to do with the chest wall and its ability to self-seal. With a stab wound or a wound from a small caliber projectile, the layers of the chest wall—skin, subcutaneous fat, muscle, etcetera—collapse upon themselves, partially or completely sealing the hole. Thus, a significant amount of air does not enter the chest cavity except through the damaged lung. The air leaking from the lung cannot get out, either through the bronchial tree or through the wound, and is trapped. With each inhalation, a little more air becomes trapped, causing the air pressure to rise between the chest wall and the lung. As this continues, the air bubble expands, collapsing the lung. As the pressure continues to build, the collapsed lung and intrapleural-free air begin to push on mediastinal structures, including the inferior vena cava, superior vena cava, and heart. This results in the inability of blood to flow back into the right atrium of the heart, leading to cardiovascular collapse and death. This is called a tension pneumothorax. And how is that treated?"

Karanja answered without hesitation, "Needle decompression and chest tube."

"And how does one perform a needle decompression? Walk me through it."

Lu started to answer.

"No, Dr. Lu, this is your colleague's party. You'll have your chance. Dr. Karanja?"

"Take a large bore needle, find the second rib interspace in the midclavicular line, and insert the needle into the chest cavity. There should be a rush of air, followed by a degree of stabilization of the patient's respiratory distress."

"And how does one recognize a tension pneumothorax?" asked James.

"Respiratory distress, shock, distended neck veins, and a trachea that is deviated away from the affected side."

"And did Mr. Colbert have a tension pneumothorax?"

The interns shook their heads in the negative.

"Correct. Mr. Lucky here had a nice big hole in his chest, so his chest cavity was open to the outside world. Tell me what to do in that situation, Dr. Lu. Dr. Karanja, will you step in here please and relieve Dr. Lu on that Allison Retractor? It looks like her hand's about to fall off. Thank you."

"Wouldn't you want to seal the hole?" asked Lu.

"Nope, not completely anyway. Otherwise, you predispose to the development of a tension pneumothorax. Think of the hole as a *really big* needle decompression. So, sealing it completely is a recipe for disaster. Let's take this step-wise."

Good Lord! Could I be any more pedantic? But if it helps them to learn, it's worth it, James thought.

James continued, "With a sucking chest wound, air is sucked into the thoracic cavity through the chest wall instead of into the lungs through the airways. Air follows the path of least resistance. When the hole in the chest wall approaches two-thirds of the width of the trachea, a sucking chest wound can occur. The average male trachea is roughly twenty millimeters in diameter, and the average female trachea is about three-quarters of that, and a kid's trachea will be even smaller. An easy way to remember this is that any wound roughly the size of a penny or larger can lead to a sucking chest wound. Patients with a sucking chest wound manifest the general signs and symptoms common to all pneumothoraxes. In addition, the patient will have an open wound in the chest that bubbles blood and wheezes with inspiration and expiration."

"So, what do you do for a sucking chest wound if you shouldn't seal it?" Karanja asked.

"If you're doing this out in the real world and not in a trauma room, find something to use as an impermeable patch. It'll need to be at least three times as large as the wound itself. Then tape the patch down on three sides, leaving the other side open. This will allow air to escape but will impede its reentry into the chest cavity. Just about anything occlusive can be used. Plastic wrap or a credit card works well. Some of the EMS units have premade plastic patches with a Heimlich valve built into them. It really doesn't matter what you use. I even heard a story once about a guy who came in with a Polaroid photograph taped over his sucking chest wound. He lived, so it must have worked. Pay close attention to the victim, however. If you start seeing signs of a tension pneumothorax, release the tape to allow it to decompress, then reapply."

Changing tack, James said to the OR as a whole, "All right, I think that about does it. Let's flush the chest with antibiotics and make sure we've got all the bleeders. Check the count and verify that Dr. Lu hasn't lost her watch. I don't think Mr. Colbert wants to spend the rest of his life ticking like Captain Hook's alligator."

The circulator and scrub nurses scrambled to count needles, sponges, and instruments. After a moment, the scrub nurse reported, "All counts are correct, Dr. Hamilton."

"Everything okay up top?" James asked, nodding to the anesthesiologist.

"All's well, Doc. Gonna start backing down on sedation now," came his immediate reply.

"Good! All counts are correct and no bleeders are evident. Dr. Karanja, do you think that you and Dr. Lu can close everything up?"

The interns nodded enthusiastically in the affirmative.

James looked over his glasses at his scrub nurse, Tana, a veteran who'd worked with him almost exclusively since his arrival at Vanderbilt. He raised his eyebrows a fraction and motioned with his eyes to the two interns. She gave him an almost imperceptible nod and half wink, which said, "*Of course I'll watch over the two newbies and make sure they don't do anything stupid.*"

"Excellent! Well done, everybody! Lu, Karanja, I'll see you back in the TICU," James called over his shoulder as he strode out of the OR.

Each day on the Trauma Service was the same. There were shootings, stabbings, motor vehicle accidents, and industrial accidents. Only the cast of characters changed.

There was always a Humpty Dumpty who needed patience, glue, and a gifted trauma surgeon to put them back together again. It was stressful. It was tiring. Frequently, it was heartbreaking. But James loved it, and by the end of the month-long rotation on the Trauma Service, the residents and interns loved it too. His enthusiasm for the field was too infectious to be resisted.

CHAPTER 40

JUNE 2022

J AMES'S MONTH AS TRAUMA SERVICE attending ended, and as was his practice, he invited the entire team to his house for a post rotation dinner. Since it was June and the Nashville weather was pleasant, dinner morphed into a barbecue and pool party. He believed it was good for the team to be able to relax and "let their hair down" after a stressful month. Luckily, Robin didn't mind. She enjoyed playing "proxy Mom" for his team, and it was an unusual night when at least one intern, resident, or medical student didn't share their family's dinner table.

This month after the party, James planned a two-week family vacation to Washington, DC. He might have been perfectly happy working year-round without a break, but Robin had put her foot down and he was wise enough not to defy his wife.

"Stop whining! The hospital won't close in your absence, and Rick Greene is more than capable of running the Trauma Service while you're gone."

James started to object. "I know, I know. Rick's great in the OR but can be a little abrasive with the house staff, and I—"

Robin's look cut him off mid-sentence. His wife of almost thirteen years, she was the only thing in the world he was afraid of and the one thing in his life he was certain he could not live without. She knew him to his core, and she loved him anyway.

"I know you're a very good surgeon," she said. "You actually *care* about your patients. You're an excellent teacher, father, and a more or less passable husband."

"Ouch! Damned by the faintest of praise."

"Part of what I love most about you is that you *do* care."

"It's just that—"

"No! You've looked forward to this trip forever. It's your chance to tell the kids your story. You need to tell it, and they need to hear it. They deserve to know who they are and where they come from, and now they're old enough to understand."

"Where they come from? We've had that talk already. You remember the one...when a mommy loves a daddy, they—"

She slapped him playfully on the side of the head. "It's a good thing we already have kids. Otherwise, Daddy might be out of luck! As is, he might still be in for a long dry spell." Robin wrapped her arms around James's waist and purred, "On the other hand, this particular mommy is looking forward to having a certain daddy's undivided attention for the next two weeks, nice meals that she's not had to prepare, being able to actually *finish* a bottle of good wine for a change, no cell phones ringing at, ummm, inopportune moments." She gave him a lingering kiss.

James raised his eyebrows and stroked her back. "You know, you could have my undivided attention now."

"Maybe tonight, lover-boy. Now, you've got packing to do." Robin ducked into the closet, returning with an armload of skirts and blouses.

James sighed. "Yes, ma'am. So, what's our itinerary? You're the big planner for this family adventure." He tossed shorts, shirts, socks, and underwear into his suitcase.

"For a hotshot trauma surgeon and a details guy, you sure seem to like flying by the seat of your pants. How do your patients ever survive? Hmmm, this red stuff is squirting from this bullet wound. What should I do? Maybe we should patch it, or maybe we should—oh, *look*, a squirrel!" she teased.

"Ha, ha, ha! Sometimes it's more like that than you'd think. Yes, there are *some* things that absolutely *must* be done with every case, but in reality, you can't *really* know what you're going to do until you open somebody up. What looks to be a nice, straightforward case often throws you a curveball. There's always some unanticipated anatomical variant or something damaged that wasn't anticipated. Sometimes, things are damaged more than preop imaging suggested, and the next thing you know you're doing a completely different procedure than the one originally planned. And you can't let any of this throw you. *Nothing* good comes from a trauma surgeon appearing frazzled or unsure. Fear is contagious. If you're too set in your ways or too excitable, bad things happen. Furthermore, an effective surgeon also learns to delegate tasks to his team. On my team, you are the schedule maker and timekeeper. So if you're doing the job, I don't have to."

"Furthermore? Really?!" Robin laughed and rolled her eyes.

"You know, as much as you do that, you must have some incredibly well-developed extraocular eye muscles. If there's ever an Olympic event for eye rolling, you'll be a shoo-in for the gold!" he teased.

"Keep it up, funny man, and you'll find yourself sharing the couch tonight with Clara Barkin and Mary Puppins!"

"Well, whereas I do love those dogs, I see your point. No more laughter. I shall be as lugubrious as a mortician's convention." He then dropped his voice an octave and continued in an overly soothing, somber monotone, "You were about to detail plans for our imminent family vacation to our fine nation's capital?"

"Lugubrious? Really? Let me guess, you memorized a thesaurus when you were eight?"

"Actually, I was seven and I only made it through the *P*'s."

"Of course you did, Rain Man. What do you mean you can't remember the itinerary? We talked about it last month."

"My memory doesn't work that way...only for things that I read or experience. For conversations, I'm just like anybody else."

"Well, *that's* awfully convenient," she replied.

"And besides, I figured it was a work in progress and therefore subject to revision."

Robin shook her head in mock disgust. "Again...what-*ever*! As for our schedule, there are only a few activities that are chiseled in stone, and those only because I've booked tours for certain dates and times. Tomorrow's a travel day. We drive up and get settled into our condo. We'll probably all be pretty tired from the drive, so I haven't planned anything for tomorrow night. Maybe we just walk around the National Mall or something as we feel like it. Our condo's within easy walking distance to the mall. After that long in a car, I'm thinking walking will be a welcome change of pace."

"Walking as a change of *pace*? Very punny, sweetie. And you say *my* puns are bad."

Robin stuck her tongue out at him, then continued, "Monday, Tuesday, and Friday we have guided tours at the Capitol, White House, and Mount Vernon, respectively."

"Check. Tours Monday, Tuesday, and Friday."

"After that, there's nowhere we *have* to be until next Sunday. That said, there are places that are nonnegotiable for each of us. For Katherine, it's the Museum of Natural History and the National Gallery of Art."

James nodded appreciatively.

"For Chuck, it's the National Air and Space Museum and the International Spy Museum."

"Yes!" James pumped his fist. "I knew I loved that kid."

Robin rolled her eyes again. "For me, it's the United States Holocaust Memorial Museum and Martin Luther King Jr. Memorial. We take the kids to them..."

"...and we have a loooong talk with them afterward," James finished for her. "I'll be interested to hear Katherine's take on those museums. I think even Chuck will find them sobering."

"Precisely," she replied. "After that, seeing the pandas at the National Zoo or maybe the National Aquarium would be pretty nice, as would be the Museums of American History or African History. I wouldn't mind making a day trip to Monticello or Georgetown while we're there. Of course, we'll see all the monuments. No doubt Katherine will want self-ies at the Lincoln Memorial and Washington Monument. Chuck mentioned something about us maybe taking a day trip to Fredericksburg. They have a museum there for the Battles of Fredericksburg, the Wilderness, and Chancellors-ville."

"He's showing an interest in Civil War history now? Let me guess, there's a cute teaching assistant from Belmont University in his American History class? Still, if he's showing an interest in something, we should probably support it. What else is on the agenda?"

"Then Sunday is *your* big day. That's the Vietnam Veterans Memorial and Arlington National Cemetery. Have you thought about what you're going to say?"

"Just short of constantly," he replied, clicking his suitcase closed. As he carried the case to the door, he thought, *How do I sum up a life lived within the time afforded by two eleven-year-olds' attention spans—even for kids as above average as the twins, that is asking a lot. And then there's Mom...* "God, I hope I can keep it held together," he murmured to himself as he descended the steps to the garage.

Robin's outline of events played out like clockwork with no hitches whatsoever. James was able, with much effort, to curb his natural inclination to serve as a walking encyclopedia at each destination and *only* corrected their guide *once* during the White House tour—an achievement for which Robin was both impressed and thankful. The International Spy Museum, which, before going, had been met with eye rolls from Katherine—clearly, she was Robin's daughter—was a hit with the entire family. Everyone was disappointed to find the Washington Monument closed for renovation. James had been looking forward to riding the elevator to the top as he'd once done on a school trip as a child, but he was out of luck.

C'est la vie. Guess we'll have to come back again someday.

Chuck, not surprisingly, developed a deep-seated interest in art when their docent at the National Gallery turned out to be an attractive Art History major from Georgetown.

After their visit to the Holocaust Memorial Museum, Katherine disappeared for a few hours into her room with her laptop. She later reemerged with an article she'd written about the experience that she planned to submit to her school paper. After reading her article, James was certain of two things. First, he'd never been more proud of his daughter. Second, he was going to talk with her about possibly submitting her article to *The Tennessean*, Nashville's major newspaper, for publication upon their return home.

Sunday morning dawned bright and clear. A front had blown through during the night, so the temperature and humidity were pleasantly temperate, quite a departure from the usual clime for DC during the summer.

At the war memorials, James was in full Wikipedia mode. Even Robin had to admit that it was kind of nice not having to carry around a guidebook. At the World War II Memorial, he took his time walking around the memorial, pointing out its design features and explaining their symbolism. He discussed the Atlantic and Pacific baldacchinos and the fifty-six granite pillars placed in an oval around the memorial pool and fountain, one for each US state and territory during the war and one for the District of Columbia. He paused before the curved Price of Freedom wall with its 4,048 gold stars, explaining that there was one star for every 100 Americans who died or went missing in the war.

Before long, a group of twenty tourists attached themselves to the family, mistaking James for a Park Service Tour Guide. If James noticed, he didn't mind. He was lost in his world. At the stations for Tunisia, Sicily, and Italy, he spoke in greater detail, especially about Anzio and the push to Rome.

When he pointed out one of the two *"Kilroy Was Here"* engravings, Chuck asked, "Dad, why would anybody want to memorialize graffiti?"

"True, son. It was graffiti, but in World War II, Kilroy had a special meaning to American soldiers. That piece of graffiti represented their presence and protection. Wherever Kilroy was inscribed, that meant, 'The Yanks are here. All friends are safe, and all enemies beware.' In truth, I cannot imagine this memorial *without* Kilroy being here!"

At the Vietnam Veterans Memorial, the usually unflappable James seemed uncharacteristically disconcerted, almost flustered. Although still a font of information regarding facts and figures, he appeared troubled.

Recognizing her husband's distress, Robin slipped her arm through his and began slowly walking with him along the polished granite wall.

Bolstered by her support, James resumed his recitation. "The wall was designed in the shape of a large *V*. It is wider and deeper in the apex and tapers to the ends of the *V*. Viewed from above, it gives the appearance of a healing wound. When the wall was dedicated in 1982, there were 57,318 names, each representing someone who died during the war or was listed as missing in action, presumed dead. Since then, another 379 names have been added. After the names of those known to have died, there is an engraved diamond. After the names of the missing, there is a cross. For the missing who have later been found or proven to have died—" He paused, having become choked up for a moment.

Katherine and Chuck glanced at one another, curious at seeing their normally imperturbable dad appear ruffled.

He cleared his throat and then continued, "For the missing who have later been found or proven to have died, the cross is overlaid with a diamond. For the missing who have later been found to be alive, the cross is overlaid with a circle. Although to date, this has yet to occur.

"The names on the wall are arranged in chronological order with the first from 1959 and the last from 1975 being found at the apex of the *V*. This is meant to suggest that there is a full circle, first to last, and represents closure. So, if you're looking for a name from, say, 1967, it would be about...here," he said, turning and gazing toward the wall. A moment later, he walked on, but this time, strangely, in silence.

At Arlington, the family stopped to admire the US Marine Corps War Memorial depicting the raising of the flag at Iwo Jima. By then, James's composure had fully returned, as had his effusiveness and love of detail.

"The memorial is a sculpture created by Felix de Weldon, based upon the iconic photograph by Joe Rosenthal from February 23, 1945, depicting the raising of the second flag over Mount Suribachi during the battle for Iwo Jima."

"The second flag?" asked Chuck.

"Yes, the second flag. The first was a flag from the USS *Missoula* and was carried up Suribachi by First Lieutenant Harold Schrier. He affixed it to a water pipe, and with Marine Sergeants Ernest Thomas, Oliver Hansen, and two other marines, raised it at the summit. This flag looked too small, so a second, much larger flag was raised later in the day.

"Remarkably, Rosenthal initially thought his photograph was of poor quality since most of the faces of the six depicted marines—Block, Keller, Sousley, Strank, Schultz, and Hayes—were turned away or obscured. But the world thought otherwise, and his photograph won a Pulitzer Prize. The very fact that the faces *are* obscured made it the perfect symbol to represent *all* marines."

"If the memorial is based on a photo from 1945, shouldn't there be a forty-eight-star flag on it?" asked Katherine.

"Good question, sweetie," James responded with a smile. "The memorial is meant to represent *all* marines from 1775 to the present, therefore a modern flag is always flown over it. Furthermore, by edict from President Kennedy, this memorial is one of the few federal sites where the flag is *never* lowered or placed at half-staff."

"That's pretty cool, Dad!" said Chuck with a nod.

CHAPTER 41

JUNE 2022

A FTER THE MARINE CORPS WAR Memorial, the family made its way into Arlington National Cemetery. There, James launched into a short lecture on the history of Arlington House, Robert E. Lee's former home, and the land's evolution into perhaps the most hallowed grounds in the United States. Chuck was impressed to find the final resting place of Audie Murphy, the most decorated American soldier of World War II. Katherine was equally awed to find the memorial headstone of Glenn Miller.

"Dad! Did you know that Glen Miller's grave is at Arlington? Glenn Miller! He had sixty-nine top-ten hits. That's almost as much as Elvis Presley and the Beatles *combined*! Elvis had thirty-eight and the Beatles had thirty-three over their *entire careers*, and Miller got his in only four years. Can you believe it? He totally *rocked*!"

"If ever you doubted that she was your daughter," Robin deadpanned, "this should allay any possible concerns."

James laughed. "I don't have the heart to tell her that it's a memorial headstone rather than a gravesite, or that

Miller's body was never recovered after his plane crashed into the English Channel in December 1944."

"Let her have her moment."

"Good call," he said, smiling after his daughter before leading the family to JFK's burial site with its eternal flame.

At the Tomb of the Unknown Soldier, the family watched the ritual changing of the guard ceremony.

An impeccably uniformed relief commander appeared on the plaza and announced the changing of the guard. The new Tomb Guard, known as a Sentinel, appeared promptly thereafter. The commander inspected the Sentinel's uniform and M14 rifle. After passing inspection, the relief commander and new Sentinel met the old Sentinel in the middle of the black mat. There, the three saluted the Unknowns and posted orders. "Remain as directed." Thereafter, the relieved Sentinel and commander retired, and the new Sentinel began walking guard over the tomb.

After the ceremony, James pointed out details that the children may have overlooked. "Did you notice the number of steps the Sentinel took in each direction? No? It was exactly twenty-one. Similarly, he took twenty-one seconds each when he faced east and north before marching the other direction at a cadence of precisely ninety steps per minute. The Old Guard practices this to get it perfect every time."

"Why twenty-one, Daddy?" asked Katherine.

"Twenty-one is the highest honor that the military can bestow. Think twenty-one-gun salute. It is the ultimate sign of respect for our military's unknown dead."

"That's pretty awesome, Dad. Where do we go next?" asked Chuck.

"There's one more place I want you to see before we go. I've only been there once, but I want you guys to see it. But first, let's swing by the Visitor Center and get a bottle of water because this might take a while."

Overhead, the sky was a Wedgwood China bowl accented with occasional fluffy white cumulus clouds. With the temperature still hovering in the low eighties, it was a perfect day for a walk, and the rolling, manicured hills of Arlington National Cemetery made a pleasant venue for a family hike.

From the Visitor Center, James led the family down Halsey Drive, past Leahy and McClelland. Uncharacteristically, he walked in complete silence with his eyes fixed off in infinity, as though he was walking in a dream—or to the gallows. He took a right onto York Drive and veered off again to the right just before they reached Eisenhower Drive. There was a light easterly breeze that occasionally freshened enough to rustle the leaves of the grand old white oak under which James brought the family to a halt, and where he, unexpectedly, took a seat on the ground.

Katherine and Chuck glanced at one another as though wondering why dear ol' Dad had gone so totally off the rails. Sensing that something important was about to happen, they each took seats on the ground opposite their father. Robin sat to his immediate right, with her hand resting lightly on his knee. She nodded and gave him a reassuring smile.

After a moment, James began speaking hesitantly, like a train leaving the station, and then picked up both in strength and cadence as his thoughts developed greater fluency. "I want...to tell you...a story...."

The children waited expectantly.

"It was a terrible accident—a senseless tragedy—and it had been entirely preventable. After terrible accidents and senseless tragedies that are entirely preventable, there is no shortage of blame, recriminations, vitriol, or anger. This occasion was no different, and the lion's share of the blame, re-criminations, vitriol, and anger—rightly or wrongly—landed firmly upon the shoulders of a heartbroken eight-year-old little boy..."

Over the next hour and a half, James related the story of his father as he'd learned it from Becca and hundreds upon hundreds of letters. Throughout his narrative, the children sat mesmerized before him, hardly daring to breathe, as he spun a tale of love and loss and love again. Robin, who'd never heard the story in its entirety, silently dabbed away tears, only to have them return again and again.

"...and fifteen years ago, I was invited to a ceremony in the Oval Office, where he was awarded the Congressional Medal of Honor. He was the greatest man I *never* knew. He was...my dad."

After a moment, Chuck shook his head in wonder and said, "I can't believe Grandpa actually won the Medal of Honor. He was a hero!"

"And I can't believe they got married at the county jail. That was a *great* story, Dad!" Katherine replied, then added excitedly, "You should write it down and make it into a book or something!"

"Indeed, he was, son! Indeed, he was. And thanks, Kat, I agree. It *is* a great story, and maybe someday I *will* write it. Or maybe *you* should. After all, you're the author in this family, aren't you?"

James rose stiffly and walked toward a grave marker a few meters away. "I think it's time that the two of you met your grandfather."

The twins followed and then gazed reverently down at the headstone before them.

JAMES WILEY

HAMILTON

SSGT

US ARMY

VIETNAM

AUG 27, 1947

NOV 19, 1967

MEDAL OF HONOR

SSM

PURPLE HEART

James turned toward the grave, came to rigid attention, and snapped off a crisp salute. Then he took the backpack from his shoulder and removed a brushed aluminum urn from it—his first horcrux—and knelt by the grave. James sprinkled his mother's ashes atop his father's grave and murmured a few words only God and his parents could hear. Then he replaced the lid on the urn and returned it to the backpack.

After a moment, he stood and turned back to his family. Together they strode toward the Visitor Center with James happily chatting about the history of Arlington House.

EPILOGUE

"Next up on *Antiques Roadshow*, an antique trunk and contents..."

"Yes, yes...now what can you tell me about this beautiful old trunk?" asked Roger Llewellyn, appraiser for *Antiques Roadshow*.

"Thank you, Mr. Llewellyn. I found the trunk while cleaning the attic of my grandfather's house. From the contents, I think it was from around the time of, or just after, the Civil War but have no idea what it or the contents may be worth," James replied.

"Well, let's take a look. This is a classic barrel-topped trunk. It has longitudinal wooden staves but no cross-pieces. The metal on the top is zinc with rather intricate scrollwork. The lock appears to have been sprung, and the buckles and leather straps are in poor repair. You will notice that there are metal clasps, which were used to supplement the straps in securing the trunk. Clasps such as these began to be used in 1872. Now, upon opening the chest, the ornamental scenes lining the walls are in excellent condition, as are the trays." Llewellyn pointed to a tarnished brass plate. "This identifies the manufacturer as Wilkinson & Frost of

Springfield, Massachusetts. Wilkinson & Frost manufactured trunks, saddlery, and harnesses from the 1840s until they went bankrupt in 1930. This is an excellent example of their work, and I would value it at $3,500–4,000."

James nodded appreciatively.

"What can you tell me of the contents?" asked Llewellyn.

"The uniform tunic and shirt were those of my great-great grandfather, James Wiley Gibson, who was killed during the Battle of Secessionville in 1862 and was returned home in his uniform for burial. Also, there are personal papers and letters to my great-great grandmother directing that, in the event of his death, the two slaves he'd inherited at his father's death should be released as free men and each be given one hundred dollars for their service. They also detail that if either or both elected to stay and help with the farm after being granted their freedom, in addition to the money, they should be given twenty acres of choice farmland and a house. Additionally, there is a great deal of what appears to be Confederate currency of varying denominations."

Llewellyn nodded. "The Battle of Secessionville, also known as the First Battle of James Island, was fought on June 16th, 1862. In this battle, Union Brigadier General Henry Benham, with 6,600 troops, attacked a Confederate force of approximately 1,500 troops under the command of Brigadier General Nathan Evans. The Confederates were victorious and thus repulsed the only Union attempt to capture the city of Charleston by land. The uniform is exceptionally rare. Officer uniforms are commonly found, but the uniform of a private in the Confederate Army is rare, indeed. That the uniform tunic and shirt still show the bullet hole in the breast, with clearly evident blood stains, makes this a piece any museum would be proud to display.

I estimate that the uniform, with its accompanying letters, would easily fetch $60–70,000 at auction."

James nodded in silence.

"The Confederate currency has a face value of slightly over $40,000, but of course lost all its value when the Confederacy lost the war. At *Antiques Roadshow*, we generally do not place values upon paper currency, but I have seen examples in similar condition for which collectors paid par or slightly higher than face value."

Again, James nodded. "There was one other item of interest in the trunk. It is a collection of bird lithographs. My father found it in the trunk when he was a boy and carried it with him all over the world."

Llewellyn appeared almost giddy. "This book, *The Birds of Asia* by John Gould, is easily the most amazing find of the day!"

"You've got to be kidding!" James blurted before he could think.

"Most certainly, it is," replied Llewellyn. "John Gould was born on England's Dorset coast in 1804. His father was one of the chief gardeners at Windsor Castle. Finding the trade of gardening not to his liking, young Gould elected not to follow in his father's footsteps. Instead, he taught himself taxidermy and became a taxidermist of great renown, once stuffing a pet giraffe for King George IV.

"In 1828, Gould won a competition and became the chief taxidermist for the Zoological Society of London, and later the curator for their museum. In this role, he developed a close association with Charles Darwin and many other of the prominent naturalists of the day. They frequently sent him specimens to be preserved and prepared for display.

"Gould was also noted for his knowledge of ornithology. In the 1830s, he began publishing high-quality ornithological volumes consisting of exquisitely detailed color lithographs with accompanying explanatory text. His works are among the most famous and important 'bird books' of the nineteenth century.

"In 1850, Gould began work on an expansive seven-volume set, *The Birds of Asia.* Unfortunately, he died in 1881 before its completion. However, his work was completed by Richard Bowdler Sharpe and the First Edition was published in 1883. It is considered by many to be the most comprehensive work on Asiatic ornithology of its time.

"This First-Edition copy of *The Birds of Asia* is truly amazing! The blue Morocco half-leather binding is in immaculate condition. The gilt-edged pages show minimal wear, and only minor foxing is evident on the color plates within. If, as you say, you've never had this book restored, then it is obvious that it has been lovingly cared for by someone. Original Gould color lithographs, individually, often sell for upwards of $2,500 each...and there are seventy-six color plates in this volume. In 2007, another First Edition in less pristine condition than this one was sold by Sotheby's for $190,000. If this First-Edition copy of Gould's *The Birds of Asia* went to auction today, it would easily bring $230–240,000!"

The monitor just off screen flashed to a display of what viewers at home were seeing at the end of this segment:

Barrel-top chest	$ 4,000
Enlisted Confederate uniform	$ 70,000
Confederate currency	$ 40,000
First Edition Gould's *The Birds of Asia*	$240,000
Total:	$354,000

After a crash from off screen, the camera panned to the floor.

"Dr. Hamilton? Dr. Hamilton, are you okay?" Llewellyn asked as he knelt by James's prostrate form.

Like father, like son...

THE END

Thank you, dear Reader, for allowing me to share the Hamilton family's story with you. I hope you enjoyed reading *Roses in December* as much as I did its creation. Please tell a friend and share a review. Your feedback will mean the world to me!

HISTORICAL FACTS AND MISCELLANY

"Photographic memory" is a topic that has been hotly debated by neurologists and cognitive psychologists for decades. Contrary to historical claims, the condition has never been proven to exist. Eidetic memory—the ability to capture a visual snapshot of an image—does exist but is generally limited to children, fading well before adulthood. Hyperthymesia (Highly Superior Autobiographical Memory) is well-described but has been reported no more than 100 times in the medical literature. Famous individuals who were purported to have HSAM include Julius Caesar, Napoleon Bonaparte, Nikola Tessla, and Marilu Henner. As depicted in this book's text, the condition has the potential for devastating consequences, with sufferers being at risk for "becoming lost in the past."

The concept of the memory palace, or castle, is nothing new. It was described centuries ago by Cicero in his *De Oratore* and is still employed today as a memory aid. It is a strategy for memory enhancement that employs visualizations of familiar spatial environments to enhance the recall of information.

The memory horcrux, however, is purely a product of this author's imagination.

The uniform and private papers described in the epilogue actually exist. They once belonged to my great-great grandfather and were donated by my family to the Charleston Museum where they've remained on display for over fifty years.

The seven buildings of the World Trade Center Complex were designed by architect Minoru Yamasaki and Associates of Troy, Michigan. The North and South towers—WTC 1 and WTC 2—were completed in 1972 and 1973 respectively.

Most skyscrapers of the day employed multiple structural support columns distributed throughout the interior to support building loads. In order to maximize floorspace and allow tenants to avoid the necessity of designing floor layouts around structural support columns, the Twin Towers employed a relatively unique "tube-in-tube" structural design style.

The tube-in-tube design called for an 87-by-135-foot rectangular central core containing 47 steel columns that ran from the bedrock to the top of each tower. Additionally, the core housed elevator and utility shafts and three stairwells. The building's façade served as the outer tube. Each outer wall contained 59 narrowly spaced steel columns to share gravity loads with the central core and provide for lateral stability in wind. The design allowed for use of 40% less structural steel than conventional designs and provided tenants on each floor almost an acre of unobstructed floorspace.

Occupying 50,000 square feet of the 106th and 107th floors of WTC 1, the North Tower was an entertainment venue and restaurant known as Windows on the World, which was once the world's highest grossing restaurant.

At 8:46:40 a.m. on September 11, 2001, hijacked American Flight 11 crashed into the North Tower between the 93rd and 99th floors. At 9:03:11, hijacked United Flight 175 struck the South Tower between the 77th and 85th floors. The aircraft tore through the outer walls and critically damaged the inner core of each building, severing the elevator shafts, stairwells, and fire suppression systems. The towers' damaged structural supports ultimately could not withstand the fires triggered by the crashed aircraft but held long enough to allow for evacuation of the majority of tenants. It is estimated that 99% of the people located below the impact zones in each tower had time to safely evacuate before the collapse. There is much more information available online about the total death toll of this tragic event and how those numbers continue to grow with the long term affects still being realized by survivors and first responders decades later.

There were no survivors from above the impact zones from either tower, including 73 employees and 91 guests of Windows on the World.

ACKNOWLEDGMENTS

Dear Reader, I thank you for joining me on this journey with the Hamilton family. *Roses in December*, and *A Song that Never Ends* before it, has been, for me, equal parts a labor of love and an "earworm" with which I've annoyed family and friends almost nonstop for the last two years. If you've enjoyed my story, well...that makes all their annoyance worthwhile.

First and foremost, I'd like to thank the police, firefighters, paramedics, and other first responders out there. "Normal" people run away from danger. Heroes, like you, rush toward it, often with little thought to your own safety. Thank you for doing what you do!

Next, thank you Charles Campbell, my friend and partner down the hall. Your unflinching support and belief in my ability as a writer has been invaluable, as have been your insights regarding PTSD, memory castles, and so many other topics. I hope you like your characters in both books I and II. Sorry we couldn't fit you on the cover, my friend.

For all the friends and members of my family who've put up with me chattering away nonstop about the scenes I'm writing, I thank you for your forbearance and for at least giving the impression of listening.

Again, I thank my colleagues who helped me with technical details outside the scope of my military and medical knowledge. "Christ, Jim, I'm a doctor, not a _____!" Any errors that persist are mine alone.

Finally, I must again thank my editor, Debra L. Hartmann of The Pro Book Editor (TBPE). Throughout the process of creating these two novels, you've worn many hats. You've been my cheerleader, my therapist, my sounding board, and my teacher. If readers enjoy my books, a large part of the credit goes to you and your alchemical ability for transforming leaden prose into gold.

Doc

ABOUT THE AUTHOR

Mark A. Gibson is a physician who practices Cardiology in the mountains of rural North Georgia. He was raised on a small farm in upstate South Carolina—the last postage-stamp sized sliver of a much larger parcel granted to the family by land grant from King Charles II in 1665—and may or may not have once gotten in trouble for digging up his mom's calla lily bed in search of the family's long-lost charter.

Dr. Gibson graduated from the Citadel in Charleston, SC with a BS in Biology. Afterwards, he received his medical degree from the University of South Carolina School of Medicine in Columbia, SC. He received his Internal Medicine training through the University of Tennessee Medical System and Cardiology training through the Wilford Hall USAF Medical Center. He served for eight years on active duty with the US Air Force, before leaving the military for private practice.

Although a cardiologist by profession, Dr. Gibson is a dreamer by nature. He is a self-styled oenophile who enjoys travel and fine food. In his spare time, he builds sandcastles and dreams of distant shores.

Roses in December represents Dr. Gibson's second offering to the world of literature, and the conclusion of his *Hamilton Place Series*. All previous publications have been of the professional, peer-reviewed, medical variety, and make for lovely sleep aids.